# WHISKED AWAY

## THE DOVE POINT SERIES
### BOOK 1

## M. COLETTE

*This one is for me.*

Hi friends!

Welcome to Dove Point!

I'd just like to say that I'm excited you've decided to dive into the world of sunshine and sandy beaches.

This book started on my phone and the notes app. I had no idea that I'd actually publish a book. It's tiring and exhausting...but so worth it.

When I wrote this story, I was at a low point in my life. I felt alone, unwanted, and unloved. So, I decided to escape reality and create a world that I wish I had.

I'm pretty sure I manifested my own Rowan William's with this story, because four months before this published, I'd met the love of my life.

Someone who I'd never thought would give me the kind of love I've always wanted. If you want something bad enough, it will come to you.

Now, let's get down to the nitty gritty.

Ellie and Rowan's story will have a happily ever after (obviously). But, there will also be tough situations that both of them will need to push through in order to ride off into the sunset.

Some topics that will be discussed are; parental abandonment (off page), infidelity (off page), anxiety/panic attacks, and self-worth.

Both Ellie and Rowan have a small part of me included in them. So, their stories have been written with the knowledge of going through my own struggles in life.

Lastly, there are sexually explicit scenes in this book. It's recommended for adults 18+ and up. DO NOT LET THE BOOK COVER FOOL YOU.

Anywho, I hope you enjoy Ellie and Rowan's story. And I hope you'll be back for more!

xx

M.

# PROLOGUE

## ROWAN

Ten Years Ago

*"With the final check-in underway, the captain will order the doors to close in five minutes."*

The echo of the flight attendant's announcement fills the airport. I inhale to soothe my anxiety as I watch passengers board the plane. The girl I love, Ellie, is being taken away from me. Well, not actually being taken away. She's leaving Dove Point and going to New York.

I'm cherishing each moment, every second, I spend with her and absorbing it all. Ellie and I have always been together. Her dreams are the reason she's leaving the West Coast.

I raise her hand and press my lips to the top of it. The mere essence of her calms my body and clears my thoughts. Tears gather at the tips of her lashes, making her already vibrant blue eyes brighter. I brush away the tear that runs down her cheek.

The sound of people walking past us is a haze, and I almost forget that we aren't alone. Her parents, our friends, and August, her younger brother, are all here to say goodbye.

"You promise to call me every day?" she asks.

I raise her head, holding onto the bottom of her chin. "I'll call you morning, noon, and night. You'll end up getting sick of me."

My heart pushes me to board the plane with her and leave Dove Point behind to start a new life in the city while she goes to culinary school.

Then my doubts come flooding in.

*Am I going to become a burden? What if she thinks she's happier without me? Maybe I'll get in her way.*

Ellie's my best friend and girlfriend, so the thought of her leaving for a long time to move across the country is overwhelming. It's only for a couple of years. She'll study, work on her craft, and come back home.

And I'll be here with the engagement ring I chose for her. She's my endgame.

"I love you, Rowan," she mutters, pressing her cheek deeper into my palm like she wants to remember how this feels so she could carry it with her.

"I love you too, El. Before you know it, these two years will be over, and you'll be home."

She agrees with a nod and takes a deep breath before exhaling. I sense her anxiety overwhelming her, but I know she's still about to board that plane. She glances behind her, noticing the line getting shorter. "I guess I better get going," she says, turning to look at me.

With her face in my hands, I lean down to kiss her. She rises on her toes to reach me halfway, and I savor this moment. A salty tear falls on our lips, attempting to separate us.

"I love you," I say again before kissing her.

"I love you." She gazes at me before grabbing the strap of her backpack, placing it over her shoulder, then heads over to the others to give one last goodbye before leaving.

Her mom's voice rings out, "We love you, sweetie."

Riley, one of her best friends, shouts, "Stay safe, El."

Ellie gives everyone a smile that doesn't reach her eyes and then turns to give her ticket. The girl who stole my heart at fifteen disappears behind the doors. The taste of her tears still lingers on my lips.

# ONE

## ROWAN

Present

*Buzz... Buzz... Buzz*

My phone vibrates against my nightstand, dragging me away from my sleep. My fingers fumble against the hard surface in search of the annoying wake-up call. The sun streams into my bedroom, and I attempt to wipe the sleepiness from my eyes.

"What?" My hand continues to rub against my eyes.

"Please, don't freak out," my sister, Addie, utters in a calming tone.

I lift myself up from my bed, awake now, and enter straight into panic mode. If someone calls and tells me not to panic, how am I supposed to respond to that? If this is how my day starts out, I'd rather go back to sleep and avoid whatever catastrophe is going to happen.

"What? What is it? Did anyone get hurt? Who died?"

"No one is dead or hurt. Calm down." Addie sighs.

I stop and close my eyes, exhaling through my lips. A wave of relief washes over me, and my shoulders drop to relax. I run my fingers through my dark brown hair, pausing when my fingers brush at the nape of my neck. It's longer than usual—a change I haven't bothered fixing, especially after Ellie mentioned during a video chat a few weeks ago how much she likes it this way.

"We've got the company's merchandise, and um..." Addie replies.

"What?" I ask.

"So, our logo's wrong, the color's wrong, and they sent wine glasses instead of beer glasses," Addie notes.

"I'll be right there."

My sister groans on the other end of the line. Meanwhile, I'm already out of bed, laying my cellphone on the bedside table and hitting the loudspeaker button so I could listen while getting ready.

"What time did everything come in?" I ask, shuffling in my room for clothes.

"They delivered it this morning at four. I went through the items, and that's when I called you. I wanted to let you know before you come in. But I should have known better, because it's you."

I pull my shirt over my head and grab a pair of dark jeans.

"Rowan?" she yells out. "Don't control this situation when I have it handled. You should trust me."

"Keys, keys...where the hell did I leave my keys?" I say to myself, feeling my jean pockets as if they might appear.

My eyes drift to the dresser, where my car keys and wallet sit next to a photo of myself, Addie, and Mom.

"Milo," I shout out.

"Ro, are you even listening to me?" Addie says over the speaker.

I hear Milo sprinting up the steps, the sound of his nails tapping on the wood floor, his honey-colored fur shining in the sunlight as he enters my room. Milo, my golden retriever and constant shadow, howls in excitement.

I pick up my phone from the small table. "Yes, I'm here. Trust issues, control freak, got it," I answer while hurrying down the flight of stairs and toward the front door. Milo tags along behind me.

"You're insufferable, you know that?"

"Yeah, well, I wouldn't be a big brother if I wasn't." I joke.

I grab my dark Vans, tugging the first one on while balancing on the other foot, my cell phone stays wedged between my shoulder and ear. Milo looks up at me, tail wagging, letting out a soft whine of eager anticipation.

"I'll meet you in five minutes."

"Ro, you don't—"

I hang up before she continues to talk. She'll only slow me down, and I'm prepared for the wrath she's about to unleash on me when I meet her.

Everyone, including my family, always jokes that I need to be in charge of every single thing—that I have to ensure things happen how I want them to. I'm not seeing a problem. I have expectations. Setting them is something I do, and I follow through.

With my business, The Salty Dog, of course I'm going to have an opinion on everything. This is a prime tourist attraction in Dove Point. I've poured my blood, sweat, and a lot of tears into it.

I move to open the door before Milo walks out, holding his leash in his teeth, and doesn't wait for me to come to the car. I had never planned on having a dog, but when I came across him as a puppy on the side of the road only outside of town, that changed.

I took it as a sign from the universe that it was me who

had found him. As if we needed each other. Both of us experienced abandonment in our lives.

The porch creaks under my shoes when I lock the door then go down the wooden stairs, almost falling off one that's loose. I glare at it while muttering a curse word under my breath and continue to walk.

Milo spins in a circle, waiting for me to let him into the front seat.

"I know, I know. I'm going as fast as I can. *You* don't have to worry about getting dressed and putting shoes on," I tell him.

Opening the car door, Milo leaps in, and his paws thud against the cushion. His exciting gaze tracks every move I make. As I circle the car, his eyes follow me, then return to the door as I slip into the driver's seat and fire up the car. The engine hums to life.

"Alright, let's buckle up."

I lean over to strap Milo into the harness that functions as a seat belt for dogs.

"Good to go?" I ask him.

Milo woofs in approval before I give him a scratch on his head.

"Alright, buddy, let's go."

# TWO

## ELLIE

Meanwhile, 2,801 miles away in Brooklyn, New York.

"Ellie, cupcake, let's just work this out."

I stuff my suitcase in the backseat of my deep green Volkswagen Beetle, then take off my yellow cross bag to throw in the car. My braid snags in the strap, and my frustration reaches its peak.

The sticky morning air clings to my skin now that summer is here. Stray bits of hair from my braid glue to my neck as I push some of my chestnut-colored hair behind my ear.

Turning to Charlie—my now ex-boyfriend—planting my hands on my hips. My stance says it all—I'm done, and he knows it. At five-foot-two, I might need to tilt my head to meet his eyes, but I'm so pissed off that my glare could melt ice.

"There's nothing to work out, Charlie," I wave my hand before letting it slap my thigh.

"Look, I know I messed up, okay?" Charlie says, dragging a hand through his blonde hair. "She meant nothing to me."

I look at the man I love—or thought I loved—and grimace. His golden hazel eyes stare into my icy blues as he pleads for me to stay.

"She meant nothing to you? You were talking to her for months, Charlie. In comparison, I was breaking my back at work. You weren't there for me. You were there for someone else."

Charlie wraps his hands around the back of his neck, tugging it in frustration. It's a telltale sign he knows he fucked up and is scrambling for what to say.

Turning my back to him, I shove my giant suitcase in the backseat. I packed everything I own, ready to leave him, and this place behind. At least for the summer. I push it in and slam the door shut, using everything in me to further prove my point.

"You did this to yourself, Charlie. Not me."

"I know, and I screwed up." Charlie raises his voice, his eyes drift to some of the early commuters who are on their way to work. He takes a deep breath as he attempts to gather himself and calm down. His gaze traces back to me, and tries to reason with me, but I'm done.

My chest feels heavy, almost unbearably so. I force myself to push down the lump in my throat and the emotions wanting to tumble out of me. I *will not* shed a single tear because of him. At least not while I'm standing in front of him.

"I'm an asshole, and I'm selfish," he begins with an edge in his voice that I don't recognize. "While I was home alone, you were at work. You weren't like that when we met. You've changed."

I rear my head back, startled.

Maybe I'm not the same person I was when I met him. I was twenty-five years old. A lot has changed since I started working at one of the most well-known restaurants in the country—The Red Table. My career turned into a relationship. I worked twelve hour days. Sometimes I'd be traveling to work on an exclusive event.

It was exciting, exhilarating even. I was at my peak and then, I turned into someone I didn't know.

I'm not the carefree, happy-go-lucky person I used to be. The thought of baking outside of work felt like a chore now. I'm too drained to even pick up a whisk. I can't remember the last time I took a real vacation. The kitchen has consumed my life.

"Why didn't you try to talk to me?" I ask in defeat.

"I don't know. I didn't want to bother you. When I did, you wouldn't give me the time of day. I gave up." He brackets his hips and his head falls.

"So your solution was to go on a dating app? Instead of going to a therapist?" I narrow my eyes at him so hard I want red beams to shoot out and obliterate him.

"I just needed to talk to someone."

My eyes almost bulge out of my head. I can hear my heart pounding in my ears and I can't tell if it's rage or heartbreak. Maybe both.

"Talk to your parents! Your friends!" I shout. "The dog that sits on the stoop of our building!" I point to Bear the Lab, who's witnessing this mess. "You downloaded a dating app, you knew what you were doing! You didn't care. Talking to someone doesn't mean putting your dick in them. Unless your dick talks? Were you holding out on me?"

"Ellie, I'm sorry. I don't know how many times you need me to say it to you so you can forgive me and come back upstairs." He gestures toward the brownstone building with a wave of his hand.

I throw my hands up, fed up with the endless back-and-forth. This is going nowhere, and I need to leave before I say something I'll regret—even if he deserves every bit.

"So you're going home for the summer? You don't want to fix things?" Charlie pauses and stares at me. "You can't just end this relationship because of a minor mistake, Ellie. Everyone makes mistakes. I love you."

Tucking my arms across my chest, I glare at him. The audacity of this man to tell me he loves me after he confessed last night that his talking dick was in someone else.

"You figure your shit out and I'll figure out mine. Don't call or text me, okay?" I say.

He opens his mouth like he's going to continue, but thought better of it. I need space to figure out my next steps. Should I forgive him after this summer and start over? Maybe an entire summer away from this city, from my job, is what I need to clear my head.

I open the car door and slip inside, not bothering to say goodbye or even glance at him. Because if I do, I'll lose the courage I have right now to walk away.

# THREE
## ROWAN

"Rowan, give me the clipboard." Addie holds her hand out.

My eyes look down at everything in front of me that needs to be fixed: shirts, tote bags, coasters, glassware. I trust my sister, I do, but I can't help it. My mind tells me that if I don't fix it, it's on me.

"You're not helping. I know what I'm doing." She looks at me with innocent eyes.

Addie follows me around the table as I spread out the merchandise. She's right. Everything is wrong. Our coasters that are supposed to be circular are square. And the logo on the shirts that says, 'Salty Dog' should be 'The Salty Dog.'

"Addie, I love you, but if you know what you're doing, then how the hell did this happen?" I gesture toward the table with everything on it.

"Okay, this kind of thing happens. It doesn't mean it's the end of the world."

"This is a big accident."

"Rowan, give me the damn clipboard!"

The pen in my hand stops writing and I turn to my sister. She has the same dark chocolate hair and blue-gray eyes as me; it's like staring into a mirror. Only my sister is five-foot-five. Her thick, wavy hair dances on top of her head in a messy bun as she speaks.

Occasionally I thought about what it might be like to be an only child. "Just make sure that you write every little thing that's wrong with the merch," I hand it over to her. "The t-shirts, the glassware, the tote bags—everything."

Addie rolls her eyes at me, shaking her head as she turns on her heels and jots down notes. "Un-freaking-bearable," she mutters under her breath.

Over my shoulder, I say, "I heard that." Approaching the long, glossy wooden bar, I pick up a hand towel, slinging it over my shoulder. I count the glasses, napkins, and coasters in my head. The glasses are under the bar, the napkins stacked, and the coasters' logos are slowly fading away.

"Please tell me you're not here because of the merchandise mishap?" A deep voice calls from behind.

I don't turn around to look at James. One of my best friends I met in elementary school. "Are you that shocked?" I give myself a small smirk.

Behind me, I hear him climb the ladder. "I'm an optimist."

"You have so much faith in me. I admire you for that." I stand up and turn around, leaning back onto the slick, cool bar counter, crossing my arms.

James writes the specials for today on the big, wide chalkboard that hangs above the bar. "Someone has to," James mutters.

"You shouldn't want to change your best friend. You should like them for who they are."

"Not when they self-sabotage themselves."

"Coming from a guy who turns down every woman that throws themselves at him."

James gives me the finger over his shoulder before coming back down from the ladder. He may appear an asshole, but once you get to know him, you learn he has a heart of gold. He's quiet, reserved, and keeps to himself.

Sometimes a little grumpy.

"Good morning, everyone," a chipper voice filters from the entrance.

Riley, Ellie's best friend, walks through the wooden door with a smile on her face. Riley's ponytail bounces, blonde hair swaying. The empty brewery slightly echoes as her sneakers tap on the wooden floor.

"What's with the good mood?" James asks, pushing his dark hair out of his face.

She sits on a stool in front of us. The giant purple water jug she carries around makes a thud sound on the counter. "Wait, she didn't text you?" Riley says. "Wow, I thought she would have let you know something."

Addie sits next to Riley. "Who texted you?"

"Ellie," Riley says.

"And how is that new?" James shrugs.

Riley gives him a deadpan look and then glances back at everyone. "She said she's coming home for the summer."

"Wait what? Why?" Addie almost falls off her seat.

At the sound of her name, I attempt to hold back a huge smile. A million feelings run through me. Ellie always has this effect on me. My palms get clammy, my heart race picks up, and I get giddy inside like a boy on Christmas Day.

"I wish I knew. She wouldn't tell me. All she said was that she's coming home this summer and will talk to us when she gets here. I tried calling her, but she wouldn't pick up."

"Ooh, what if Charlie proposed to her?" Addie's eyes go round.

"Doubtful," Riley says. "She would have told us before coming here." Riley looks at me, and I could read her mind without her needing to speak it.

Me and Ellie, it's not in the cards anymore. She's a bigshot pastry chef in NYC, and I have a business here, a life here. The last thing I would ever do is get in the way of that, knowing damn well how hard she'd worked to get to where she is.

I've always known she was going to be a star baker when she made me a cake after my first girlfriend dumped me. It was my favorite. Funfetti with vanilla frosting. She made the frosting from scratch, and I remember the moment I tasted it; I almost fell to the ground. I didn't know food could make you weak in the knees, but there I was, floored. She didn't bother cutting slices. Just grabbed two forks from my kitchen, and we ate it straight from the pan, laughing between bites.

She dipped her finger in the frosting and put it on my nose when I wasn't paying attention. I couldn't get mad even if I tried. Not when she let out a laugh and looked at me with that smile that won me over.

A small flutter ran through my chest when I'd see the small dimple in her left cheek. A cartwheel in my stomach. She had just the one, but anytime I'd see it, I felt like the world got a little brighter.

"Rowan, do you know anything about this?" Addie pulls me from my thoughts.

"Wish I did." I shrug and bite back a smile.

# FOUR

## ELLIE

There isn't another car in sight. My hair becomes tangled by the wind, and my hand moves through the air when the windows are down. The sun's heat is a gentle caress on my face.

It's nothing but the lane ahead and birds singing as if greeting you. I'm surrounded by tall trees that rise on either side, their branches wide and protective, while the grass gleams bright and green in the sunlight.

Stopping my car, I hear the tires crunch on the gravel. My body aches from the long ride from New York and back home to the West Coast. I move my neck to work out the strain in my shoulders, and lean against the door, lifting my face to the sun. Its warm, calming rays offer a rare sense of peace.

The drive had been relentless. Small bathroom breaks and quick stops. Audiobooks and music had been my only companions, minutes ticking by as I tried to push Charlie and my job out of my head.

No time for rest.

Seven hours have passed, and with my last coffee a

distant memory, I'm running on empty. Sleep hasn't come since Charlie shattered everything. Every moment I closed my eyes, I pictured him and his body tangled with the mystery woman.

My tiny town is only noticeable with binoculars—too bad I don't have any with me. One sight pops out, and that's the vivid blue ocean and the white water smashing in. From my vantage point, I view all the homes spread out.

If I concentrate hard enough, the sound of the tide thundering on the surface flows by me. I take a deep breath and focus on the smells: flowers, sprouted tree leaves with redbud, and a hint of saltwater.

I can't remember the most recent moment when I was at peace. The constant noise in New York has gotten familiar to me. Trains, car horns, people yelling. My mind has gotten chaotic, never giving me a moment of silence. If it wasn't New York being loud, it was my own thoughts about work crashing around in my head. The next dish, review, or event.

I don't want to be trapped or anxious anymore.

I'm lucky to do what I love—creating dishes that draw people from all over the world. It's a dream come true, and I made it happen. The owner had presented me with a lifetime opportunity to become the head baker. This is something past Ellie would've jumped at in a heartbeat. However, I'm having doubts now.

I continued my training for another two years after my initial two years with the most talented chefs. The crème de la crème of the pastry world. I couldn't pass up the chance. Graduate and then continue with the best. So I stayed.

Letting go of Dove Point was a hard choice I faced. I went back home for a couple of weeks to talk to my parents about it because their opinion meant everything to me. I wanted to make them proud, and they were one hundred percent supportive of it all. Including my brother August and our friends.

The decision, however, depended on the most important person. Rowan. At fifteen, I fell for the boy. He asked me to be his girlfriend when we were sixteen, and that was that. I knew he was my forever person.

But the memory of that heartbreaking conversation still haunts me.

*"I'll be going back in about a week to start more training," I said, then grabbed his hand.*

*"Do you have to go? You've already been gone for two years. I don't know if I can deal with two more. Please don't leave." He squeezed my hand before looking away into the distance while we sat on the roof of my house.*

*"Come with me," I blurted out, startled by my own words.*

*Was that selfish of me? To ask him to leave with me, drop everything he has here? Rowan and James are talking about opening a brewery. That would be big for them.*

*"I can't."*

*We both looked in the distance from the roof. My parents' home is just a few blocks from the beach. Rowan and I always showed up on this roof to study the stars, talk, and kiss. During high school, we'd chat about our futures. The imaginary house we'd have or the bakery I once dreamed of opening here in our small town.*

*"So what does this mean for us?" I swallowed, and felt the lump in my throat.*

*He held onto my face in his hands and kissed me. He kissed me again at dusk, when stars emerge.*

Since that time, we've only been friends.

Driving past the welcoming sign, *Welcome to Dove*

*Point Est. 1801. Population:* 10,000, nerves thrum through me. Entering the town, I glance around at the familiar buildings. The brick sidewalks come together with the storefronts. Trees flank white light poles going down the curb. The town is small, and everybody knows everybody, no matter how hard you try to keep your life private.

Scanning all the connected shops: small square buildings, chalkboard signs display out front, doors prop open, inviting anyone in, people outside fill the coffee shop tables while enjoying the weather or working on their laptops. Others bob their heads in time to the guitar strumming, played by a guy on the sidewalk.

Then there's Ollie's, my beloved ice cream place, as the streetlight turns red on Ashburn Road. It's a shack with a yellow roof, white body, and painted frozen desserts covering the walls.

I'm pretty sure I drool when I think about the warm chocolate sundae I love. Rich homemade vanilla bean custard with hot fudge swirled around it, a tower of whipped topping and nuts, and a cherry on top that completes the dessert.

When I was young, I found doing chores exciting. After I received my allowance, I would skip my way straight to Ollie's, rewarding myself. There's no indoor seating, so people sit outdoors or take a stroll. Customers give their orders at the window. I remember having to stretch up on my tiptoes to peer over the ledge to place my order.

While I look at the line of people getting ice cream, I hear a woman call out my name. Before I pulled into town, I folded down the soft top of my car, turning it into a convertible. It's gorgeous out, and I wanted to take advantage. Now, I think I regret it.

Dove Point is...gossipy.

"Ellie!" a familiar female voice says. "Oh my gosh, is that you? I can't believe it. It's been so long! How have you been? Are you back in town for a visit?" Beatrice exclaims.

Beatrice Anderson, the town's vibrant artist who owns Art Fusion, the local gallery, looks at me with her spiky silver hair, thick tortoiseshell glasses, and mango-colored overalls paired with Dr. Martens. She somehow pulls off a look that defies age.

"Hi, Mrs. Anderson." I smile and nod. "Yep, I'm here for the summer. I just got in."

"Oh, how wonderful! I saw your mom a couple of days ago, and she mentioned nothing about your visit." She smiles.

I didn't tell her. My dad included. Or my brother, August. The only person I told was Riley. I can only hope that it doesn't reach my parents before I tell them myself. I should have kept the damn car top on.

"Well, here I am." I force an awkward laugh and grip my steering wheel tight.

"I'm having an art show soon. Would you be around to make those amazing peanut butter chocolate squares? Of course, I would pay." She beams with her hands clasped together.

Opening my mouth, I wait for words to tumble out, and then close it. My plan didn't involve working or touching any sort of utensil during my visit this summer. However, my savings are small, so extra money would be helpful.

"Sure, I'd love to. I can swing by in the next couple of days, and we could talk?"

Mrs. Anderson claps her hands in delight before she says, "Wonderful! I'll let you know more of the details soon. It's good to have you here. Tell your parents I said hi." She waves. The light turns green, and I nod and say my goodbyes, not wanting to hold up the line of cars behind me.

"Will do," I mutter to myself and sigh.

Two more blocks up ahead, I spot the brewery in the distance. My heart speeds up for a multitude of reasons.

Riley is the only one who knew I was coming back. She sent continuous texts and even made a few phone calls, but I didn't answer any of them.

Second, Rowan. The connection we have has always been different, deeper, than with anyone else. We just get each other. He's my closest friend...and, well, my ex. When we broke up, it wasn't messy—no hard feelings. We both knew it was for the best, and we wanted to salvage our friendship.

Thankfully, we've done just that because I can't imagine losing someone like him from my life. Rowan has always taken up a large part in my heart. He was my first teenage love.

I drive into the lot connected to the brewery and turn off my car, needing to take a minute to myself before walking in there. The Salty Dog is a beautiful building. It was once a candy factory years ago, before my parents existed.

A year after I was born, it closed and was vacant for a long time until Rowan and James bought it to build their business. Dove Point received multiple offers from people who didn't live in town. It didn't feel right to give it to someone the town didn't know.

It's a two-story building with a brick exterior, a pair of large windows on each side of the oversize door, and two tall palm trees standing ahead of it, wrapped in twinkle lights.

I try to prepare myself. Addie, Hailey, and Riley will

freak out, but I don't want to deal with their sympathy or pity.

This needs to run as smoothly as possible. Tell them the situation and move on to a relaxing, stress-free summer. Maybe I should have told Riley the entire story? Everyone would understand, sparing me awkwardness or embarrassment.

I'm tired, hungry, and getting my period. Since I'm stressed, I have a craving for sweets. Charlie is still contributing to that moodiness. I'm on the verge of tears because all I want is a cupcake.

Pulling down the sun visor, I flip the cover to look into the mirror. My under-eyes have a purple hue because of lack of sleep. Reaching for my bag in the passenger seat, I dig through it, wondering if I left concealer in there. No luck.

"Dammit," I murmur to myself.

Looking in the mirror, my fingers trace the bags under my gaze. They tell the story of what I've been dealing with, and now my friends will get to see a side of me I hid when I visited home. I lean back and close my eyes for only a second before getting out of the car.

I let out a breath, trying to hype myself up. "Just walk in there with your chin held up high and tell them, '*Hey guys, I don't think I can handle life anymore. Charlie cheated on me because I paid too much attention to work and not him, and I might hate my career now. I'm fine. Everything's cool.*'"

One more time, I close my eyes, taking a deep breath in, before letting it out. I study my reflection one more time before lifting the visor and head out of my car.

# FIVE

## ELLIE

Stepping into the brewery gives me a warm, fuzzy reaction every time I visit. Rowan and James's goal was specific; they hoped to create a welcoming environment. It was a shock when I saw the final setup. James ended up taking all the credit when I learned most of it was Rowan's idea.

After grabbing the brassy gold handle on the large wooden doors and pausing, I shake off my nerves before opening the door. The interior appears more spacious, with high timber beams running across the top.

The place comes off rustic because of the rich brown wood floors and brick walls. Amber-colored decor spreads throughout the brewery, with some of it tucked in corners for more intimate gatherings. Wooden stairs lead up to the second floor, where there is more caramel-leather furniture and tables and chairs. String lights hang from the ceiling and cast a warm glow at night. Tall, narrowed windows line up across the back wall, displaying a wide view of the ocean.

With the vast brewing equipment behind a glass display, Rowan showcases how they create the beer, and explains how the machines function. I've asked him at least ten times to clarify to me again how it all worked. He was always happy to re-explain it to me. It was his pride and joy.

The sun shines through the brewery during the day. At night, it comes to life. The ambient lighting throughout the room creates a relaxing atmosphere. The beer garden out back displays string lights that hang along the long wood fence and wraps around trees that give the area more privacy.

"Ellie!" Riley gets up from a bar stool and runs to me with open arms, she towers about six inches over me, and tugs me into her lean body. She's the instructor at the town's yoga studio, and her body is always in peak shape. I made the mistake of attending one of her classes, not realizing it was hot yoga. About halfway through, the heat got to me, and I fainted.

I never did it again.

I choke, "Ry, I can't breathe."

"Sorry! I've just missed you so much!" Riley's words are a fast-moving jumble. "I know I only saw you a few months ago and video-chatted a couple of days ago, and text all the time but still! It's so nice to have my bestie back for the entire summer."

With her buttery blonde hair bouncing, the corners of her gaze crinkle from her wide smile. In our friendship, we talked every day, no matter what. She video-called me, even from the bathroom, because she couldn't wait to talk about her late-night hook-up.

Addie extends her arms out. "I'm so happy you're here." She jumps on me and I almost fall over. "How are you?" she asks. "I've missed you so much."

"I've missed you too."

James looks at us. His golden tan skin contrasts with his

dark hair, and his silver-gray eyes seem to catch the light. With a friendly grin, he walks toward me, saying, "Look who it is."

"Wow, growing some facial hair, Jameson? Looks nice." We give a quick hug. James and his brother, Beau, have always been like family to me.

"No, Hailey or Beau?" I glance around the large space.

"Hailey has a full day of appointments," Riley replies.

James says, "I don't know where my brother is."

"Probably getting a tattoo by my sister." Riley chuckles and rolls her eyes.

My heart thrums for the one person I see after I laugh and agree. Rowan.

He stands off to the side with his arms crossed, that signature pose making him look almost impossibly serious. The minute his gaze meets mine, everything changes. His eyes are like the ocean, deep and quiet. They hold a calm power over me. The blues and grays shift, catching the sunlight in a way that makes my chest tighten.

My heart continues to pound, the rush of blood moving through my veins, pushing straight to the tips of my fingers. His dimples show when he smiles. The same ones I haven't kissed in what seems like forever.

Tattoos play along his muscular arms, causing my eyes to trail the black ink. Of all of them, there's one that catches my eye. One he had me choose after high school graduation.

The memory is still so vivid in my head.

*"You want me to pick one out for you? Are you sure that's a good idea?" I laughed.*

*Rowan shrugged. "I know you well enough that you won't choose something ridiculous. You love me too much."*

*"Shut up." I bit back a smile and nudged my shoulder*

*into his. I looked at the flash sheet in front of us. "That one."*
*I pointed to a blue butterfly.*

*"My favorite color." He glanced at me and grinned. "How'd you know?"*

*I rolled my eyes. "Rowan, your favorite color has always been blue for as long as I've known you."*

The butterfly shows off in the middle of his forearm, surrounded by others that are not colored, causing it to stand out more.

"Ellie Thompson," Rowan says in his deep tone that makes my toes curl and the hair on my arms rise.

"Rowan Williams." I suppress a smile, trying to stay serious.

My arms open in embrace, smiling so hard that my cheeks hurt. The warmth of his body that presses against mine does things to me. Unspeakable things. He wraps his arms around my waist, and I tug him down with mine that wrap around his neck. The familiar embrace makes my heart go into hyper-speed. The tension in my shoulders melts away.

He makes me feel safe and secure knowing Rowan could protect me. I breathe him in and my heart slows down to a healthy rhythm. His scent is refreshing. A fresh breeze of coastal air and blue cypress.

"I've missed you so much, El," Rowan whispers in my ear.

Just like that, the hairs on my arms rise. "I've missed you too." My lips brush the skin of his neck when I say those words. Four words that mean more than he could understand.

"Should we, uh, leave you two alone?" James chimes in.

We've been hugging longer than I realize. I pull away but in no rush to separate. His grip loosens, matching my speed. Then large hands unwrap themselves on the lower side of my back. My hand brushes the skin of his neck, and a shiver runs down my spine.

I tilt my head back to meet his gaze. I wouldn't mind permanent neck pain to continue looking into his beautiful, hypnotic eyes.

"Okay, I don't know about you guys, but I'd love to know why you're here for the summer. Any big news?" Addie pushes her brother out of the way.

My body tightens, and a familiar knot forms in my stomach. Riley and Addie loop their arms into mine on each side, guiding me outside to the garden. I hear the guys shuffling behind me and peer at Rowan with pleading eyes to save me. He smirks at me, and I narrow my eyes.

"What's going on? I'm dying here," Riley urges, swaying my attention to her.

"I'll spill everything when we sit down," I say.

"Oh my God, there's spilling. This is going to be good," Addie says, stretching out the last word. "Wait, if it's something bad, then it won't be good." She shakes her head.

Each person settles onto a chair near the fireplace outside. I glance at Rowan and spot him watching me, waiting to see where I'm going to sit. I give him a knowing stare, and he rolls his eyes while he walks to sit in the chair next to me.

"Okay, spill," Riley says.

I spin the ring on my thumb; the smooth motion grounding me. If I think my anxiety is creeping in, I use this fidget ring. The rose gold has dulled over time, worn down from the countless times my fingers have twisted it, seeking comfort.

Addie looks at me with her storm-blue-doe eyes, while Riley leans herself forward in her chair. I'm sure she's about to fall out of it and face-plant onto the ground. I glance around at everyone. Maybe I should have pulled only the girls aside. It's too late now.

I clear my throat, sit up straight, and spill it all. "You guys know how busy I am with work, right?"

They all nod.

My eyes rest on the pavement, and I purse my lips before I continue. "I haven't been at home much because of how crazy work has been." I pause and look at them and then take a deep breath in before continuing. "That's part of the reason I've come back for the summer."

"Are you quitting? Are you moving back home?" Riley claps her hands with a giant grin on her face.

"No, I'm not quitting." I tilt my head and peer at her.

"Wait." Addie holds her hands out. "If you're here for the summer, is Charlie coming to visit?"

Rowan's moon-lit eyes gaze at me, concern written all over his face. His perfect eyebrows furrow, before his jaw muscles tick while he keeps his eyes on the ground. He's the only man I know who can look handsome while pissed off about something.

My lips to the side before saying, "I haven't been happy for a while. With my job and the city. I felt—feel—burnt out." I peer down at my lap and play with my fingers. "Charlie said that because of the stress I was dealing with at work, it also affected him, and that he felt alone."

"Wait," Riley says, "please don't say what I think you're going to say."

With Riley, we're so close that sometimes we can read each other's minds. It's kind of creepy, actually. We can have an entire conversation by facial expression alone, and right now, she looks like she wants to hurt someone.

I attempt to hold back the tears that want to fall from my eyes. "He cheated on me."

Riley looks ready to body-slam Charlie, with her eyes wide and mouth open. I turn to Rowan; he's still not looking at me. His eyes focus on the ground, but his leg bounces and he cracks his fingers one by one with his thumb.

"Get the fuck out," Riley exclaims.

I scrunch my nose at the tingling sensation and attempt to pull my legs up on the chair, wrapping my hands around my knees. I'm smiling on the outside like I'm not at all affected; yet I'm screaming and punching the air.

"That shriveled-up shrimp cheated on you?" Riley grips onto the sides of her chair, causing her knuckles to turn white.

"If you keep shouting, you're going to lose your voice," I say. "Charlie was begging me to stay and fix things. Obviously, I couldn't do that. If I had stuck around, I think I would have stayed with him."

"So, are you on a break, or are you broken up?" Addie asks impatiently.

"At this moment, we're broken up." I nod and let my body rest and go slack again. My head falls to the side because I don't have the strength to keep it up.

"Wait, you're thinking about going back to him?" Riley questions in shock, her eyebrows flying up to her hairline.

Leaning my head back and glancing up toward the clear blue sky, a bird flies by, and I pray it doesn't shit on my face. That would tip me over the point of no return.

"I don't know." I shrug. "We were together for four years." I pause, looking at Rowan, and I see a muscle tick in his jaw. My head swings back to the group. "It's not that simple."

"It is! It's a very simple solution. You say '*fuck you*', give him the finger, and never look back," Riley says.

"Is there anything we can do to help?" Addie asks.

Letting out a heavy sigh and shaking my head, I answer, "I just want to go home. I'm so exhausted, and all I need right now is sleep." Attempting to put on a brave smile, I continue. "I've gone almost four days without sleeping thanks to work. I can't tell whether you guys are real or a hallucination." Everyone doesn't laugh when I try to lighten the mood. "Is Milo here? I'd love to see him," I turn to Rowan.

He turns his attention to me, offering me a weak smile. "Yeah. He's sleeping in the office. Come on."

Rowan stands up from his chair, and I follow. Everyone else glances in my direction, sending sympathetic stares. I know damn well they're going to talk once I'm far enough out of reach to hear them. Riley is coming up with a revenge plan.

We get inside and go straight to his office, where the door is ajar. I grab Rowan's arm, pulling his attention. He looks at me, and I put my finger on my lip, telling him to stay quiet. He grins and moves to the side, gesturing with his hand for me to walk in front of him.

I poke my head in the doorway and see Milo sleeping on his back in his very large dog bed that's next to Rowan's desk. The wooden door makes a slight creaking sound and wakes him up. He flips over onto his stomach and sees me walking in.

He barks with excitement, and I push the door open and got on my knees, ready for him to greet me.

"Milo," I shout with my arms wide.

He whines and gallops toward me, his body too excited to stay calm as he licks my face.

"I've missed you so much, how've you been, buddy?" I scratch behind his ears and then on the side of his neck. He continues to whine and lick me. "I know, I know," I coo. "Come on." I get up from my knees and walk to the three seated couch against the wall. The soft fabric makes my body relax.

Milo jumps onto the sofa with me and sits down next to the armrest.

"You are just so cute," I say in a baby voice.

"Oh, he knows. That's why he gets away with almost everything he does," Rowan says, leaning against his office desk before folding his arms across his chest.

"As he should." I continue to baby talk while scratching his ears and kissing his head.

I hear Rowan clear his throat before asking, "Are you okay?"

My eyes find him, and my heartbeat picks up. His biceps bulge and I try not to drool.

"I will be," I say with a smile.

"Are you staying at your parents' place? Do they know you're here?"

When I sit down, Milo follows, propping his head on my leg. I shake my head. "Nope."

"Do you want them to know you're here?" He raises his eyebrows.

"Well yeah. I'm not going to hide from them for an entire summer."

The corner of his lips tilt downward while he rocks his head from side to side. "I think we can accomplish that."

I huff out a laugh. "How? Should I wear a mustache as a disguise? Change my name?"

"We can call you Joe."

"Do I look like a Joe?"

"Only if you have a mustache." He grins at me with a shrug.

"You're ridiculous, you know that?" I smile and shake my head.

"I know." He doesn't take his eyes off me.

We sit in comfortable silence, and I continue to pet Milo, who's fast asleep on me. My head gets lost in the way Rowan looks at me, as if I'm the only person in the world. It sucks that we aren't as close as we used to be—more than friends.

I've always loved him, and I knew that he always loved me.

"For what it's worth, I'm glad you're back home for the summer," he breathes.

I nod. "Yeah, me too."

## SIX

### ROWAN

When Ellie and I arrive at her parents' house, I park the car and look at her. She's sleeping in the passenger seat. Her light brown hair falls over her eyes, and her lips part.

Milo's face said it all when he saw his favorite girl. He missed her just as much as I did.

It's one of my favorite sights; seeing her with Milo. She's the only one who knows those secret scratching spots that make him groan and collapse in pure bliss. It feels like ages since he'd seen her, even though she was home over the holidays.

I questioned whether she was fine. Ellie is tough. She knows how to handle herself and doesn't need any of us to help keep her on her feet. But I know this broke her heart.

Charlie. That piece of shit. He was never good enough for her. I can only hope to run into him so I can knock him on his ass. And I'm not a fighter. I've never allowed myself to get to that level of anger. But Charlie has a punchable face, so maybe it's time I break my knuckles in.

Five minutes into our conversation, she'd fallen asleep on the couch. I didn't feel comfortable with her driving when she'd been this tired. Falling asleep in my office meant she shouldn't have been driving her car.

I scooped her up from the couch and brought her to my Jeep, thinking about getting her car tomorrow instead. Her body was limp, and I could feel exhaustion radiating from her.

Ellie opens her eyes and lets out a sigh. "Thanks for bringing me home. I didn't think I'd fall asleep on the couch."

"You know I'm always here for you," I tell her.

She leans her head back on the headrest and turns to look at me. Her sleepy blue eyes look bright and clear. The color always shines the brightest when she wakes up. I was always eager to see them right away when she'd open them.

Ellie always took a nap after coming home from school. By the time our favorite show would come on, I'd have to wake her up by rubbing her back and whispering her name. She would huff a breath through her nose in annoyance. But she was always stunning, no matter what her mood was.

Sometimes I would pepper her with kisses on her cheeks and head. A slow smile spread across her face while she pretended to still be sleeping.

She places her hand on top of mine, wrapping her fingers around my palm. Her soft skin rubs against my rough skin. I resist the urge to wrap her hand in mine, pressing my lips to each knuckle, savoring the feel of her skin on my lips.

"Do you want me to go in with you? Help you break the news to your parents? Is August here?" I ask, circling her palm with my thumb in soothing motions.

She shakes her head. "Your guess is as good as mine."

We both look at her parents' house. The long porch showcases the white wicker furniture and powder-blue cushions. Pale blue couples with purple hydrangeas spilling over the staircase flanks, which leads toward the entrance.

Ellie loves this house. It carries a lot of character, and she knows her mom tries to keep it that way.

"Shit, I'm so exhausted. The thought of talking to my parents sounds brutal." She says annoyingly while rubbing her face. "Let's sneak into the guesthouse."

"Maybe it could work, but I doubt it."

I turn my focus back to Ellie, once again asleep. The clock on my dashboard says it's five, and I need to get back to the brewery sooner rather than later before it gets too busy. People were already trickling in when I was carrying Ellie.

"El," I whisper.

"Hm," she murmurs.

"I can take you to my place and you can sleep there." I brush a strand of hair behind her ear. The simple gesture is so familiar and nostalgic.

She breathes out through her nose in an approving yes and tries to nod her head. "You can take me," she mumbles.

It's at this moment that I realize Charlie has just pushed Ellie back into my arms. This is my second chance to get the girl I love back. I'll do anything I can to get one more chance with her.

# SEVEN

## ELLIE

I wake up in a dark room and adjust my eyes to my surroundings.

When I look behind my legs, I notice Milo tucked in next to me. The bed I'm on is huge, king-size, yet this dog needs to be so close to me I can feel the heat coming off him.

I love Milo too much to bother him.

Massaging the side of his stomach while he continues to sleep, I lean up on an arm, rubbing my free hand over my face. I spot my phone on the nightstand next to me, plugged into a charger. I don't remember doing that.

Two in the morning? How long have I been asleep?

The wheels in my head start to turn. I met everyone at the brewery, spent time with Milo, and fell asleep on the couch in Rowan's office. The next thing I remember was being in front of my parent's house in his car.

I was worn out, wanting to cry from tiredness, and I'm sure I asked him to take me to his place.

Searching around the room, I spot Rowan lying on an inflatable mattress. With his bare back facing toward me, the muscles in his shoulder blades move with each breath he takes. I let my eyes trace the long tattoo that goes down his spine. A sword with a snake wrapped around it, all in black. I remember when he got that tattoo. He read a fantasy book that he became obsessed with. He couldn't lay on his back for a week.

The crickets outside are chirping, but everything else is silent except for the little snores Milo lets out every other minute. When my eyes adjust to the darkness that surrounds me, I spot Rowan's dresser on the far wall across from the bed.

A few music posters hang in frames around his room. One poster displaying Vampire Weekend—the same poster he bought when we traveled to watch them in concert. It hangs above his desk, which has two large desktop screens. A complete setup.

When I turn back to Rowan, I notice the closeness of the air mattress. He doesn't move or make a sound; he looks peaceful.

Crawling over the bed, not wanting to disturb Rowan, I attempt to figure out what I'm going to wear. I think my suitcase is still in my car. Shit. I'm going to have to borrow his clothes.

I don't know where he keeps anything. Cool. This is very cool.

When I get to the edge of the bed, I peek at something on top of his dresser. In the darkness, I narrow my gaze and move silently. A piece of paper lies on a stack of clothes.

*El, I picked out some clothes for you to change into if you get uncomfortable. You went to sleep right away, and I didn't want to bug you.*

I stop reading the note and scan the clothes. A large shirt that looks extremely cozy, and he gave me a choice of basketball shorts or sweats. I continue reading the note.

*I gave you shorts and sweatpants; I wasn't sure which one you would want. But if the sweats are too long, shorts might be better.*

*You might trip, so be careful of that. Sleep tight. I'll see you in the morning.*

What great hospitality. He's always one step ahead of me, like he knows I'm going to wake up from being uncomfortable in my tight clothes.

I grab what I want, walk into the master bathroom, and change. After a bit, my muscles relax after removing my bra and jeans.

When I glance down, I realize he was right, and I can't see my feet. But I still stand by my choice. The fabric is warm and a bit fuzzy on the inside. The material is nice and breathable, a bit thin.

My legs and feet swim in his sweatpants. The fabric drags on the smooth wooden floor while I creep back into bed. One foot at a time, I'm almost there. Almost—*thud.*

Rowan shoots up in panic and looks at the bed. "What happened? Ellie? Are you okay? Milo, where's Ellie?"

Milo lifts his head and spots me, and Rowan turns to where he's looking. I'm on my back; my head turns in Rowan's direction. I lift a hand in a lazy finger wave.

"Hello," I say in a hushed tone while embarrassment rushes over me, and I let my hand fall.

Rowan covers his head with his hands and looks at me. "Are you okay? Why are you on the floor?" He pinches his eyebrows together and looks at my legs.

My gaze returns toward the ceiling; I wait for him to figure that out alone. A chuckle comes out of him; all I can do is close my eyes and accept my fate.

"I told you."

After I ignore the comment, I get up and walk over to

the bed. My knees press into the soft mattress as I crawl back into bed. Rowan continues his laughter at my pain.

It's not until I'm situated back in my spot that I stare at his bare chest.

*Oh. Well. That's nice.*

Rowan sees where I'm looking and covers his nipples with his hands. "Hey, this isn't a free show, Thompson. Don't ogle me."

My eyes go up to his, and I raise my hands in defense. "I'm sorry if I made you feel uncomfortable. Can't blame a girl for looking."

Rowan smiles at me and shakes his head. I tuck myself under the covers on his bed and lay down to face him. He does the same.

"Thanks for bringing me here. I appreciate it," I say.

"I figured you'd need a clear headspace before seeing your family."

I rub my face out of pure exhaustion before holding my hand toward him, hoping he will take it. His thumb traces small rings on the back of my hand, and he doesn't stop. The sensation lulls me back to sleep while he continues.

---

AS I AWAKE from my dream, I feel wetness against my neck and jaw. I block the warm breath in my ear by lifting my shoulder. After opening my eyes, I'm met with big chocolate brown eyes.

"Milo, is this how you wake up your dad?" I whine before I peek at him from beneath the blankets.

After giving me a quick lick on my cheek, he runs out of the room. Then I rub my eyes, and attempt to get up and stretch.

The aroma of wood-smoked bacon reaches my nose. It ends up leading the way to the hall, down the stairs, and into the kitchen; I'm almost sure my body levitates like a cartoon character.

Rowan, who's wearing a shirt, stands by the stove with his back to me. Well, that sucks. I start to think back to last night when he slept next to me, his smooth skin, muscled back, and his —

*Focus, Ellie, and stop daydreaming. You just got home, and you're already drooling over your best friend.*

The sun streams through the window and lights up the white ceramic farmhouse sink. The light wooden counter spread across on either side of the sink. From the windowsill, small pots hold soil with green leaves beginning to grow. All edible plants: mint, basil, parsley, cilantro, and rosemary.

More natural light enters the kitchen thanks to the skylight window. Rowan grabs a copper cast-iron pan from a hook above the stove.

Milo's nails tap on the hardwood floor and disappear as he lies down on a rug below the sink, while the sound of crackling bacon echoes in the kitchen.

After pulling a chair and sitting down, I rest my elbow on the table, and my cheek in my palm. Rowan opens one of the glass cabinets and pulls out a deep blue and purple mug that's sprinkled with stars all over it. Mimicking the night sky.

Thinking about how much tea I drink when visiting Rowan is an embarrassing thought. His entire drawer is organized with every tea you can think of. I always felt bad for using his mugs and dirtying them, telling him I'd buy my own to keep here.

The deep swirls of blues and purples have golden flecks

of stars. Softness filled his eyes as he spoke. *"It reminds me of the nights we'd spend on your parents' roof, watching the night sky,"* he said.

Rowan is right. The night sky and its twinkling stars are my favorite. You can't see one star in the bright lights of New York the way you can see them in Dove Point. I reached a point where I stopped trying and gave up.

He sits my mug filled with chamomile tea down in front of me. He smiles and turns back to the stove to finish cooking. I pick it up, warmth going around my hands, and take a deep sniff. He added honey–my favorite–for sweetness.

"I don't deserve you as a friend." I hum and lift my shoulders up in comfort.

Rowan's shoulders bounce, letting out a laugh while he continues to cook. "Why is that?" he asks, not looking at me.

"Well, for one, you let me crash in your bed. I didn't realize how exhausted I was until I fell asleep in your office."

He flips over a pancake. The sizzling sound hits the pan and then subsides.

"You're making breakfast, and you made my favorite tea, too. I feel so spoiled." A giggle escapes from me.

"I enjoy spoiling you," he said, grabbing his mug and moving around the kitchen.

My heart flutters in my chest, and my neck feels hot. I take a drink from my mug to hide my smile. I couldn't remember the last time Charlie's done anything simple like make me tea. Rowan's reminding me how the small things can make someone feel.

Rowan places pancakes and fruit in front of me. Steam rises from the mug as he pours himself coffee.

My eyes track every movement he makes. The way his biceps flex when he picks things up and sets them down. A single wet strand of wavy hair falls next to his temple. The tip of his tongue sticks out with pure concentration.

Rowan nods at me to pile food on my plate, and I don't hesitate. Every time we ate together, he made sure my plate was full before serving himself.

"So, are you ready to see your parents?" he asks, pouring syrup onto the fluffy stack.

I chuckle with a mouth full of food before saying, "No."

"What do you think will happen when they see you?" he asks.

"August will be happy. I'm his favorite besides you, James, and Beau. My dad will be surprised at first, but then he'll get excited. My mom will be happy, but upset I didn't tell her."

"I can already imagine what she's going to say." Rowan looks down, shakes his head and laughs.

I mimic Mom's voice. *"Ellie Alexandra, why didn't you tell me you were coming home? I didn't have time to clean the guesthouse. I need to go buy more food to feed you. I can't believe this."*

Rowan tilts his head back, laughing more. "That sounded a little too close to your mother."

"I know it's scary." I dip my bacon in maple syrup before I take a bite.

"You want me to tag along?"

"I figured you'd go to work today." I cock an eyebrow.

I grab a blueberry and examine it before popping it into my mouth. The ripeness of it bursts with sweet and sour, causing my lips to twist. Rowan's eyes land on my lips and then go back to mine. The heat in my cheeks bloom.

Rowan clears his throat. "James will be there. I'll just text him and let him know; he won't care."

"I think it'd be smart to have you around." My head tilts.

"I can tell her the worst news, and she'll keep her tone in check because she doesn't want to scare you off."

Rowan gives me a cheeky smile. "I like to think I'm her favorite out of everyone."

"Oh, yeah, you're super lovable," I say, grabbing a blueberry and throwing it at him.

He catches it in his mouth, which wasn't supposed to happen, and smiles at me.

I point to him and say, "Don't get cocky."

He wiggles his eyebrows at me while tossing another blueberry and catches it in his mouth.

# EIGHT

## ROWAN

Ellie sings Celine Dion while it blares through the speakers —I feel the vibration near my legs. She attempts to hit the high notes, and I applaud her for her effort, no matter how terrible it sounds.

After breakfast, we went to pick up her car at the brewery, and she offered to drive. My head is touching the car ceiling, so I put the seat back as far as it would go. My knees still hit the glove compartment, digging into my skin. I won't complain or say anything because this is her car, and I don't want to make her feel bad.

She'd been back home for one day, and it's been a breath of fresh air. Anytime I'm with her, I worry less about work, my anxiety, Mom, Addie. She took all the stresses in my life and tucked them away into a jar that she hid from me.

We pull into the driveway of her parent's house; she shuts off the engine and slumps into her car seat. I reach for the door handle to get out, but Ellie doesn't move.

"You ready?" I glance at her.

Ellie peers at me, and the corner of her lip tugs upward.

Her eyes break away from mine, and she looks down at her ring. The sound of the metal circling over and over can put someone into a trance. Her teeth pull at her bottom lip, and I can see the wheels turn in her head. The space around us fills with her anxiety, trying to suffocate her.

I hold her hand to pull her attention away from her own thoughts. "It's going to be fine." A small smile escapes me. "I'm going to be right next to you the entire time. I know your mom can be a little overexcited."

"A little?" She turns to me in her seat. "Remember sophomore year during homecoming? When I said everyone was meeting at our house for photos, she was decorating with balloons and flowers. Matching the balloon colors to the homecoming theme took her a week. Rowan, she called the principal for the colors."

"There's nothing wrong with that."

"We were only there for ten minutes. You know I love my mom, but I always worry about the way she overreacts to things. She gets stressed easily."

"It'll be fine. I think they'd rather you were home and not in New York, anyway." I open my door and step out of the car.

My muscles scream as my body stretches after being cramped in the car. The drive from the brewery to her house takes less than ten minutes, but my neck feels like it took an hour to get here. I stretch it from side to side, relieving the soreness.

I grab Ellie's suitcase from the back and shut the car door. Ellie, 'Ms. do it all herself' tries to take it. I swing the suitcase away from her and put it behind my back, the wheels hitting my ankles, and I try not to wince.

"I got it." I grin.

Ellie puts her hands up and backs away. "Okay, muscle man."

"Muscle man?" I arch my brow.

"You're carrying that thing as if it weighs one pound." She points to it. "It's pretty heavy."

"It's not." I show off and lift it above my head as if it's nothing. My workout consists of lifting bags of barley that are almost two hundred pounds.

"Considering you carry around bags of grain every day at the brewery, I'm not surprised. You aren't the scrawny boy you used to be." She tilts her head, scanning my arms, then peers back up at me.

"If you want me to toss you over my shoulders, just say the word, El." I give her a wink.

"I've always wanted to be thrown over a man's shoulder. Sounds kind of hot."

"Oh yeah?" My eyes trail her up and down when I take two steps toward her and cock my head to the side with a playful smirk.

Ellie takes one step toward me and lifts her chin to meet my gaze. She shrugs and says, "Yeah."

We stand still in that spot, waiting to see who'd break contact first. Suddenly, I feel hypnotized, like I've stepped back in time, thinking about the days when this is all we'd do.

My mouth goes dry and air escapes from my lungs while I drown into those ocean blue eyes.

I clear my throat. "Okay, quit stalling and let's get going."

"I'm not stalling. I was just complimenting you on your new muscles." She wiggles her eyebrows at me.

"I'll take the compliment when you step through the

front door." I hold the back of her neck softly, leading her toward the front steps.

The pinks, purples, and blues of hydrangeas come into view, bursting from the front porch. The smell of honey surrounds us when we walk up the stairs. Ellie hovers her finger over the doorbell, and she hesitates before pushing the button. The loud sound of chimes from inside the house echo.

My brows pinch together in questioning. "Why are you ringing the doorbell?"

"I don't know. I was in a panic." She gestures to the door. "They leave this door unlocked, even though they shouldn't."

"This isn't New York."

She glares at me. "You would lock your doors too if you'd seen what I've seen. Now, zip it." She turns back toward the white door.

The large lavender wreath bounces on the door when it swings open, and we're greeted by August. His smoky blue eyes go wide, and his lips pull into a grin of excitement. He's coated in sweat while in his running gear.

"Holy shit!" August looks at her shock. He pushes the screen door open and grabs Ellie into his arms, enveloping her. Then pulls her off the ground, squeezing her.

"Oof, you just cracked my back," Ellie grumbles as he sets her down. "Thanks." She grinned up at him.

"What the hell are you doing here?" August pushes his round glasses back up his nose.

"I'm... uh, well, I guess I'm home for the summer?" The corner of her mouth tugs up in an awkward smile. "Surprise," she says more in a question, raising her hands to her sides.

August's dark eyebrow arches, and a cruel grin pulls at his lips. "Did you warn Mom?"

Ellie sucks some air through her teeth, the awkward smile still playing along her lips.

August's shoulders bounce as he laughs. "Oh, this will be fun."

He looks past Ellie and sees me with a suitcase. "Rowan." August nods, still smirking at me. "I'm assuming you're here to soften the blow?"

"You know how much your mom loves me."

Ellie turns to look at me with a deadpan expression.

I laugh, throwing my free hand out in questioning. "What?"

She turns and looks at August. Her brother looks at us, smiling, and turns around to walk back into the house.

"Mom, Dad, you have a delivery," August announces.

Ellie peers at me again, her head falling back with a groan as I guide her inside the house and toward the kitchen.

"Surprise," she lifts a shoulder, stretching the word out. She shifts from foot to foot, waiting for their reaction.

I stay close behind her and lower the suitcase to the oak floor. Ellie's parents sat at the white marble kitchen island, drinking their coffee.

Mrs. Thompson's jaw drops. She attempts to talk, but her words sputter before she can speak, "Ellie." She sits her mug down with a soft click against the counter and rises from her chair. Her light brown hair, which falls just past her shoulders, sways when she moves toward us. Her smooth, glowing skin makes her look younger than she is.

"Honey, what are you doing here?" She pulls her daughter in for a hug. "Is everything okay?" She steps back and looks Ellie up and down.

"I'm fine, Mom."

"What a pleasant surprise," her dad says.

Ellie's parents wouldn't let her drive all the way here by herself. They would have bought her a plane ticket right away if she had told them she was coming home for the summer. Ellie doesn't like to burden others with her problems. She's always been that way. She's the type to handle things by herself and not ask for any help.

She's stubborn.

"No, I drove here." She tilts her chin up.

"You drove?" Ellie's mom calls out.

"Sweetie," Mr. Thompson responds to Mrs. Thompson, "Let me hug our daughter first, and then you can interrogate her."

He grins down at Ellie and brings her into a bear hug. His body towers over her, and Ellie smiles. His arms tug her into his strong and sturdy frame. "Hello, my sweet girl. I'm so happy to see you."

Growing up, I watched the bond Ellie and August shared with their dad. It always tore at my heart. Mr. Thompson was the dad who'd do anything for his kids—a kind of love I would've given anything to have with my dad.

My last memory of Dad is of him kneeling and saying he and Mom were separating, and that he might see me again.

I ran after him, begging him to take me with him. He just kept walking, and when he got into his car, I yelled and cried, hoping he'd change his mind. I sat on the front porch, crying, convinced he'd come back for me.

"Hi, Dad." She looks up at him.

Mr. Thompson pulls away, and her mom cuts in, "So, is this just a surprise visit?" Mrs. Thompson looks at me, standing behind Ellie. "Rowan." She grins and opens her arms to greet me with a hug. "How are you?" She pats my back. "I just went out to dinner with your mom and Aunt the other day. I always forget how much of a riot those two can be. We're thinking about starting a book club with some of the other women in town."

"That sounds cool."

Ellie's parents have known Mom and Aunt Rosey since they were kids. Mr. Thompson was already friends with Dad. I never asked him whether he still talks to Dad. What if he does? Does he talk about me? Did they stop talking when he left town?

"Do you want to sit down?" Mr. Thompson gestures with his head toward the living room.

She walks next to her dad and into the living room, his arm wraps around her shoulder, comforting her, while her mom follows behind them. The kitchen and living room connect in an open-house concept. Large oval windows go from the ceiling to the ground, letting in natural light.

"What's going on? Why didn't you tell us you were coming home to visit?" Mrs. Thompson sits on the powder-white sofa chair, crossing her legs as she pulls down her maxi dress to cover her feet.

I glance at Ellie, sitting beside her dad on the other end of the couch sectional. Her throat bobs, and her shoulders tense. She meets my gaze. I give her a small and reassuring nod as we communicate in the same unspoken way we have always been able to.

*You can do this, Ellie.*

"I need you to promise me you will listen and not interrupt me. Not until I'm finished talking." She raises her eyebrows.

Her dad and August agree before giving her a hesitant, worry of a smile. We all turn to look at her mom.

Mrs. Thompson looks at all of us for a beat. "Okay, okay." She holds up her hands. "I won't say a word."

Ellie sits up straight and clears her throat. Everything she tells the group at the brewery, she repeats to them. Mentioning work stress and feeling run down, she holds herself together, similar to the brewery. Before telling them about Charlie, she pauses, then continues.

"Are you okay?" August looks at her with worry in his eyes.

"I think so. It happened so fast that I don't think I've processed anything yet. I just... left." Ellie stares straight ahead of her at nothing.

"Are you two broken up then?" her dad asks.

Ellie looks at him and nods with a smile that doesn't reach her eyes.

"You did the right thing," her dad responds. "I'm glad you came home, even if it's just for a little while."

"I was hoping I could crash at the guesthouse." Ellie looks between her mom and dad.

"You know you don't need to ask," her dad responds, pushing a hand through his salt and pepper hair, then folding his arms across his chest.

"What about work? What's going on with that then?" Her mom crosses her arms.

"I don't know, Mom. It's only been a couple of days since it all happened. I just want to get settled and spend time with everyone."

"We'll get everything set up for your stay." Her dad rises up.

"I'll grab your favorite knitted blanket in the upstairs closet. Give me a list of food you want me to get from the store." Her mom walks around the kitchen.

"Thanks, mom but you don't need to do that. I just need somewhere to sleep, nothing grand."

"You sure you don't want to stay in your old bedroom?" August leans against the wall in the kitchen with his arms crossed and smirks.

"Sleep in my very tiny childhood bed? No thanks." She turns to her parents. "I'm not gonna lie, I was kind of dreading this conversation with you guys."

"You mean you were dreading discussing Mom." August smirks again, and a laugh rumbles through his chest.

Ellie narrows her eyes at him. "Shut up."

August shakes his head with a laugh. "It's good to have you back, Ellie."

"Ro." Ellie turns to me. "Thank you for everything." She grabs my hand and squeezes it.

"It's not a problem, but I need to head out and see my mom and Aunt Rosey."

"Can I see you tonight? At the brewery?" She raises her eyebrows.

"Always, El." The corner of my mouth tips up.

"August." I glance at her brother. "I'll see you around."

He walks toward me and holds out his hand to pull me in, slapping his other palm on my back. "Always a pleasure. I'll see you tonight too."

"Oh, I'll just ride with you then." Ellie points to August.

August rolls his eyes. "I guess you can come with me."

Ellie gives August a playful shove, and he staggers back, though he's a foot taller than her. She's stronger than she looks. "Shut up, you love me."

August grins and pulls her into a messy headlock, ruffling her hair. Ellie squirms, shouting at him to stop, her voice a mix of annoyance and affection. "You smell terrible, August! God, how long did you run for?" She wiggles in his grip, trying to break free, then turns toward their parents. "Mom! Make him stop!"

"Alright, that's enough. August, let go of your sister," Mrs. Thompson calls out from the kitchen sink.

I watch the scene unfold, a warm feeling settling in my chest. It's chaotic, it's loud, but it's perfect.

It's so good to have her home.

# NINE

## ROWAN

After dropping Ellie off, I knew taking some time to myself was the right choice.

Even though I was uncomfortable all night and my shoulder hurt, I didn't let go of her hand. Not even an earthquake would tear me from her.

I push back my hair with both hands. My head tilts toward the sky as I stop. I haven't let myself indulge in a woman for a long time. *243 days. 8 months. 5,840 hours.* That part of my life is something I haven't allowed myself to enjoy.

My habit of pushing people away resulted in my ending relationships prematurely, before anyone else could. I knew I was blaming something that I knew wasn't there.

That was never Ellie's experience. When she was nineteen, New York became her new home. We tried staying together long distance, but when you live on opposite sides of the country, it gets tough. Especially when you both are teenagers who can't afford to see each other anytime you want.

After two years, she came back and delivered the

biggest blow. All I thought about was the ring in my pocket, which felt like a heavyweight pulling me down. My mind went blank, and I lost my voice. I couldn't think. All I could do was nod and tell her I understood.

I did nothing to make myself happy for a long time after that, not for another six months, when I woke up one morning and felt like everything was going to be okay.

As I get closer to Mom and Aunt Rosey's house, my aunt's smirk comes into view as I look up. She and Mom are sitting in the wicker chairs on the porch. Hanging potted plants sway in the wind down the rest of the porch.

"Here he is! I'm so glad we are worthy of your attention." Aunt Rosey waves her fingers at me.

Rosey suggested we move in with her after Dad left. It was large with plenty of room. She nagged Mom until she gave in. And she's the younger one.

The yellow two-story house has become my home. It's fuzzy around the edges of what my first home looked like with Mom, Dad, and Addie. I hold a lot more memories here than I didn't in the other one. Memories that involve me and my friends—Ellie. The first time we kissed was in my bedroom when we were supposed to be studying for a science test.

My heart thundered in my chest when I felt her lips on mine. She was my first kiss. I can still go into my old bedroom and feel somersaults in my stomach.

Mom and Aunt Rosey were downstairs making dinner and singing while Addie danced in the living room. Our cheeks flushed, Ellie and I were called to dinner, facing the scrutinizing gazes from all three.

They teased us for years.

Addie and I look more like Dad than we do Mom. Both Mom and Aunt Rosey have strawberry blond hair, hazel eyes, and freckles scattered on their faces. There're no freckles on mine or Addie's face. I started out very blonde, but that changed as I got older. I do think my eyes look nice.

Mom is a typical coastal mom. She always wears light blue, different shades of white, sage green, and tan. She wears the necklace I bought her for Christmas when I was eighteen. A simple chain necklace with a turtle charm. Her favorite sea animal. Aunt Rosey leans more on the boho side —more hippy with dresses and skirts that always flow in the wind.

"Sorry, sir, we don't take solicitors." Mom peers at me and grinned.

I roll my eyes and walk up the steps to the porch.

"Can I get you a drink? Do you prefer water, lemonade, tea, or beer? It's not your beer, but you know, hospitality and all." My aunt waves her hand around.

My lips turn downward.

"Rose, would you mind getting your nephew a drink and leaving him alone?"

Aunt Rosey gets up, muttering something under her breath about my mom, which Mom ignores.

"Come sit." Mom pats the seat of the other wicker chair next to her, beaming at me like she hadn't seen me in months instead of days.

Mom overcompensated as I grew up, showing extra love after Dad left. Sometimes, it felt like she was trying to protect us so much that it felt forced. I never blamed her for doing that. She wanted us to know that it wasn't our fault. How do you convince a young child that they aren't to blame for a parent leaving?

Just to make her feel better, I'd always nod my head in understanding, give her a kiss on the cheek, and tell her I loved her.

My body slumps into the chair, and I let out an exaggerated sigh. My head falls back and then closes my eyes for a moment, but when I do, all I see is Ellie. The way her hair always smells like vanilla and strawberries, how the sun makes the swirls of blue in her eyes look like a calming sea, or when you get her to laugh just hard enough that a snort slips out of her, making her laugh harder.

"Tell me what you're thinking?" Mom pulls me away from Ellie's crystal-clear eyes.

"Ellie's back in town." I bite the inside of my lip.

She smiles at me and nods. "Your sister told me after you and Ellie left the brewery. How's she doing?"

"Addie didn't tell you why she came home?" I arch my brow.

"She mentioned something about an ex-boyfriend, Charlie, and her job."

I can feel my face grimace when she mentioned his name. There were no issues with him when they first started dating—of course I wallowed in despair when I saw she was moving on.

I questioned him as a person after noticing things as I learned more about him over the years.

One time we went to the Christmas market Dove Point has for the season. Ellie saw a booth where there were handmade aprons. There was one in particular that she wanted. The color was white, with these little flowers embroidered on the upper half of the apron and then on each pocket on the bottom.

To this day I remembered the look on her face when she saw it. She let out a small gasp, her eyes bright with excitement at what she'd found. Ellie said she needed to have it, but Charlie told her she had enough at home and that there wasn't enough space.

I went back and bought it for her. Charlie glared at me while I grinned back after she opened it in front of him.

He's not a fan of me either.

The screen door opens, and I jolt out of my memories when Aunt Rosey comes back out with my drink. She hands me fresh lemonade and then sits down.

"So." Aunt Rosey swings one leg over the other. "What's going on with that blonde guy? The one with Ellie. Are they still going out?"

Rosey always loves to gossip. Now that I am older, I've learned to watch what I say, because it'll be in the Dove Point paper before I know it. I can see the headline now: Ellie comes home after cheating scandal.

"No, they're not together right now." My hand rubs the stubble on my jaw.

"What happened?" Mom looks at me with worry in her eyes.

"Ellie mentioned she had a lot on her plate at work. I guess she was so wrapped up in it that it caused some issues between them." I feel my jaw clench when I think about my next words. "He cheated on her."

"He cheated on her?" Rosey leans over Mom and stares at me.

I nod.

"She found out?" Mom turns to look at me.

I huff a laugh and shake my head before looking at them. "He had the balls to tell her."

"What a little asshole," Rosey snips.

"Rose." Mom looks at her and shakes her head.

"No, he's an asshole. Ellie is a sweet girl. She doesn't deserve that." Rosey stares at Mom with furrowed brows. Her lips press into a line but continues on, "How did her mom handle the news? The woman is such a worrywart about everything. She is always making a fuss over her daughter."

My brows pinch when I think back to conversation. Mrs. Thompson was—calm. She didn't make as big a fuss as she would have with anything else. "She was fine." I look at them. "Her parents listened and said they would help her set up the guest house since she's staying for the next three months."

"Maybe because they didn't like the pretentious little shit," Rosey utters to herself.

"I'm sure you're excited to have her back for an entire summer." Mom grins at me.

I avoid the comment and turn my head away to look at the other houses, trying to hide the smile that wants to betray me and come out.

"Did you guys make plans for anything?"

My attention turns back to Mom. "Not yet. We'll plan to hang out soon after she settles in at her parents' place. I'd like to have as much time with her as possible before she leaves for the city again."

Aunt Rosey eyes me. "*If* she goes back."

"What reason would she have not to? She works at the best restaurant New York offers." I pick at a piece of lint on my jeans, trying to distract myself from this conversation I don't want to have.

Aunt Rosey leans over Mom in her chair before she counts on her fingers. "She just got cheated on. She's burnt out from her demanding job. Her mother says she doesn't have many friends in the city because her life revolves around said job. She's unhappy. It's as simple as that. Considering Ellie's intelligence, it's a wonder why she would return to a place that makes her miserable."

Again, my head falls back onto the chair, while I think

about her words. She makes a good point, but that determines nothing. This summer can be the recharge that Ellie needs to get back to how she was when she first started there.

"I think deep down she came here for another reason.Not just to get away for a summer. What do I know, though? I'm just an old woman who's had a long life and many lovers." Rosey leans back in the chair.

"Alright, I get it." I hold up my hands and think more about it.

Her life is there. She's lived there for almost ten years. People from all over the world visit the restaurant where she works. Considering the situation, what could have led her to leave?

My thoughts spiral, and I go into that dark place that's hard to get out of when I overthink about my worth to someone. She ran away from a messed-up situation, and I have my own baggage that I've been wanting to disappear on its own.

There are things I need to fix in my life. I need to find self-worth for my mind to settle. Good enough for Ellie, for my business, and as a son. I don't want to worry about being left behind again.

I'll only allow myself to have Ellie when I decide to close that chapter of my life and talk to Dad. This could be my second shot at having her and not letting her get away this time.

# TEN

## ELLIE

"Hi, can I get a campfire sundae, please?" Addie stands in front of the window where a teenager nods.

I dip a spoonful into my own sundae, scooping up the fresh-smelling strawberries, melting hot fudge, and caramel sauce. I let out a deep, satisfying breath. The thickness of the custard mixed with everything else melts on my tongue.

"I shouldn't have asked for a tall swirl. It's already dripping down my hand." Riley licks her chocolate and vanilla ice cream, the colors swirling together in the large waffle cone that wraps around it.

"That's why I stick to a bowl," I say before lifting up the clear container that shows off the swirls of my ice cream.

"Life is about risks, Ellie," Riley says and licks her finger.

"Not when it makes you sticky," Addie says.

"Leave me and my ice cream alone," Riley says.

"You're the one who complained." I cock an eyebrow.

"That's beside the point." Riley says.

Wisps of clouds and the bright blue sky blanket the

town. The shining sun embraces everyone. Dove Point's summers are similar to a fairytale. We have our rainy days, but it's always sunny and warm.

Living in New York for as long as I have, I've developed a thicker skin—thanks to the brutal winters. When I saw snowflakes during my very first cold season there, I was giddy, like a little kid. The way it blanketed the streets, turning everything into a winter wonderland—it felt magical.

That magic faded fast as the years passed. The snow changed from pure white to black and gray. The thick fluffiness turned into mush. I cursed the weather gods every time I slipped on a patch of ice or trudged through piles of slush.

"Why couldn't Hailey come along?" I glance at Riley.

"She's meeting up with us later tonight." She takes another lick of ice cream.

We walk toward the heart of the town, passing under an enormous sign that hangs from two lampposts on either end of the sidewalk. Across it, someone wrote 'Dove Point Music Fest.'

The streets shut down, with groups of people taking advantage of walking down them. Apparently, it's what we do when a road is closed. Everyone flocks to it as if they've never seen one before.

We watch small children run past us; a lion, Spiderman, a unicorn, and something that resembles a terrifying SpongeBob SquarePants.

Toward the end of the street, a large stage looms, with the hum of activity surrounding it. I watch a band setting up their instruments, adjusting the microphones and tuning guitars, preparing for the night ahead.

Meanwhile, a DJ plays upbeat tracks through the speakers, the music spilling into the streets, giving an energetic pulse that seems to ripple through the crowd.

"Okay, so who came up with the idea of Milo carrying drinks to the customers?" Riley asks before we sit down at a table.

The tray has a simple circle design with 3D-printed cups that hold the glasses and a strap that can clip on Milo. He's very careful and doesn't mess around with his snacks.

"When you're getting paid in treats, anything is possible. Plus, it took forever to train him to do that. Rowan taught him a trick that lets us know when he wants to do it. So, he chooses his own hours." Addie licks some ice cream off her thumb.

"I also noticed someone staring at James almost the entire night." I wiggle my brows at her.

She winces and fans her hand toward her mouth after shoveling it in. "Cold!" she wailed.

Riley cackles before scrambling to eat as much of her ice cream as she could as it runs down her fingers and into the napkin around the cone.

"I wasn't staring. He was talking, so my attention was on him," Addie murmurs, brushing her brown hair behind her ear.

"He answered a question that Rowan asked, and you kept your eyes on him after that," Riley taunts.

"I didn't know it was a crime to look at someone, sorry." She raises her eyebrows with attitude.

"There's a difference between looking and eye-fucking," Riley says.

"I was not doing that."

I glance at Riley with a smirk, and she mirrors my expression.

Addie sits up straighter and puts her hands between her legs. She peers around before whispering, "I had a crush on him once during middle school, and you guys will never let me forget it."

Riley and I glance at each other. Addie hides her red face in her hands, shaking her head.

"Aw, it's fine, Adds. We all had little crushes growing up," I say.

She looks at me. "You're one to talk! I still see how you look at my brother. It's all over your face."

"She's got you there," Riley rucks in her lips, holding back a smirk.

My eyes narrow at both of them, and I continue to eat my sundae in silence. Addie's right. I'm not good at sneaking glances at Rowan when I stare at him like an owl.

My phone vibrates through my cross-body purse, making me set down my delicious ice cream to unzip it and take out my phone.

> Charlie: I miss you.

I roll my eyes and groan. This isn't the first time he's texted me since I left.

"What's up?"

I show them the screen.

"Ew," Addie grimaces.

Riley cackles, "What a fucking tool. You better not respond to him."

"I'm not? Why would I? I have no desire to talk to him."

"I have no clue where your head is at." Riley shrugs. "I was just making sure."

"Trust me, he's very far from my thoughts. I know I've

only been home for about a week, but I kind of already forgot he existed." I put my phone back in my bag.

"Good for you. He doesn't deserve any space in your pretty head." Addie points her spoon at me.

"I'm just hoping he stops bothering me at some point this summer. I told him that we need some distance."

"He needs to go into literal space and leave you alone," Riley says.

"I love having you as a best friend, you know that, right?" I look at Riley.

"Duh. And I adore you."

"Hey, I'm sitting right here," Addie says.

"I love you too," I say.

Being around my family and close friends makes me miss who I used to be.

---

THE NIGHT SKY is in full effect. I sit on the beach and take in the ocean while everyone else clusters near the main stage to check out the band.

I look up at the beautiful dark blue sky, watching the stars twinkle. This is my happy place. The sounds of the waves crashing onto the surface, the seagulls flocking above while they call for each other, the calm of everything around me. I don't have a towel with me, so I've sacrificed my clothes and hair to lie down on the sand.

I've tried many times to spot stars when I lived in New York. I'd go on the rooftop of my apartment, sit in a chair, and just try. When I wasn't successful, I'd stare at the moon, hoping Rowan was looking with me all those miles away.

I've gotten used to the chaotic lifestyle of the city. The hustle and bustle. The loud noise you can't escape from.

When I settled my life there, it all enamored me. The people, the lights, the energy folded themselves around me. It was like nothing I'd ever experienced before.

I took the negatives and tried to reframe them as positives. Every compliment and praise I received toward my work made me hope those words would ignite that flame in me again.

It never did.

"Ellie!" Riley screams from a distance.

Looking behind me, I see her waving at me. I get up, brushing the sand off my shorts, legs, and hands. She turns back around when I approach her.

"How old do you think the drummer is?" Riley tilts her head.

"Why? You think he's cute?" My eyes follow hers toward the stage.

"I'm going to say twenty-eight," James butts in.

"If that guy is your next meal, then I suggest making your move quickly." I jut my chin toward the group of women flocking him.

"I've always enjoyed a bit of competition," Riley says, strutting away.

We hear noise from up front, and a man with a guitar strapped to him speaks. A sound behind me pulls my attention away while he introduces everyone.

"Hey, guys." Hailey walks up to me and James, Beau trailing close to her. Hailey gives off a cool vibe, with light brown hair and curtain bangs, one section dyed a striking icy blond. Tattoos wind down her arms, and her septum and nose rings glint as she moves. Her winged liner is always perfect—sharp enough to cut through anything.

"Hey." I pull her into a quick hug before stepping back. "How was your date?"

"It was fine. He told me about this cool club, thirty minutes from here. We should check it out."

"I can totally use some dancing in my life right now." I nod.

"I'm in." Beau looks at Hailey with a smirk.

She turns to glare at Beau, who looms at our backs, his tall, broad frame hovering over us. They're like two peas in a pod. He's covered in tattoos, even on his neck, with a nose piercing to match what Hailey has. He and James share similar features, making it obvious they're related.

"Who invited you?" She peers at him.

"You're saying you have no desire to watch me do the robot?" Beau shoves his hands into the pockets of his rugged jean jacket.

"I see your face enough at the tattoo shop," Hailey responds.

"How is it my fault I enjoy getting tattoos?"

"You don't see me going to the barbershop and bugging you all the time."

"Oh, please. You love seeing my handsome face." Beau lifts his hand from his pocket and wraps an arm around Hailey, tugging her body into him.

She rolls her eyes and takes a swig of her drink. I hide my smile when I eye James, giving him a knowing look that says, *Can your brother be more obvious?* He shrugs and lets out a quiet chuckle.

The band plays a familiar melody, and Hailey grabs my hand, her eyes lighting up as she glances at me. The first chords of "Teenage Dirtbag" by Wheatus thrums among the audience.

"I love this song," Hailey shouts in excitement and sings.

We serenade each other while dancing through the

crowd. My arm bumps into James, his grip holding his beer up.

"Alright, alright, calm down." He wipes his drink off his shirt.

I wince. "Sorry."

"Hi, guys!" Addie calls out, running toward us. "I was just up front with Riley, and she's glaring at the drummer."

"That checks out." August comes up behind me, scaring the shit out of me.

"Where the hell did you come from?"

"Ha, good to know I'm still capable of scaring you."

An hour later, I feel sweat dropping down my chest from jumping, singing, and dancing with my friends. Another melody ends, and the lead singer bends down to pick up his drink, taking a swig before setting it down.

"This cover is slower, but it's a good one." Sailor Song plays through his guitar.

My thoughts get lost in the music as I rock back and forth on my feet. I stop thinking about my career, Charlie, and feeling alone.

Someone warm and solid presses themselves against my back, and I think nothing of it. It's gotten more crowded since we've been here, so I expect people to lose self-awareness with personal space. But then I feel a hand on my shoulder and look up, ready to fight whoever's touching me.

Dark blue eyes frame thick lashes that gaze toward me, along with a smirk that showcases a dimple I'm all too familiar with. The pounding in my chest settles. I grin up at Rowan and look toward the band again, trying to steady my breathing. A simple touch like this makes me want to turn around and tug him against me. But I push my body into his. *Maybe* my ass pushes toward him a little more. I blame it on the alcohol.

"Hi," he says, smiling down at me.

"Hey."

I feel his hand go from my shoulder and down my arm. Stroking my skin. For just a second, I let myself get lost in his caress. The way it relieves and helps ground me. The simple act of his touch lets me know that he's here. That everything is going to be okay.

The song ends, and the crowd erupts with shouts and applause. The band announces they'll be playing one last track for the night. I recognize the melody of the music, and I can't contain my excitement as "Adore You" by Harry Styles blared from the stage.

My eyes find Rowan again, and I grab his hand, dragging him through the throng and toward everyone up front.

"What are you doing?" he asks.

"Come on."

His tall frame helps separate people as we get through them, and when we get as close as possible, I turn, still gripping his hands to steady myself from the dizziness.

My hair whips this way and that, and my smile beams across my features. Rowan spins me around and holds me, pulling me tight. I want to be consumed by him, to kiss him. I need him.

But I can't.

I don't let go of his hold, mostly because of the spins because I'm drunk. I crane my neck up and sing to him, serenading him until I'm blue in the face.

His grin is beautiful when he looks down at me. I feel his grip on me tighten, pulling me as close as possible. The heat on my cheeks feel like they're going to burst into flames from the touch. My mouth curves into a smile, and I take in the warmth of his body onto mine.

A feeling of happiness spreads through me, from my

head to my toes, and I hold on to that while I dance with my best friend to one of my favorite songs. I lock this moment into my memory as we spin in each other's arms.

The night eventually turns into a blur, and all I remember is Rowan and his beautiful eyes and his infectious laugh.

I feel like a teenager again.

# ELEVEN

## ROWAN

"Morning, sunshine," I greet Ellie, seating myself opposite her in the booth.

She groans, her head resting on the cool table. She isn't fond of the idea of meeting me for brunch, considering how late we stayed out last night, and how many beers she drank.

We chose our town's well-loved diner, The Breakfast Nook. Each window has a booth connected to it and square tables are placed throughout. It's a more modern look since it was updated.

Her forehead moves back and forth on the table, and her thick hair falls over her back.

"What are you doing?" I ask.

"I'm cooling my face down," she says.

"You had a lot to drink last night."

"You don't say," she mumbles.

It's impossible not to feel bad. Moving my fingers through her hair, not thinking anything of it other than trying to make her as comfortable as possible. I see her slump, and her face tilts to one side on the table.

The sound of a moan slips through her lips, and my

hand stops. The desperation I feel running through my body, wanting to hear it again and again, is agonizing. I bite the inside of my cheek and attempt the thoughts that want to run through my head.

"Why did you stop?" she whines.

"Sorry." And despite my better judgment, I start again.

"This feels incredible. Oooh, my God." She moans again.

*Don't get a boner, don't get a boner, do not get a boner.*

Images in my head start to appear after hearing the sound; her pretty little mouth letting my name slip out while she's bent over a kitchen counter, on her knees in bed.

I shake them away, but still feel my dick getting hard, and I'm not dealing with this right now. I remove my hand from her just before the server approaches the table..

The server glances over at Ellie, still facing down on the table. My lips tug into an apologetic grin and I give her my order along with Ellie's usual. She jots it down on the notepad and leaves with a smile.

Ellie picks up her head and keeps her eyes closed as she laid it back on the headrest of the blue booth.

"You remember my order?" Ellie rasps.

"You've ordered the same thing since we were small. It's your go-to breakfast here."

I cross my arms and look at her. Her skin is vibrant, it shows every freckle you can spot across her nose and sprinkles across her cheeks. Her pouty lips look so delicious that I need to withstand the urge to reach across the table, cup her face, and taste them.

"Did I tell you that Charlie is clueless about what my favorite breakfast is? I've told him a million times what I like, but he never remembered," Ellie says. "One year of being friends, years of being together, and he couldn't remember. I chalked it up to a poor memory." She sighs. "He forgot a lot of things that involved me."

My hands clench into fists as my arms remain folded across my chest. Just the sound of his name spikes my blood pressure.

Considering they've been together for four years, why doesn't he remember that? What drew her to him?

"I guess it must be a good thing you aren't with him anymore then, hm?" I say.

"He texted me yesterday." She rubs her temples.

My body goes rigid while I hold my breath, wondering what he texted and if she responded to him. I didn't think he'd have the balls to reach out to her, considering she ended things with him.

"What did he say?" I ask, swallowing the lump in my throat.

"Telling me he misses me. You know, bullshit."

"Did you respond to his text?" I'd like to think that I know Ellie better than she knows herself. My head tells me she didn't text him, and I hope I'm right.

"I didn't. I looked at it, showed Riley and Addie, then ignored it."

My shoulders slump in relief, not knowing they were up to my ears. "I'm sure they both had something interesting to say about that."

"Oh, Riley wanted to go through the phone and punch him in the dick."

"I wouldn't blame her if she did."

"That's dramatic."

"Well, Riley is the definition of dramatic."

"You should avoid saying that if you're near her."

"If I go missing, you know who to investigate."

The server comes to our table with our dishes. "French

toast and milk. She places a plate in front of Ellie, "and the works." An extra plate of hash browns and sausage links sit next to her French toast.

She gives us a smile, asking if we need anything else, and heads back to the kitchen.

The maple syrup drops off the edge of the bread that's fried to perfection. Chocolate chips melt on top, and strawberries, powdered sugar, and whipped cream scattered across the plate. She pulls a hair tie from her wrist and wraps her hair in a loose bun, not taking her eyes off her dish.

"Rowan," she says without looking at me.

"Yeah?"

"I'd appreciate it if you would eat your food, and stop staring at me."

"Whoa, how did you know I was looking at you? I was looking at your food."

She gives me a blank stare. "If that's the case, then look away because you're not getting any of this."

I hold back a laugh, knowing that if I were to grab something off her plate, she'd stab my hand with the fork. She's very territorial with her food, but I've mastered picking a fry or two.

I lick my lips, looking over Ellie's shoulders, and say, "Mr. Frank is stuffing two breakfast burritos into his mouth. Holy shit, he just unhinged his jaw."

"Wait, what?" Ellie whips her head behind her.

Mr. Frank wasn't doing that; he was drinking a cup of coffee and talking to the cook. I use this opportunity to taste the whipped cream, licking it from my finger.

She narrows her gaze at me, then peers down at her plate and then back to me. "Did you just..." She points to her food.

I give her a questioning look, picking up my glass of water. "I don't know what you're talking about."

"Mr. Frank wasn't even eating anything."

"Sorry, I must have been seeing things." I stab my fork into my hash browns, which are crispy and soft at the same time.

Ellie places her elbow on the table and then points at me. "Rowan Andrew Williams, I swear, if you touch my food... you don't want to know what I'll do to you."

My eyebrows rise. I set my elbows down on each side of my plate, holding my cheeks in my hands. "Please tell me what you'll do to me."

"Don't try to be funny," she says, forcing her smile at bay.

"Aw, you like when I'm funny." I pout, leaning back in the booth before folding my arms.

"You're lucky you're cute." She stuffs a piece of bread that carries all her toppings into her mouth.

"Only for you, baby girl."

Her cheeks flush at the comment, making my heart leap in response. All I crave is to spend more time with her. I need her. If I put in the effort to bring back our intimacy, we might rekindle our connection, forgetting about our problems for a short while.

# TWELVE
## ROWAN

"Ellie, would you mind checking the back of my hair to make sure it looks okay?" Riley asked. "I don't want a repeat of the prom tragedy, where clippings from my extensions were showing off."

"The back of your head looks fine." August looks at Riley in the rearview mirror.

"I didn't ask you, Augustus." She turns to me. "I cannot wait to get to this place. All I would like to do is dance with my bestie and have a fun time. I don't want any guys bothering us."

"Your hair is good to go, Ry," Ellie says.

Laughing and chatting, Ellie, Riley, and Hailey sit in the back, and their voices merge with the car's hum. Ellie leans against the window, her eyes flicking between the passing city lights and her phone, checking messages or snapping photos.

I'm upfront with August; the familiar sound of his music fills the space between us. His hand taps on the steering wheel to the beat while he glances at me with a grin when he hears Riley talking. Beau and James will meet us at the nightclub, but for now, it's just the four of us, the laughter and energy building as we near our destination.

"My outfit tonight is so good. I thought long and hard about it," Riley says.

"I have something long and hard you can think about." August grins at her.

"Ew, August." Ellie grimaces.

"Augustus, you would be so lucky if I were to consider your small penis."

"Hey, it's not small. It's large and in charge. It's a shower and a grower. You would know if you took a chance on me."

Riley ignores him while adjusting her top.

As we pull into the parking lot, I watch flocks of people exiting their vehicles. The five of us pile out while other partygoers rush toward the music. The sound thumps from inside when the black doors open and close. Outside, people separate into groups, talking or looking forward to others arriving.

Beau yells, standing in front of the entrance, "Took you guys long enough."

"Sorry. We were waiting for these three." August gestures with his head toward Ellie, Riley, and Hailey.

"Sorry for wanting to look good tonight," Riley says.

"Come on, let's go." Ellie pulls Riley's arm.

We follow the girls, and I keep my eyes locked on Ellie. This evening will be interesting. I'm going to glare at any man who goes near her. The outfit she has on tonight proves I'll need to keep myself in check.

The snow-colored halter top shows off her cleavage while skinny, small tassels hang on the hem in the front, making it look more playful. She's wearing these incredible jean shorts that should be illegal and paired them with a brown belt and her white high-top Converse sneakers.

She looks like a goddamn smoke-show.

"This is my heaven." Beau glances around as if he were a kid in a candy shop.

Hailey glares at him. "Beau, please don't get us kicked out."

"Looks like we have a bachelorette party here with us tonight. Guys, care to join me?" Beau asks with a smirk.

"I guess," James says with a huff.

"Don't need to ask me twice," August says.

I push my hands into my pockets. "I'm gonna stay back."

"Suit yourself." Beau pats me on the shoulder.

Everyone disperses in different directions, except for Ellie and Riley, who stick by me.

The nightclub is buzzing with music and laughter. People pack the dance floor, and their bodies move in sync with the pulsing beat. Reflecting light, the disco balls, a cluster of varying sizes, adorn the ceiling above, creating shimmering spots across the room.

I watch the guys saunter over to a table filled with women. Deep maroon vines and foliage hang above the long section of tables, with a white glow emanating from them. Behind the DJ booth is a neon light that displays, 'Dance first, think later.'

"I'm going to get us some drinks. I'll be right back." Riley gestures to the bar.

The bar is the showstopper.

Red lighting shines under the entire counter. Crystal racks run across the wall behind the bartenders, filled with bottles of liquor. There are three separate arches below the display, stocked with different brands of alcohol, all lined up in their signature glass bottles.

"Are you gonna dance?" Ellie stands on her toes.

To hear her better, I bend down to her level. "The floor looks crowded, and I'm not sure if anyone wants a tall man bumping into people."

She shakes her head. "It'll be fine!"

"I like the sparkles on your cheeks," I say, after pointing to my own.

*Sparkles? I like the sparkles on your cheeks? I couldn't have said anything better than I like your damn sparkles?*

She tilts her head back and laughs while I lower my head down even further, trying to hide my embarrassment, and she surprises me by meeting my eyes. Her head angles down with a grin plastered on her face.

"Thank you. It's a highlighter blush. It gives me a bit of a glow." She places her hand under her chin and beams.

"Well, it looks beautiful on you."

The lighting in here is dim; however, I can almost make out her cheeks turning red. She's blushing and attempting to mask her smile by covering her face. I grab her wrists and pull her hands away.

"Don't hide that smile from me."

She locks her eyes with mine and pulls at her bottom lip. My grip still holds on to her while we enjoy this moment alone together under the moody lights of the nightclub.

"I come *beering* gifts." A smile tugs at Riley's lips. "Get it?" She clutches five beers in her hands.

"That's pretty good," Ellie admits and grabs her beer from Riley.

"Eh, it was fine." I grab mine and salute her in thanks.

She deadpans and walks past us, glaring as she sets down her sister's beer.

The music changes to something upbeat. Ellie takes another swig of her drink before she and Riley go to dance.

"Wanna come?" she asks.

"Nah, I'm good."

A hand lands on my shoulder, and I turn to see August standing next to me. I follow his gaze going onto Riley.

August watches Riley the same way I watched Ellie. Their friendship is interesting. They were close years ago, and then, one day, they started hanging out less and less. The only difference I noticed between the two of them is in their banter.

Sometimes it can be entertaining; other times it gets annoying.

I trail my eyes back to Ellie, her skin glistening under the party lights, her hair moving as she turns her body. I notice a guy shifting his body closer to hers, and knowing Ellie, she won't shy away from someone wanting to dance. He's tall, not as tall as me, but enough for Ellie, and she smiles at him.

I tighten my grip around my beer bottle, and if I don't relax, it's going to shatter in my hand. I loosen it and instead put the pressure into my jaw, tightening it while I clench my teeth.

Heat surges through my blood as I stare at him, embracing her. She gives him a smile that doesn't reach her eyes, while returning the gesture.

I attempt to control my annoyance and remind myself that she's friendly. I watch him gesture with his head in the opposite direction of us to a table filled with a couple of men and women.

"August, do you see this fucking clown?" I turn to look at him, but he's disappeared somewhere else.

Ellie smiles and shakes her head. I can see her trying to walk back toward us, but the guy is being relentless. My jaw muscles pop while my chest rises and falls in an unsteady rhythm. She holds up a hand toward him, and her facial expression changes from pleasant to irritated.

I put down my beer on the round high-table, and when my eyes connect back to them, his hand tugs at her wrist, and all I see is red. My body moves fast as I approach the two of them.

My pulse quickens by the second, fueled by rage, as I grit, "Hey."

He turns his head, and I have a slight height advantage, causing him to lift his chin up to speak to me.

"Do you mind? I'm talking to someone." His beady little eyes stare back at me.

"I do mind," I say, keeping my voice steady and my breathing in control.

"Who the hell are you?" he asks.

"It doesn't matter who I am. Why the fuck are you touching her?" My hands clench into fists, my nails biting into my skin.

"Look, man, all we were doing was talking."

Ellie chimes in, "Yeah, and then you wouldn't let me go back to my table."

Red-hot anger rushes through me, and I almost bare my teeth at him like some wild animal. Emotions take over me I've never felt before.

"Hey, I thought we were having a good time, sweetie," he says.

After unclenching my fists, I walk towards him. "Get your fucking hands off her, or I swear I will rip you into shreds."

The man narrows his gaze at me before letting her go. Ellie takes her arm back and wraps her hand around her wrist where he was holding her. He stares at me, not averting his gaze, and I'm more than happy to stare back. Just for the hell of it, I grin at him.

"She isn't worth the trouble." He turns his back on us.

I stare at him, making sure he doesn't backtrack and bother Ellie again. Soft hands tug on my arm, but I don't let my eyes falter until the man reaches his table with his friends.

"Come on." Ellie pulls me toward her, and I feel her hand run down my arm, into my hand, and she locks her fingers through mine.

We head back to the table where our friends stare at us. Each of them carry a unique expression: shock, surprise, pleased, giddy. Ellie doesn't drop my hand when we get to them but grips it tighter, like she's nervous about the man coming back. I give her a gentle squeeze, reassuring her I'm not going anywhere.

"What a creep," Riley says.

"I'm sorry I didn't see what happened, Ellie," August says with worry, his eyebrows creasing together. "I would have stepped in."

Ellie shakes her head. "It's okay. Rowan got to me just in time. My knight in shining armor." She looks up at me with a beaming smile.

I feel my heartbeat quicken at the small compliment. "It was nothing." I wave her off while heat creeps up my neck.

She takes another long swig of her drink, polishing it off, and sets it back down on the table while everyone continues their conversation over the loud music.

"You wanna dance?" she asks.

I glance toward the dance floor behind me. It's more intimate in the way people are dancing.

Bodies press against bodies, hands roaming each other. We didn't even dance like this during homecoming or prom.

Before I let my fear get in the way, I nod my head yes, and she leads me to the dance floor. It's fine. We're both grown adults, and we have an intimate past. We dry-humped ... a lot when we were younger. This is nothing. This is fine.

It's fine.

# THIRTEEN

## ELLIE

Anger radiated from Rowan that I'd never seen before. Feelings for him bubbled to the surface, and I couldn't hold them down. It was...*hot*. Then, the next thing I knew, I asked him to dance with me; or rather, I blurted it out. It may have been my reason for getting closer to him and for letting myself touch him.

A slow song plays, and intimate couples, engulfed in their own world, crowd the dance floor, grabbing one another as if being pulled apart. My hands find his shoulders, then trail down his biceps and onto his waist. I resist the urge to tug at the back of his shirt and pull him into me.

He caresses my arms and strokes them, giving me goosebumps with the light touch. I lick my bottom lip before I tug on it with my teeth. Rowan's eyes follow, and his strong Adam's apple bobs.

The dim lights cast a glowing sensation over the dance floor, turning everyone's bodies into shadows and slow movements, almost mesmerizing. I couldn't get enough of his calloused hands that wander along my body, pulling my hips into him.

My body turns to Rowan, and my back presses against him. I gaze at him—his smoldering eyes—and feel myself drift off in them. I'd be okay with not finding my way home if I were lost in them. The intimacy builds, and my ass grinds into him, wanting to feel him get hard against me.

Everything fades around me, and it's just the two of us here. I fight with myself to push away when I know we're trenching into dangerous territory. With the space between us being only inches apart, the heat of his body wraps me up.

*This can't happen.*

My eyes cast down at his lips, and I'm taken to our first kiss again. I still remember how soft they were on mine. My hands go up his chest and then to his shoulders, moving toward the back of his neck, where I feel strands of silky, thick hair running through my fingers. I know he wants to taste me just as badly as I do him.

My heart hammers inside me, and a dull ache between my legs reminds me of his power as he moves closer. With his lips inches away from mine, he cups my face in his hands, only for mine to caress him once I closed my eyes.

*Is this happening? Do I want this to happen?*

Something fierce pulls me toward him, meeting him halfway when the music changes to something with a quicker tempo. The smoky orange glow of the sultry lighting turns deep blue.

I compel myself to leave that bubble of lust and regain my footing. My eyes roam to his chest, which continues to rise and fall. The adrenaline courses through our bodies. We stand still on the dance floor, frozen for a heartbeat.

And neither of us dares to move.

Ellie: I'm in deep shit.

Ellie: HELP

Riley: Whoa

Addie: What's wrong?

Ellie: Pizza, chocolate, movies.

Hailey: Please stop blowing up my phone and let me sleep.

Addie: Emergency movie night? Oh, this is code red.

Riley: I'll bring the pizza.

Addie: I'll get the chocolate.

Hailey: I'll bring the tequila.

"I'M HERE." Riley sings out when she comes into the guesthouse an hour later, a pizza box in each hand. My mouth salivates thinking about the melted cheese I'll consume. Lactose intolerance be damned.

Addie follows, carrying hefty bags that fill with assorted chocolates. "My fingers feel like they're going to fall off from carrying all of this."

"What's up bitches." Hailey raises her arms holding two tequila bottles with an up to no good grin on her lips.

Everyone here is in their loungewear, with no makeup, no bras, and no guys.

Our emergency movie night started when Riley lost her virginity. Every time something monumental happened we'd call for an emergency movie night.

"I have all our movies queued up and ready to go." I

point to the television that hung above the fireplace, where it's surrounded by the couch and lounge chairs. We end up moving everything, including the coffee table, to make a large pillow and blanket bed. We lie together, eating and gossiping while Bridget Jones's Diary plays in the background. I'm sure the guys envies us.

"Hand me the tequila." I grab the bottle from Hailey.

# FOURTEEN

## ROWAN

This morning, I messaged Ellie, hoping she was free to hang out. Over and over my thoughts became consumed with everything that happened between us. When our bodies pressed together, I thought I felt a lightning strike.

Unfortunately, she was already taken by the girls. She let me in on the secret of emergency pizza night. What I've learned from that is, it's nothing good. The topic could be questionable, and I hoped to God it's not about me.

Instead, the guys came to my place to hang out and grill. Three men, ready to devour everything after a grueling workout, found food stacked on my kitchen counter. We ran ten miles after lifting weights in the town gym. Milo wanted to join the run, but I wouldn't allow him to go ten miles. That's animal torture. So, I gifted him with a new chew toy and bone.

"Where the hell is your mustard?" James rifles through the fridge.

"Bottom shelf inside the door," I say.

The guys pile their plates to the brim with juicy burgers, grilled corn on the cob, fresh greens, and other small sides.

"Hey, what happened last night at the club?" Beau asks before he picks up his burger, taking a large bite out of it.

"What happened last night?" I glance at everyone, breaking my gaze away from my food, and they all have shit-eating grins on their face. Apart from August, who displays a grimace.

"You know what we're talking about," James says, pointing a pickle at me.

Thoughts drift back to last night; us dancing under the mood lighting, the bass vibrating off the floor and into our bodies. I still feel the handprints she's left on me. When they landed on the nape of my neck, I wanted to go feral. My body felt like it was on fire, but the desire poured out of me when I slid my hands over her waist and hips. I let myself go a step further when I passed the hem of her shorts.

Teenage Rowan would lose his absolute shit if he saw that happening.

"I had to turn around the minute I saw my sister get all handsy with you," August says. "Why would you do that in front of me?"

"And I'm the one to blame?" I bite into my cheeseburger.

"We're not blaming anything," James says.

"Yeah, we're just bringing up that you two were humping each other," Beau says.

August groans, hitting him on the shoulder with the back of his hand. "Dude."

"What?" Beau chuckles. "Can't we be happy that he's getting what he wants?"

"Dude!" August blurts before he punches Beau in the arm.

"Ow," Beau says.

"What about the guy she was with?" James asks.

"I'm just happy that Rowan stopped whatever could have happened." August shakes his head. "I left for five seconds to talk to Riley, and then that shit happened."

Beau looks at August and grins. "And what were you talking about?"

"None of your business," August says.

"August and Riley sittin in a tree k-i-s-s-i-n."

"Beau, I swear to God, I'll hit you again." August points at him.

Beau giggles and bites into his corn.

"Back to Rowan," James says.

I roll my eyes. "Nothing happened."

# FIFTEEN

## ELLIE

"So much happened," I breathe.

"I can't believe I missed this!" Addie shouts.

Hailey looks at her with pinched brows.

"You want to see your brother and Ellie make out?" Riley replies.

Addie slumps her shoulders and rolls her eyes. She pushes her hair from her face and composes herself. "No, that's not what I mean. I mean, I wish I had seen Rowan almost beat the shit out of a guy. My brother can't hurt a fly. Remember when I saw a spider crawling on top of his desk at work, and I told him to kill it?"

Addie pops a piece of a chocolate bar into her mouth. "He got the creepy thing in a glass and brought it outside to put on a bush. Who does that?"

"The guy wasn't rude to me. Just a little aggressive, I guess. He wanted to continue hanging out, and I didn't want to. That's when he grabbed my wrist, and I didn't even hear Rowan come up behind me." I shrug. "Do I attract assholes or something? All the guys I've met outside of Dove Point are creeps or jerks. Remember the one guy who thought the government put microchips in our brains when we were born?"

Hailey cackles. "What the fuck?"

"Yeah, I stayed the entire time because I was scared to end the date." I smiled, nodded, and never saw him again." I shiver.

"Okay, going back to what we were talking about," Riley states. "Did you want to kiss Rowan?" She leaned across the floor with a gleeful smile.

"I won't lie and say no."

Addie shrieks like a teenager.

"You know, it's weird that you're excited about your friend and brother almost kissing," Hailey says.

"It's not weird when we all know they're meant to be together. Why can't I be happy for both of them?" Addie narrows her eyes on Hailey.

When Rowan and I dated in high school, Addie took that as us planning to get married and started calling me her sister. It was very cute, and of course, I never told her to stop. Rowan didn't either.

"We're not getting together," I say.

"Why not?" Addie frowns.

"For a multitude of reasons. I've created a life in New York. I have an apartment there. A career."

"Jobs come and go, but love is forever," Addie says.

"God, you're such a romantic," Hailey says.

"So what if I am?" Addie crosses her arms. "I'm sorry that I'm all for a happily ever after. They can happen."

"El, do you love your job?" Riley asks.

Biting the inside of my cheek, I start questioning it. Do I love my job? It's all too complicated now. They stare at me, waiting for an answer.

"Do you want the surface-level answer or the deep-level answer?" I ask.

"As deep as the ocean, girly pop," Hailey says.

My palms push into my eyes before I peer at them. "I loved my job. I loved every minute until I didn't. I feel like I can't complain though."

"You can totally complain," Riley says.

"Yeah, but this is something I've wanted since I was little, and now that I'm twenty-nine, I'm questioning my passion for it. I mean, take Hailey for example." I point at her.

"Why am I an example?"

"Because you're obsessed with what you do." I say.

"Uh, I have my days where I fucking hate it too," she says.

"Yeah, I love teaching yoga, but sometimes I don't feel like telling people to bend down and breathe because there are days when I want to fall down and scream." Riley says.

"Okay, that's a little dramatic," Hailey says.

Riley gives her sister the finger while she keeps her eyes on me. Hailey sorts at my side.

"Look, I've chosen the wrong path in my life. I went into something I loved, and maybe it should have stayed a hobby or something. It pulled me away from home and my friends, even Charlie. It was my fault he cheated on me because I became consumed by the kitchen."

"I'm going to stop you right there." Hailey puts up a hand, showing off her black stiletto nails. "You will not blame yourself for what that worthless piece of a man did to you. He should have ended things if he knew he was going to cheat."

Addie and Riley nod in agreement.

I let out a sigh. "I don't know what I'm doing with my

life anymore. I miss the simple things. I miss the type of baking that brings people joy. The things I've created were incredible, but sometimes they looked so..."

"Lifeless?" Addie says.

My chest feels heavy, and my eyes prickle without me stopping them.

"When did you start feeling like this?" Riley asks.

I huff a laugh because I remember the day. "It started the day we were prepping for a big event. I was under a lot of pressure. On the day of the event, I messed up the main dessert dish, a fucking soufflé. Something I've made a million times. It was just me and two other chefs who had to prepare it."

"What happened to them?" Addie asks.

The team was told to make one hundred soufflés for all the guests that would attend the charity event. The head chef designated me as the team lead on it. Everything had to be perfect, so I prepared for anything that could have gone wrong.

Pain in my jaw radiates over the dumbest mistake I'd made in my career. "I forgot the butter."

The girls look at me perplexed.

Inhaling through my mouth, I close my eyes before continuing. "I could've fixed the problem. I knew it wasn't the end of the world, but it was for me. I never messed up. Ever."

"So then what did you do?" Riley asks.

"I dropped to the floor and cried. I cried and cried until my eyes had no more tears left. I screwed up." A dull pain shoots from my palms. I look down only to realize my nails dug into them, creating crescent moons. "I sat on the floor for two hours."

"Did you get in trouble?" Hailey asks.

A weak laugh escapes my lips. "No, I didn't get in trouble. But there is something I need to tell you guys."

The three of them perk up at my words. I haven't mentioned the promotion I received at the restaurant since I've been home. I haven't decided yet, and this decision will solidify what direction I'll be taking in my life.

"They offered me a new position to be head chef at the restaurant."

"What?" they say in unison.

"Mhm." I nod.

"Did you say yes?" Riley asks.

"If you said yes, then that means you're for sure staying in New York." Addie says.

"I mean, you should say yes because the opportunity is insane, but, shit, would we even have time to see you anymore?" Riley says.

"Did you tell my brother?" Addie asks.

"Oh, shit." Riley says.

"Take a fucking breath. You won't even let her answer." Hailey says.

Riley and Addie both take a deep breath, saying sorry.

My eyes bounce between the three of them. "I didn't give them an answer. I'll need to when I go back."

"Do you want the job?" Addie asks.

Exhaling a large breath through my cheeks, I shrug my shoulders. "I don't know. It's part of the reason I came home for the summer. To figure my shit out."

"Well, I don't think there's a point in asking us," Riley says. "We're never voting you off the island."

Addie nods. "She's right."

The upper half of my body falls onto the floor as my mind spirals. If I stay , I could start over with my career.

Maybe I could work at a small bakery or take some time off to find my love for it again.

Then Rowan pops into my head. What would he do?

# SIXTEEN

## ROWAN

Today is boating day. It started as a celebration when the doors opened at The Salty Dog. Everyone enjoyed it so much that we've made it a yearly thing.

We gather our money and rent a small one or a sailboat. This year, we opted for a yacht to celebrate Ellie being home this summer.

The breeze mixes with the sun—balmy but not terrible. We're close to approaching June, which is when it gets too hot outside and you sweat in places you didn't know were possible.

It's been a few days since I've seen Ellie. The brewery has gotten busier, and it pulled my attention away from everything else. Today, I'm taking full advantage of being with her.

There'd been no talk about Charlie lately. No texts or calls, at least that I know of.

"Woo, boat day!" Beau throws his hands up.

Milo barks as we stroll up to Beau.

"Boat day!" James says.

Over and over, they continue to repeat themselves.

They'd be voted most annoying brothers. Both of them wore matching tropical shirts—bright green leaves and neon-colored flowers—paired with their swimming trunks.

"It's boat day, baby!" August says.

"If you guys don't shut up, I will gag all of you." Riley walks up to us with her sister and Addie.

"Promise?" August grins.

"You're first in line," Riley says.

"I love you too, sweetie." August blows her a kiss.

The girls are wearing similar outfits with a see-through cover over their bikinis. Riley lifts her large pink tote onto her shoulder.

"What do you have in there?" August asks.

"What, this?" She gestures to her bag. "Oh, you know, the usual things to bring down the male population."

"Hot," August says.

While the rest of the group continues to talk, I glance at my surroundings, looking for Ellie. Biting the corner of my lip, I wait and wait. A couple of minutes later, Milo whines in excitement and bounces on his paws.

When I turn around, my breath hitches at the sight of Ellie walking towards us. She's wearing the same sheer bikini cover as the girls and I almost strain my eyes to get a look underneath. She looks like a snack I'd become addicted to.

"Hello, everyone."

Milo runs in her direction with his tail wagging and tongue sticking out of his mouth. I'd do the same thing.

"Milo," she coos.

He continues to whimper as he licks her cheek, chin, and jaw.

I whistle. "Milo, that's enough."

Can a guy cockblock his dog?

"Hey, Ro." She walks up to me and places her palm on my bicep.

"Hey, El." Heat creeps up my cheeks.

My body tenses at her touch. If she reaches for me again, I might have to throw her over my shoulder like we talked about a week ago. I'd wave toward our friends, wishing them an enjoyable excursion.

"Let's get this started. We're wasting precious boat time." Beau exclaims. "Let's go, let's go, move, move, move."

"You need to breathe." Hailey says.

"Are you asking or are you demanding?" Beau wiggles his brows.

Hailey tilts her head to the side and gives him a bored look. "I'm going to go tan now."

The captain quickly let us know the rules. Jumping is forbidden anywhere on board the boat. Refrain from leaning over the edge during the boat's transit. Keep all glasses on top of the counter.

Above all, *"no one can impersonate Jack and Rose at the ship's front."*

Fair.

"I'm going to the top to tan. Would anyone like to join me?" Riley asks.

August opens his mouth to say something.

"No," Riley says.

"You said 'anyone,'" August shouts.

She smiles at him. "Anyone but August Thompson."

August turns to the others. "Do we have time for me to go change my legal name? This is an emergency."

The corner of Riley's lip tugs up before she schools her features. When I search around at everyone else, I notice I'm the only one that caught that. I guess I'll keep that to myself.

The boat glides through the water, away from the pier. Beau poured oil into his hand, then rubs it all over himself.

"Why are you doing that?" James asks.

"Doing what?" Beau stops and looks down at his body.

"You're oiling yourself up like you're going to a Magic Mike audition." James says.

Beau grins before he pats his brother on the shoulder. "Thanks, man."

James winces when he glances at his arm covered in oil.

August connects his phone to the Bluetooth speaker he pulled from his bag. The guys created a music playlist for this specific occasion. There's over two hundred songs on it, and I'd lost track of who added what. It'd become chaotic.

A song with a piano melody plays, followed by an upbeat sound and a woman singing.

"What is this?" James asks.

"Hell yeah, I chose this," Beau says.

"Is this... Is this Demi Lovato?" August asks.

"Damn right it is." Beau starts lip-syncing the words.

"How do you know all the lyrics?" James asks.

Beau ignores his question and continues while looking at his brother, putting on a full-on performance.

"You need to stop." James laughs.

"I guess he was auditioning for Magic Mike." August chuckles.

Once the chorus of the music hits, Beau sings for his life. He raises his hands into fists triumphantly, then gestures at all of us, giving the greatest show of our lifetime.

"Dude, this song is a fucking banger. Don't diss Demi." Beau points to James.

"Do you understand the lyrics?" I ask.

Beau shrugs. "Yeah, we're just being cool for the summer."

August and I laugh.

"What?" Beau asks.

"You're singing about women hooking up with each other," August says.

With a shocked expression, Beau glances towards us, shifting quickly into a smile, then nods. "Nice."

# SEVENTEEN

## ELLIE

"Did I just hear a Demi Lovato song?" Riley gives me a quizzical look.

The boat provides tanning chairs where the four of us are lying in a row. It took all eight of us to pay for this boat just for today. It was... a lot. I won't tell my parents the amount of money August and I spent just to be on it for a day.

When the guys said annual boating day; I ran to the bikini store. How hot did I want to be? I'm a modest person, but I couldn't decide between a thong bikini and a simple one-piece. The devil on my shoulder favored the thong, while the angel suggested the one-piece.

The devil won, and I kicked the angel right off my shoulder.

I'm not one to wear something like this, but since I'm home to have some fun, I said to hell with covering my ass cheeks! Single Ellie's in town!

"Have you heard anything from Charlie?" Addie asks while spreading sunscreen on her legs.

"Since showing you two the text he sent? Yeah," I say.

"Ew, when?" Riley sits up.

"Yesterday while I was with my parents."

"What did it say?" Addie asks.

"He wanted to video chat with me. He said, *"I miss your face."*" I gesture my fingers in quotation marks.

Hailey pushes a finger down her throat, mimicking a gagging sound.

"Did you answer him?" Riley asks.

"No, I didn't answer him."

"What if you block his number until you go back?" Hailey asks.

My teeth graze the bottom of my lip. I've thought about blocking him while I'm here, but never did. One might say that I have a bad habit of putting others and their happiness before my own.

"I don't think she needs to go that far," Addie says.

"You think he isn't worthy of a block?" Hailey asks.

"I've blocked no one before," Addie says.

"Well, you're a lot nicer than I am," Hailey says.

"How are things with you and Rowan? Anything new between you two?" Riley smiles ear to ear.

The muscles in my cheeks want to fight against me, wanting to show off a smile. "We haven't hung out. He said work is busy." I look at Addie.

"This is our busy season. Trust me, he'd rather hang out with you." Addie raises her brows.

My lips betray me and tug up into a shy smile.

"Aw, look who's getting in her feelings," Riley says.

"Shut up." I push Riley's shoulder before adjusting myself back onto the seat.

My eyes scan at the surroundings. Being here makes me feel luxurious. No wonder rich people are always happy. Daydreaming about being served cocktails and sweets all day made me swoon. The long, soft chairs are a step up from the plastic ones pools provide.

My role as a pastry chef pays well, but when you live in New York, that doesn't matter. With this job, owning property here seems possible. However, staying here means I won't have my current job. Considering Rowan, along with his business and home, I question just how different things could've gone.

If I keep thinking about it, I'd drive myself insane.

"I'm going to see Mrs. Anderson tomorrow to talk about catering for her art show coming up." I say.

"Oh, that's exciting!" Addie sits up and looks at me.

"It's nothing big, just a few treats." I shrug.

"I thought you didn't want to do any of that while you're home?" Riley turns her body toward me.

"I'm living off my savings at the moment and could use the money." I sit up on the chair, crossing my legs.

"Are you excited at least?" Addie asks.

"I don't know. Maybe a little?"

"Do you want any company? I don't mind being around," Addie says.

"Yeah, so you can eat them while she bakes," Hailey cocks an eyebrow.

"She wants the peanut butter squares, the ones that I used to make all the time for the bake sales at school."

"Ooh, I love those," Riley says.

"It's cool you're doing that for her," Addie says.

The wind blows through my hair before I grab it and pick it up so the wind could caress my neck. "Does anyone have an extra hair tie?" I fan my neck.

"Here." Hailey hands over a black scrunchie.

"Thanks." I take it from her and wrap my hair in a high bun.

"Would you care if we showed up? You know, to support both you and Mrs. Anderson?" Addie asks.

"If you want, sure," I say.

"How much is she paying you?" Hailey asks.

"Hailey, you can't just ask people about their money," Addie says.

A laugh escapes me before I lay my body back down. I turn to the girls. "It's fine. She's paying me enough to last through the summer."

"That means it's *a lot*," Riley says.

"El, you know how the town holds The Taste of Dove Point?" Addie asks.

"Mhmm," I hum.

"What if you sign up? You know, have their own table and sell some stuff they love? You can make more money from that."

"Eh, I don't think so." I shake my head.

"Why not? Sounds like a great idea." Riley turns over onto her stomach, brushing her hair over her shoulder.

"I don't know. It just doesn't seem like something I would do."

"You ran the bake sale throughout high school, Ellie," Hailey says. "That should be a piece of cake."

"Well, yeah, but it was to raise money for something. There was a purpose behind it."

"This can have a purpose too. You can choose the charity you want to donate to," Addie says.

My lips tug downward when I consider the idea. Raising money for a charity is a great idea. I'd be able to bake what I want. It'd be my menu and simple desserts.

Addie gasps and sits up straight.

"What? Is there a bug? What?" Hailey sits up, glancing around herself.

"I just had a genius idea." Addie says.

Hailey settles in the chair, releasing a breath. "You could have said there wasn't a bug."

Addie waves her off. "Ellie, I know you're only here for the summer, but..."

# EIGHTEEN

## ROWAN

"Man, I wish I could live on this boat." August glances at his surroundings.

The sky is clear, with no clouds. An hour ago, Beau was a rule breaker and attempted to play both Rose and Jack at the front. The rest of the guys laughed when he was scolded by the captain.

"You could get yourself a sugar mama," Beau says.

"I think I'm past my prime for that." August scrunches his nose.

"Are we having a bonfire after this?" James swipes a piece of cheese and meat from the platter in front of us.

"Hell yeah, we are. Nobody can deprive me of my s'mores." Beau looks each of us in the eye.

"You'll get your s'mores, princess, don't worry." August turns his head to the side and looks at Beau.

Beau pumps his fist in the air.

Someone comes down the stairs, then Riley appears, walking toward our table of food that was provided for us. It held finger foods like beef sliders, bacon-wrapped jalapeño poppers, and pineapple BBQ meatballs. The guys and I almost demolished it, realizing we needed to save some for the girls.

August whistles when he looks at Riley. She gives a pinched expression and narrows her eyes at him.

"Wanna take a seat, sunshine?" August pats his lap.

"I would rather be eaten by sharks," she says.

"Damn, that's cold," Beau says.

"He'll live." Riley gives August a tight-lipped smile.

"Are you guys doing anything fun up there?" Beau asks, stretching his arms on the booth we're sitting in.

Riley saunters over to us and eats the beef slider she grabbed. The color of her skin looks like it had picked up a tan already. "Addie was persuading Ellie to sign up for the taste festival and donate to charity."

"That'd be cool," I say.

"But then Addie did a complete turnaround and suggested she could raise money to open her own bakery here, almost convincing her," Riley says.

August looks perplexed by the words that come out of Riley's mouth. "Wait, do you think she'd do that? What did she say?"

Riley's shoulders shake with laughter. "What do you think?"

"Did she laugh in Addie's face?" James asks.

"I think she's still laughing as we speak," Riley says.

"As crazy as the idea is, I don't think it's a bad one." Riley shrugs.

"Our mom would cry with joy if Ellie came back home." August says.

"She would one hundred percent do that." Riley nods. "Plus, she isn't happy with her job at the restaurant."

"Wait, what?" My posture straightens when she says that.

"Crap. I shouldn't have said that. Pretend I never said that." She waves us off.

"No, no, no. That's not how this works." August narrows his gaze and shakes his head. "What did she say?"

My eyes bounce between Riley and August. We don't see this side of him—serious and demanding—let alone toward Riley. The rest of us wait for her to bark back at him, but she doesn't. She freezes and looks at him with wide eyes.

Before she reboots herself and schools her features, she lets out an exasperated sigh. "She kind of had a breakdown at work."

"What do you mean, kind of?" August says.

"There was a big event that she was in charge of. She said that she messed up the dishes and when she did, she—" Riley trails off.

August's eyebrows rise, and he gestures with his hand for her to continue. "She what? Did she quit?"

My head swivels in his direction. There's no way in hell Ellie would've left her job without telling us. I'd like to believe she wouldn't hide something important from our group. My attention turns back to Riley.

"She fell to the floor and cried," Riley says.

Everyone stays quiet as we digest this new information. My heart sinks at the thought of Ellie at her job, weeping, alone. Technically, Charlie should have been there for her, but he wasn't.

"Shit," August says, leaning back.

"Yeah. Shit." Riley says.

When we spot Addie and Hailey coming downstairs, we clear our throats or adjust ourselves in the seat like we weren't just talking about Ellie and her breakdown at work.

Riley turns to head toward the girls, while the guys change topics.

There's no sound or showing of Ellie joining the rest of us. I can take my chance and join her now since she is alone and everyone else is busy. My heart urges me to go to her.

Before anyone spots me, I sneak upstairs to be with the woman who needs me.

Ellie's towel wraps around her shoulders. She focuses on the sea in front of her while the cool breeze dances through her hair. The sunset casts a glow around her.

"Hey," I mutter.

When she turns to look at me, her grin is infectious. "Hey, you."

The tension in my body disappears at the sound of her angelic voice.

"Can I join you?"

"You know you don't need to ask." She scoots further down the chair.

"Thanks." I sit down next to her and leave her enough room, but to my surprise, she comes closer to me, our knees almost touching.

A chill runs through my body, not knowing if it was the breeze or our skin brushing each other.

"So how have things been? I haven't been able to catch up with you," I ask. My elbows lean down on my knees, and I clasp my hands together.

She exhales a breath, and her shoulders drop at the question. Her eyes are still on the water, the sun reflecting off it, causing ripples of sparkle.

"It's been nice being home. I'm taking advantage of doing nothing, for once, you know? Lounging on the couch and taking naps." She glances at me. "You remember how much I loved my naps."

"I've had my fair share of waking you up, consequences be damned," I tease.

Her eyes crinkle when she laughs. The sound was infectious and beautiful. I'd do anything to hear it more. It's been a long time since I've heard a genuine laugh from her. When she'd visit during the holiday's—Charlie, unfortunately, being present—she didn't have that spark.

When she did, it sounded forced. Charlie and Beau competed to bring out the most laughter. Beau was in the lead, of course, grabbing everyone's attention. Ellie watched Charlie's personality change. He sneered and scoffed. She'd make herself laugh with a tone that wasn't at all familiar to me.

I felt like I was losing the girl I once knew.

"And what about you? Has anything exciting happened?" she asks.

"Hmm. I taught Milo a new trick."

She gasps as her eyes widen. "What is it?"

"He learned how to open the fridge and grab a beer for me."

"No, you didn't."

My lips break into a smile, and I shake my head. "No, I didn't. I did, however, teach him how to use his inside voice."

"Inside voice?"

"Yeah, if he's being loud trying to grab my attention, I'll tell him 'inside voice', and he'll whisper bark. It's the cutest fucking thing I've seen him do."

"Ugh, I love him so much. I'd die for him." She stares at me.

"Okay, I hope it doesn't come to that."

Ellie snorts and then shoves her shoulder into mine. We

sit in comfortable silence, both of us watching the sunset as the colors wash over us.

"Have you heard from work?" I ask.

She shakes her head. "I don't know if that's good or bad." She peers at me. "They gave me some pretty big news before I left and are letting me mull it over."

Big news can mean anything. A promotion or relocation. I don't smile at either choice; both are there to remind me of her leaving. Maybe if I lay out my intentions, tell her how I've been feeling, she'd reconsider going back.

"What's the big news?"

Ellie tilts her head down, then back up at me. "They offered me a promotion." She pauses, and her gaze bouncing between my eyes. "They want me to take over as head chef."

My mouth opens, then closes while I try to find the right words. Of course, part of me wanted to tell her to take it; it's what she'd always dreamed of. I'm also ready to get down on my knees and beg her to stay with me.

"Are you going to accept it?" I ask.

She twists her lips to the side. "I'm conflicted."

Her body shifts toward me, and she lifts her leg onto the chair. I watch her knee brush my leg and press into it. "What do you think I should do?"

Only two things can happen. I could encourage her to stay, or I could disappoint her and suggest she go.

My fist covers my mouth when I clear my throat. "I know everyone here would be happy if you stayed. I also think they'd be happy if you took it. It's like a bittersweet moment, if that makes sense."

Ellie looks down at her hands, a slight feeling of disappointment in my answer. She doesn't need to say it when I could tell by the way she's quiet and not looking at me.

"But," I said.

She peers back up with hopeful eyes.

"I'm going to be selfish and tell you to stay. It would be wrong of me not to tell you the truth. Of course I want you to stay here. It'd be like old times."

"Thanks for being honest with me," she says, one eye squinting against the sun.

"I'll always be honest with you." My hand finds her knee, and I brush her skin with my thumb, something that's second nature to me, something that I don't think about before taking action.

Ellie wets her lips, and my eyes catch the way her delicate throat bobs. "Rowan, I—"

Her phone rings from behind her on the chair, and she twists her body around and looks for it. When she picks it up, her face turns into a scowl.

"Who is it?" I ask.

A heavy exhale leaves her lips. "Charlie."

My jaw tightens at the name. "Are you going to answer it?"

She shakes her head out of frustration and rubs her forehead. "This is the fifth time he's called me today. I don't think he'll stop until I do." Her eyes find mine while she gives me an apologetic smile. "I'm sorry. I just want to get this over with."

I break eye contact and nod because knowing she's going to talk to him feels like my heart is being ripped to shreds.

Ellie rises from the chair and then moves away before responding. "Hello," she answers with a bite in her tone.

I refuse to stay here for this. The last thing I want to hear is Ellie giving the guy another shot. The possibility of that is low, but I'm not taking any chances.

I stand up from the chair and keep my eyes on her while she paces back and forth. Her eyebrows show annoyance as she scrunches them together.

Just as I step onto the first stair, I overhear what she says.

"Charlie, we aren't together right now. Why can't you understand that? I swear, you never listen to me."

I force myself to take one step at a time as her voice fades.

# NINETEEN

## ELLIE

Being in the sun for five hours sounded like an incredible idea, but maybe it wasn't. I lie on the sand while everyone else sets up for the bonfire. I feel like a dried-up grape and look like Rudolph's red nose. Here's hoping I at least get a nice tan after this.

"I am the master of the flames," August says.

"It's just fire," Riley says with a cocked brow.

"If the world goes to shit and you need someone to create a fire for you, don't come running to me," August says.

Other groups of people surround us with their own fire. When summer arrives in Dove Point, you can spot a bonfire every night on the beach, with groups of family and friends spread out across. The stars shine with the same intensity as the fire.

"Where are my s'mores?" Beau rifles through the bags sitting around us.

The bags in question consist of marshmallows and a tub of marshmallow fluff. The fluff was Addie's idea after she watched a video of someone dipping a strawberry into melted chocolate and fluff. At first, I thought the idea was genius, and then I realized the mess it created.

"They're right here," Hailey says, pointing at the tote next to the towel that's out on the sand.

All the girls and Milo sit on a large beach towel Riley brought. James flattens out the sand so we wouldn't deal with bumps and ridges. It's one of the many uncomfortable things about sand. The guys stand around the fire or sit on the sand.

Through all the movement and chatter on the beach, my focus stays on the man who comforted me on the boat a couple of hours ago. Thinking back to our conversation about my promotion, the honesty about what he thought I should do creates more conflict in my head.

He wasn't shy about telling me he wanted me to stay, and when he said those words, my stomach danced and I felt a blush creep up my neck.

I didn't expect him to touch me, and I flinched at the contact, but then relaxed. The calming motions he played along my skin sent tingles all over.

All of it—the buildup of emotions, the physical touch, the honesty of him wanting me to stay—pushed me to wanting to tell him I needed to be here; with him, our friends, my family. But he wanted me to stay. This could be the second chance we've both needed.

Then Charlie called. And well, no need for an explanation on that.

"*Ellie? I know I've been calling a lot, and I'm sorry. I just—*"

"No. Stop. *You need to stop calling and texting.*"

"*I need to talk to you. I'll beg on my knees for you to forgive me. Please. I've thought a lot about it, and I was being selfish. I should have asked how you were doing at work.*"

*"It's a little late for that when you fucked that other girl. Did she know you were in a relationship?"*

*Charlie stayed silent on the other end of the line for a beat. "She didn't know."*

*My eyes closed as I let out a pathetic laugh. "Are you fucking kidding me? You didn't tell her you had a girlfriend? Is she still talking to you?"*

*"Stop talking in the past tense."*

*"Is she still talking to you?"*

*"Yes."*

*Another laugh slipped through my lips.*

*"But I keep telling her to stop texting me."*

*"Maybe if you tell her you were with someone, she'll stop talking to you. You should try that."*

*"Ellie, please—"*

*"Goodbye, Charlie."*

Rowan was gone when I turned to look back, and I don't blame him. I wouldn't want to stick around either if he were on the phone with an ex. Since then, he's stayed his distance since we left the boat.

"Look at this beauty," Beau says.

He holds the bottom of a graham cracker followed by a marshmallow and chocolate bar, then another marshmallow and chocolate bar, and then two more of the same, tucked into another graham cracker on top.

August says, "They should paint that and hang it in the Louvre."

"How are you going to fit that in your mouth?" James says.

Beau shrugs. "By the grace of the s'more gods." He opens his mouth and surprises everyone by showing that it could fit. But after one bite, it falls apart and crumbles onto the sand. Milo sniffs at the area, trying to find what he could get as a treat.

James and August keel over in laughter along with the rest of the girls. As I peer around the bonfire, I don't see Rowan. My neck cranes and my eyes squint. He isn't anywhere in sight until a few seconds later, and I find him sitting closer to the water.

"I'll be right back," I say to Riley before I get up.

The sand pushes its way in-between my toes, and nothing makes me feel as awkward as walking in sand, causing me to stumble around and trudge through. I watch as the waves glide onto the sand when I get closer to Rowan.

"Hey, what are you doing?" I ask.

"Oh, hey." He turns to me. "Just hanging out by the water."

"Did you want to be by yourself? I can go back?" I point behind me.

"Nah, I'd like your company." He grins; his dimples showing under the moonlight.

The cold sand covers my legs, and there was a bite in the air. Goosebumps raise along my arms, and I wrap myself up for warmth.

"Here." Rowan moves beside me and takes off his black hoodie before he hands it to me.

"I'm fine," I say.

"Don't be stubborn." He holds it out again.

My eyes narrow at him while the corner of my lip tugs up. "Thanks."

I pull the hoodie over my head and inhale the scents that surround me—sandalwood and bergamot that's always made my knees wobble. The heat from him wearing it a few seconds ago wraps around me, and the goosebumps disappear.

"So what brought you here and away from the bonfire?"

"I've just had a lot on my mind."

"Wanna talk about it?"

Rowan turns his attention back to the dark ocean. "I've been thinking about my dad."

"What? Why?"

He sighs. "I've always thought about what my life would have been like if he hadn't left."

"Yeah, I know." I nod.

"And now that I'm turning thirty soon, I think I want to leave that all behind." He places his chin on his arm and focuses on me.

"It doesn't sound like a bad idea. You've dealt with the hurt for a long time, and maybe moving on can help you figure out other things in your life."

"I think I should see him."

My eyes widen, and uneasiness ripples through me. Rowan seeing his dad can be a good thing or a bad thing. Something in the back of my head wonders what could happen if he sought him out and no good comes from it. What if his dad turns him away again? And if that happens, what mindset would that bring Rowan?

I've witnessed the hurt and anger toward his dad as he grew up. He questioned his self-worth for years and blamed himself for his dad leaving, an emptiness inside him that needed to be filled again. I've tried filling that emptiness, but I wasn't enough.

I clear my throat. "Do you think that is a good idea?"

"I still haven't talked about it with my family. After sitting with it to understand my feelings, I think I'm ready. I need to know why he left because my mom never told me. If I don't do this, I'll wonder 'what if' for the rest of my life?"

"I just don't want you to get hurt again." I follow my

instincts and grab his hand, holding it in mine, like I'm protecting him. It's the best I could do without getting my feelings tangled up.

He squeezes my hand, and God, I wish I'd feel it roam all over my body like it did when we danced. I'd take a kiss on top of my hand if I could. I'd just gotten out of a relationship, and I'm here to find myself again, my passion, and if Rowan distracted me, I don't know what path that would lead me to. Maybe heartbreak again for the both of us.

"Come here." He lets go of my hand and puts his arm out, gesturing for me to scoot in closer to him.

In a matter of seconds, I move over; he wraps his arm around my waist, and tugs me closer to him. His touch is icy, and I bring his hand that's placed on me under the hoodie to keep warm.

"You know how lucky I feel to have you as a best friend?" he says.

"Way too lucky. You get free desserts and in return, I get Milo." I glance at him and smirk.

"Are you just using me for my dog?"

We share a soft laugh together, and our eyes meet while we breathe in the same air. My chest tightens when his stormy eyes drop to my lips, and I feel a pull of energy that causes me to lean in closer.

"Milo," Rowan says after he barrels into us.

I lean back, letting him come between me and Rowan. He licks Rowan's face and then nudges him.

"What's going on, buddy?" Rowan asks. "You wanna hang out with me and El?"

Milo whines and turns to me, licking my nose. "Hi, cutie." I scratch under his jaw and kiss him on his cheek. I'm sure I see Rowan pouting when I look at him. "Jealous?" I cock an eyebrow.

"Completely," he says.

"Aw, I'm sorry. I can give you a kiss on the cheek?"

"If you do, then I might ask for more." He winks.

A shy smile lifts at my lips before Rowan leans closer to me with his cheek. I press my lips onto his stubble. The sensation prickles at me. And I want more.

It's been two days since the bonfire. Since Ellie and I came so close to kissing. It's all I've thought about. All I've dreamt about. Neither of us expected it; however, I'm glad it almost happened because it sparked a fire under me.

I massage my temples while trying to erase all the emotions that built up over years of missing her. Two knocks at my door pull me away from a daydream I wrapped myself in.

"Yeah," I shout toward the door while I keep my fingers on my temples.

"Am I bothering you?" Addie asks.

"No, come in." My head lifts as I watch Addie come into my office and shut the door behind her. "What's up?"

She sits on the sofa across from my desk, shuffling the top of her hair with a hand, and pushing it to one side. Her skin changed from olive to bronze from the other day.

"I wanted to check in with you, see how you're doing." She crosses one leg over the other and folds her arms.

My lips purse while I shake my head and shrug. "Everything is cool."

Addie nods and says, "Okay, so you aren't freaking out about almost kissing Ellie?"

I'm certain my thoughts halt at those words. I cock my head to the side. "Come again?"

"You and Ellie," she slows her words. "Kissing."

The corners of my lips turn downward, and I shake my head again. "I'm not sure what you're talking about?"

Addie reminds me of Aunt Rosey 2.0. I wouldn't say Addie meddles in people's lives, but she also doesn't mind if people allow her to. She more or less does it because she thinks she'd help people find a solution to their problem.

She narrows her gaze at me, and a wicked grin lifts on her lips. "Don't play stupid with me, Rowan. I witnessed it myself. Now, let's try this again. You aren't freaking out about almost kissing Ellie? Your best friend, your soulmate, the one who got away."

"It wasn't a kiss. It was two friends talking who sat close next to each other. You should get your eyes checked." I lean back in my office chair and cross my arms.

"Oh." She sits up straight and unfolds her arms. "So I could go ask Ellie about it then? I mean, maybe she'd say the same thing or maybe she wouldn't. With us girls, she'd just tell me." She lifts off the couch to walk away.

"Fine," I say, annoyed. I sit up straight and lean my arms on the wooden office desk. "If I find out you told anyone, even Hailey's cats, I'll show everyone the video of you and Rick the vacuum cleaner."

Her eyes go wide with fear. "You wouldn't."

My eyebrows lift in a *try me* gesture.

She pushes herself onto the couch and mutters under her breath and says, "Why would you stoop that low?"

"Maybe it's payback for threatening to tell Mom about what happened at work." I smirk.

"Fine," she snips.

My jaw clenches for a beat. "We were talking about something, and it almost led to a kiss."

"What were you talking about?"

"Milo."

"You almost kissed because of Milo?" She tilts her head in confusion.

I tilt my head from side to side and nod. "Yeah."

She licks her lips and shakes her head. "No, you're not telling the entire story."

"I swear." I hold up my hands. "We were shooting the shit. I said something about her using my friendship for Milo, and I guess we didn't realize how close we were sitting together until we looked at each other. It was... unexpected."

"And then Milo cock-blocked you." She raises her eyebrows in amusement.

My mouth opens and then shuts. "Is this karma for clock-blocking him?" I mumble to myself.

"What?"

I shake my head. "Nothing, but how did you even know? Were you spying on us?"

Addie scrunches up her nose. "I wasn't spying. I, um, accidentally..." She trails off and looks the other way.

"Accidentally what? What did you do?" I ask.

"I was playing fetch and didn't realize you two were in that direction, so I guess Milo saw you and ignored the stick," she rambles.

I run both hands down my face. Addie meddles without realizing she meddles.

"Maybe it's a good thing we didn't kiss."

"Shit, I'm sorry."

"Don't apologize. She came home to escape the bullshit. I'm not adding on to that."

"Okay, but you're not just anyone. You have Ellie... you two are like out of a romance book. Your tropes would be second chances and friends to lovers."

I snort a laugh. "Those are unrealistic. Which is why they're in books and don't happen in real life. We both witnessed Mom's heartbreak when Dad disappeared."

"Dad was the villain in Mom's story, and I couldn't give a shit about him. Plus, you are not him. He didn't care about breaking Mom's heart and never tried to contact either of us. We're better off without him." The light in Addie's dusty blue eyes fade.

Addie and Dad got along just fine, but she hung out more with Mom and Aunt Rosey. When Dad left, Addie felt like it was her job to console our mom. She was only five-years-old and wise beyond her years. From the outside, it could look like none of that affected her. She rarely talked about him, and when she did, it seemed as if her heart turned to stone toward him.

I need to tell her about Dad. But now is not the time.

"Alright, enough about Dad. You asked me about the kiss. I told you what happened, and now we can move on."

"You're giving up? Oh, come on. You've let yourself be miserable for years because all you want is her. Because her idiot ex did something incredibly stupid." Addie holds out both hands with her palms facing up. "He gave her to you on a silver platter. And now you won't take advantage of it?"

"Ellie is not someone to be taken advantage of."

She scoffs. "Don't be dumb; you know exactly what I mean."

"What would you like me to do? Ask her on a date? See if I'm worth her giving up everything back in New York?"

"That's what you should do."

"Do it. Ask Ellie out on a date. The worst that can happen is her saying no. But she's just as in love with you as you are with her. If she says no, then I'll never meddle in your life ever again."

"Wow, that's like winning the lottery."

"Do it, do it, do it," she said, chanting.

She continues and claps her hands with every beat. She knows she would drive me insane until I give in, and I don't know what would be worse; dying of annoyance or giving in.

Addie watches me pull out my phone, which stops her chanting, and gives me a smile that gloats with her victory.

# TWENTY-ONE

## ELLIE

Today is a rot on the couch kind of day.

Riley is settled on the floor, consuming Sour Patch Kids, mirroring the image of a person being offered grapes from the vine.

"Ry, you're going to choke. Sit up," I say before I stuff my own face with Flaming Hot Cheetos on the couch above her. The overwhelming spice makes me feel alive and depressed at the same time.

I woke up this morning and decided that I would wallow in despair while I thought about where I'd gone wrong in my life and reevaluate my choices.

My intention wasn't to be dramatic; however, this represented my last year in my twenties, and it blew up.

"If I die, I die. Death by Sour Patch Kids," Riley says.

My phone buzzes on the floor next to Riley's head, and my arms are too limp to even care.

"Who is it?" I ask while I stuff chips into my mouth.

Technically, I shouldn't be eating these chips. My gut isn't having it anymore, and it likes to remind me I'm not sixteen with a stomach of steel. I knew the consequences of my actions and ignored them.

Riley slaps her hand onto my phone as if she were playing whack-a-mole. She sighs and looks at the screen. "It's Rowan." Her fingers tap along the screen and unlock my phone.

When I chose my password to be my birthday, I expected nothing less than for her to let herself in. In kindergarten, she came up to me and demanded we be best friends because she liked my dress. It was light blue with small daisies on it.

She gasps after she reads it and sits up, sugar sprinkled off her shirt and onto the wooden floor.

"Riley, my mom just cleaned this floor. I'm not taking the wrath of her, I'll tell her it was you."

"Rowan just asked you what you're doing tomorrow."

"Okay, and?" I stuff another chip in my mouth before I suck the red residue off my fingers.

She cranes her neck toward me with wide eyes, an open mouth, and a beaming smile. "He just asked if you'll go to dinner with him."

I sit up and snatch the phone out of her grip. Loose strands fall, flanking my cheek, as my bun tilts.

> Rowan: Are you free tomorrow night?

> Rowan: I was wondering if you wanted to go to dinner.

Riley lifts to her knees and shuffles toward me, where I still sit on the couch. Where this might lead occupies my thoughts. Two friends going to dinner to catch up and spend time together?

He couldn't possibly ask me on a date, since I'm only

here during the summer. My mind wouldn't forget about the kiss that—almost—happened on the beach. What would have happened if Milo hadn't interrupted us? Would he still suggest a date, or would we ignore each other?

"Is he asking you on a date?" Riley asks.

"No." I shake my head and glance at her. "There's no way he's asking me on a date."

"Why not?"

My hand holding the phone drops onto my lap. "I'm home for the summer."

Riley stares at me and blinks once.

"Why would he want to go on a date knowing that I'm leaving in a few weeks?"

"Maybe he wants to determine if there's a chance of reigniting something?"

"And then what? We see how the rest of the summer goes until I need to leave again? I've already done this to him—twice, might I add—and I'm not doing it for the third time."

Vibration runs through my fingers when I look down again, expecting another text.

> Charlie: What are you up to?

"Oh, you've got to be fucking kidding me. He's still bothering you?" Riley gives me a quizzical stare.

"The man won't give up." I give her a tight smile.

"Give me," Riley reaches for my phone, but my movements are too quick for her. I hold it above my head.

"What are you doing?"

"What do you think I'm doing?" She reaches for it again, and this time I stand up. "I'm going to tell that asshole to leave you the fuck alone and then block his number."

"Riley." I sigh.

"It's not like you're talking to him, so why does it matter?" She stands up and brackets her hips.

My nose scrunches, and I give her a guilty look. No one knows about the call I took from Charlie, except for Rowan, a couple of days ago. I knew he wouldn't tell anyone, and if he did, Riley would have already destroyed my phone.

She tilts her head to one side with pinched lips. "What did you do?"

"When we were on the boat, he called me, like, five times. When I was with Rowan, he called again, and I couldn't take it anymore, so I answered."

Her eyebrows lift, almost touching her hairline. She closes her eyes and holds up a finger. "What did you just say?"

"I told him to leave me alone. Trust me, we didn't talk pleasantries."

Riley's head turns down, and she covers her face in her hands. "Ugh, Ellie." She focuses her attention on me. "That's exactly what he wants!"

"I know, but it's not like I was telling him I missed him, which is what he wants from me. I'm not running back to him."

She inhales and forces a smile onto her lips. She's a natural at deep breathing to calm down considering she instructs classes at the yoga studio in town.

"Fine, okay. I will not tell you what to do. You're my best friend, and I love you. I know you're not going back to him." Her eyes soften when she looks at me.

A tiny smile touches my lips. "You don't think I know all of that?"

"He needs to take the fucking hint. I mean, you haven't reached out to him at all, yet he continues to bother you.

You're being way too nice, but that's just you. If it were me—"

"You would have chopped his dick off by now, I know."

She crosses her arms. "You're damn right I would. Now, ignore him and text Rowan back. He's probably spiraling by now."

A breathy laugh escapes me when I look back down at my phone. Before I answer, I go back to Charlie's text and delete it.

"That's my girl," Riley says. She pats my arm and turns on her heel and walks toward the kitchen. "That candy made me so thirsty, and now I'm starving. Wanna order some Chinese? I could go for an egg roll or four."

"Yeah, that sounds fine." I sit back on the couch while my fingers hover above the keyboard. My teeth bite onto my bottom lip as I type.

> Ellie: I'm free as a bird.

After I hit send, I cringe at what I'd said.
*Free as a bird? Who am I? Nelly Furtado?*
My phone buzzes again.

> Rowan: Awesome. Can I pick you up at 6?

> Ellie: That sounds good. Where are we going?

> Rowan: Well, if you wanna ruin the surprise...

> Ellie: I do

> Rowan: Let's just say it's zesty.

A gasp escapes from me when it hits me. We're going to Zesty Ziti.

"What is it? What did he say?" Riley asks from the kitchen connected to the living room.

I sit up and skip my way to Riley. I pull a stool from under the small marble island and sit down. "He's taking me to Zesty Ziti."

Riley gasps while I nod in excitement. "Do you know how hard it is to get into that place? It's been open for three months, and there's still a waitlist. I heard their calamari is to die for. How did he even swing that?"

"I do not know; I didn't even ask."

"You know what this means, right? This is a date."

My eyes go round. This is a date. *This is a freaking date.* I'm a food fiend, so of course all other thoughts slip away when he mentions the restaurant.

Riley spots the look of fear on my face.

"No, do not freak out; this is fine."

I shake my head. "No. No, this is not fine. This is a date. What if this leads to more dates? What if our feelings get tangled up again?" My fingers weave through each other in a jumbled mess to add emphasis. I lean across the counter, both palms on the solid surface. "What if we have sex?"

"Whoa." Riley's hands rise. "You just took thirty steps forward. How did your head even get there?"

A hot flush creeps across my cheeks as I attempt to swallow the giant lump in my throat. I let out a self depre-cated laugh while I tap my nail on the counter.

"Well, Charlie and I haven't slept in a while."

"What's a while?"

My eyes roam the ceiling above me while I think about it. "A year?" I squeak out.

Riley's mouth gapes, and she shakes her head. She

attempts to speak, but her words tumble over each other. "How did I not know this?" she exclaims and throws her hands out.

"Well, uh." I wince.

"Well, uh, what?" She splays her hands out again.

"I didn't want to burden you with my sex life."

"Burden? You didn't want to burden me? Ellie, I'm your best friend. We tell each other everything. The other day I told you I thought I had a hemorrhoid!"

"Oh yeah, what happened?"

She waves me off. "The doctor said it was just a minor cut and to be careful. They gave me some medicine for it." She rolls her eyes. "That's the last time I'll ever try butt stuff."

I grimace. "Thank you for sparing me the details."

"It's the least I could do because I'm your best friend, and I tell you everything!"

My head rolls back, and I groan. "Riley."

"I'm not mad at you, just disappointed."

"Okay, Mom." I scoff and cross my arms. "Can we get back on topic? Zesty Ziti? A date with Rowan? My ex-boyfriend."

"Okay, let's pretend this is a date. I mean, it is, but for your sake, we'll just pretend."

"I appreciate that." Sarcasm oozes from my mouth.

"Let's role play some things that could happen." She walks around the counter and sits down next to me, the stool skipping on the floor.

"Why do you think we'll sit this close?"

"Because if this is in fact a date, then he's going to request a booth. It's more intimate. Now, you're you and I'm Rowan."

"I figured."

She clears her throat then relaxes her body in the chair.

"So, how do you like the place?" Riley says in a burly voice.

A snort escapes me. "Is that supposed to sound like him?"

"Of who? I'm Rowan, and we're at Zesty Ziti." She gestures with her hand around the bright white kitchen.

Attempting to suppress a giggle, I roll my lips inward. For Riley's sake, I relax in my chair and push back my bun that wiggles around on top of my head.

"Thanks for bringing me here. I didn't think I'd ever get to try this place out." I cross one leg over the other.

"It's worth the thirty-minute drive." Riley, I mean, Rowan, stretches their arm around the back of my chair.

My gaze follows the movement and swings back to her. "So how'd you even get a reservation here? It's impossible to get in."

She polishes her nails on her chest and then admires them before she looks back at me. "Let's just say I know some people. I did some favors for them, so they told me I could come back anytime."

"Rowan wouldn't scrub his nails on his clothes, but okay." I clear my throat. "Well, you should take advantage of coming here as much as you can. Try every item on the menu. I doubt any regular restaurant-goer could say they did that here." I pick up my imaginary drink. "Oh my God, this wine is so good."

"I only get the best for you, honey." She winks at me. "Get whatever you want from the menu." Riley passes me the imaginary menu.

"Thanks," I say, opening my hands and looking at my palms. "Oh wow, these prices are insane. Are you sure you can afford this?" I turn over a palm, pretending to look through it.

"You're worth going bankrupt for. Heck, get the lobster and steak if you want it." She brushes her fingers along my shoulder and smirks. "You have the most beautiful eyes. It's like staring into a clear blue sky on a beautiful day."

"Oh, thanks," I say before I pretend to blush and peer down at my lap.

Riley uses her other hand and lifts my chin with her fingers. "Ellie Thompson, you are the love of my life, and the only woman for me." She gazes into my eyes. "No other woman could compare to you. You are my destiny, and I'll walk to the ends of the earth for you and destroy any man who comes your way. Forget Charlie. Forget New York. Come back home."

My eyes blink before I notice just how close our faces are to each other. I pull back, speechless at what I'd just heard.

"If I were a lesbian, I'd already be in your bed," I say.

She sits up, pleased with herself. "Why do you think men fall in love with me?"

# TWENTY-TWO
## ROWAN

Strands of wet hair fall over my eyes when I look at myself in the mirror. My skin is pale, and my stomach feels sour from the nerves my body holds.

If it's only two friends going to eat, why am I nervous?

To clear my mind, Milo and I jogged and then we laid on the grass at the park.

It'd been hotter than I expected, my shirt drenched in sweat. I tugged it off and tucked it into the side of my shorts. My shirt usually stays on, since I prefer to avoid the older women's early morning comments. But this morning, I couldn't get away from it. I waved and kept moving until I reached my house and sprinted inside.

Ever since then, I've been staring at my reflection in the foggy mirror.

Addie was thrilled when I asked Ellie out to dinner.

*"There." I showed her my phone. "I texted her. Now will you get off my back?"*

*"Oh please. Don't act as if you aren't happy. You've wanted to do it since she's been back."*

"It's not like she's going to say yes." I placed my phone on the desk and crossed my arms.

"Okay, but what if she does?" Addie mimiced my stance.

"I don't know. Then I'll take her to the Dockside Burrito's."

"Um, no? Ellie deserves more than a burrito."

"Okay." I placed my hands behind me and leaned back. "Then where would you suggest?"

Addie tapped her chin and glanced away. Then looked toward me, a smile on her lips, her pupils expanded. "You should take her to Zesty Ziti."

"That place is fancy as shit. This isn't a date. It's just—casual."

My sister stood up from the couch and walked toward me. She rested her palms on my shoulders, staring at me. "Rowan, I'm going to say this slowly."

"You're scaring me."

"You're going to take Ellie to a nice place and show her how a real man should treat her. Of all people, she deserves it after what she's been through." She patted me on my right shoulder.

The vibration from my phone shook against the wooden surface, and we both peeked at it. I bit the inside of my cheek before I grabbed it. My hand wouldn't move, yet my heart continued to ricochet in my chest.

"Are you going to read it or stare at your phone all night?" Addie gestured to it, then slapped her thigh.

"Calm down," I said, then gripped it in my hand.

Ellie: I'm free as a bird.

My fingers tapped on the screen, and I told her what time I'd pick her up.

*"Well?"*

*"I guess we're going on a date? Or just dinner as friends. I don't know what this is, but it's happening."*

My phone vibrates on the bathroom counter and pulls me back to the present. Mom's name slides by. A photo shows her in front of a field of tulips when I took her to the tulip fest last spring.

"Hey Mom, what's going on?" I pick up my toothbrush before I open the drawer and grab toothpaste.

"Oh, nothing, just calling to ask how you're feeling before your date with Ellie."

My hands stop what they're doing. "How—"

"Your sister told me." A sound of glee radiates from Mom's voice.

"Of course she did," I mumble and close my eyes.

"Why can't I know?" she asks.

"That isn't it. I just don't need anyone making a big thing because it's not. We're just going out to eat."

"But aren't you going to that fancy new restaurant out of town?"

"Well, yeah," I said, then brushed my teeth.

"Okay, so then it's a date."

"I don't know if I'd consider it one. Addie is the one who suggested it."

"Oh," Mom said.

My eyebrows pinch together. "Oh?"

"Well, I just thought it was your idea to take her to that restaurant. If I had known it was your sister's idea, then I'd have put the pieces together that she was meddling." Mom tuts on the other end of the line.

"It wasn't her idea. It's not that I don't want to go out with Ellie. I just don't want people getting ideas in their heads since she's only here for a visit." I turn on the speakerphone.

"As long as Ellie doesn't find out Addie is the one who put this idea in your head. I don't think she'd be too happy knowing that it was your sister getting in the middle of whatever is going on between you two."

Milo gets up at Mom's voice, puzzled at the space.

"I don't plan on telling her that. In fact, I don't plan on mentioning Addie at all during dinner because she isn't the topic of our... date."

"Ooh, so it is a date?" she teases.

The thought of it being a date quickens my heart. I clear my throat and shake off the feeling.

"I don't know. Maybe? I don't know," I reply.

"Well, you'll know once you see what she's wearing. Alright, well I'll let you finish getting ready. I want to hear all about it. Good luck, honey. Bye."

Ellie's outfit could determine what this dinner is. What the hell does that even mean? Maybe I should text Addie.

Rowan: Question

Addie: Answer

Rowan: Will I know if Ellie thinks this is a date by how she's going to be dressed?

My palm scrub at the stubble along my jaw while my mind goes a mile a minute. I shouldn't feel stressed like this; my hands shouldn't feel clammy or shaky.

I stand in my bedroom, startled when my phone buzzes in my hand. Addie's name moves across the screen with a photo of her double-fisting two beer bottles.

"Yeah?" I answer.

"You don't know what you're wearing, do you?"

"No idea," I admit.

"Do I need to do everything for you?"

"I didn't even ask you to help! You called me." I glance at Milo with a '*do you believe this*' expression and gesture to the phone.

He cocks his head.

"Go to your closet and tell me what you have," she demands.

"Okay," I say before I slide one side of the closet's double-door open.

"What is the first thing that catches your eye?"

My eyes dart around the shirts that hang up in front of me: polos, button-ups, regular shirts, sweaters.

"I don't remember having this many clothes." I run my hand along the fabric of a button-up, wondering if it'd be thin enough to wear on a hot day. "Hey, how do you know if a button-up is cotton or whatever?"

"Is it soft and thicker than a regular t-shirt?"

The material feels coarse, but thin.

"Hold it up to the light and look at it. Is it kind of see-through?"

"Uh," I held it up by the hanger in front of the window. "Yeah, it's a bit see-through."

"Okay, so it will be airy. Just wear a plain t-shirt under it. What color is it anyway?"

"Dark blue, like navy." I flip it back and forth.

"Okay, that's perfect. I know you have chinos, so wear those."

"You work fast." I throw the shirt on the bed and rifle through my drawers to find the tan pants Addie suggested.

"Yeah, I know. Anyway, I've gotta go. Text me later. Good luck."

# TWENTY-THREE

## ELLIE

"I don't know, Ry. Isn't it a little... much?" I face Riley, moving away from the large mirror inside the bedroom. My light brown wavy hair sways across one shoulder.

She sits on the bed with different outfits piled next to her. I lack nice outfits, given my summer-only plan and expectation that no one would ask me out. Rowan included.

"I think it's hot." She cocks her head.

"Didn't you wear this last New Year's Eve?" I ask.

The silky red fabric clings to my body, and I peer down at the sequence pattern in an intricate design. Thin spaghetti straps and a square neckline shows off my golden tan.

"Yeah, and I made out with that one hot guy half the night." Riley smirks to herself and picks up the ends of her hair, examining the strands.

"Oh, yeah," I say.holds out a casual dress.

"Here, unzip me. My hands are too sweaty."

"Are you nervous?"

"Ah, cold, cold." My body flinches at the icy feel of Riley's hands, and a chill goes down my spine.

"Sorry, sorry."

"And no, I'm not nervous. There isn't anything to be nervous about. It's just a regular dinner with a friend." The silk dress falls off my body, showing my black, strapless bra and lacy booty-shorts that match.

Riley understands me, despite my blank, bored expression. Before I put on the fifth dress of the night, I run my hands down my bare thighs as sweat sticks on my skin.

"Okay, I'm a little nervous. I don't know why," I call out and turn to her. "I shouldn't be. He didn't even say the word 'date'. Just... dinner."

My hand grabs the dress Riley picks out next. The fabric was soft and light, perfect for summer.

"What if you act like it's more than just dinner?"

"What if I embarrass myself by doing that?" I pull the dress over my head and tug it down.

"The history the both of you guys have, I don't think you could embarrass yourselves."

There were plenty of embarrassing stories. Once, he tickled me hard enough that I let out a fart. Both of our eyes widened at the sound, and he sucked in his lips trying not to laugh.

I examine the dress in the mirror. The sage-green baby-doll dress is flouncy and flows toward the bottom. It's cinched underneath my breasts, causing them to lift. It makes them perkier than they already are while small pink flowers spread along the fabric.

"That's the one; it's so cute," Riley squeals and claps.

"What about—"

"You'd think I'd forget heels? Here." She grabs her tote bag, which carries three pairs of block heels in three different colors: white, black and nude.

"Thank God we wear the same size shoe. I don't know

what I would've done," I say and grab the black pair when I sit down on the bed next to her.

"Your makeup looks flawless, by the way."

"Aw, thanks. I had five pimple patches on my face earlier." My hands work the strap on the second heel before I put my foot down and place my hands in my lap.

"Is it hot in here? I'm hot." I lift my hair with my hand off my neck and fan myself with the other. My body feels like it's overheating.

Riley grabs my hands and pulls them down. "Hey, look at me."

My mouth feels dry, and I smack my lips trying to gain moisture. Again and again, I clear my throat.

"Ellie, what on earth are you doing?"

"I think I need some water."

She snickers, "Hurry, he'll show up soon."

Both of us hear a knock; our attention shifts. The beat of my heart pounds in my chest while I feel a tingling sensation down my arms.

"He's here. Why is he here so early?" I urge and whip my head toward her.

She looks down at her phone and shows me the screen. "It's five till six, so he isn't early. I'll answer it. Give yourself one last peek in the mirror." She pats my knee and sits up.

"Alright." I respond, then stand and revisit the mirror. I inhale through my nose and hold it for five seconds before I let it out. "You're fine. It's just dinner," I repeat to myself while I push the fabric of the dress down.

"Ellie?" Riley calls out.

"Coming." I grab my black clutch bag and walk out of the room. The sound of my heels tap on the floor.

When I pass through the hall and turn the corner, my sight catches Rowan. He stands next to Riley, but she becomes blurry when I scan him up and down. He tucks his hands into his tan chino pants. A dark blue button-up paired with it, even with his black Vans.

He pushes his hair back before he stuffs his hand back in his pants. My eyes catch a glimpse of his fingers fidgeting in his pocket. The corner of my lip tugs up, knowing he's been just as nervous as me. At that, I feel my body calm. My shoulders drop, and my hands unclench my purse.

"Hi," I say.

"Hi," he replies, and then beams.

I become addicted all over again.

"HOLY SHIT," I mutter to myself. "People did not exaggerate. It's beautiful here."

Together, we enter the waiting crowd in the lobby. The atmosphere is elegant yet stylish. A sign hangs above the hostess in cursive that read, *'Enjoy a taste of Italy'*.

Rowan walks up to the stand, a hand tucked in one pocket, and it makes his ass look... incredible. My head tilts to the side as I bite the corner of my lip.

The red brick wall holds mirrors of varying sizes, along with framed photos of different places in Italy. Vintage style pendant lights hang around the ceilings, a warm glow illuminating the space. Along the wall sits a deep brown tufted booth; across from it paired with a wooden circular bistro table and chairs.

"Hi, reservation for two under Williams." The sound of his voice could make any woman's toes curl. It's deep, soothing, and stoic.

When I peer at the woman looking at the screen in front

of her, I catch her glance through her eyelashes; a playful smirk dancing along her lips.

*Oh, hell no.*

A spark of confidence hits me, and I stroll up next to him with a devilish grin. My hand finds his biceps, and his gaze finds mine. His cheeks flush, and I glance toward the woman at the stand.

She clears her throat and states, "Right this way." Her eyes meet his.

Her gaze locks on him like I wasn't standing right there, grabbing his arm.

"What are you doing?" Rowan murmurs to me.

My hand slips away from his arm and wraps around my purse with my other hand, and I shrug. "I don't know what you're talking about?"

A breathy laugh escapes him. His warm hand caresses my lower back through the dress, and a rush of air sweeps through my lungs.

He keeps it there until we approach the outdoor patio. The same round tables from inside and square marble tables flank us, with green cushioned chairs that arrange around each table.

Small trees, shrubbery and plants create an intimate atmosphere. Above were globe string lights that cover the area. A slight breeze passes us and kisses my cheeks, while the sun glows in the sky.

The hostess speaks, "Here we are," before she situates the menus next to one another in front of the chair.

"Thank you," Rowan and I speak in unison.

"Enjoy." She gives one last look toward Rowan, practically eye fucking him.

My eyebrows rise at the bold move as I place my clutch on the wooden table.

Rowan catches me glaring at her when he looks back at the woman and then to me. "Are you okay?" he asks skeptically.

My attention shifts back to him and I feel the muscles in my face relax. "The hostess seems to have eyes for you."

He cocks a brow, then smirks at me. "Huh. I didn't even notice considering I'm already with the most beautiful woman in this place."

A smile tugs at my lips. "Alright, enough of the compliments."

"Let me get the chair for you." He walks behind me and pulls the seat out.

"Thanks," I say.

For a moment, he hesitates, not sure which chair he should sit in.

"Rowan." I giggle.

"Sorry, sorry." He pulls out the chair next to me and sits down.

While biting back a shy smile, I pick up my menu and browse the vast options. My gaze sweeps toward him and over my menu; his eyes catch mine at the same moment. This night should be interesting.

# TWENTY-FOUR

## ROWAN

My heart stopped for what felt like minutes when I watched Ellie walk into the living room at the guest house.

A breath escaped me when my gaze shifted to her, and she robbed me of all my oxygen. She could claim me, and I'd fall to my knees. Hell, I'd wear a shirt that displayed *'Ellie Thompson's bitch'* if she'd asked me to.

All the blood in my head went straight to my cock.

The sensation made me pinch my thighs while my hands were in my pockets. It helped. And the way she walked up to the hostess—when she touched my arm—I had to pinch myself again. By the end of the night, I'd have multiple bruises.

"Get whatever you want; don't worry about the cost," I tell her.

Her eyes flick to mine above the menu. "Are you sure about that? I could make you go bankrupt from food alone."

"I'd go bankrupt for you any day."

She snorts at the comment and closes her menu then looks at me. "Would you attempt a jewelry heist for me?"

A grin pulls at my lips. My gaze wanders around our

surroundings before I lean in and whisper, "How did you know about that?"

Ellie places an elbow on the table, her chin on her palm, with wide eyes. "Tell me more."

"I've been keeping track of the world's most expensive pink star diamond. It's worth seventy-one million dollars. One of the most expensive diamonds in the world," I whisper.

She gives me a puzzled look. "Wait, is that real?"

"Of course it's real."

"How did you find out about it?" She sits back in her seat, and a huff of laughter slips from her lips.

"August watched a documentary about diamonds and told me all about it."

"That checks out considering it's all he watches." Ellie picks up her menu again to browse through it.

"Knowledge is power." I give her a one-shoulder shrug and pick up my menu.

"Not always. He watched one about the meat industry, and he almost scarred me for life. I begged him to stop." She shivers.

"Is that why you didn't eat meat for a year? Why keep it a secret from me?"

The group held a BBQ once or twice a week the year she gave up meat. She'd bring her own food: veggie burgers, veggie hot dogs, and dairy-free cheese.

"Wait," I say. "Is that why you vomited all night after Hailey's party? I thought it was all the beer you had."

She was five hot dogs deep.

Ellie grimaced. "Yeah."

A laugh rumbles through me. Throughout the entire day, my shoulders tensed, but soon, that tension vanished. Every time I breathe, it's slow and even, instead of rapid and short. Conversation flows between us, calming like river streams; it puzzles me why I anticipated it to be awkward. We spoke almost every day when she lived in New York, or we video-chatted.

"Although," she went on, "I watched a dessert documentary with him when we were kids. That's where my love of sweets started."

"Do you remember the cake you made for me our freshman year of high school?"

"Oh yeah. That was when um." She snaps her fingers and sits up straight.

"Jessica." My lips press together, and a nod rolls from me.

"Yes! When she broke up with you." She takes a sip from her glass of water and sets it down. "You know, I never liked her."

"You think I don't know that? You didn't talk to her much when she was around."

"She broke up with you two days before the Valentine's dance to go with Evan. I'm surprised I remember all of this."

"You were my hero by bringing cake and going to the dance with me." I clutch my chest.

It feels like yesterday when I think about the dance. At that point, my voice was changing, which caused a lot of laughs within our group. It would crack and squeak. When Ellie and I were together, I cleared my throat to prevent it, until the evening of the dance where I asked her to join me during a slow song.

She didn't laugh or cause a scene. Instead, she took my hand and led me onto the middle of the gymnasium floor.

"Did I tell you how she glared at me for a week after that? Ellie says.

No, she didn't. Even if she did that, I wouldn't have noticed it, since I paid attention only to her after the dance.

"Hello there, welcome to Zesty Ziti. Have you dined here previously?" A server with red hair and many freckles greets us.

"It is," Ellie answers.

"Welcome. My name is Evan, and I'll be serving you this evening. Here is our wine menu." He set the small black book down on the table. "And our specials for the night. Do you wish to pursue the drinks, or do you already have a choice?"

Ellie points a finger on the menu. "Can we get the bruschetta with the burrata and the bacon-wrapped asparagus?"

"Of course, and for the wine?" Evan asks.

"Does the Napa Valley Cabernet Sauvignon sound good?" I ask her.

"Fine by me." She perks up.

"Sounds great. I'll get those appetizers in and bring out the wine shortly." Evan walks back inside.

The sound of a pleasant hum slips through her lips. "I feel like such an adult."

"What? You've never been to an upscale restaurant before? I've never been able to bring you before, but since you were in New York, I just assumed."

"Just because I worked in one, didn't mean I could afford them. Well, not that I couldn't afford it. I used that as an excuse when Charlie didn't feel like going out. It's sad, having to lie to myself that money was tight when he was not interested in the idea."

Is it wrong to ask her not to bring up the person I'd like to punch? I don't want to seem like a psychotic ex-boyfriend. Then again, I showed that side when that guy annoyed her at the nightclub.

"I guess it's a good thing I get to do it first then. But now that means I'll need to step up my game and keep impressing you."

She gives a low whistle before she says, "You might have to. Who knows, I could meet a billionaire one day who whisks me away."

"I guess I need to save up for a private jet then."

"You would do that for me?" The red creeping up her neck doesn't cover the shy smirk on her lips.

"It doesn't hurt to see you with a smile on your face. Happiness looks good on you, Thompson."

*Shit, I'm fucked.*

# TWENTY-FIVE

## ELLIE

"Oh my God, I can't eat another bite or I'll explode. Go ahead, poke my stomach," I say to Rowan.

I knew I was pushing it when I asked for the dessert menu, but I'm a glutton for punishment.

My mind couldn't decide whether I wanted the three medallions steak with a Parmesan crust or braised short ribs. It was easier for me to choose sides than it was the main dish. Evan returned, taking our orders, but I still couldn't choose, forcing Rowan to order for me.

He went with the three medallions, medium rare, and I don't regret it one bit. The chef cooked it perfectly, and the tender meat melted in my mouth while the buttery flavor exploded on my taste buds. That twice-baked potato made me think of how I'll propose. It was creamy, cheesy, and loaded to perfection with bacon bits and green onions.

I also enjoyed the steamed broccoli.

A small laugh slips from him. "Didn't I tell you the three-layer chocolate cake was a bad idea?"

"It came with vanilla bean ice cream!" I roll my eyes.

Everything was amazing, and I wouldn't complain

about a single thing. I don't know who I'll marry or when, but I'll need to have my engagement party here.

It's been well over an hour since we sat down, and the sun is telling us it'll see us tomorrow. The sherbet-colored sky surrounds us while the string of lights above us sparks to life. Earlier, it didn't feel romantic like it does now. We stay here, enjoying each other's company while the wine bottle stays on our table.

The sounds of summer wrap around us; birds sing, the chirping chorus of crickets is faint, while music plays in the background. Behind, a group shouts 'cheers', with laughter echoing, and glasses clinking.

"How did you get a reservation here? Isn't it impossible?" I ask, laying a hand on my very bloated stomach.

Rowan crossed an ankle over his knee, relaxing his posture. "I can't divulge my secrets. That would be no fun," he said.

A grumble pours out from me, and I pout my bottom lip like a five-year-old.

"That's not fair; you know I give in when you give me that face. All Bambi-eyed." He moves from the comfortable position he was in and sits up.

My expression doesn't change while I bat my eyelashes at him. During childhood, I became familiar with techniques to persuade him. Of course, there was trial and error. Like the time I found out my birthday gift was a baking class at a local kitchen supply store that was too expensive for my budget.

"We work with them; James and I. Since Addie handles marketing, she checks out potential partners, and when we got wind about Zesty Ziti opening, she sent them sample products. Things have been going well."

"That's so cool," I say, beaming as a rush of excitement pierces through me for him.

Rowan rubs the back of his neck. "Yeah, I'm hoping we get to work with them for a long time. We give them updates on new products we're working on."

"I'm so proud of you. You guys have outdone yourselves with the brewery. I remember when you first shared the idea with me."

We were sitting on the beach, eating pizza and drinking beer that Rowan wasn't too pleased about. He complained that the taste was bland, but drank enough of them that we both were a bit buzzed.

*He drawled, "I could brew better beer."*

*"Then do it," I said, poking his arm.*

*He scoffed before he took another drink from the bottle. "I don't even know how to. It seems so—" He twirled his finger and said, "complicated."*

*"If I can learn how to bake, you can learn how to brew beer. You should ask James if he'd want to do it with you." I shrugged. "You could open your own place."*

*His arm wrapped around my shoulder, then tugged me into him, placing his lips on top of my head. "You're incredible, you know that?"*

While the memories swirl, we glance at each other for a beat. I fell in love with this person. Marriage and kids while we grow old together and we sit on a porch watching our kids grow up to have their own kids. He wasn't the one who pushed me away. I left to follow a dream that I'm now questioning.

"So have you talked to your family about seeing your dad?" I ask while my stomach churns from my previous thoughts.

Rowan scrunches up his face, giving me the answer in his expression alone.

"That gives me the answer I need." I chuckle.

Brushing a hand through his hair, he creates a rumpled look. People spend hours in front of the mirror to make their hair elegantly disheveled, and he does it in one swoop movement that creates this ache between my legs. I fight the urge to run my own hands through the thick, soft locks.

"Okay, if you were me, how would you tell them?" he asks.

"Why ask me?" I point to myself.

"You came back home without explanation and then told our friends plus your family what happened. I'd say you have better practice at this than I do."

Damn. He's got me there.

Without realizing it, I've started spinning the ring on my thumb. Telling my friends what happened was easier than telling my parents. When we pulled up at my parents' house, my body felt sweaty and prickly, like I was going to throw up. The thought of disappointing my parents made me feel sick. I left home only to run back because I couldn't cut it.

Even though I kept my cool in front of them, I felt like I was going to shit myself. I chewed on my lip the entire time I was talking and was blinking rapidly to keep myself from crying and crossed my arms to keep from covering my face in embarrassment.

My eyes find him, and a slow breath leaves my lips. He deserves to close this chapter of his life and move forward. It could either destroy him or change his life in a way he never expected it to.

"I don't think I'm the right person for this. I was terrified throughout the entire situation." I cross one leg over the other and tuck my arms into my chest.

"But you did it. I think the hardest part was leaving New York to come back home."

"You mean run away." My eyes cast down to the floor, and shame flows through my body.

"You didn't run away."

I can only scoff. What else could that result in? I might've stayed, resolved matters with Charlie, enjoyed a small hiatus, then returned to work. Instead, I grabbed a suitcase and drove away from things I should have faced.

"Your mom and aunt are just as supportive as my parents. I can't tell you how Addie feels because she avoids bringing him up in conversation." Uncrossing my legs, I lean toward Rowan, and grab his hand. "If finding your father helps you move forward, then do it. Talk to your family."

My thumb travels toward his wrist, where it circles underneath. His pulse beats against my finger, and I count each one that passes. I'm almost positive that my heart matches the rhythm of his.

He glances down and clears his throat. "Can you come with me?"

A slow smile grows on my lips. "It's the least I can do since you were there for me." My other hand finds the strands of his hair that fall down toward his eyes. It's soft, thick, and my fingers run through it seamlessly as I push it back for him.

He takes my wrist with his free hand and looks up at me. Both hands wrap in mine while our eye contact is steady. I wish I could blame the sweat building on my neck on the sun, but the stars are out now, and there's a cool breeze.

He places a finger on my ring and spins it in slow motion. The tip of his shoe touches mine, and it's now that I realize how close we are.

Rowan licks his lips and peers at me for a beet before asking, "Do you wanna get out of here?"

# TWENTY-SIX
## ROWAN

Ellie shouts over the roaring wind, "My hair is tangling up and smacking me in the face."

The top is gone from my Jeep as we drive along the coast while the moon shows off the sparkles it's creating through the ripples. I've missed these moments—spending time together, not knowing what the day will bring.

My focus stays on the road when I remember she left behind a hair tie the last time she was in my car. I feel the soft elastic band on my fingertips and hand it to her. "Here. This is yours."

She glances down at it with a quizzical expression. "Why do you—"

"I found it on the seat when we went to my place." I peer at her. "You were half asleep, remember?"

Ellie wraps her hair up, pulling at the loose strands around her neck. A few of them escape from her grip and fall down her neck. The road is empty in front of us. I steal a few sidelong glances at her and notice her body relax while she shifts her knees toward me.

A few minutes later we enter the town, and it takes five

minutes to get to my place. The only sounds that surround us are the grasshoppers that hide in the darkness.

When my car beeps after I lock the door, Milo props up onto the windowsill, his tongue hanging out the side of his mouth. The tip of his nose makes a mess of my window, which I'll need to clean again. I clean that window at least four times a day.

"Milo!" Ellie puts her arms out in front of her even though she can't get to him.

He barks in excitement, jumping off the ledge, then back up.

I open the door with my house key, and Milo comes barreling out, almost knocking both of us over. He jumps and licks and whines.

"Milo, down," I tell him. He continues to whine, but sits down, his tail wagging on the wooden porch. "Let's go inside, buddy."

Ellie takes off her heels and jogs to the couch, throwing herself onto it, and burrows in it. "Oh yeah, that's the stuff. My feet are killing me. I don't even remember the last time I wore heels."

I follow her lead, kicking off my shoes and throwing my keys on the coffee table. "Want something to drink?"

"What do you have?"

"Beer, wine, orange juice, seltzer water, lemonade, milk, sweet tea, regular tea, coffee." I open the fridge door, scanning inside when I hear Ellie laugh from the living room.

"Why do you have so many options?"

"Can a guy enjoy a variety of drinks without being judged?" I peek at her while she makes herself more comfortable on the dark blue couch, taking up at least three of the five cushions.

She laughs some more before she says, "Sorry, I was just

curious. Pick whatever you want; you know I'm not picky." She hums to herself.

Milo follows me around the kitchen while I grab us two cans of seltzer water. "You wanna treat?" I baby talk to him.

"Uh, yeah? Are you really asking me that?" Ellie says from the other room as she scrolls on her phone.

"I was talking to Milo. But, if you want a treat too, I'm right here, baby girl." I splay my arms out before I grab the container of treats that sits on top of the fridge. Milo became too smart for his own good and figured out all the spots I would keep them. "El, watch this."

She sits up on her elbows and peers over at us. I stand in front of the marbled counter, making sure she gets a good view. I hold the treat between my fingers as I look down at him. "Sit down, Milo," I whisper. He does as I say and adds a bark, causing me to lift a finger to my lips. "Whisper." His tail swings back and forth across the wooden floor. He hushes a bark twice before I toss the treat up. Milo jumps on his hind legs and catches it perfectly in his mouth.

Ellie gasps and claps her hands. "Good job, Milo!" she shouts, pulling his attention toward her. He runs to her and soaks in the praise she continues to give him.

"I'm the one that taught him that. Where's my credit?" I gesture my arms out.

She waves me off. "Training him was the easy part. It was his decision if he wanted to do it." She scratches under his chin and kisses the tip of his nose.

"Show off," I mumble as I walk toward the couch. "Wanna watch a movie?"

"Ooh, yeah. Can we watch that one movie where the girl stays at this house and another guy is there, which makes them both confused, and they find something in a basement? I hear that's good." She lifts her legs up, how generous of her, and she lowers her feet down onto my lap.

My eyes narrow at her. "That was vague, yet I somehow know what movie you're talking about. Can you pass me the remote right there?" I gesture to the corner of the table.

Ellie stretches her arm out, the tips of her fingers grabbing it before she tosses it to me. "Want me to turn off the lights?" I ask while pulling up the movie.

"It wouldn't be a scary movie if the lights were on." She wiggles her brows.

I clap twice, and the brightness vanishes, replaced by the screen's illumination. The movie cover lights up the living room in deep red.

"Oh, my God." Ellie chuckles, causing her drink to bounce on her stomach. "You did not just clap your hands to turn your light off. When did you install that?"

Beau suggested we watch old commercials. Knee-deep in puffy Cheetos, the idea popped into his head when he smoked a bit too much. We started talking about the ones we remembered and pulled up some videos. "The Clapper" came on, forgetting that it existed.

*"I've always wanted one of those," I said.*

*"You should one hundred percent get that for your house. Do you understand the power you have in handling that thing?" Beau said.*

*"Please don't say—" James said, but Beau cut him off.*

*"When you had a lady friend over, you could use it to set the mood. Picture this: You two are getting close on the couch, music plays in the background, and then it's off to Sin City, baby."*

*Beau nodded with an excited grin on display; it's one that I wouldn't want to come across in an alley when it is dark.*

I look at Ellie and shrug. "A few months ago. I wanted to surprise you with it. Did it work?"

"Teenage Ellie would have felt impressed and charmed."

---

WE'RE HALFWAY through the movie, and a jump scene is coming up.

I might not have mentioned to Ellie that I'd already seen this film. I think it would be fun for her not to know that little tidbit since I already planned on scaring her at one of the creepiest parts of the movie.

I'm laser-focused on the screen, counting down the seconds when the deformed woman appears on the screen.

Five... four... three... two... one.

"Watch out!" My hands pounce on her stomach, and before I can let out a laugh, her foot kicks me in the jaw, my teeth clamp together. "Fuck." I hold my face as my back lands on the couch.

"Oh, my gosh." Ellie gasps and sits up right away to assess the damage she's done. "Oh my gosh, oh my gosh," she continues to repeat those three words. "Are you okay?" She sits on her knees, looking down at me.

"Yep." My head wobbles, agreeing and disagreeing simultaneously, since I don't know what the fuck just happened. "I'm good," I answer, still covering from my nose to my jaw.

"Let me see." She reaches down to grab my hands away from my face, and when she looks, she winces.

"Is it bad?" The ringing in my ears has died down, but the pain around my jaw doesn't fade away. It's going to be bruised and swollen tomorrow morning.

She shakes her head and waves me off. "It's fine. You're fine. You just... I think my toes left an imprint on the bottom of your jaw." She peeks down to get a better look, then brackets her hips. "You did this to yourself. How was that a good idea?"

I move my jaw from side to side and continue to feel my cheeks. Ellie continues to scold me, and all I can do is smile through the pain because she is so goddamn cute when she gets serious. I watch her eyebrows pinch and her lips press down into a line.

Is it strange that I feel aroused after being kicked in the face by her? Or is it because she's chastising me?

"I'll get some ice." Before she leaves the couch, I grab her wrist and pull her into me, causing her to yelp. "What are you doing?" A quiet giggle slips from her.

I'm not sure what I'm doing. But I need her. Maybe she kicked me so hard that my brain is upside down in my head, and a surge of confidence kicked in. Day by day, I can't stop thinking about her. When I'm near her, my body pushes me to get closer. I need to feel and taste her before I go out of my mind.

She brushes one side of my cheek, and the comfort in the motion causes me to close my eyes. The pain that took over eases. I ask her the only question that's on my mind.

"Can I have you?"

# TWENTY-SEVEN

## ELLIE

"What did you just say?" I ask in confusion. The touch of his thumb on my jawline comforts me as he brushes it.

My eyes cast down to his throat when he swallows, trying to find his own words again. I must be hallucinating because I think he just asked me if I'll let him have me. He needs to elaborate on that. Those words can mean many things.

Maybe he didn't finish his question? Maybe he's going to ask me if I can bake him a cake.

Can I have you bake a cake for me? Can I have you tell my family that I'm going to see my dad? Can I have you get off me because you're digging your pointy elbow into my rib?

"Can I—have you?" He gives himself a puzzled look when he repeats himself. "I'm sorry." I see him sit up, and I ease my body off him. "That wasn't supposed to come out of my mouth. Word vomit." He blurts out with an awkward laugh.

I lean back on my heels, keeping my gaze on him, and tilt my head. I don't want to make him feel awkward. The screaming from the movie plays on in the background, but the man I've longed for since sixteen captures my attention, and I forget all else.

"Tell me," I ask.

"Tell you what?"

"What did you mean by that?" Curiosity tramples my thoughts like a stampede.

He scratches the back of his neck and breaks his gaze away from mine in embarrassment. I can pinpoint his emotions like a pirate finding the treasure on his map. When you know someone as long as I've known him, you develop a sixth sense for that kind of thing.

"It was nothing. My emotions got the best of me when you were scolding me." He shrugs and lets out a quiet laugh.

I rear my head back. "What emotions? And I wasn't scolding you." I cross my arms. Okay, maybe I was scolding him, but I won't admit it. He had to be, or he wouldn't have learned his lesson. I've also learned my lesson. My mighty kick is ready to be used on some men.

I wonder whether Charlie would come here if I asked him to.

"It's nothing..." He runs his hand through his hair, letting out a sigh before he sits down to face the movie. If I weren't looking at him, I wouldn't see the way his jaw muscles tick, like he's kicking himself for saying something he wishes he hadn't said.

I've already used the pouty lip and Bambi eyes on him at dinner. I guess I'll need to go stern mode on him. Scooting closer to him while still on my knees, I take his face in my hands and turn his eyes back on me, making sure he looks straight at me.

"I'm going to ask this one more time." My attempt at not

getting swept away in his grey, cloudy eyes is a test I will fail. "What did you mean by that?"

I search his eyes while waiting for an answer, trying to find it on my own before I make myself go crazy. Then they drop to his lips, which look soft and delectable. I need to feel them pressed against mine. I've forgotten over the years how it feels to get lost in his kiss when it's nothing but us and the stars outside.

One minute we're looking into each other's bright eyes and the next our lips are crashing together. He asked if he could have me, and this is my answer. This is his answer to how I feel about him. It's not a want; it's a need. I'm taking what I can get from him with no remorse.

My lungs scream for air, but I ignore the call when his tongue sweeps against my bottom lip, causing a soft moan to leave my throat. I beg for more when I swipe my tongue up the tip of his lip. His fingers travel through my soft brown hair before he cradles my neck.

Our tongues dance together, following each other's movements. He follows my lead, and I realize he remembers the way I like to be kissed. His teeth nip at my bottom lip, and then he sucks on it. If my eyes weren't closed, he would see how he makes them roll behind my head in pleasure.

I feel his hands grasp me on my waist, and he pulls me on top of him.

I didn't bother wearing underwear. When an occasion calls for a dress. But dammit, right now I'm feeling Rowan's hard length underneath his pants. Moving my hips makes him groan under his breath as his lips trail from mine and onto my neck.

My head tilts up before I bite my lip when I feel his teeth bite the skin on my neck, and I am about to lose control of myself. "Wait," I say, catching my breath and pulling back. His lips are already red from the pressure of our kiss.

"What's wrong? Are you okay?" he asks through panting breaths.

Nodding to him, I push both hands through my hair and down my neck. "I'm just thinking—this." I gesture between us. "What are we doing? What is this?"

Do we want this to happen?

This familiar sensation of my heart beating fast echoed what I felt when my existence shattered following the dessert mishap. When everything crumbled and I couldn't glue it back together. Except, nothing is falling apart. In fact, it's the opposite. The pounding of my heart comes from the heaviness I've carried these past 10 years. It's escaping, and I think my mind and body are trying to process it all happening within ten seconds.

I'm the one who stopped whatever this is.

"Well," Rowan says. "I think we're kissing?" He looks behind me and squints, then nods. "Yeah, I think that's what it is." A slow smile creeps onto his lips, and I melt—again—when I see his captivating dimples that make the world a little brighter. "But if you want to stop..."

His hands grip my hips like he's ready to help me get off him. My thumb finds his jaw and brushes over the rough stubble. I blink as I weigh the pros and cons. The pros; we're kissing. The cons; I go back home in three weeks.

Fuck it.

My lips find his again, and I feel his large hands roam up my waist and then back to my hips. "Just this once," I say between kisses. "This can happen."

His head nods in agreement before slipping his tongue into my mouth and caresses mine. My hands find his hair, and I tug on it, pulling a groan from him. It sounds so delicious that I pull at the strands again.

I can feel myself getting wetter as I continue to grind into his stiff cock. "Take me upstairs," I whisper against his lips. Three words that must remain in my memory escape like one in trouble.

I'm a damsel in distress and he's the only person who can save me from my chaotic life.

# TWENTY-EIGHT

## ELLIE

"Are you sure?" Rowan asks.

The incredible sensation of my clit rubbing against the rough jeans and his hard cock has me going in a tailspin. No more questions. No more thinking. Just doing.

"Take me to your room. Now," I demand.

Before I can take my next breath, he scoops me up, and my legs wrap around his waist, locking in. "You don't need to ask me twice," he murmurs against my neck.

"Technically, I did." My nails dig into the nape of his neck, and his fingers dig deeper into my skin once we reach the top of the stairs. The dress I'm wearing is just above my knees when he places me on the bed and looks over my body.

His breathing is uneven. "Ellie," he asks huskily, causing me to clench my legs together. "Are you wearing any underwear?"

The smile that shows on my lips tells him my answer.

His hands flex at his sides, and he tilts his head. He possesses an animalistic gaze, almost as if intending to tear the dress. "You walked around naked under that dress this entire time? Do you want me to kill every man who looks at you? Because I will."

*Oh, fuck me.*

"Open your legs for me." The tip of his tongue pokes out when he licks his lips, like he's ready to have his dessert.

The hem of my dress still sits above my knees, showing off my smooth, tan legs. Thank God I shaved this morning during my shower. It was definitely overdue. I bite the inside of my lip and notice his eyes continue to lock between my legs. I'm terrified of his judgment seeing my body. It's not what it used to be.

Stretch marks have developed on my breasts and outer thighs. My once-smooth back carries small acne scars. There's a burn scar on the bottom of my wrist from two years ago when I wasn't paying attention while taking a pan out of a five hundred degree oven.

Yes, he's seen my body in a bikini, but this is different. This is me showing him my imperfections up close and personal.

The smooth blanket under my legs glides along my skin while my heart races. The thin material of the dress rises, and I feel the fresh air brush my clit. It feels freeing and reckless.

"Fuck." The sound that comes from his mouth is raw and deep. "Seeing you in person like this." He pauses for a beat, swallowing down whatever emotions he's currently carrying. "Imagining you in this position is nowhere near as perfect as it is in real life."

Those words—they do something to me. It ignites something that was buried deep. They have me spreading my legs wider. My right hand creeps onto my thigh, inching closer to my pussy that's begging for friction.

"Don't," Rowan whispers. My hand stops. "I'm going to

tell you what I want you to do. And you, my darling Ellie." I watch him step closer to me and meet my eyes. He grips the tip of my chin and kisses me. I want to beg for more. "You will be a good girl and obey."

My chest falls when I realize I've been holding my breath. I don't know this part of Rowan. Outside these doors, he's still the sweet boy I grew up with. But inside this bedroom, he's the one in charge. Dominant. I'm familiar with the sex world of dominance and submissiveness. I haven't dived into that world.

Internal heat blazes within at the idea of him learning his desires elsewhere. Discovering what he wants from a partner. And I hate it.

All I do is nod in agreement. His lips perk up into a grin that the devil himself would whimper at. He stands up straight, walking backwards until his lower back hits the dresser. One ankle crosses over the other, and he makes himself comfortable before folding his arms.

He tilts his head. "Do you remember the last time you touched yourself?

My mouth opens and then shuts when I try to remember. It's been a long, long time. Long enough that I don't remember when my toes curled while an explosive orgasm ran through my body. Embarrassment heats my cheeks.

"I... don't know." I stare down at my feet and huff out a laugh.

"Good," he says slowly. "That means I can remind you how it feels to have a man make you feel so fucking good that you'll be begging for another." He uncrosses his arms and places his palms on top of the dresser. The dark button-down shirt tugs at his chest, straining to come undone. "Now touch yourself for me."

My hand slides down my inner thighs, and the simple

touch of my fingers gliding down my slit causes me to catch my breath. My eyes flutter shut when I drag my finger down my slit.

"Lay down for me, baby." I open my eyes to find Rowan clenching his fists before I lean myself back onto the bed. "Put your feet up on the bed." I do what he tells me and feel my dress slipping down onto my hips when I open my legs wider. Rowan lets out a heavy breath. "Your pussy looks fucking delicious."

I lift myself, supported on one elbow, so I can gaze at the man who will set fireworks through my body. My teeth bite into my bottom lip, and I slowly play with myself. A soft moan slips from me, and my fingers move up and down, feeling myself.

I'm soaked and haven't even circled my fingers around my clit.

"Put your finger in your pussy for me," Rowan demands, and I listen.

My index finger pumps in and out of me at a controlled pace while I grind against the movements. "Add another finger, baby."

My middle one follows as I continue to ride on my hand. The only thing we hear is the sound of my fingers stroking into my wet pussy.

"Imagine your fingers as my cock. Except thicker and longer. Then it gets to a point where you don't know if you can take another inch of me." The corner of his lip tilts up, and his eyes roam my body. His usual calming blue-gray eyes have turned into a thunderstorm.

Both a whimper and a moan fall from my lips as I continue to pleasure myself. His left hand lands on the button of his pants, and he unbuttons it fast enough that I don't catch the way his zipper is already down.

He doesn't tug at his jeans or strip down to his briefs. All he does is stand there. I can see his cock pushing out of his pants, trying to set itself free. A shiver runs through my body, and I pound my fingers harder into my tight pussy.

"I want you to sit up for me, Ellie baby," he says before he walks up to me. He grabs the hand I was using on myself and looks at my fingers. He peers back at me and brings my fingers to his lips and into his mouth, sucking them one by one. Rowan hums in appreciation. "I think this might be my favorite meal."

My lips part, and I can feel my eyes widen. He just... tasted me. The ache between my legs becomes almost unbearable, and I can feel them wanting to buckle.

"You want to touch my cock, baby? Want to feel what you do to me?"

I shift my gaze from his eyes and down to his pants. His length twitches in anticipation. "Yes, please." He drops my hand and doesn't tell me what to do next. He waits for me patiently, like he gets off on torturing himself.

"Touch me," he whispers.

I cup my palm around balls first over his pants. The sound of him sucking air through his teeth pulls a smile onto my lips. If there's one thing I remember about what he likes, it's this. He used to love it when I played with him before giving in to what he wanted. Something that hasn't changed.

"You remembered?" He smirks.

I rub at them and then take my hand up the rough fabric of his jeans and push my palm into his hard cock. Memories I've kept locked up in my mind have escaped. Flashes of us tangled together in bed.

His hands work at the buttons on his shirt and undo them one by one, then his lean muscles peek through one he slides it off. Both my hands tug at the sides of his jeans, showing off his muscular thighs and the large tent that's pitching in his briefs. My mouth salivates.

At the sight of that, I become feral. I place my hands on his hips and push him back, letting myself kneel in front of him, and he says nothing. He doesn't stop me. My eager hands pull at the waistband of his underwear, and I rip them down until his cock springs up.

It's large and beautiful. He grabs the back of my head, wrapping my hair around his hand. "Shit," he hisses. "I'm going to burn this image into my head. I want to die with it."

A huff of a laugh escapes me before I wrap one hand around his thick, warm length, and I lick the tip of his head. The taste of his pre-cum sits on my tongue, and I twirl it around his base before filling my mouth inch by inch.

"God fucking dammit," he breathes out. "That fucking mouth of yours."

I hum in appreciation and hollow my cheeks as I take him in further, making sure I concentrate on not gagging, which I think will be impossible. Only half of his cock is in my mouth before it hits the back of my throat and my eyes water.

"Tell me if it's too much for you, baby. I don't want to hurt you."

My head shakes in answer, and I take another breath before going down even further, adjusting my jaw. This is a challenge I'm going to overcome. I've given Rowan head plenty of times before, but I don't remember it being this... full.

When I feel more at ease, my mouth works around him. His hand grips my hair harder, and I pump him into my mouth faster. My other hand wraps on top of the other, allowing myself to give my throat a break, and I suck the tip of him as I tighten my grip.

The sound of him panting makes me work harder; his hand pushes my head as he jerks his hips in the same rhythm. "Touch yourself for me."

I let my hand drop between my legs, and my vision spins at how wet I am. His breath quickens, my moans becoming louder while my fingers circle my sensitive bud.

"Fuck right there. Keep fucking going."

My other hand grabs onto his hip, and I use my mouth to take him in deeper, my teeth scraping him.

"Holy fuck, that felt good," he groans out.

I smile while his cock is in my mouth, pulsating, and dripping on my tongue while I let my teeth scrape against him again. Pressure builds below when I quicken the pace on myself; my eyes shut as they continue to water from the pleasure I feel thrumming through my body.

His movements jerk and my knees wobble even though I'm already on the floor. "Come for me, Ellie. Be a good girl and come."

At his command, I let myself go, all the weight that built up on me these past years lifting off me as my body submerges in satisfaction. A few seconds later I hear Rowan gasping and panting, and he thrusts once, twice, and a third time before warmth pours into my mouth.

We groan as our bodies release together. My toes curl so tight that they may be stuck this way for months. After we calm our breathing, he lets go of my hair and moves his hand to my cheek.

His voice is all gravel when he says, "You did so fucking well, baby." He smiles down at me, and all I feel is accomplishment and praise. "Now, be a good girl and swallow."

# TWENTY-NINE
## ROWAN

Peering down at Ellie on her knees is a fucking sight to behold, as if she couldn't get any more beautiful, she proved me wrong. And having her mouth filled with my cock and cum is the cherry on top.

She swallows without even blinking. I follow her eyes when they cast down and notice I'm rock hard again. That's the power she holds over me.

I reach down for her hand and lift her to her feet. The way her chin tilts up and her baby blues shine, she shows some sort of pridefulness, like she's gained her wings back and doesn't feel defeated anymore. Her flowery dress falls over her knees again, and I already miss the sight of them.

Her hand finds my waist, and she gravitates toward me. "Did I do well?" she asks.

That she's even asking me is mind-blowing. I don't have the words to describe how incredible she was. The softness of her tongue sliding on the tip of my cock or the way her cheeks were so hollow she sucked my soul out of my body.

My lips tug up into a smile while I hold one side of her face. Our lips press together again, and I melt inside.

"There's too many words to describe how incredible you are. We might be here all night if I tried," I tell her. Ellie's cheeks turn crimson under my touch, and she's still as radiant as ever. "I wish you could have seen what you looked like on your knees and your mouth filled with me." My index finger lifts her chin up. "So fucking perfect." I kiss one side of her cheek.

She shudders a breath and her lips part, almost begging me to take her again. My other hand lifts her dress up and trails between her thighs and onto her drenched clit.

"Fuck," I murmur before digging my head into the crook of her neck. A gasp falls from her, and then a sharp breath. "Were you ever this wet for anyone else?"

I feel her head shake, and the grip of her hand tightens around my waist when she shakes her head.

"Good." I shove one finger into her warm pussy, and her other hand finds my shoulder, holding onto me while I push deeper into her. I add another finger before pushing back into the tightness of her. "Ride my hand, baby." I lift her leg up and hold it against my hip.

She rocks back and forth, fucking my fingers while I match her rhythm. The beautiful sting of her nails digs into my shoulder, piercing my skin. I hold her tighter while she lets herself go. Her head falls back, and she moans out my name.

"Rowan," she pants.

*Fuck.* Hearing my name escape her lips in a beautiful moan made me want to rip off her dress and fuck her until she couldn't speak.

I slip my fingers out of hers, turning her around before she can even process what she's doing. Her back is against my chest, and my hands roam over her breasts and between her legs again. I dip my head down toward her neck and nip at her skin.

"You don't know how badly I want to fuck your tight cunt. My cock is begging to remember how it feels to be inside you," I rasp, pushing my throbbing dick against her ass.

She pushes her ass into me. "Then do it." All movements stop. My thoughts pause. Ellie turns to face me and slips her hands onto my shoulders, pushing down the shirt that I'm still wearing. "I need you, Rowan. Please," she begs. "Do what you want with me."

"You sure you wanna do this?" I ask, needing to know that she's in the right headspace for this. "You've just had me in your mouth, but if we take it one step further." A deep groan comes out of me. "Do you know what you do to me, Ellie?"

She kisses my chest as my shirt falls onto the floor. "This is what I need right now." Another peck. "You are all I need right now." She lifts her eyes up to me. "I'm giving myself to you. Take it. Now."

One arm lifts her small body while the other runs through her hair. Our lips clash and our tongues sweep together in chaotic movements. The sound of our breathing is uneven and pleading. I neglect my strength when I pull down the sleeve of her dress, causing it to rip. "Shit."

"What?" She doesn't stop kissing my lips, my jaw, my neck.

"I ripped your dress." I walk her to my dresser and sit her on top. She's level with my hips, and I'm thanking my past self for buying a dresser at this height because it's come to better use than just storing my belongings.

Ellie moans and tugs at my hair. "I don't care. Just take it off." She grabs the hem of her dress, lifting one thigh at a time to hike it over her hips. Her long, caramel-brown hair spills onto her back after she pulls the fabric over her head and throws it to the floor.

Seeing her breasts bounce causes me to bite the inside of my cheek, forcing myself not to come in my pants when I glance at her pert nipples.

My head tilts while I scan every part of her and rub a hand over my jaw. "The things your body does to me, Ellie." She covers them as my eyebrows pull together. "Why are you covering yourself?" I wrap my hands around her small wrists.

Her slender throat bobs. "My body has... changed since the last time you've seen me like this. It's not what it used to be." She breaks eye contact with me, and my jaw clenches.

"Look at me," I ask her in a gentle tone. It takes a moment for her to raise her eyes to mine, and I smile at her. "Every part of you is perfect." Her hands drop, and I let go of one of her wrists. My finger traces the small stretch mark. "Your body is unique in every sense. It's yours and no one else's. Every bit of you tells a story." I glance back at her. "And I can't wait to learn about it all over again."

Her legs wrap around my waist, pulling me closer toward her. She leans back, showing her body off after giving her the confidence she needs. It doesn't matter what anyone else says because *she's mine*. All her perfections and flaws.

She keeps her focus on me and says, "Thank you."

I lean in toward her, my lips hovering over her ear. "Tell me what you want, Ellie. What do you need from me?" I whisper. Her words alone will have me give her everything she desires. She's in control of this, and I want her to be. "How do you want me to fuck you?"

Her full breasts rise and fall with each breath she takes.

My knuckles turn white as I grip the edge of the dresser, keeping myself from wanting to touch her hard nipple that's begging me to suck on it.

"I want you to take away all the pain I've carried for the past five years," she asks. "Help me forget about everything that's waiting for me." Her nails trail down the center of my abdomen, following the trail of hair that meets my cock, making it twitch in anticipation. "I need you to fuck me until I see stars again."

The corner of my lip tugs into a pleased smirk. My hands grip her ass and I tug her forward, my tip almost touching her wet pussy. "Please," Ellie begs before biting down on her lip.

"Let me grab a condom." I turn to walk toward my nightstand, but she stops me. Her hand wraps around my wrist.

Her lips press together almost in embarrassment before she says, "I'm on birth control and—I haven't." She huffs out a breath. "The last time I had sex was about a year ago," she mumbles under her breath and peers up at the ceiling above her.

Surprise causes me to raise my eyebrows. However, I know not to ask her about it. I also won't mention the person who played a part in her running to me. "Okay," I utter before turning toward her and cupping her face. "I haven't been with anyone else either."

I watch her shoulders relax at my words. Did she think I craved for other women when she was gone? That discussion can wait. Right now, she's about to wreck me in the best way possible.

"I'm all yours, Ellie."

# THIRTY

## ELLIE

Rowan's large hands grip my ass, tugging me toward the edge of the dresser. His hard cock aligned with my hips.

This might fix my problems, or it could create new ones. The last thing I'd want to do is drag him into my problems. Shit. I'm overthinking, and when I overthink, I blurt things out.

"Wait," I say, holding on to his biceps that he's one hundred percent flexing at the moment. That isn't helping. But he freezes and waits for my next words. "Should we be doing this?" My gaze flits to him, and I let out a sigh. "I mean, I know we just talked about this and we're full-on naked, but—I just don't want to mess anything up between us."

My heart hammers, and I expect the worst.

"We don't need to do this, El." He brushes his thumb on my cheek, and I'm comforted by the touch.

When he smiles at me, I twist my lips to one side, and peer down at the very large, firm length he still has. With a wince, I glance in his direction. "I'm so sorry. I feel so embarrassed."

"Come here," he whispers and pulls me into him. A cocoon of warmth surrounds me as he wraps his arms around my body. He kisses the top of my head and then my temple. "We're not letting something like this get between us or make you feel embarrassed. We're two adults who care about our friendship."

Okay, we may be way past the "friendship" point after what we just did. And we're holding each other while we're nude.

"I don't know about you, but I'm craving some pizza." He pulls away, and a flirtatious smirk is on his lips. "Would you wanna stick around? Hang out more?" I nod with a smile, and he bends to pick up my dress. His lips turn down when he looks at it. "I'll buy you a new one."

A snort comes out of me when I take it. "Technically, you'll be buying Riley a new dress," I say before hopping off the dresser. I hang it in front of me with my hands and tilt my head. "She's going to kill me." I watch Rowan open a dresser drawer and then hand me a pair of sweat shorts along with a faded band t-shirt. "Thanks."

He kisses my forehead before grabbing his own clothes to wear, and I notice he doesn't bother putting on his briefs under his grey sweatpants. Grey sweatpants that are thin. And he's still hard. How is he still hard? I'm kicking myself for stopping what could have happened.

But I think tomorrow I'll thank myself. I slip on his black shorts and tug at the drawstring before pulling on his shirt. I'm drowning in his clothes, but I wouldn't have it any other way.

"Hey." He walks up to me and holds my face in his hands. When he tilts my head up, places a kiss on my forehead. "Thank you."

My eyebrows pinch together. "For what?" He lets go

and swivels next to me, wrapping an arm around my shoulder as we walk out of his bedroom.

"For being you."

"Ah." I nod. "A nervous wreck that overthinks every-thing?" I side-eye him and see him roll his eyes.

"That's my role in this friendship."

There's that word again. *Friendship.* I can't tell if he's trying to convince me or himself. Maybe he regrets what we did earlier. There's not one ounce of regret running through my body because I've regretted a thing with this man. Except for my leaving him.

That's the only thing I'll always regret. I bury that part of my life.

Riley: Let's go to the beach today. I'm in the mood for some eye candy.

Ellie: As thrilling as that sounds (sarcasm), I'm having lunch with my mom.

Riley: I wonder what it's like to have a mom who wants to hang out with their daughter.

Riley: Tell your mom I said hi!

Ellie: Wanna come with?

Riley: Nah. I'm gonna wallow in my apartment and ponder my mommy issues.

Ellie: STOP. We've talked about this. Do we need another emergency pizza night? Two in one year sounds about right.

Riley: You still need to tell me what happened between you and Rowan. The date was like three days ago, and every time I bring it up you totally sidetrack the conversation.

Ellie: Way to turn the conversation around.

Riley: Come on, I'm DYING HERE.

Riley: Are you ignoring me?

Riley: You can't avoid this conversation forever, Ellie.

Riley: Fine! I'll ask Hailey and Addie to annoy you until you talk to us about it.

"KNOCK KNOCK." Mom taps her knuckles on the white wooden door to the guesthouse. She greets me with a toothy, excited smile. It's adorable. Her shiny brown hair sits just above her shoulders, and she doesn't have an ounce of makeup on. The shining sun that follows her complements her hazel eyes. "Are you ready to go?"

"Just about." My head does a double take on Mom's outfit. Her long, off-white dress flowed to her feet, showing off her robin egg colored toenails, and she paired it with a dusty blue crocheted purse. "You look so cute. If I'd known you'd dress up, then I would have tried harder." I gesture with my hand up and down toward my outfit. Black running shorts—ironic since I don't run—and a plain white v-neck shirt I've paired with my white Crocs that are looking worse for wear.

Mom waves me off, and her chunky bracelets clink together. "You look fabulous."

I give her a lop-sided grin before playfully rolling my eyes. "Would you want to go to the farmers market before or after lunch?" I ask while I sling my 'farmers' market tote bag' that's twice the size of a regular tote bag, over my shoulder.

She looks at her phone and says, "The market closes at two, so we have plenty of time."

"Sounds good to me," I say in a chipper voice.

The farmers' market in Dove Point is one of my favorite places to be. It happens only during the summer each Saturday. The vendors stay similar each year; however, a couple of new vendors have shown up since I left the town.

You can find anything from goat's milk to lavender or handmade soap. But nothing tops the all year round apple cider donuts. Even when it's hot out, they hit the spot.

When we step into the diner, almost every person at their own table greets Mom with a wave or hug. Mom held the cool mom status, even if she is a worrywart. But she's always prepared for any situation that may arise.

Her bags are like a pharmacy. If there's a cough, she gives a cough drop. If someone scrapes their knee, they can find a Band-Aid unwrapped and ready to go. She even brought homemade chicken noodle soup when all five of the Johnson kids came down with the flu.

We scoot into a booth, and a teenage server fills up our glasses with water in silence and then walks away. Thinking about James working here makes me chuckle. Any time he'd fill up the glasses at a table and customers said thank you, he'd just mumble, 'You're welcome' and go on to the next table.

Even as a teenager, he was quiet and a tad bit of a grump. I'm pretty sure he came out of his mother's womb with a grunt.

"Hey Mrs. Thompson, how are you?" A different bubbly teenage server stops at our table. Her shiny jet-black hair bounces in a high ponytail. "Are you gonna get the usual? Green goddess salad?" When she smiles, colorful bracelet bands cover her teeth.

"Hi Valentina, how's your summer going?" She places one arm over the other on the table and gives all her attention to the girl. Her olive skin tone complements her warm brown eyes. She doesn't look familiar to me at all. It's just another reminder of how long I've been away from home.

Valentina's shoulders drop, and she tilts her head to the side. "I've been studying all summer."

"Oh yeah, your parents mentioned you're getting ready for your ACT and applying to colleges."

My eyes bounce between Mom and the girl as they continue to talk about the potential colleges she wants to attend: Harvard, Yale, and Northwestern. Then they speak about her brother—who left for college—and how he's doing.

"Have you met my daughter, Ellie?" She gestures to me. "She's a big-shot pastry chef in New York City." Mom beams.

Valentina's features perk up as if a lightbulb turned on. "Oh yeah. Mom told me you were back in town. It's nice to meet you." She gives me another bright smile. "It must be cool living in a big city like that."

"Oh, it's great," I say awkwardly. How do I tell this innocent teenager the truth?

*The pitfalls of adulthood: tough choices, heartbreak, accompanied by workplace sadness over butter.*

"I can't wait to graduate and live in a big city," she says in a cheerful tone.

All I do is nod and smile because I can't lie to this girl anymore and squash her dreams.

"So what can I get ya?" she asks, and I open my mouth to tell her, but she stops me. "Wait! Let me guess. I love guessing. Hmm." She taps her pen on her chin and then squints her eyes at me. "A double patty melt, extra cheese, with a side of fries." Her posture straightens. "Am I right?"

I raise my eyebrows in pure shock and terror. "That was —scarily accurate." A laugh rumbles out from me, and I nod. "Yes, that's it."

She gives me a closed-lip smile and walks away, her ponytail swinging as she does.

"Isn't she just the cutest?" Mom says before taking a drink of her water. "I would be shocked if she didn't get into an Ivy League college. She and her brother are so smart." She places a napkin on her lap before looking at me. "What have you been up to? It still feels like you're in New York with how much I see you these days." She jokes.

An apologetic sigh escaped me. "I'm sorry. I've been keeping myself busy so I don't think about work or Charlie." My hands rub my face.

"I get it." She reaches out her hand and places it on top of mine. "Life can be rough sometimes. But I promise this will all pass. You'll forget about Charlie and go back to work happy again."

Each day, I attempt to stay positive. But that's difficult when I lack the spark that tries to revive with baking. As well as the night with Rowan, leaving my thoughts scattered. I can't stop thinking about it. Also, it isn't only the intimate aspects, but just... him.

The way he makes me feel both mentally and physically. He makes the hard days a lot easier just by looking at his smile when he sees me. Being home is a daily reminder of how much I love him. I will always love him, even if I don't have him.

"I ran into Mrs. Anderson, and she told me about her upcoming show and how you're baking some things for her. Why didn't you tell me, sweetie?" Mom says sweetly.

I shrug. "I don't know. It's just peanut butter squares."

She cocks her head, and her features soften. "Ellie, you should be excited. This could open opportunities, letting others reach out."

"It's just not the same anymore."

She puts her chin in her palm. "What are your plans after summer?"

I've always had a plan growing up. Goals that I want to achieve. But now what? I'm slowly losing my love for something that brings a smile to everyone who eats my desserts. I don't have the foggiest idea which direction to move toward.

"I don't know," I say, defeated. The thought itself is scary.

Mom hummed to herself. "As much as I don't want to ask this, I'm going to because I'm your mother and all I do is worry. Have you heard from Charlie?"

Mom and Dad thought Charlie was fine. They would ask how he's doing, but never went above and beyond.

"He texted and called me. I haven't heard from him in a week. Maybe he took the hint." I crossed my fingers.

The hint being me telling him on the phone call to give me space.

Mom presses her lips in a tight line. "You aren't considering fixing things with him, are you?"

I can feel a grimace spread across my face before controlling it. "At the moment, no."

"At the moment?"

"Probably not."

She places her elbows on the table and looks at me sweetly while her chin rests in her hands. "I loved when you and Rowan were together. Would you give that another chance?"

"I doubt it would happen."

"I don't know, Ellie. You were head over heels for him. And I know he was with you. I think he still is."

"What makes you say that?"

That question is the dumbest I've asked. I'm not naive. He still holds these feelings. But we both know we can't act on them.

"I can just tell. He reminds me of your dad." She smiles to herself. "A sweet man who isn't afraid to express his love for someone. I swear I don't know how I got so lucky."

"I'm sure Dad is the one who feels he's lucky to have you."

I grew up in a house that was filled with love. Fairytales drew inspiration from those two. Dad always looks at Mom like she's his queen. They still hold each other, snuggle on the couch, and offer positive affirmations.

I look down at the ring on my thumb, slowly spinning it when I think about how our relationship used to be. He always catered to my needs, even when I didn't ask. He would listen to me talk about my day and ask questions.

As the years went on, that dwindled.

He'd ask about my day, but not listen. It was like he'd checked out.

"Well, I hope you find what you're looking for, honey. You deserve the best, and I hope you realize that," Mom says, pulling me out of my thoughts.

I smile at her. "Yeah, I hope so too."

# THIRTY-ONE
## ROWAN

"Anyone home?" Stepping inside Mom and Aunt Rosey's house, I'm greeted with silence. Sound drifts from the living room. A record player spins with static, showing the music has stopped. The wooden floor creaks underneath my shoes as I walk toward it to pick up the needle and turn it off.

Rosey called from the sunroom toward the back of the house, "Yeah."

I go through the dining space. Frames of family photos cover the walls. Brightness surrounds them as they sit across from each other. They hold a paintbrush in hand with laser focus on the canvas in front of them.

My lips curve into a smile. "What are you two doing?"

"We're painting each other." Mom tilts her head in concentration.

"Each other?" My eyes flit between them.

"We saw this thing on social media." Rosey peers at Mom, then at her canvas. "You paint the person in front of you and they do the same." She squints. "Then we show them."

"We're almost done," Mom murmurs.

Curiosity gets the best of me as I walk toward Mom and stand behind her, hands on my hips. A snort comes out of my nose, but I clear my throat to cover the sound. "This looks great." I turn my hat backward and lean down for closer inspection.

"Okay, I'm done," Mom says proudly.

"Just one more thing." Rosey makes one more swipe at the canvas. "Alright, I'm done. On the count of three," she says. "One, two, three."

I clamp my lips together at the sight of Rosey's painting. She should stick to crocheting.

"What the hell did you do? I don't have pink hair." Rosey gapes at Mom. Walking between them, I tilt my head at the canvas Mom holds and examine it with my aunt. It reminds me of cotton candy.

Mom flips the canvas back to her with downward-turned lips. "I thought it'd be creative, you know? Out of the box type thinking."

"You made me look like one of those troll dolls," Rosey exclaims.

"I think it looks great." I shrug a shoulder and give her a toothy grin.

"Don't encourage her." She points at me.

"At least I didn't give you a unibrow. I don't even have one." Mom touches them.

"Sorry to break it to you, but you have one." Rosey gives her a tight-lipped smile.

Mom gasps. "I do not."

"Then what are you plucking at every morning, hm?" Rosey retorts with a cocked eyebrow.

My head falls back as they continue to bicker. This is a common occurrence when they don't agree on something.

Exhaling a breath, I cross my arms, and clear my throat

loud enough for them to stop. "I'd love to watch you argue over the worst painting; but I showed up to talk with you."

"Is everything okay?" Mom asks, setting the canvas down.

"Depends."

"Take a seat." Rosey gestures to a white wicker lounge chair against the back floor to ceiling window. "What's going on?"

After taking a seat, I place my hands on my knees, the jean fabric absorbing the anxious stress building on my palms. "It's about Dad."

Mom and Rosey exchange glances and then look at me. "What about your dad?" Mom asks.

I bite the inside of my cheek, and my legs bounce. I rehearsed what I was going to tell them. In front of the bathroom mirror, in front of Milo, in the rearview mirror while I drove here. Yet, my mind goes blank. Like someone took an eraser and wiped the board clean.

"Alright, I'm just going to spit it out. I think it's time I saw Dad. It's been on my mind a lot. This is something I need to do. But I want your opinion." My hands clasp together over my stomach.

"Oh," Mom squeaks out.

Rosey peers at Mom, tilting her head toward me and raising her eyebrows. Her eyes widen, and I think she's scolding Mom. "Okay, okay," Mom mumbles under her breath and holds her hand up toward her sister. She turns to me. "Can I ask why you'd like to see him?"

My finger taps on my knee. I shrug, then I mutter whatever pops up. "I'm just wondering how he's doing." If I tell them the truth, this will become a therapy session I don't feel like having.

"He's doing just fine," Rosey quips.

He's doing fine? I cock an eyebrow in curiosity. Mom whips her head toward her sister, raising her own eyebrows. "How would you know how he's doing?" I ask. Neither of them answers while they continue to stare at me.

What are they keeping from me and Addie? I'm afraid of continuing the conversation or regret even having it to begin with. My thoughts spin with the possibilities of what they're about to tell me, and I feel antsy.

Mom places her elbows on her knees and rubs her temples. A heavy sigh leaves her lips.

"You knew this time would come, Laura." Rosey leans back in her chair, crossing her arms and glances at me.

"Can someone tell me what the hell is going on?" My heart stammers in my chest while my breathing picks up. Did he die? Did Mom lie to me? Was she the one who pushed him away?

Mom lifts herself up. Worry pinches her eyebrows. I brace myself for whatever it is she's about to tell me. "Your father and I—we're still in touch." She rubs her palms on her yellow skirt.

My head shakes in disbelief while my heart sinks. The rock in my throat won't let me swallow the shock and nausea I feel coming up. I shift my gaze toward my aunt, who sits there, glaring at her sister. Thinking about Addie makes me push my feelings aside.

This isn't good.

"Okay." I situate myself in the chair and cross my ankle over my knee. A million words want to fall from my mouth, and I can't seem to gather them to come out in a coherent sentence. Instead, I clench my jaw and nod. "When? Why?" I ask without looking at her.

Betrayal and confusion are the only two words I feel right now.

Her body relaxes, and the small smile that pulls at her lips is—almost—comforting. "We spoke last week."

"Last week?" I shout. "What the hell did you mean, last week?"

"Rowan Andrew," Rosey scolds.

"It's fine, Rose." Mom gives her a side glance. She sits up straight, and her chin tilts up. "We speak once a month; that's it." Both her demeanor and tone are gentle.

My lips press together, and I break eye contact for a beat. Nausea creeps up more and more, causing my stomach to twist in knots. I'm so terrified of throwing up that I'm letting Mom keep talking.

"He asks about both you and Addie." She can read my mind with the questions I need to ask. "I've always updated him on how you guys are doing because he asks. There's no ill-will between your dad and me." Her throat bobs, and a shade of pink develops on her neck. "A few months after he left, I started receiving checks in the mail." She huffs out a laugh. "I didn't know how to process it."

"I thought he was being a pompous ass. Showing off his money once a month like we needed his help," Rosey says in one breath. Her mouth tightens, then relaxes before continuing. "But—I knew we needed his support." She inhales a deep breath. "I had my reasons, and I don't need to elaborate."

"Why?" I say, forcing the guttural word out.

"Why did I take his money and continue to speak to him?" Mom's eyebrows rise in questioning, and all I do is nod, still feeling too nauseated to talk. "I was a single parent who had two kids I needed to provide for."

"We wanted to give both of you the life you deserved," Rosey says. "You wouldn't have been able to join the surf team or afford the clothes you had. The tuition alone for you and your sister was a lot. Our priority was the two of you. If you want to shame us for taking his money, his help, then so be it. But now that you're an adult, maybe you'll understand the choices we made."

My mom reaches out for my hand. I look down at it when I wrap mine in hers. Holding my mom's hand makes me feel like a kid again. Walking on the beach to collect seashells. Tagging along on her morning coffee runs.

Pulling myself together, I find my voice again. "Why didn't he visit? Or ask to talk to us over the phone? All the bullshit he put us through? Why didn't he want me or Addie?" Mom squeezes my hand once.

"I know you're angry and upset right now. But I think it's best if you speak to your dad about this. Ask him those questions. Just—please don't go in with bad intentions. Don't give him a hard time. You need to listen."

"What about Addie? How can I keep this from her?"

Keeping this from her is painful. She's carried these feelings of resentment and dislike around with her.

"Addie is a whole other story." Rosey waves us off. "That girl is as stubborn as anyone gets. She still holds a grudge toward me since she was two because I wouldn't let her eat ice cream made of clay."

Mom scowls at her sister and comes back to me. "I'll handle your sister. Look, I'm not getting between you and your father. We have no problems with each other. He wasn't around, but he still took care of us. He's a good man."

Exhaustion thrums through my body like I've just worked a twelve-hour shift at the brewery. This new information changes everything. He cared about us. More than I could have ever imagined. What does this all mean now? Can we salvage our father-son relationship? "Do you know where he lives?"

She nods. "I do."

---

THE NAUSEA HASN'T DISAPPEARED since leaving the house.

Keeping this information from Addie feels—wrong. It's not my place to tell her. I know that. But I'm two seconds away from approaching her apartment and need to force down the bile rising in my throat. I stare at the white door in front of me, my hand on the brass knob that opens to the hallway filled with doors to different suites.

I shove my key into the lock, and the doorknob turns. I pause, debating whether I should delay this until I feel normal. "Just get it over with. She's your sister. She'll understand," I mutter to myself.

After closing the door, I climb the stairs to the second level. Normally I take two steps at a time, but not today. When I reach the top, I freeze. My skin tingles, and I feel hot. I ran down the steps, barreling through the entryway, before reaching the alley, and vomited.

I hear footsteps pass by, but I don't bother looking. My hands brace on my knees, and I inhale long breaths through my nose and out my mouth.

"Rowan?"

My eyes open, and I wipe my mouth before turning to see my sister, standing with a paper bag of groceries. She looks at the ground and back at me.

"Oh my gosh." She strides toward me. "Are you okay?"

"Yep, I'm good. I must have eaten something bad." I pat my stomach for dramatic effect. "Since I'm here, can I talk to you about something?"

Addie glances up and down at me wearily. "Uh, yeah,

sure. Let's go inside." She gestures with her head toward her building. "Is everything okay?" A floral wreath with bright colors hangs around the peephole when we arrive at the third door down the hall.

"Yeah, everything's fine." I wave her off.

She sets down her bags and then walks to her fridge, grabbing a ginger ale and then passes it to me. "For your stomach." I nod, grabbing it. She walks around her quaint kitchen. There's no window, and the only light she gets is from the ceiling. It's a standard kitchen that isn't showy, just the way Addie likes it.

I clear the taste of throw-up from my mouth and chug the drink Addie gave me. The cool, fizzy soda settles my stomach. How should I bring this up? I could butter her up. Or just rip off the Band-Aid. She's smart. She'll realize something is wrong.

I close my eyes and hope for the best. "I'm going to see Dad." The sound of a box dropping on the floor catches me off guard, and peek through one eye. She's much closer to me, causing me to jump back. "Christ!"

"I'm sorry, I think I just had a stroke. You're seeing Dad?"

The corners of my lips tug up in a smile that doesn't reach my eyes. "I need to do this."

"No, you don't. You don't need to do this." She shakes her head, causing my eyebrows to crease in confusion. "This isn't a good idea. He left for a reason. He wants nothing to do with us."

"You don't know that."

She folds her arms across her chest. "Okay, and how would you know?"

All I do is stare at her. Because I can't tell her what I've learned. That our Dad cares about us and has taken care of us. We wouldn't be where we are if it weren't for his help.

"Did you tell Mom? Aunt Rosey?" she asks suspiciously.

When I close my eyes, I answer her with a nod because I'm too nervous to see her reaction to this.

"Okay, what did they say? They think it's a bad idea, right?" Her eyebrows shoot up.

I rub the back of my neck. "They're fine with it. They gave me their blessings."

Addie gapes and lets out a breathy laugh. "This is a terrible idea, Rowan. I had to watch you grow up, blaming yourself for something that wasn't your fault. You know it wasn't your fault."

"Listen, you don't need to understand why. I just needed to tell you." I place my hands on your shoulders, making sure she knows that I'm listening to her, but she needs to listen to me. "You don't need to agree either, but don't make me feel like shit for doing this. Please."

She shrugs out of my hold and crosses her arms. "I don't agree with it. You're running to someone who doesn't care. You're going to come back home hurt. I can't watch you destroy yourself."

Everyone saw the damage it caused me watching him leave. Addie picked me back up. She saw the true darkness in me I hid from others. "I need to do this."

With her arms still crossed, she huffs out a breath and glances away. "Fine. But don't say I didn't warn you."

A pang of guilt hits me in the chest like a football. But I didn't expect her to jump up and down with enthusiasm. The most important thing is telling her. That's all I can do.

I just hope she's wrong.

# THIRTY-TWO

## ELLIE

After the successful trip to the farmers' market, I headed to Riley's apartment since she lives near where the market takes place. I grabbed a fresh apple-cinnamon bread for her. I know she'll devour it within two days.

Technically, I should go to the art studio to speak with Mrs. Anderson. I can't help but keep putting it off. Every time I think about it, I get this nervous twist in my stomach. It's the simplest dessert I can make, and it still causes anxiety.

Today's weather is peaceful. Trees remain motionless, devoid of welcome wind. There's chatter throughout the town as people walk and shop. Flowers blossom when I pass storefront troughs.

There's also a relaxed atmosphere that surrounds us. Everyone knows fall will meet us as summer days end.

The smell of coffee pours itself outside as people open and close the door to the local coffee shop, Sip-Sip Hurray. Not only is Riley's apartment above it, but it's just a single space. She gets it all to herself, and I envy her. Not needing to worry about neighbors and other noises.

I press the gold button, and the door buzzes, signaling it's unlocked. Again, I'm hit with smelling roasted coffee. I take advantage and inhale while my eyes flutter from the aroma.

Who needs candles when you can smell coffee all day? Her apartment is only scent-free when the shop's closed. During that time, she opens the windows to waft out any lingering smells and lights her candles that fill the space with citrus.

My favorite is pink lemonade.

When I open the door, I'm met with a cozy atmosphere. A couch, sage green, velvet, with decorative pillows sits toward the wall's right. Frames of different sizes and shapes adorn the wall above it. Wooden shelves hang on the opposite wall above a decorative vintage table covered in candles, more photos, and small cactus plants.

A soft rug covers the center, accompanied by a round, wood table.

The real showstopper is the bay windows. Connected to it is a bench-like seat that's also decorated with blankets and pillows. It's perfect for people-watching. Sometimes I feel like a total creep when I do. The tiny disco ball in the corner bounces off the sun's rays, casting a prism throughout the living room.

Her apartment's space is generous. It could hold two people if it needed to.

"Ellie?" Riley calls out.

"Hey," I say as I walk into the small kitchen that connects to the living room, grabbing myself a drink before plopping down on her couch.

"I hope you don't mind, but Hailey is coming over." She walks into the living room in lazy attire. We sit together, and I grab a decorative pillow.

I give her a lazy wave. "That's fine. She can help me rethink my life decisions and where they've led me." I throw my arm over my face and attempt to bury my body in the couch.

"What happened?"

"Just feeling existential dread. I've realized that I don't know what I'm doing anymore, and I'm almost ready to give up."

"Is there anything I can help with?" She picks up her legs, wrapping her arms around them, and tilts her head on the back of the couch.

"Everything feels like it's bubbling to the surface. I know it won't stay like this forever." I peer at her. "Do you know that feeling when everything... I don't know, feels hopeless? The impending doom—that it won't change for the better?"

"I'm living in a small but cute apartment, working at a yoga studio half the time and at my dad's dentist office the other half. And then lie on this couch with a pot full of macaroni and cheese.

"You don't like the idea of coming home to someone? They ask about your day. You spend the evening together and go to bed holding each other."

Riley mimics a gag before saying, "Sounds gross."

A snort escapes me because that answer was obvious. Riley isn't someone who likes to commit. In fact, I can't remember when her last relationship was.

"What up," Hailey says before tossing her bag onto the floor. A beanie—which I find insane of her to wear considering it's eighty degrees outside—covers her black and blonde hair.

"Hi." I wave lazily.

"Hey, Hails," Riley replies.

"Uh, are you okay?" Hailey asks and sits down on the floor.

"She's having a life crisis. Just your normal Tuesday," Riley says.

Hailey tilts her head back and says, "Ah, that'll do it."

"Did you get a new tattoo?" I point to the clear wrap on Hailey's forearm, trying to change the subject.

She holds out her arm. "I sure did."

"What did you get this time?" Riley asks.

"Whiskey and Butterscotch." She gets on her knees and scoots over to us. The tattoo has one orange cat and one grey, in a yin and yang symbol, curled into each other.

"That's so cute," Riley squeals. "Have you had any hot clients lately?"

"There was one guy who came in. Totally my type." Hailey wiggles her brows.

"Oh, so Beau?" I tease.

"Really?" Hailey quirks a perfectly shaped eyebrow.

"What? You're a match made in heaven." I raise my eyebrows and smile.

Riley cackles. "More like hell."

Hailey points a manicured, almond-shaped nail at her sister in agreement. All three of us jump when the buzzer rings in the apartment. It continues and doesn't stop, just a consistent buzzing.

"Who the hell is that?" Hailey asks.

Riley gets up from the couch, gives us a confused expression, and hits the buzzer.

"Are you seriously letting someone in that you aren't expecting?" I ask.

"Ellie, we live in a tiny town, not the city," Riley replies.

"Why does everyone keep comparing things to the city?" I ask.

Hailey looks at me. "Because you compare it."

Someone opens the downstairs door and runs up the stairs. I sit upright, questioning if I should pick up the candle to attack them. Maybe this is why everyone pokes fun at me. My shoulders drop when I see Addie. She's huffing and puffing like she's about to blow this house down.

"Whoa." Hailey looks up at Addie from the floor.

Addie turns to close the door and drops her backpack on the ground. Her dark brown hair whips around, and she goes to the kitchen to get a glass of water. She slams the cabinet before filling her glass, then chugs the water. "My brother is out of his damn mind. Idiotic." She sets down the glass and rubs at her face. "He decided to tell me he's going to see our dad." She splays her arms out and gives us a sarcastic smile.

"Don't you think it's a little harsh to call him idiotic for this?" I say. Yes, it's unnecessary, but I've talked to Rowan about seeing his dad. Addie isn't a fan of the guy, but she should at least support her brother.

She walks toward us with determination and a crazy look in her eyes. "What other word would you use?"

I raise one shoulder and say, "Brave? Courageous? Bold?"

Addie rolls her eyes, not at me, but at the situation itself. Why should he find this man? I don't understand." She sits next to Hailey.

"Did you ask him why?" I ask.

Addie glances at me, her lips parting like she's about to say something, but presses them together. Riley peers at me, then looks at Hailey with raised eyebrows.

"I didn't."

"Then why are you giving him a hard time?"

Addie lets out an exasperated sigh. "Our dad hasn't

been around for nearly twenty-three years. He's never reached out to us, never tried to come back home. So why now?"

"Had you asked him about the situation, you wouldn't be here wondering." I love Addie. She's like a little sister to me, and we don't have the type of relationship where we argue or stop talking.

But when it comes down to Rowan—this protectiveness takes over.

"Maybe we should hear Addie out?" Riley says, her eyes bouncing between us.

"Yeah, sorry. You're right." I give an apologetic smile to Addie. She looks at me with a weary expression.

"I just don't want him to get hurt. If he's awful, then what? I know Rowan blames himself for our dad leaving. And we all know he did nothing wrong. It just didn't work between our parents."

"What did he tell you? Give us a breakdown," Hailey asks.

Addie composes herself, inhaling a deep breath before letting it out. "He came over, saying he wanted to talk. I thought maybe it was about the date you guys went on. Wrong. It was about him wanting to see our dad. And apparently our mom is totally okay with that. I told him it was a terrible idea."

"What happened after that?" Riley asks.

"We just kept butting heads. I told him it wasn't a good idea, and he told me I don't understand." She looked down at her hands. "Then he left... shit. I'm such a shitty sister."

"No, you're not," I say. "You're protective of your brother. I am too. However, I think this will benefit him."

"You know about this?" she asks.

My lips turn downward, and I feel like a dog with its tail

tucked between its legs. It felt as if I had done something wrong and got caught. "He shared this with me on the boat. He asked for my opinion, so I told him to visit."

"You told my brother to go see our dad?"

"I'm pretty sure that's what she just said," Hailey says.

Riley rolls her lips inward and then gets up from the couch. "Anyone thirsty? Hungry?"

"Why would you do that?" Addie chides.

I sit up straighter on the couch, almost in a defensive pose. "Then he can move forward. He can get the answer to all the questions he's had since he was young. Then maybe he won't blame himself for something he didn't cause."

"And what if that doesn't happen? Then what? Do you plan on staying here? Or are you going to leave? Again." she says taut. "Then drag him out of a dark place? *Again.*"

My head jerks back in surprise. I blink a few times, and my mouth goes slack. I'm at a loss for words after she just shot an arrow at my heart.

"Rowan isn't the only person you left behind. And now you're agreeing he sees our dad—who left us—to maybe have a relationship with him. I'm not going to see him heartbroken for a third time, Ellie."

The silence here is deafening, uncomfortable, and awkward.

Addie never speaks like this. She's the one that uplifts someone and turns a negative into a positive. And mentioning that Rowan wasn't the only person I left behind. Suddenly, I feel nauseated.

"That was harsh, Addie," Riley says, her voice small.

I lower my head and huff out a breathy laugh, then clear my throat. "Okay." Riley and Hailey glance at me, but Addie turns her head away. My hands rub on my legs before standing up and grabbing my bag. "I need to go. I'm supposed to meet with Mrs. Anderson about the art show."

"Ellie, wait," Riley says, grabbing my wrist.

"No, it's fine." A tight smile pulls at my lips. "It's none of my business. I'm not family, and I'll be leaving in a couple of weeks. Addie's right." My eyes find her while she is still glancing out the window. "I'll talk to you guys later."

# THIRTY-THREE

## ELLIE

After yesterday's fun conversation with Addie, I thought it'd be best to go home and think about the consequences of my actions.

I crawled into bed, set my phone on DND, and fell asleep. I woke up to missed calls and texts. Rowan, Riley, and even Addie.

I'm too much of a chicken-shit to open Addie's text. I hate confrontation. This is what I do. I avoid arguments.

But I would also like to put on the record that I did have an argument at the start of the summer. With my ex-boyfriend. So technically, I've met my quota for the year.

Contemporary music greets me when I step inside Art Fusion. The walls fill up with bright—or depressing—paintings. I never understood art in this sense. In movies, people will stand in front of a painting and decipher the meaning. I actually find it comical because they're so serious.

"Ellie." I'm greeted with enthusiasm from Mrs. Anderson.

She's wearing black-and-white checkered pants, paired

with a black belt, and a loose-fitting black sweater tucked in the front. She's the epitome of coolness.

"Hey Mrs. Anderson." I wave and smile. "I love your glasses. Are those new?"

She touches the geometric glasses that she's wearing. The multicolored layers are the only pop of color in her entire outfit. "Thank you so much, sweetie. I just got these last week. Aren't they cool? Every time I buy a new pair, I say to myself, 'This is the last one,' and well..." She raises her eyebrows and shrugs.

I laugh and nod. "I'd do the same thing. Except with baking supplies." The thrill of buying something shiny and new filled a gap in my heart. It sounds depressing, but it worked. Especially with new appliances, I could use for work. New knives, spatulas, and a torch lighter. Even a cute apron.

Mrs. Anderson places her hands on her lower back and cocks her head. "I've been meaning to ask how your career is going. It must be exciting, huh?"

There's something about her that soothes me. My shoulders dip, and the surrounding space is Zen. The urge to open up to her is strong. I have no qualms about it. "To tell you the truth, that's why I came home. I sort of..." I wince. "Ran away from it. It became too much, ya know? It's sort of embarrassing. Not being able to handle something, I've become passionate about."

She shakes her head. "That's not embarrassing at all. Things happen. Life happens. Sometimes you grow out of something you once loved. Finding passion and thinking, 'This is it.' Or sometimes, you get so overwhelmed and end up coming back home. Only to create something that's special for you." Her eyes roam around the bright studio.

I follow her lead and admire everything around me. "Wait. You left Dove Point and came back?"

Her smile was as inviting as sunshine. She stuffs her hands in her back pocket and peers back at me. "I sure did. I was eighteen when I left. First, I lived in Austin, Texas, for the art scene, and then, sure enough, I was living in New York. Just like you."

I'm stunned by this. I never heard her story about her life. She was just a cool artist in town. She's confident in what she does. Her chin is always high, and she expresses herself without fear.

I bit my lip before asking, "Can I ask why you left?"

She shrugs. "I think my time outside of Dove Point was done. I was in my early thirties when I realized I wanted to come back home and settle down. But this—" She gestures around us. "This wasn't in my plan. At all. I burnt myself out. The sight of a paintbrush drove me to scream. I know it sounds odd because people look at painting as something relaxing."

I can definitely relate.

"But when you're working for others and not yourself, the excitement fades. I didn't remember the last time I had painted for myself. At that point, I came home to consider my future. Either stay in a fast-paced environment, make others happy, or become miserable. Or, I could find myself again within my roots. And I'm so glad I did."

Is it creepy or ironic that she spoke about my past, present, and—possible—future? It's been a ride trying to get people to understand where I'm coming from. They say that they do, but I'm too nice to tell them they don't get it. I'm not an asshole. But it's refreshing to see someone's perspective in what I'm dealing with.

It's refreshing. It even makes me feel a little hopeful that things will be okay. That no matter the decision I make, it's mine and no one else's. This is my life. My happiness. My body feels lighter, and my thoughts become brighter.

"Alright." Mrs. Anderson claps lightly. "Enough about boring old me. Let's get down to business. I'm so excited that you're helping me with the exhibit. I don't believe paintings will be the show's focus. We get to have a table filled with desserts created by Ellie Thompson." She gives me a wink, then gestures with her hand for me to follow her.

A thrum of excitement takes over my chest, and I feel like I'm one step closer to taking over the pastry world again.

AFTER LEAVING THE ART STUDIO, everything seemed brighter.

The shame I've been feeling is slowly disappearing as I wave goodbye to it. We talked for another hour about the ideas storming in my head.

We're keeping the peanut butter squares—obviously—along with creamy strawberry shortcake cups, and mini cherry cheesecakes.

My catering services increased the guest count from ten to thirty. That alone makes me feel both happy and frightened. It's a small event—to me—I've whipped up desserts for over one hundred people in one room. I display a personality that thrives on approval, aiming for the satisfaction of every person.

Blasting "Dancing Queen" by ABBA could help overcome that funk. I can feel my mood shifting from nervous to relaxed. I wrap my hair in a tight bun to avoid any hair disasters because that is very gross. The lemon scent from the hand soap hits my nose, and I'm ready to bake.

All the tools and ingredients line up on the kitchen counter. "Hello, old friends." I pick up egg out of the carton and stare at the different specks of color on its tan shell. It's cold to the touch, and before I know it, I crack it with one hand on the edge of the silver bowl. The golden yolk sliding toward the middle.

My body is in motion. My hands move around grabbing the whisk, brown sugar, strawberries. Everything comes naturally to me. No need for recipes or second thoughts. It's like riding a bike again—hoping not to fall off the bike.

An hour later, I've made ten of each dessert. The kitchen is a mess; there's flour on my shirt; and One Direction is playing in the background.

I allow myself to rest while the goodies cool down before finalizing the final touches. And by rest, I mean cleaning up the kitchen. I'm usually a clean as you go person, but I was enjoying myself too much to do it.

The mess in front of me is invigorating. Throughout the years, it's been engrained in me to keep my station clean. Spotless.

I hear the door open behind me when I toss all the empty eggshells in the trash.

"Wow," August says.

"Hey."

He shuts the door behind him while I continue to clean the counter. "I didn't know you were in here baking the entire time." August walks to one of the cooling racks showcasing the mini cheesecakes. His hand swoops in to grab one, but I'm faster and slap it away. "Ow." He pulls his hand back.

"They're not for you," I scold. "It's for the art exhibit

Mrs. Anderson is having tomorrow night. I don't need your greasy paws all over them."

"You should've made extras. You know better. Remember the brownie incident of 2009?"

"Don't remind me." I deadpan and lean my hip on the kitchen counter, crossing my arms. "I baked for two days. And it wasn't even for you."

"I inhaled those two pans like it was my job. They were delicious." He pats his stomach.

"You ruined the bake sale."

He gives me a shrug and raises his eyebrows in a 'what can you do?' type look. A bowl of bright green apples catches his eye on the kitchen table, and he scoops one up, tossing it in the air before catching it and taking a bite. "So now that summer is approaching its end, what are you planning to do?"

A groan comes out of my mouth, followed by an eye roll. "You just had to go there."

"What?" The pitch of his voice rises, along with his hands. "I can't ask my sister a simple question?"

"That's just it. It's not a simple question, August. It's an annoying question. Like a fly buzzing near your ear that won't leave you alone."

"Did you just call me a fly?"

I sigh. "No, August. I just don't wanna be responsible right now. No work. No ex-boyfriend drama. Nothing."

"Look, I'll make it easy for you." He widens his stance and lifts his hands, one still holding a half-eaten apple. "Stay home."

My eyebrows pinch together. "You act like that's something easy to do. I can't just snap my fingers and everything goes away."

"You're a grown-ass adult; you can do whatever you

want. If you want to come back home, you know you won't be alone." He finishes the last bit of his apple and tosses it in the trash. "It's not like you have nowhere else to go if you decide to leave your job."

"I hate when you're right," I mutter and look away.

He lets out a giggle, and I respond with another eye roll toward him. "Don't you have somewhere to be? Like a date with a random girl?"

August walks toward the fridge and pulls out a water bottle, taking a generous chug from it. "I do. Her name is Claire."

"And do I know this Claire?"

"Nope. She's from the town over. I met her at the club we went to. Sweet girl." He gives me a wink, and I grimace.

"Right. And are you going out with her because you actually like her? Or are you trying to make someone jealous?" A smart-ass smirk tugs at my lips.

He gives me a blank stare. "I don't know what or whom you're talking about."

"Don't play dumb with me. You look at Riley the same way Beau looks at a chocolate cake." I wince.

"We're friends, nothing more." His facial features take over with sadness when he looks down at the floor, avoiding eye contact. I didn't mean to strike a chord with the topic of Riley.

She and August were actually close a long time ago. They hung out more than me and her, and she's my best friend. One day they were laughing and flirting; the next they were distant, and didn't talk much. They don't know I witnessed the shattering of their friendship. But it's none of my business.

"Here." I grab one of the peanut butter squares and hold it out to him.

He narrows his gaze at me and the treat I hold in my hand. "Is this a pity dessert?"

I give him a bored look and tilt my head. "You have three seconds to take it or—"

His hand swipes the square out of my hand, and he stuffs it in his mouth. "Thanks," he says with a mouth full. "I've gotta get going. I have to pick up Claire in two hours." He walks toward the door to leave, then turns to me. "For what it's worth, I'd really like it if you came back home. I miss my big sister."

I give him a smile that doesn't reach my eyes. "And I miss my little brother."

# THIRTY-FOUR

## ROWAN

Tonight is a very important night for Ellie. One that—I think—will determine her fate with knowing if she should continue doing what she loves.

The Jeep is serving as a dessert-mobile, and I'm not complaining. Yes. Maybe I'll complain a week later when it still smells like sugar and there's none around to satisfy my craving. As I drive up to the house, I see Ellie in the drive-way, alongside roughly twenty boxes.

The short white dress that hits just above her knees sways in the wind. My gaze moves to her cleavage. The fabric ties in a bow, pushing her breasts together. And her hair. The caramel brown shines in the sun.

I've dreamt about the night we both pleasured each other. Whimpers escaped her lips while she begged for more. The way my name sounded from those pretty lips. Fuck.

*Control yourself.*

Shaking the memories from my head, I pull into the driveway, watching Ellie wave eagerly. She's so fucking perfect.

"Rowan," she shouts, waving in excitement. "Thanks so much for helping. Seriously. You're a lifesaver." She bends down with her knees closed to pick up three white boxes and hands them to me.

"Well, I wouldn't be your knight in shining armor if I didn't help. We both know that can't happen." The paper boxes have a clear lid, showcasing the sweets that I drool over. "What are those?" I gesture with my chin.

"Strawberry shortcakes," she gleamed, stashing a box in the back.

"If there aren't any leftovers, I may need to riot." I grab three more boxes and set them in the car. "Now that I think about it, I've had zero desserts from you this summer." When I turn to her, I cross my arms and give her a frown.

She tilts her head and smiles. "Are you stealing my move, Rowan? You think pouting is going to get you anywhere with me?"

"Absolutely. Is it working?" I push my lip out a bit and give her the saddest puppy-dog eyes I could come up with.

Her eyes take on a hypnotized look, turning her body toward one box, and lifts it up to me. "Don't be sad. Here is a full box of peanut-butter squares," she says in monotone.

"That is the creepiest thing I've seen someone do."

She lifts the box up more, continuing to stay in character. "Please. You must take these. Or I will not satisfy your needs."

"Oh, trust me." A laugh escapes me. "You've satisfied my needs."

Ellie breaks character, her jaw dropping and eyes widening. "Ew. Don't be so crude!" She swats at my arm.

I continue to chuckle, grabbing the box and placing it in the car. "Alright, you ready to go?"

She fiddles with her fingers, and when I peer down, I see no ring on her finger. The faded rose gold ring that's sat on her thumb for almost the entire summer has vanished. "I can't lie to you and say I'm not nervous. I'm ready to run for the hills."

"I'll have no choice but to chase after you. I'm not letting you out of my sight." A smirk pulls at my lips. She drops her hands and takes two steps closer to me before grabbing both my hands in hers. "It's going to be great. I promise."

When she lifts her gaze to me, her soft brown lashes can't hide those baby blue eyes. "Thank you for believing in me. I don't know what I'd do without you."

My love for her causes me pain. I love her so damn much that I don't know if I can handle her leaving my side again. The thought of getting down on my knees, begging her to stay, is strong, and I don't know how much longer I can fight it.

"You're a star in my eyes, Ellie. You always will be." When I lift her hand up to me, I press my lips to her skin gingerly. Her feelings mirror mine, without a doubt. It's always been there. That chemistry—it's never left us.

First, I need to see Dad. And then, I'm getting the girl.

---

I CONSIDER MYSELF ARTISTIC. I've built a business from the ground up, and behind that business involved a lot of creativity that James and I have perfected. At least, that's what I tell myself. There's always room to grow.

The theme tonight is 'Identity.' And I sure as shit think how ironic it is considering the minor crisis I've been dealing with this summer. Trying to find my identity within my father. Wanting to figure out who he is and what I've taken from him.

Three thumbprints hang in front of me on one large canvas. It's about the size of a sixty-inch television. The curves in each line represent the person we are. Each one that I gaze at is different. Underneath is a small plaque sign that signifies each fingerprint.

When I tilt my head to look at the first one; it's a simple whorl. Around and around. The longer I stare at it, the more lost I get in it. Then there's the second one; a tented arch. It resembles a hill, except one on top of the other. Kind of like if you reach the top of one hill, only to notice there's another above it. And the final one is a radial loop; the ridges flow toward the thumb. Similar to ocean waves.

I can't help but look at my thumb and learn that mine is a radial loop. I wonder if Dad has the same print as I do. Or if it's like Mom's instead.

"Thumb prints. Interesting," James says next to me. He takes a swig from his beer bottle and leans his head to one side like I did moments ago. "Would it be weird to say these paintings are giving me an identity crisis?" He continues to look ahead.

"Maybe that's the entire point of this exhibit. To cause reflection on identity. If we're our own person or if we walk in the shadow of someone else." My hands slip into my jean pockets while I continue to examine the colors next. Each fingerprint is in its own color—navy blue, forest green, and deep red.

"Thank God I didn't take an edible before this or I'd probably have a midlife crisis," Beau says on the other side of me.

Both James and I turn our attention to him. "You're twenty-eight," his brother responds.

"Okay." Beau turns toward James. "The man had two heads that were trying to escape from his real one. Check that out, then you can talk all the shit you want." He stuffs two peanut-butter squares in his mouth.

"Dude. There's one that's a shattered mirror. I didn't like what I saw." James rubs the stubble on his jaw. "One eye was in one corner and the other in the middle. There will be nightmares tonight."

"All I know is Mrs. Anderson will receive my therapy bill after this." Beau downs the rest of the amber liquid in a crystal glass.

A snort slips from me, but I continue to stare at the painting. It won't let me look away. Like it's telling me what I already know. Who am I?

When I force my feet to move to the next one, I catch Ellie glaring at it. Not looking. Glaring. Like she wants to rip it off the wall and throw it across the room, Hulk style. "Everything okay?" I ask cautiously.

Her focus snaps to me, as if she were in a daze. "Oh, yeah." She turns her attention back to the painting. "I've been glaring at it for what feels like forever, and I suspect I'm losing my sanity."

My eyes shift to the black and white painting. There are five staircases, but each one leads to five different doors. No signs. No directions. Paths intertwine, creating confusion to the eye. It's surrounded by glass windows, which causes me to go cross-eyed.

I press my fingers into them, trying to set them straight again.

"Yup. I just did that five minutes ago," Ellie says. "This

painting is freaking me out. It's like—telling me my life story, and I'm suddenly very overwhelmed. Riley stood here with me for two minutes before she said she couldn't take it anymore."

"She was probably treating it like one of those mazes you get as a placemat at a restaurant." I chuckle.

A laugh comes from Ellie, and she breaks eye contact to look at me. "Which one did you come from?"

"The next one over." I gesture with my head. "It wasn't as...abstract as this. But it definitely turned some gears in my head."

"Oh yeah? And what might those gears be?" She turns fully toward me, her eyes roaming my face as if I'm a painting.

I shrug. "It just made me think more about my dad. Who I am as a person and how much we actually share. Not just in looks but in personality. Identity. Will we have the same quirks or body movements? I don't even know what his voice sounds like anymore."

Ellie gazes at me with focus, and her tone softens. "Do you want any of those things?"

My eyebrows raise as I think about it. "I'm not sure. I don't know what to expect. You know? I understand not to go in with high hopes." I find Addie talking with other observers. If there's one thing she's great at, it's striking up a conversation with people she's never met.

"I heard about what happened when you told Addie about seeing him. I'm sorry it didn't go the way you wanted."

"I knew what I was getting myself into. Not to mention she caught me throwing up in the alley." I rub my neck in embarrassment.

"Oh shit. Were you okay?" She touches my forearm, and a shiver runs through me.

"My nerves got the best of me." I give her a sad smirk.

"When do you plan on seeing him?"

"This Saturday." My stomach churns with nerves again. Ejecting them did not solve the issue, apparently.

"Okay." She folds her arms. "What time are we going?"

"You still wanna come with me?" I say a little too eagerly.

"Of course I'm still coming. I'm not letting you do this alone. I'll have your back no matter what you choose. We can wait outside for three hours if you need to. Or if you want to punch him in the face, I'll support your decision."

"Whoa, no one's punching anybody." I grin.

She rolls her eyes and smiles. "You know what I mean."

A chuckle escapes me, and I tug her into a hug. I smell lavender and feel my heart slow to a steady beat. The effect she has on me needs to be studied by scientists. No one can change my mood the way Ellie can.

My biggest need is bringing her and this visit can resemble the stairs in that painting. And I hope I open the right door.

***

"MY KITTENS ARE MEOWING," Ellie practically throws herself into the passenger seat of my car.

I snort and look at her as I turn on the car. "Your kittens are meowing?"

She throws her head back before turning to look at me. "Yeah. Instead of my dogs barking, my kittens are meowing. It's cute."

"You've had success tonight. I'm sure plenty of people

asked for your catering services." We leave the art gallery and head onto the road, back to her house.

"Catering services? I don't provide catering services. This was a one time thing." She looks forward, her eyelids heavy, her hair blowing gently in the wind.

The night sky is like a velvet blanket covered in diamonds. It's one of those nights that reminds me just how insignificant we all are on this tiny planet. We could vanish instantly within the endless universe, blind to it.

Shit. That art exhibit did a number on my thoughts.

I pull into the driveway of Ellie's parents' house and put the car in park before closing my eyes for a second. Tiredness takes over my body.

"Want to come inside for a bit? Hang out?" Ellie says and unbuckles her seatbelt.

My hand rubs my sleepy eyes. Should I stick around and unwind? I can tell we're both mentally exhausted.

Ellie's desserts stole the show. Person after person asked her question after question. Will you be catering other events? Have you thought about opening your own business? What's it like living in a big city?

I kept my attention on her even though I stood across the room from her. I planned to swoop in quickly to support her if she seemed overwhelmed. Everything she made was gone within ten minutes, and she badgered herself for not making more.

I have a knack for helping Ellie escape her thoughts. She needs to quit blaming herself for that. Word had spread around town regarding her catering. It caused a flood of guests to arrive.

We both open our car doors and walk toward the wooden gate that leads to the backyard and guesthouse. I unlatch the lock as I tower over her and hold it open. She turns around to give me a tired 'thank you' smile and we walk through the massive yard.

Mrs. Thompson decided that her project for the summer would be gardening. The brick path guides toward the quaint guesthouse; stalks of vegetables line each side. Tomatoes, peppers, carrots, even some strawberries. Crickets chirp and cicadas buzz around us.

Ellie lets out a yawn when we step inside, both of us shrugging our shoes off before we stumble toward the couch and sit down. We let out comfortable sighs in unison.

"What a day," Ellie says.

"I'd say it was a successful one." I dig my body into the couch and rest my head on the back.

"I'd forgotten how it felt when people appreciated my baking. I feel accomplished knowing I'm skilled at something that brings happiness."

When I turn my gaze on her, all I see is happiness sketched in her features. Her lips pull into a pleasant smile. I can't look at her without falling harder for her. My chest is tight, and my feelings become overwhelmed with love and admiration.

"I'm glad that spark is gradually coming back. You deserve to be proud of yourself and the talent that you carry. You've been smiling all night. I miss that smile."

She gives me the same smile that tugs at my heartstrings. I would do anything for this woman. I would battle a thousand men to reach her if I needed to. Hell, I'd climb the tallest mountain just to reach her.

"I'm your number one fan, Ellie Thompson." I give her a wink.

"You want an autograph?"

"Only if it's on my butt cheek."

"Ew." Ellie laughs and gives me a shove. "Can I ask you something?"

"Anything."

"What's the goal with your dad? What do you want out of it?"

My body deflates when I let out a heavy sigh. "Closure, I guess? I need to move on. I think it's about time."

"Why now?"

"You want the truth?" I raise my eyebrows.

She breaks eye contact for a second and then back to me. "Well, yeah."

I wait for a beat to gather my thoughts. "You," I say simply.

"Me?" She cocks an eyebrow.

I nod. "Yep."

She huffs out a laugh. "Why?"

"You prioritized yourself. You knew you'd find solace by coming home. Right?"

She nods.

"That's what I need to do. Figure out who I am. It's like my dad is the missing puzzle piece. You kind of gave me the courage to face my issues head-on."

Ellie's eyes narrow and her eyebrows pinch together. "I'm not facing my issues. I ran away from them."

I roll my eyes. "You didn't run away. Didn't you face Charlie when the whole cheating thing went down? It could have ended differently, but you spoke with him about his stupidity."

"And what about my job? I ran away from that."

"You took a well-deserved break. When did your last vacation happen? Christmas and Thanksgiving don't count as a vacation."

Her lips turn downward while she thinks about it. I look

at the watch on my wrist jokingly, and she catches me and then laughs. "That's not funny."

"I'm just saying. This summer was your vacation. So no, you didn't run away, and you faced the bullshit with Charlie, who's a douche. I never liked that guy," I mutter in the last part.

"I knew you never liked him," she says in a defeated tone, and suddenly I feel guilty for saying that.

I bite the inside of my cheek and scold myself for saying that to her. Her hand wraps around mine, helping release the tension in my jaw. "I'm sorry."

"Don't be. To tell you the truth." She turns her body toward me, her knee touching my own. "I wasn't happy anymore. In fact, I kind of—resented him? Gradually, affection died down. However, I did nothing about it."

This information comes as a total shock to me. Ellie never mentioned this to me and definitely not to Riley. She'd come running to me. It's no secret to Riley how I still feel toward Ellie.

"Does anyone else know this?" I can't help but ask.

She shakes her head. "I didn't want to bother anyone with my relationship drama. We just grew apart."

"Why didn't you end things sooner?"

She shrugs. "I was comfortable. I know it's a dumb reason, but it's the truth."

"Ellie, I know you know just how much I've screwed up my relationships. I couldn't handle them."

I watch her chew on the corner of her lip before she looks away with crinkled eyebrows. "Why did you do that? End one after another? Is it because of your dad?"

A bundle of nerves appears in my stomach at the question. Of course, part of the reason is my abandonment issues, but the biggest one is the woman sitting in front of me. How will she react if I tell her the truth? This summer has been nothing but truth bombs, but this is the biggest one.

I clear my throat and pick at my jeans. The words hover on my tongue, but I struggle to say them. Why do I suddenly feel like a teenager? Telling Ellie all over again that I—still—have feelings for her?

"None of them were right for me. They weren't... you."

# THIRTY-FIVE

## ELLIE

All I can do is blink as my thoughts shift into motion.

They weren't me? Like she wasn't a five foot two girl with brown hair and blue eyes? Or just super funny? Cool?

Okay, I'm giving myself too much credit. But still. What does that mean? I'm too scared to ask. My feelings toward him are already out of control, and if he tells me what I think he's going to tell me, I don't know if I can handle it.

My memory returns to Addie's statement to me at Riley's place.

'Do you plan on staying here? Or are you going to leave? Again. Then drag him out of a dark place? Again.'

The taste of bile rises in my throat, and I suddenly feel overwhelmed. I've let Rowan down once. I can't do it again. But my lizard brain has other plans.

"What do you mean... like me?"

His lips part before he drags his tongue over the bottom one, tugging at it with his teeth. I can almost feel his hand trembling on my own.

*Oh wait, that's me.*

He gives me a flat look that says, 'Ellie, are you really

asking me this?' But I need to hear it from him. From his mouth. That will solidify everything between us. Of course, what we did a few nights ago should have already solidified whatever this is between us, but I'm stubborn.

"Every woman I've ever been with wasn't you. And I'm not talking about your features. I'm talking about the complete package. There's no other woman like you, Ellie Thompson. Even if things don't work out between us, I'll die knowing that you were my endgame."

Such simple words cause an ache between my legs, knowing that this man would give his all to me. But I also feel guilty, knowing we can't be together because of me.

"I'm sorry," I utter.

"For what?" he asks with pinched eyebrows.

I swallow the pit in my throat. "It's my fault we can't be together. It's my fault that we broke up." The lump I tried to push down comes flowing back up. Tears pool around my eyes, making Rowan blurry when these feelings hit me at once.

The look of alarm tugs at his features. His eyes bounce between mine, and he lets go of my hand so he can cradle my face with both of his. A small laugh slips from his lips, and my eyebrows knit in confusion. "None of this is your fault. If anything, it's my fault for not leaving with you. I should've fought harder for you."

All I do is shake my head, disagreeing with him. It's nice that he wants to take this burden off me, but it won't work. I can't let him take the blame. I didn't need to leave and go to school in New York. Attending college here, staying home— it would've been simpler.

He smirks at me, and his blue-gray eyes carry nothing but kindness. "Fine. Would it make you feel better if I said it was both of us? Fifty-fifty?"

An ugly snort rumbles from my nose. He presses his forehead against mine before giving it a kiss. I want him. I need him. I love him. He's my best friend, and I know he's the only person I want to spend the rest of my life with. But I can't choose between him and my career. Not again.

Am I wrong to want him all for myself?

My eyes peer down at his lips before I crash into them. Initially, he wavers, becoming rigid, but afterward, he loosens and returns my kiss. His tongue slips into my mouth, warm and soft. It pulls a whimper out of me, and I feel like melting into this couch.

His hands still cradle my face but move into my hair and then down my body in one quick motion. Suddenly he grips my hips and pulls me into him; my arms wrap around his neck. His lips break away from mine, and he trails toward my jaw and onto the sensitive skin of my neck.

He remembers my weak spots, and that makes me want him more. I moan and let my neck follow his lips, not wanting him to stop. He nips at my earlobe, and I bite my lip. Another spot that he knows makes me go feral.

"Rowan," I pant out.

"Hm." He continues to kiss my neck, my jaw, my collarbone.

"I need you... I need you to fuck me. Please." I beg while swallowing a moan.

The movements stop. His lips stop. "We don't need to do that."

My hand trails on his thigh, inching closer and closer to his cock. Our eyes meet, and his eyelids are heavy. It seems he's in a haze.

I shake my head. "I was in my head, overthinking. I wasn't giving myself what I knew I needed. And I need you, Rowan. I need you in every way."

He lets out a heavy sigh while his head hangs low. I keep my hand where it is. "I don't want to ruin anything between us, El." His assertions disagree with what his gaze tells. There's fire in them and hunger. He wants me just as badly without having to say a single word.

I break eye contact and nod my head. "I understand. You shouldn't feel obligated to apologize." I gaze back at him. "Everything I've said is true." My hand squeezes his thigh in reassurance.

"Then again. You're very hard to resist." He kisses my jaw. "I'd have you bent over." His lips go to my neck. "Grabbing the headboard," he says huskily. "screaming my name and telling me you can't handle it anymore while I make you come again and again."

What's this man doing to me? Does he realize he's making the situation worse and not better? I can feel my panties becoming soaked and my breasts aching. My breathing comes out in pants as my chest rises and falls.

"Please, Rowan. Don't make me beg anymore. If you—" I gasp when I feel his large hand trail up my dress, so close to my pussy that I move my hips closer. "If you think it's a bad idea." My neck falls back when I feel his index finger trail the hem of my underwear. "Then we should stop. Right?"

He bites my collarbone. "Yeah, we should stop." But he doesn't. His finger continues to roam and then finds itself right on top of my clit. My underwear gives away just how much I need him. "God, fucking dammit." He groans. "You're so fucking wet."

My hand creeps up his thigh, and I roam over his hard cock. He sucks in air, and I feel him twitch in anticipation. "I thought." I take a breath in. "We wouldn't do this? I don't." He sucks my neck and I moan. "I don't want you to feel like we need to."

"I take it back," he says quickly and presses his index finger onto my clit, the material of my underwear causing a barrier.

I let myself have him and press my palm onto his hard length, massaging it through the rough fabric of his jeans. He lets out a guttural groan, and the hair on my arms rises. The sound sent a shockwave of pleasure down my chest, into my belly, and between my legs.

I continue to rub my hand over him and let myself unbutton his pants, then his zipper. Going slow is pointless; my body needs him. His abs clench at my touch, and my finger trails down the strip of hair that dips into his groin.

His head falls onto my shoulder when I loop my finger between his briefs. At the same time he lets his fingers slide underneath my panties, two of them feeling what he's done to me. I move my hips for better friction as he continues to tease me, not giving me what I want.

"Show me how much you need me." The tone of his voice is demanding and raw. "Show me what you dream about every night."

My teeth scrape at my bottom lip, and I press down hard enough that it gives me pleasure. I peer at his hungry gaze. The way his lips part and his eyes nearly roll back when I guide my hand under the soft fabric of his briefs and down to his hard cock.

The tip is wet as I swirl my thumb over the head. Rowan whimpers. I've never heard a man whimper for me. I won't lie to myself and say I don't enjoy hearing that sound because I absolutely do. My thumb rubs at his head some more, causing it to be slick enough that I grip him tighter and stroke him.

"Fuck yes, baby," he mumbles, barely getting the words out. He doesn't forget about me and pushes my underwear to the side, letting his fingers explore my sensitive bud. The friction causes my hand to grip his cock tighter, pulling another deep groan from him. "Just like that."

My breathing becomes jagged, and my eyes are heavy with desire. The ache in the bottom of my belly wants more. I need more. "I don't know if I can wait any longer. I need you now," I plead.

A wicked grin grows on his lips when I feel his own hips rocking. Before I can get another stroke in, his hand leaves my pussy then grabs my hips and settles me on top of him. The feel of his cock presses into me.

"Oh my God," I whine. I didn't feel him against me like this last time. My hips rock on top of him of their own accord, not waiting for my brain to signal the movement. The tips of his fingers dig into my hips.

"How badly do you want my cock, baby?"

"So fucking bad," I say between each breath.

"Then take it. Take what's yours, Ellie." He lifts himself up, not bothering to slow things down anymore, and lets go of me to dip his hand into his briefs and release his massive cock. The length itself makes my mouth water. "Sit on my cock, baby. Ride me." He pushes my underwear to the side, and I lift on my knees, centering myself onto his tip.

I tease him with just his tip. Letting him feel the wetness and warmth of me. "Mmm," I moan.

"Giving me just a taste of you? Fuck. You want me to beg, don't you?"

He pulls a smile from my lips before I let myself slowly take him in me. It's been so long since I've been with someone, let alone Rowan, and I forgot how incredible it feels when he stretches me.

"Look at that. A perfect fit, baby." His hands find my hips again. "Now ride my cock like a good girl."

My hands brace on the back of the couch, and I let my head dip into his neck, peppering it with kisses. I bounce up and down in a slow rhythm, enjoying every second of this. The only sounds I hear are our skin slapping together and the moans coming from Rowan's mouth.

The speed I'm going at isn't enough for him when I feel his hands take control of my movements. My legs tire out—which tells me I'm severely out of shape—and I slow down.

"Are you getting tired?" he asks softly. I answer with a nod, and then he pushes deeper inside me, lifting his hips. He holds my lower back and slowly slides off the couch, my pussy still wrapped around his cock. It's like he's afraid we'll separate and won't find each other again. My back settles on the rug that covers the wooden floor. "How's that?"

"So much better. I'm sorry." I wince.

"Why are you sorry?"

"Because my legs suck and I get tired within like two minutes." I laugh at myself, and he smiles down at me. God, he's so beautiful. His grey gaze dominates the current blue. The dimples that showcase with his smile pull at my heart-strings.

"Baby." He lifts my left leg up, pressing it gently onto my chest. "This just gives me a reason to fuck you harder." He kisses my cheek before thrusting himself into me, and I moan in pleasure. He clutches my knee; his other palm rests beside my head, supporting himself. Each movement is pleasurable torture. His cock slowly leaves me, then he rams it back in. Over and over.

I attempt to catch my breath, but it continues to flee from me. My breasts bounce with every pump he gives me. "Fast, harder." I beg.

My request sets his eyes ablaze, and he gives me what I want. He pounds into my wet pussy; my back rubbing against the rug oddly adds to that pleasure. I can feel my hair turning into a knot in the back as he continues to fuck me harder and harder.

He lifts himself up, turning me on my side while putting my foot on his shoulder. I brace myself, my hands holding onto the ground, and my eyes roll so far back when he shoves himself inside me again. It's so deep, I didn't think it was possible.

Rowan holds onto my ankle before letting his other hand onto the floor. He bends toward me and goes in deeper, causing my nails to dig into the plush rug. "Holy shit," I yell out.

"Your pussy drives me crazy. You're perfect." He continues to praise me while fucking me faster. His cock goes deep and hits a spot I never knew I had. I think I'm going to climax without touching myself.

"Oh, my God," I cry out. "Harder, harder," I pant.

"If I go any harder, I won't last."

I squeeze my eyes shut, and my jaw drops when I suddenly feel a rush of pleasure run through my body, from my head to my toes. "Holy shit. Rowan, I'm coming. Oh, my God."

I hear him whimper. A sound that makes my toes curl. He gives me one last, heavy thrust before his own pleasure takes control of his body. Rowan gives me three more thrusts until he stops, still inside me, panting. When I open my eyes to look at him, his forehead gleams with sweat. I can feel mine sliding down my neck.

My head falls down onto my arm as I try to control my breathing. The pounding of my heart fights against my chest. If I weren't already lying down, I'd collapse. A small whimper escapes from me when I feel him pulling out, still hard, and soaking wet.

He sits on his knees and looks down at me. There's still fire in his eyes, and when he gazes down at my pussy, that's filled with him, I watch his fingers push in everything that's dripping outside of me. Almost as if he's marking his territory..

My eyes are heavy, closing of their own accord, and before I drift off to sleep, I see him lick his fingers that are covered in both of us.

*Holy hell.*

He fixes my panties, putting them back the way they should be, before fixing himself. A pleasurable sigh is all I hear when I close my eyes, and I feel his body pressing against mine. "Lift your head up for me, baby." I do as he says as he tucks his biceps under me and he pulls me into his chest, his other arm wraps around my stomach.

I feel like I'm floating as I drift off to sleep, everything around me fading away peacefully. Just before everything goes dark, I hear three words I never thought I'd hear again.

"I love you."

I'm woken up by the sun and Ellie's soft snores. We're still on the floor, but now I'm on my back, her head on my chest and leg sprawled over mine.

I rub my face and wake up out of my haze. I realized I hadn't gone home the night before. Shit. Milo. My hand reaches for my phone in my front pocket, and I text Addie.

> Rowan: Hey, I'm sorry, but can you check up on Milo? I didn't get home last night.

> Addie: Sure. Why aren't you at home? Is everything okay?

> Rowan: Everything's fine. I fell asleep at Ellie's place.

Three grey dots appear, disappear, and reappear again.

> Addie: Oh, okay. I'll be at your place in five minutes. I'll make sure he eats and then I'll take him for a walk.

I set my phone down, then turn my head toward the

window; the bright blue sky greets me. I'm surprised Addie didn't blow up my phone asking question after question. Whenever something comes up regarding me and Ellie, she turns into a love guru, trying to decode our relationship.

Maybe she's just tired, and it'll hit her when she's fully awake. I'll need to prepare myself for the annoyance.

The sound of a tired grunt grabs my attention when I notice Ellie waking up. I feel her foot point as if she's stretching it out. Her arm raises from my chest, stretches, and then settles back down. She huffs out a sigh and doesn't move her head.

"Morning," she says groggily.

I smile to myself. I wrap my arm around her shoulders and pull her close, then I kiss the top of her head. "Morning, sleepyhead."

She groans. "My back is killing me. I can't believe I fell asleep on the floor." She pushes herself up on her hand and twists her back. Her messy hair frames her face, and a grumpy frown appears on her lips. After she brushes her hair out of her face, she lifts herself up on her feet and puts her hand out to me.

"Are you attempting to help me up?" I raise an eyebrow.

Ellie scoffs and gives me a dead-eye look. "Come on."

I grab her hand, and she pulls at my arm, but I put in seventy percent at lifting myself up. I stand, then stretch my neck from side to side and in circles. I massage the knot I feel on the side. "Damn. You weren't kidding. I don't think I'll be able to move my neck for a week."

She lets out a huff of a laugh before dragging her feet to the kitchen. Her dress wrinkled, and her eye makeup smeared; she walks like a zombie. A very cute zombie.

"You want some coffee?" Her voice comes out raspy.

She rummages through the cupboards, grabbing two mugs, and then starts the coffee.

"Do you even have to ask?" I sit at the small kitchen island.

The sound of coffee dripping into the clear glass pot soothes me, along with the nutty scent that fills the room. Ellie leans her back on the counter facing me, the sun rays falling around her from the window above the sink. She crosses her arms, and then her eyes close.

"Sorry," I say, and she opens her eyes.

"For what?"

I rest my chin on my palm and smile at her. "For wearing you out last night."

Her eyes roll, but I get a laugh out of her. The coffee machine beeps, letting us know it's ready. Ellie's enticement last night fills my thoughts. The way she felt around my cock. How I whimpered her name as I felt myself filling her up.

Then I remember me pushing my come back into her, not letting a drop escape from her beautiful pussy. Shit. My dick is hard again just thinking about all of it. The clinking sound of my mug snaps me out of the beautiful memory, and I grip the handle before taking a drink.

I remember falling asleep next to her and dreaming. I told her I loved her. However, it felt odd, since the dream felt real. I tilt my head, continuing the thought.

*Wait. No. No, no, no, no.*

I choke on my coffee and slap my chest before coughing into my fist.

"Shit, are you okay?" Ellie comes around, setting her mug down, and then gently slapping my back.

Pushing myself up from the chair, holding out my hand. "I'm fine," I say, before scurrying to the front door and grabbing my shoes. "I realized I'd forgotten to do something important. Talk to you later?"

"Oh." Her eyes cast downward, and she fidgets with her ringless thumb. "Yeah, sure."

After I put both my shoes on, I walk toward her and grab her hands. "Hey, look at me." I grip her chin, tilting her head up, before kissing her lips. "I'll see you later. Okay?"

She kisses me back and then smiles at me, nodding. "Yeah, okay."

BY THE TIME I get to my house I'm panting. It's early enough that few people were out while I was driving home. No one was there to witness my psychotic driving.

My hand slams the door shut harder than I intended to before I hear someone in the kitchen.

"Rowan?" Addie calls out.

Shit. My head falls back before I catch her staring at me with wide eyes. She looks me up and down with a weary expression before Milo comes barreling at me.

"Hey buddy." I drop to my knees to give him a proper greeting and kiss the top of his head.

"Are you okay?"

I fight with myself, wondering if I should tell her. I'm not sure who else I would tell. It'd be too awkward to tell the guys, plus they'd joke around and give me shit. When I stand up, I run a hand through my hair and sit on the couch.

"Before I tell you anything, promise you won't freak out."

Addie glances both directions then trudges toward the couch to sit beside me. "Uh okay. What's up?"

I inhale a deep breath before speaking. "Last night, Ellie

and I—" God, this is so fucking awkward. "We hooked up," I say, because it's the least uncomfortable way to tell her we had sex. I don't even like saying that word to Addie. Sex.

"You guys had sex?" she exclaims. Well, at least one of us can say it.

"That's not even the worst of it," I mumble.

"Oh god." She covers her face in her hands. "What did you do?"

"Well, when we were falling asleep, I told her I love her."

She stares at me, her eyes growing beyond expectation. Her words sputter and she stands from the couch. "What the hell is wrong with you?"

The sound of a tire screeching on pavement plays in my head. What? What's wrong with me? I wasn't expecting this kind of... reaction? She usually gets excited if something between Ellie and I happens. Is there something she's keeping from me?

"Wait. What?"

She crosses her arms and her mood shifts from shock to apprehensive. "I kind of—said something shitty to Ellie a few days ago. I texted her, but she never responded to me and I haven't seen her in person."

Addie saying something shitty to anyone is something rare to come by. She sees the bright side of things. Unless it comes to our Dad.

"What happened? What did you say?"

"It happened after you told me you were going to see dad. I'd been in a shit mood and I went to Riley's place, not expecting everyone else to be there, because I needed to vent." She pauses and lets out a sigh. "Ellie was standing up for you. As she should have been. I let my careless attitude get the best of me and…" She trails off, putting her finger tips to her lips, and closes her eyes.

"Addie." I press.

"I questioned what would happen if everything didn't go as planned between you and dad." I told her she'll end up leaving you again and I'll be the one to pick up the pieces… like I did for you when she left for New York."

There wasn't a time I'd get upset with Addie. She's my little sister. She irks me like a sister does, but I rarely become angry. I guess there's a first for everything.

"Addie, why would you do that?" I stand from the couch.

"I know! I fucked up, okay? You don't think I feel guilty about it? Ellie isn't speaking to me and I don't blame her. It's been eating me up inside." She paces the living room while wringing her hands together.

"So, what? You're pissed we slept together and she's going to leave again? It's my fault too Addie. I'm the one that let her go. It's not your responsibility to protect me and my feelings. I know what I'm getting myself into." My heart races while emotions race by one by one. "We aren't teenagers anymore, Addie."

I watch her wipe away a tear and she crosses her arms again. "I know, I'm sorry," she says with some bite to her tone. "This situation is beyond Ellie. It's also about dad. I love Ellie, you know I do. But I can't watch you two hurt yourselves again. Neither of you deserve to feel like that."

The anger that built inside me evaporates when I see my sister like this. My shoulders drop and I walk up to her. "I'm sorry." I pull her in for a brotherly hug that comprises squeezing her uncomfortably. Our standard 'let's call a truce' hug.

"You have no reason to apologize." She steps back when I release her. "I was being a bitch."

"Yeah. You were." I bracket my hips and raise my eyebrows.

"Are you still seeing dad?"

"I'm going tomorrow and Ellie's coming with me."

She nods. "Okay. I'm glad she's going. I still don't know how I feel about you seeing him. But I'll support your decision."

I give her a small smile. "Thank you, Addie. Now can you do something for me?"

"Sure."

"Go talk to Ellie."

# THIRTY-SEVEN

## ELLIE

My phone buzzes on the coffee table, and I stretch to grab it from the couch. After Rowan left, I changed into cozy clothes and decided to just hang out by myself today.

A lot runs through my thoughts following the previous evening's unforeseen circumstances. The main thing at the forefront of my brain is Rowan not bringing up the fact that he told me he loved me just before he fell asleep. Maybe he thinks I didn't hear him?

When I look at my phone, I see a text from Addie.

> **Addie:** Hey, can I come over? I need to talk to you.

> **Ellie:** I'm a little occupied at the moment.

I know I shouldn't keep pushing this conversation off, but Addie's never been mad at me. She's like my little sister. The hurt in her eyes when she told me I left her too—I couldn't handle it.

Someone knocks on the door, and I sit up before

catching Addie opening it. She pops in like she usually does anywhere she goes. "You liar. You're not busy." She gestures to me.

"Yeah, I am. I'm busy lying on the couch, enjoying time by myself." I cross my arms.

She closes the door, removing her Crocs before strolling toward me. A ponytail holds back her wavy brown hair, exposing her sharp jawline and long slender neck. Addie's always been delicately beautiful. The white cotton shirt makes her skin glow and her freckles pop across her cheeks.

"We need to talk, Ellie." She mimics me and folds her arms.

I open the fridge, grab a bottle of white wine, and tug at the cork, making a popping sound, before taking a wineglass from the cabinet.

"Isn't it a little early to be drinking wine?" Addie asks.

The champagne-colored liquid fills my glass. "Yeah, well, this conversation will require some, Addie." I take a swig from my glass, savoring the sweetness on my tongue. "Want some?" I ask, trying to be friendly.

"Might as well."

I pour her a glass and hand it to her. Without speaking, I move toward the living space, seating myself on the couch while holding my glass. She sits on the couch, but leaves an empty cushion between us. We sit in silence, neither of us starting the conversation.

"I'm sorry, El," Addie breaks the tension. "I was an asshole, and you didn't deserve any of that. My emotions were high that day when Rowan told me about our dad. I didn't mean to unleash all that on you."

My nail taps at the glass, and I don't make eye contact with her. "It's fine," I mutter.

She lets out an annoyed groan and sets her glass on the

table. "It's not fine. I regret having said that. I can't have both you and Rowan pissed at me."

Finally, I look at her. "What do you mean, Rowan is mad at you?"

"I was with him this morning, and I told him what happened. He also told me what happened between you guys last night. Congratulations I guess," she says in a sarcastic tone and grimaces before picking up her wineglass and gulping a large helping.

"Look, that wasn't supposed to happen. But it did. I don't regret it."

"If things were different, you know I wouldn't care, but they are. You're going back to New York. To your busy life where we barely get to talk or see you. I'm scared that with you leaving and him seeing our dad, it won't do any good for him."

"You don't think I know that, Addie? You think I just want to sleep with him and then leave? All of this is my fault. I get that." I drink the last of my wine and lift myself from the couch to grab more.

"God. You and Rowan need to stop blaming yourselves. You had to make a choice between your career and staying home."

I snatch a fresh bottle of red wine off the counter. "I chose my career instead of your brother. It's safe to say, I think, that I'm a shitty person." Holding the bottle, I bite the cork, pluck it, and then fill the glass.

Addie sucks down her drink and sticks her glass out, requesting a refill. She tells me to stop when it passes the half mark and takes a sip. "Choosing your career over a man isn't shitty. Okay? And I was a brat when I said that shit to you."

"But you're right. It stung, but it was true. I'll be leaving soon, back to a place that stresses me out, dealing with an ex-boyfriend who won't leave me alone." I laid my head back on the couch. "And your brother told me he loved me. What should I do with that? Why would he say that? As if having incredible sex with him wasn't enough."

"Oh my gosh. You know he said that?" Addie asks, and her jaw drops.

I bury my face in the wine glass, drinking my sorrows as I nod. "He said it before we both fell asleep. I think he thought I was asleep already. Wait. How do you know he said that?"

"He told me. I was taking care of Milo and he came home all freaked out."

"Oh, God. Freaked out?" I sit up and knit my eyebrows together. "He totally regrets telling me." I drink some more.

"No! Not like a bad freak out, but like a 'holy shit I told her I love her, does she love me back?' sort of deal. You know?" Addie soothes me and rubs my back in small circles.

"I'm so sorry for leaving you, Addie." I can already feel the buzz taking over my body from the wine, and drunken tears fall down my cheeks. "You're my best friend."

The second she sees me crying; she cries. "No, don't be sorry. It's okay. I love you so much."

"I love you too," I cry before pulling her into a hug. The aromas of wine and tears surround us as we embrace each other.

---

ADDIE and I are laughing so hard, with three empty wine bottles, and tears running down our faces.

"I've learned my lesson never to trust a fart," Addie says through a laugh.

"Oh my God. I can't breathe. That was too funny." I wipe away the happy tears that coat my face.

We hear a knock on the door. I'm not expecting anyone to come over, and they're about to witness a drunken mess of laughter. When the door opens, I see Riley coming inside.

"Hello?"

Addie continues to laugh at herself and falls back on the floor. "I'm gonna pee myself."

Riley chuckles, then glances around. "What the hell is going on?" She glances at the bottles on the table, our glasses empty. "Are you guys drunk at one in the afternoon?"

I nod eagerly and sit up on my knees. Riley looks like she just came from a yoga class. The matching maroon leggings and ribbed shirt complement her skin tone. She pulls her hair out of her ponytail and runs her hand through her hair.

"How did this happen?" She points between us.

"I forced myself in. She didn't want to talk to me, but I forced her because I'm a bitch," Addie drawls while pointing at me, then her hand falls back on the ground.

"Don't worry! We made up."

"Ellie and Rowan had sex!" Addie chuckles.

"What," Riley exclaims and walks up to us, placing her hands on her hips, then glares down at me. "And you didn't tell me?"

"It just happened last night," I say nonchalantly.

"Where? Why?" she asks impatiently.

"Please don't get into details." Addie throws her arm over her eyes.

When I glance at her, I can't help but laugh before pointing toward her and saying, "Actually, Addie."

"What?" She uncovers her eyes and looks at me with wide eyes.

"You're lying where it happened." I laugh some more and cover my mouth.

"Oh my God," Addie yells. She doesn't pick herself up; she just rolls away from the spot. "Oh my God, that's so gross. Oh, my God."

Riley cackles while Addie continues to freak out. She gets up and wipes her hands on her clothes, like she's trying to get dirt off her. "You need to burn that rug," Addie says. "Burn it and throw the ashes in the ocean."

"Was it good?" Riley asks.

"Don't say a word, Ellie. You are not answering that while I'm here." Addie points at me.

I lift my hands up. "Okay, I won't." I look over at Riley and give her a subtle thumbs up.

"Why don't you tell Riley what else happened." Addie crosses her arms, and she smiles at me.

My lips press together while I try to suppress a giant grin that wants to come out. "Well, we were falling asleep after—you know. And he must have thought I had fallen asleep because he told me he loved me before he fell asleep."

Riley clutches her hands to her chest, and her eyes go soft. "Aw, oh my gosh. He actually said it? Ugh, my heart. So what happened this morning then? Did he bring it up? Did you?"

"No. Neither of us brought it up." A tight smile pulls at my lips. "He left pretty fast this morning. He choked on his coffee and said he had to go. But then Addie said he came home pacing around all freaked out, so it definitely hit him he said it to me.

"I thought I had done something wrong. But he gave me a kiss and said he would see me later." I shrug one shoulder.

"You need to tell him you love him, Ellie. What are you still doing here? You should be with him. Tell him you love him and then bang."

Addie groans in disgust. "I need a glass of water."

Riley walks up to me and grabs my hands. "Ellie, this is awesome. You guys are coming together again, and both of you deserve each other."

"That may be the case for you, but it's not realistic. It's back to reality."

She tilts her head and gives me a stern look. "No, you don't. You act as if you'll have anywhere to go if you leave your job. I think everyone, especially your family, would welcome you back with open arms."

I roll my eyes. "You sound just like August."

"Don't compare me to your brother."

"Riley isn't wrong," Addie adds before taking a drink of water. She has another glass in her hand and gives it to me. "I mean, I know you're a big deal at your job, but it's not like it wouldn't happen anywhere else. Plus, remember the idea I gave you? Opening your own place? It can totally happen."

"That sounds exhausting and unrealistic. I don't have the money nor the knowledge of Business 101. Plus, I'd have to figure out all the tiny details. The menu, the staff, the interior design. Just thinking about it gives me a headache."

"Oh, please." Riley says. "You'd have support. Not saying you need to. I mean, it'd be awesome, but I totally get it. It's probably a pain in the ass."

"You can also ask my brother," Addie says. "I mean,

hello, he has his own business. He started it with a beer kit and a dream."

"Fine. Let's pretend I have people to help me go through the process. But what about the money? It's not cheap to lease out a store. I don't know how it all works."

We all sit, thinking, the quiet around us floating in the air.

"What about the food festival?" Addie says.

"Oh yeah," Riley adds. "The Taste of Dove Point. It's a perfect opportunity to make money."

"I don't know about that. The festival is a big deal. Plus, the number of desserts I would need to make sounds stressful. Figuring out how much I'd sell them for. I don't have business cards, or even a name in mind. People will ask a bunch of questions—"

"Ellie, stop rambling for a second and let us talk," Riley says.

My mouth shuts.

"Your mind is racing a mile a minute; you're freaking yourself out," Riley continues. "Do you like the idea of participating?"

I scrunch my nose. "I don't know. It should be a relaxing summer. Now I'm just stressed thinking about a festival and a business and leaving my job. I don't know." My hands shoot up in the air. "I have to move my things out of the apartment."

"Just hire movers to deal with that," Addie suggests.

"You expect me to pay for movers and ship my stuff across the country when I don't have money to open my imaginary bakery."

"You haven't heard from him in a week. He's probably moved on with the woman he cheated on you with. Fuck him," Riley says.

The sound of my phone buzzes over and over on the table. When I bend to grab it, I stare at the screen. "Did you summon him?" I turn the phone screen toward both Riley and Addie. Charlie's name slides across the screen.

"Give me that." Addie snatches my phone from my hand and answers it. "Hello." She stands up while Riley and I look at her. "No, this isn't Ellie. It's Addie." She pauses. "You don't recognize her voice, given the five years you were together?" She stops and rolls her eyes. "Ellie isn't available to talk. Ever." Addie cocks her hip. "Why don't you run to the woman you slept with?" Her shoulders slump, and pure annoyance takes over her features. Her head tips back, and she groans. "Oh my God, Charlie. Give it up! She isn't going back to you! Kick rocks." Addie hangs up.

Me and Riley both drop our jaws in surprise. "Holy shit, Addie. That was awesome," Riley says.

Addie hands me my phone. "He's such a prick."

"What did he say?" I ask curiously.

"He said that he screwed up and tried convincing me he's a good guy. He mentioned a plane ticket. I'm pretty sure he was just talking out of his ass."

"If he actually shows up, then I call dibs on kicking his balls," Riley says.

"I'm pretty sure Rowan would call dibs on beating his ass before anyone else touches him," Addie says. "He's not a fighter. But I think he'd throw that out the window if he sees Charlie."

A man coming to my rescue sounds hot, but it's something I don't want to happen. If Charlie shows up, I don't know what I will do. Yell at him to go home? Would he even listen to me? Probably not.

Rowan punching Charlie in the face is a delightful

image. But Rowan would be the bigger person. He's bigger in other areas compared to Charlie. I need to focus.

I set my phone down and stand up. "I think I need another glass of wine."

"You're going to see your dad?" James asks.

I nod and take a drink of my beer.

"What are you trying to get out of it?" Beau asks.

The guys and I decide to hang out on the second level of the brewery while customers mingle downstairs. I look over the railing and down at the machines below us. One employee cleans around the equipment.

Another employee hands me a cold glass of beer, and I thank them before I walk back to the guys and sit down at the table. "I'm not sure yet."

"Was it Ellie who inspired this idea in your head?" Beau asks.

I shrug. "There are a lot of reasons I'm doing this. I didn't wake up one morning and say to myself, 'I'm going to see my dad.' This has been on my mind since my twenty-fifth birthday. But yeah, Ellie is one of the big reasons I'm pushing myself to do this."

"This is a lot to process for you," James says. "What if it... goes to shit?"

"Hey," Beau says, pointing at his brother. "He needs to

approach this with a positive mindset. We know it'll go the way you need it to." He pats me on the shoulder.

"When are you seeing him?" James asks.

I raise my eyebrows. "I'll be leaving in thirty minutes."

"What," Beau and James say in unison.

"You're telling us this thirty minutes before leaving? What the hell? I could've been hyping you up this entire time," Beau says before getting up from his chair. "Come on. We're getting hyped up." He stands in place and starts doing high knees running.

"Dude, chill out. You're shaking the entire floor," James says. "It's gonna come crashing down because a six-foot-five giant jumped around."

Beau immediately stops and stares at his brother. "Rude." He sits back down.

"Are you going by yourself? Or is Addie going with you?" James asks.

"Oh, Addie hates the idea of me going to see him. She kind of ripped into me when I told her." I take a drink of my beer. "But, she sort of came around to my decision."

"You're going by yourself?" James asks.

"No, I'm actually going with—"

"Hey guys!" Ellie stands at the top of the stairs and waves.

James and Beau peer at her and then at me. Beau cocks an eyebrow and James buries his face in his drink, suppressing a smile. The man never smiles. I tilt my head to the side and narrow my eyes at him. His lips drop when he pulls his drink away and goes back to stone cold.

"It's a little early to be drinking, isn't it?" Ellie says once she gets to our table. Her hair is damp, telling me she showered and came directly here. The black leggings she's wearing bring out the shape of her ass, and I stop myself from drooling.

"You have no room to talk. Addie mentioned how hammered the two of you were when she showed up this morning. She threw up in the bathroom and went home." James raises his eyebrows, waiting for her retort.

"It was an emotional day!" She crosses her arms.

"Today could also be emotional." Beau salutes his glass and then swallows the rest of his deep brown beer.

"Not sure how you're not in the bathroom yourself," Rowan asked.

"Well, I drank five glasses of water and took three Tylenol to help with a migraine I successfully avoided." A triumphant smile spreads across her lips.

"I heard you and Addie made up," I say to Ellie.

"Three bottles of wine helped. Riley came over and caught us rolling around on the floor laughing. I guess it was a sight to behold."

"Sounds like I missed a good time," Beau says, shaking his head.

Her head tilts, side to side. "I don't know. There were tears in the beginning."

"I'm sure Beau would've cried with you two," James adds.

Beau places a hand on his chest. "I'm not afraid to show my feelings, unlike some other people." He glares at his brother across from him.

James narrows his eyes in annoyance. "Shut up."

"Rowan, how are you feeling?" she asks and gives me a small smile.

"That's a silly question to ask, don't you think?" Beau says.

"Shouldn't you be doing push-ups or something?" Ellie says jokingly.

"And to think you're my favorite of the group." Beau shakes his head.

"I thought Hailey was?" She teases.

"Now she is." Beau turns his body away from her, crossing his arms, and tilting his chin up.

"Well, this has been fun." Ellie looks at me. "Ready to go?"

"Absolutely not." I stand from my chair and smile at her. "I'll see you guys later."

"Good luck, man," James says.

"Tell your dad I said hi," Beau says.

I give him a perplexed look, then shake my head and walk down the stairs with Ellie.

***

BEFORE WE EVEN STEPPED INTO the car, Ellie shoved me aside, insisting she should drive. I gladly gave her the keys to my Jeep because there was no way I'd be able to focus on the entire three-hour drive up the coast.

"How am I more nervous than you? It's not even my dad," she says while the wind whips her hair around.

"Because you care about me and my feelings." I turn my head on the headrest and give her a smile.

"Well, duh. I swear, Rowan, if that man hurts you any more than he already has." She shakes her head. "I will fight him."

"El, I can handle it. I appreciate it, but it's fine." My hand grips her neck, and I squeeze once before letting go.

She continuously brushes her hair from her face, but it's a losing battle. Reaching across the console, I gesture to a hair tie that's wrapped around her wrist. She takes her hand off the steering wheel, leaving the other one on, and hands it to me.

Her hand reaches out for it before she gives me a quizzical look when I reach for her hair. "I'm gonna tie it for you. Keep your eyes on the road."

"Thank you," she says bashfully.

After it's tied back into a basic ponytail, my hand lands behind her neck once more. The pads of my fingers massage her skin. I can feel tension radiating from her. "You okay?"

"Yeah. I'm just a little nervous. I shouldn't consider this isn't my estranged dad. If anything, I should be the one to give you a massage."

"You can give me one tonight." I wink.

She rolls her eyes and laughs. I can't express to her how grateful that she's coming along with me. This is an enormous deal. My heart races the entire ride, and my knees bounce. I'm also taking every second I have to be with Ellie before she leaves.

Even if the situation with Dad fails, she'll still be around.

We pass hills, small towns, and vineyards. I'm eager, anxious, and curious. What will he notice about me? What will I think of him?

I'm trying my damnedest not to get ahead of myself. The million questions that are running through my mind try to push themselves to the forefront of my brain. Is he nice? Will he want to see me? Should I have listened to Addie?

If Mom agrees, he can't be a terrible person. However, I'm questioning how he could take care of my family the way he did. Raising a child, let alone two, isn't cheap.

Maybe he's a drug lord.

Ellie clears her throat, pulling me from my wild thoughts. "Charlie called yesterday."

I can't help but laugh. "You're joking?" She looks at me before I release her neck, dropping my hand into my lap.

She shakes her head. "Nope. I didn't answer the call. Your sister did. And she was very drunk."

My hand twirls in a gesture, telling her to continue the story.

"I have a few favorite parts from the conversation. He wasn't on speaker, so all Riley and I heard was coming from Addie's end. She told him to go cry to the woman he cheated on me with."

"Incredible."

"She also mentioned something odd." Her voice trails off, and she stares into the distance. She shakes her head as if she's trying to scrub her thoughts away. "He mentioned buying a plane ticket." Ellie looks at me. "He wouldn't come here. Right?"

There's a pinching sensation in my palm when I realize I'm clenching my fist. That would be a dumbass move on his part if he even thinks about stepping foot into town. He really thinks Ellie will take him back.

That's peak delusion if I've ever heard one.

"He must be dumb as a rock if he thinks he's coming here. It's a waste of time and a waste of money on his end," I say.

Ellie's throat bobs as she fidgets in the driver's seat. I watch her knuckles turn white, gripping the steering wheel.

"Hey," I reach for her hand, and she yanks it off the wheel like it's glued on. When I grab it, I plant a kiss on top and tangle my fingers up with hers. "Talk to me."

She lets out a shaky breath. "What if he asks me to give him another chance? What do I tell him? That I'm no longer interested and that I hooked up with my ex this summer? I don't know whether I can face him." Ellie groans and tips her head back, then focuses back on the road. "It's bad enough that I've decided about the promotion, and now I need to deal with him in person?"

"Wait, when did you—"

She cut me off. "I decided yesterday."

"Was it a drunken decision?"

She winces and glances at me from the side. "Maybe? A drunken heart speaks sober mind, I guess."

I tug at my lip with my teeth and nod my head slowly. "Yeah," I mutter. "What did you decide?"

Ellie squeezes my hand before giving me a reassuring smile. "This day is about you. We'll deal with this, then we talk. Okay?

Suddenly, I feel dizzy.

# THIRTY-NINE
## ROWAN

My grip tightens repeatedly while I view the large house. Our mouths gape at the size while it sits on top of a hill. Who needs this big of a house?

"Holy shit," Ellie whispers.

I can't take my eyes off the house. Aunt Rosey's house isn't small, but it's not big. It'd fit the four of us comfortably. There were four bedrooms and two bathrooms. Having to share bathrooms with three other women was an experience for me. My understanding regarding the sizes of tampons and pads surpasses what it should.

But I won't shy away from buying a bunch if asked.

How the hell does someone afford a house like this on top of helping Mom? It's towering over us. Mom explained that his scholarship involved engineering.

A brick path leads up to a Spanish-style house. The creamy white exterior bounces off the clay tiles light brown color. All the windows have sleek black trim. When my eyes trail upward, large trees and shrubbery gather along the brick path.

"I was not expecting this." Ellie breaks into my thoughts.

"What did you expect?"

"I don't know. A townhouse, maybe? A small one-bedroom house? Is he a celebrity we don't know about?" She looks at me, expecting an answer as if I already know the guy and his life story.

"Or a drug lord," I mumble to myself.

"What did you just say?"

I wave her off and shake my head, then look at her. "Let's go."

The path continues, curving upward from the drive. I haven't seen such a driveway. It's very private. Ellie and I scan around us. A brick wall builds upward the higher we get and stops at my hips.

"Oh, you've got to be kidding me," Ellie says in an exasperated tone.

Again, we tilt our heads up as our eyes trail up and up. The driveway curves to our left near a large garage, and in front of us are two flights of concrete stairs. Had we known we'd be climbing Mount Everest, I would have told her to drive up here.

We finally get to the top of the stairs, and I hear Ellie panting behind me. Her hands brace her knees, and she's bent over. I bend down to reach her eyes and rub her back. "Are you okay?"

"I've gotta lay off the sweets," she breathes out.

At the front of the house resides a big oak entryway with brass. The second level has a balcony that splays in the middle with two glass doors that lead inside. The front is smaller than I thought, but I'm sure that will change if we step inside.

"You ready?" she asks gently.

"No," I reply.

Preparing to knock, my fist clenches, but I pause. I shuffle my feet and try again. Still frozen.

"Do you want me to knock?" Ellie points to the door.

I only nod, my hand returning downward. My mouth is dry, and I think my heart will stop because of the speed it's picked up now. My eyes lock onto the door in front of us. Ellie breathes deeply, then lifts her fist to knock three times.

I stop breathing when the handle on the door clicks and it swings open. A blonde woman stands in front of us. She's small, like Ellie, with chocolate brown eyes. I watch her lips tug into a welcoming smile.

"Hi, can I help you?" Her voice is angelic. She's kind, and I get this sort of, safe space energy from her.

Ellie peers at me, and I can't seem to find my voice. My attention is completely absorbed in breathing.

She clears her throat before plastering a smile on her face. "Sorry to intrude. My name is Ellie." Pressing her hands to her chest, she then gestures toward me. "And this is Rowan. We were hoping to speak with Michael Williams?"

The woman's eyes widen when she hears my name. Her smile falters, and her posture stiffens. She looks behind her back in the house and clears her throat. A smile reappears.

"Sure, yes. I'll be back in a second." She disappears into the large home, her footsteps quicken.

Out of the corner of my eye, I spot Ellie leaning her body halfway through the door. "Wow, we thought the outside was big."

Inside grabs my attention. An open-concept layout. Dark wooden floors, bright white walls, and the furniture set match in a cream color with dusty blue throw pillows.

Extending beyond, occupy large windows toward the yard. Clear glass, top to bottom.

Footsteps come back around, and I stand straight. Ellie grabs my biceps. "You're doing great."

I'm blowing this, but I wouldn't expect anything less from Ellie with her being my hype person. A man walks toward us. It's as if I'm looking into a mirror. A sharp gasp pulls at me the closer he gets. From the corner of my eye, I see Ellie looking between us. She must be noticing the resemblance as well.

His dark blue eyes and deep brown hair are just like mine. He has a slight wave in it as well. We have the same nose with a slight bump. People assume I've gotten into a fight and someone broke my nose.

The style of his hair is different from mine. Faded on the sides and shorter on the top, but his beard is clean and close to his skin.

He's wearing simple black jeans and a plain blue t-shirt. He doesn't seem to belong here. He drew no attention to himself. Not showy.

The woman trailed him; I mulled over her words. Did she say my name? Does she know I'm his son? His face doesn't show any shock or surprise. He looks at us as if we're his friendly new neighbors.

It isn't until he's five steps away that he stops in his tracks. Fuck. His thick, dark eyebrows rise, and his chest moves rapidly. I watch his Adam's apple bob.

"Honey, Rowan's here." Her tone is part surprise, part worry. If this were any other situation, I'd laugh because she reminds me of Ellie.

"Hi." Ellie holds out her hand. "I'm Ellie."

His bewildered expression remains even as his gaze shifts toward Ellie. His mouth opens, then closes, and he clears his throat. "Ellie Thompson." He nods. "Look at how much you've changed."

"Oh," Ellie says in shock. "Yep, that's me." She holds her hand out, and he takes a moment to process the gesture until he clasps his hand in hers.

The woman—who I assume is his wife—stands behind him still while she wrings her hands. Nerves radiate from her.

Ellie grabs my hand, and her thumb rubs my palm. "I assume you know Rowan. Your son."

My eyes must be tricking me because it looks like his own are turning glossy. "Yeah." The word comes out watery, and he swallows down whatever emotions try to push through him.

"Would you like to come in?" The woman puts her hand on Dad's arm, and I spot the small squeeze she gives him.

Dad turns to the side. "Please come in."

Ellie lets go of my hand, but I still need her touch to ground me. My palm rests on her lower back.

"Would either of you like a drink? We have lemonade, tea, water, sparkling water, and wine." The woman abruptly stops and turns toward us. "Oh, silly me, I didn't even introduce myself. I'm Amy." She puts a hand out, shaking ours one at a time.

"She's my wife," Dad says.

It's weird to hear him say that. His wife.

"Nice to meet you, Amy," Ellie says cheerfully. "You have such a gorgeous house."

"Well, thank you. I can't even explain how long it took me to decorate this place. I didn't want to hire an interior designer because it wouldn't have felt authentic. Created with love and care." Amy smiles.

It's hard to dislike someone like her. She's so damn nice.

"You did a great job. Maybe you should get into interior designing yourself," Ellie says.

The flow of conversation between them releases some tension inside my stomach. Knowing they could amuse each other while Dad and I stare awkwardly. I would give anything to know his thoughts.

"We can sit outside. It's so beautiful out; it would be a waste to sit in here." Her hand waves around the bright house.

Ellie and I follow behind them. My anxiety ignores the house's interior design. My eyes don't break away from Dad. I'm sure it's a beautiful house, but unfortunately, I have more pressing matters to deal with.

One of the tall glass doors slides with ease when Amy opens it. When we walk out back, the giant in-ground pool is right in front of me, and it pulls my attention. They could host a party of thirty if they needed to. I wonder if they're that type of people. Entertainers. Hosts. Showing off the luxury that surrounds them.

Beyond the pool is the vast ocean that's never-ending.

Ellie grabs my hand and guides me to the lounge chairs that surround a bonfire pit. Two chairs on either side of the stone fire pit. Dad sits across from me and Amy across Ellie. I refuse to let go of her hand once it's in mine.

I stare at Dad, and he peers back. He looks—great. Healthy. There isn't a single wrinkle on his skin. The only indent I notice are the ones that show when someone smiles. He must smile a lot. I wonder if we look alike when we smile.

His blue shirt brightens his eyes. The closer I look, the more I realize that his are lighter than mine. He must be spiraling inside just like me, but his composure says other-wise. His back is strong; his shoulders are straight.

He proves to be the kind of dad I aimed to become. That thought alone makes the little boy inside me sad all over again.

"So," Ellie says, breaking the silence.

Amy crosses her leg over the other. "Rowan. I can't believe you're here and that I'm meeting you. I feel like I'm meeting a celebrity."

My eyebrows tug together. That captures my attention, and her eyes scan my features. I don't need to ask what she means by that when my face alone tells her.

"Oh, sorry." She lays a hand on Dad's forearm. "You're famous in this household. All I've heard about since I've met your dad is his son. Of course, I've heard plenty about your sister, Addie. Was she not able to make it?"

"She's busy today," Ellie says gently.

Amy nods in recognition. I look back at Dad before Amy says, "Ellie, I would love to give you a tour of our home. Would you like that?"

Ellie hesitates, then looks at me and back at Amy. "Oh. Yeah, that would be great, thanks."

I peer at her and attempt to speak to her with my eyes, telling her to please stay, don't go. I can't do this without her. She lifts my hand to her lips and kisses it.

"It'll be okay. I promise. I'll just be inside, okay?" We let go, and she stands from the chair. She kisses my cheek and places her hand on my shoulder, squeezing it once before she and Amy vanish into the house.

# FORTY

## ROWAN

Another five minutes pass as we sit in silence. Silent staring ended; there's a tiny bit of relaxation. I scan everything around me, taking it all in.

The clear blue water in the pool. A patio table, accompanied by six chairs, occupies the yard, nestled under a tree. It's green grass, bright and trimmed.

"I don't even know where to start," Dad breaks the silence, and I turn toward him. When he smiles, it's bright and inviting, and his dimples match mine. "There's so many questions I have, it's the size of a novel." He awkwardly laughs.

The corner of my mouth moves; I'm unsure of what to do with my arms. I decide to have them relax on the wide armrest like I'm being interrogated.

"How've you been?" he asks.

I gulp down all the anxiety and attempt to get my shit together. "I've been okay," I say meekly.

He nods and smiles again. "I hear you started your own business. A brewery? That's incredible."

Another swallow of anxiety gets shoved down. "Yeah. My best friend—James—he's the co-owner."

"I heard about that. James Lewis. How's his dad? He was a great guy."

A pair of seagulls shriek in the distance, mixed with the sound of waves crashing into rocks below us. Dad doesn't come across as nervous. He's talking to me like we've just seen each other and are playing catch-up.

"He's doing well," is all I say.

I watch his finger tap on his knee. Maybe that's his tell-tale sign of nerves. "I can't believe you're here. Sitting in front of me. Gosh. You look just like your mother."

This pulls the curiosity out of me. "Really? I feel like I'm looking at my older twin. Not saying you're old. You look... healthy for your age." I wince.

"You have her cheekbones. And her ears." He tilts her head. "And her eyebrows."

"That's... detailed?" Confusion prompted my words, unsure of how to interpret it. Is it a compliment? Or just straight-up creepy?

The laugh that comes from him is full of nerves. "That sounded creepy, didn't it?"

My lips pull into a tight smile, and I give him a curt nod. The sound of another door sliding open and my eyes lock on Ellie. Her smile is wide and excited, like a kid in a candy shop.

"This place is awesome. It's like an adult theme park," she says before closing the door again. A genuine laugh forces itself out of my mouth, and I shake my head.

"Wow, you're smitten with her. Is she the one?" Dad says.

I shrug and scratch the back of my neck. My hair pokes out from underneath my hat. "We dated in high school, and she moved to New York when we were nineteen. We broke up two years after that."

He props his elbow on the armrest and plops his chin in his hand with a perplexed look. "So, is she back now?"

"Only for the summer. She'd gone through something and needed a break. So she came home. But she'll be leaving again soon." There's a slight pain in my chest when I say those words. She's going back. Leaving again.

"Can I give you some advice? Father to son."

Should I accept advice from someone who has been absent for over twenty years? Mom and Aunt Rosey were the ones who guided me through life and supported whatever path it was that I took.

He wasn't around, which made me feel unworthy of true love.

"Shoot," I say.

"When you're with her, do you learn to love yourself more each time?"

That wasn't advice. That was a question. Too deep of a question for him to be asking me. But I give in.

"Every moment of every day. She makes me feel invincible, actually. I can deal with whatever comes my way. She's the reason I have my business. She pushes me to be the best man I can be."

I'm overwhelmed by the love that Ellie gives me, so much so that it could bring me to tears. She's a wish come true. My shooting star.

Dad grins and says, "If you both want it, it will work. Good things take time. The world feels brighter when you find your soulmate."

My smile falters, and I think about Mom. "You didn't feel that with Mom?"

His shoulders slump, but he knew the topic would come

up sooner rather than later. This visit isn't just about me. It's about my family.

He lets out a heavy breath. "I fell short of the father I needed to become for you and your sister. My head wasn't in it even though my heart was. She became pregnant with you while we attended college, at twenty-one. Your mom was ecstatic. But things started to sort of crumble."

My parents were twenty-one when they found out about me. I'm trying to put myself in Dad's shoes. What might my reaction be if Ellie were pregnant? Would she have stopped her dreams to take care of a child she didn't plan on having? That's a loaded question.

"She told me to stay in school. The end of sophomore year was coming up, so she dropped out before junior year. I didn't want her to. I actually fought her on it, but she was so persistent. To my surprise, your Aunt Rosey was on my side, telling her sister to finish school." He leans toward me and whispers. "Rosey scared the shit out of me ever since I was ten."

A chuckle escapes me. I don't doubt my aunt's capability of intimidating people when she needs to. He was fixated on Mom. Sisterly protection, I guess.

"We were thrown into parenthood. Then, having Addie two years later—it caught up with me." He rubs his palms on his jeans. "I started a job that was very demanding, so I wasn't home much, and that hit her pretty hard. She was at home with two toddlers running around. We drifted apart. I was constantly working while your mom was taking care of the household. Bit by bit, we fell out of love."

That last part hits me like a train, knowing that's how things ended between her and Charlie. Minus the cheating part. Being close to someone who's been through a tough relationship that didn't end well helps me understand Dad's situation a bit more.

"I love your mom as a friend, always will. Our relationship went in a different direction than we had thought."

Something in my stomach churns. They parted due to their issues, though that explanation doesn't clarify his absence.

"Why didn't you come see me or Addie?" I blurt out.

He sits back in his chair before breaking eye contact with me. Shame overtakes his features. His large hands cover his face as he rubs them up and down. Do I face learning he was just a coward? I'm not sure what else it could be.

"I failed you as a father. I couldn't allow you to look up to me like some hero." His hands run through his dark hair. Not much moves considering his hair is short and faded on the sides.

"You didn't even try. You left and never looked back. A son needs his dad. I blamed myself, thinking I wasn't good enough for you as a son." I attempt to control my tone of voice, but it's all spilling out now. All the sadness and rage. "Mom told me you would send her money to take care of us."

"It was the least I could do for being a shitty person." His tone rises, but there isn't any bite to it, just embarrassment. "It wasn't easy for me. None of that way. Leaving you, not talking to you, or your sister. I'm lucky enough your mom kept in touch with me. I owed it to her to help."

"Yeah. It's called child support. And once you sent the check, you slept like a baby in this giant house." I gesture around us. "Why does a person need twenty rooms?"

"There's only six."

When I tilt my head, I give him a look that says, '*Seriously?*'

"Fine. I get it. You're pissed off at me." He puts his hands up.

I scoff. "You wanna see pissed off? Never get up close to Addie. She gave me so much shit for even wanting to come here." My teeth bite the inside of my cheek. "I'm not pissed off. I'm disappointed."

"That's worse than feeling angry." His elbows fall to his knees as he covers his face. A sigh echoes around his hands. "Years after I left, I've hated myself. I was in a dark place. I almost got fired from my job. My driving motivation centered on providing you and your sister the life you deserved. Even if that meant my leaving."

I can't stop my thoughts from racing. I have no idea how to process or feel. Happy, sad, relieved? I didn't expect our discussion to go well without any disagreements. At least from my end. Seeing me thrilled him. For years, I convinced myself that all I needed in my life was Dad and for him to fill the hole in my heart.

Maybe it won't be today or tomorrow, but I know that I'll want it. Processing this is making my head hurt. My eyes prickle, and my throat feels clogged. When I squeeze my eyes shut, trying to shield the glossiness away from him, my cheeks turn wet.

I wipe at them, hoping he didn't see this vulnerable side of me I'm not ready to share.

"Rowan," he says in a gentle tone. A fatherly tone. "I'm sorry. I truly am. You were a perfect son to me, and I didn't want to disappoint you. I couldn't let you see me struggle to be a father."

I clear my throat and sit up straight, sniffling. "It's fine."

Rubbing my sweaty palms on my jeans, I stand up from the chair. "I should get going. It's a three-hour drive."

He scrubs his hand over his mouth and runs it smoothly to the back of his neck. Sadness heavily blanketed him. His straight shoulders are now drooping. "Alright," his voice quivers, then he lifts himself up from his chair.

Would it be wrong to hope he tells me to stay? A dad needs his son.

"Will you come back at least? Maybe have dinner with us? Ellie can come too." He brackets his hips. "I just—I want my son back in my life. Can you give me a second chance? A do-over?"

His asking me for a second chance is something I never expected. A slight sensation of release runs through my chest. "Yeah."

# FORTY-ONE

## ELLIE

Exhaustion rolls through my body. Rowan and I are heading back home, and he looks worse for wear. I haven't had the courage to ask how it went.

One minute Amy is showing me their wine cellar—which was insanely big—and the next, Rowan's dad comes to find us, telling me that Rowan is ready to leave. Amy and I looked at each other, concern etched on our eyebrows.

An hour ago, I asked if he was okay, and received barely a response.

"The house has six bedrooms," Rowan says.

My gaze shifted toward him briefly before returning to the road. The only thing ahead of us is the pink sky mixed with the dusty blue clouds. "Six bedrooms?"

Rowan's baseball cap covers his face, and his hands rest on his stomach while his body slumps in the seat. "Not twenty. Six."

What the hell is he talking about? "Did he give you a bedroom tour or something?"

"Who needs a house that big?" he says.

"Considering there were six people living there, it

sounds like they needed the space." I glance at him again when I see him shuffling up on his seat.

"What?" He picks up his hat and turns it backward. A scientific study needs to be held so I can know why women like myself go feral when a man turns his hat backward.

"Shit," I mutter.

Rowan turns his body toward me. "What do you mean, he needed the space?"

I wince and bite my lip. "I'm not sure I should be the one to share that information, Ro."

"Okay," he drags the word out. "Does he have four kids that I don't know about? Does he foster kittens? Do they each get a room? This kind of information can't be a secret."

"Aw, that'd be cute. But no." I shake my head. "He doesn't foster kittens."

Rowan drops his head, then lifts it back up. "Okay, how about we play a guessing game? Give me clues and I'll figure it out. Then you're off scot-free."

I shift my eyes to him and then to the road. He'll continue to ask, and I want to avoid adding pressure. Then again, if I tell him what I know, it may produce more stress.

"Fine." I twist my lips to the side, thinking of a clue. "Amy's involved."

"That isn't a clue." He looks at me and deadpans.

"Sure it is. She's involved with the four bedrooms." I shrug.

"Okay. Uh. She uses each room for different hobbies? Oh god. Is there a... dirty room? Shit. Forget what I asked." He covers his face.

"Ew, no? What is wrong with you?" I grimace.

"I don't know! My thoughts feel chaotic. So, what? Do I have four siblings or something?" He peers at me.

I can't help but wince again, and that alone tells him my

answer. His mouth drops open, and he widens his eyes. Suddenly, his face turns as white as a ghost.

"Pull over," he mutters.

"What?" My head whips toward him.

"Pull over," he shouts.

The steering wheel whips to the left as gravel crunches under the tires. Rowan leaves the car, runs away from the car, and then vomits before I could park. He braces his hands on his knees as he heaves.

"Shit," I mutter before turning the car off and jumping out. "Rowan." My feet move quickly, and when I get to him, I place my hands on his back. "Are you okay?" I rub his back, trying to help calm his nerves.

He spits whatever is left in his mouth before he stands up straight. "I have siblings?" His hands go on top of his head, and he spaces out.

"Step-siblings." I keep a hand on his back and continue to stroke it. "They're Amy's kids. But that's all I'm telling you because you need to hear this from your dad."

Rowan drops his hands and wraps his arms around me, tugging me into his body. I wrap my own around him, squeezing tight, letting him know I'm not leaving him.

"Thank you," he whispers.

I pull my head back to look up at him and smile. "Let's go home."

---

DRIVING BACK HOME ALWAYS FEELS LONGER, ESPECIALLY on a three-hour trip. It felt like six.

We stopped at a gas station after Rowan's emotional turmoil. We picked up snacks, minty gum, and water.

Conversation shifted; the topic, how rough the baking industry can actually be.

"I didn't realize how stressful it could be. I never really thought about it," Rowan says as he opens the door to his house. Rowan's mom was so nice to offer to look after Milo all day.

"What did you think it was like?" I ask, shrugging my shoes off at the entrance inside the house.

"Eating chocolate, cake, and getting to take the leftover goodies home." He tosses his keys onto the coffee table. "I'm gonna go brush my teeth, but keep talking, I'm listening."

"It's very cute of you to think I get to eat what I bake." I watch Rowan walk into the downstairs bathroom where he spares an extra toothbrush and toothpaste. I cross my arms and lean against the doorway. "You were watching the wrong shows, weren't you?"

"What? Everyone is baking in a tent, uplifting others, and not yelling. It's a nice thought." He brushes his teeth and stares at himself in the mirror. "But then," he says with a mouthful of toothpaste. "There was a baking show with personal chefs."

"Hmm, and?"

He cups his hand, filling it with water, before putting it in his mouth, swishing it around with the toothpaste and spitting it out.

"Do you really make intricate designs with chocolate?" He brackets his hips.

My eyebrows rise and fall quickly as I let out a heavy sigh. "Many, many times. It's one of my least favorite things to do. Throw being an architect into baking and you're looking at a stressful night."

"How come you've never sent pictures?"

We walk back to the living room and sit on the couch. I

turn my body to face him and rest my elbow on the back of the couch, my temple resting on my knuckles.

"Because I was busy making sure it wouldn't break. Some were so fragile it took five people to move them." He nods, and I continue. "It can be a stressful environment depending on what your goal is."

"Would you ever go on one of those shows?" he asks.

"Hell no."

"But they win money at the end."

"And I'd lose my sanity."

Rowan laughs with a bright smile. "That's fair. I've seen some people break down, and honestly? It makes me wonder if it's worth it. All the stress that comes with something you're supposed to love doing."

"I guess it depends on the person. Many people can't handle a stressful environment that's fast paced and demanding. Especially if you're trying to make a name for yourself, you have to know how to handle criticism or you'll break down."

He glances at me, and I can see questions dancing in that beautiful head of his.

"What?" I ask.

"Riley told the guys what happened at your job. She didn't bring it up out of nowhere; it just kind of... flowed into the conversation."

My back stiffens.

"What exactly did she tell you guys?" I ask, trying to sound casual and not embarrassed.

There was a reason I didn't tell Rowan, especially my brother. August hasn't mentioned it, and I don't know whether this is positive or negative. He was trying to spare my feelings, knowing that I came home to avoid what made me come here.

He reaches for his hat, taking it off before setting it on the coffee table. I watch him run his hand through his thick locks.

"She mentioned the word breakdown." His jaw ticks as his lips press into a firm line. "And you cried."

Recalling that evening causes slight jaw pain from clenching my teeth. It was hard to tell them what had happened. Admitting that I couldn't handle something that I'm great at.

"Why didn't you tell me?" he asks.

A chuckle slips out of me accidentally. Rowan frowns.

"Sorry, that wasn't toward you. It was more toward myself. Reminding me how much of a failure I've become."

"Whoa, whoa, whoa. Don't say that about yourself." He scoots closer to me; our knees knock into each other, but neither of us flinches at the touch. "You're a badass who makes sculptures out of chocolate. You work at one of the best-known restaurants, and they offered you a promotion."

My eyes cast down at my hands, where I fidget with my fingers. "A promotion I'm not taking," I mumble.

"You're not taking it?"

"I can't."

"Why not?"

"It's not something I want anymore. I don't know. I don't know what I'm doing," I say simply.

He holds the tip of my chin with his fingers and lifts my gaze up at him. I watch his eyes roam mine like he's trying to read my mind.

"Talk to me, El. Tell me what's going on in your head. I can't help if you don't talk. And I want to support you. Figure out what makes you happy again. Your happiness is all I care about. If that means not taking this promotion, then that's fine. I'm going to help you figure this out. You're not alone in this."

I lean in and kiss him softly. His fingers still grip my chin while I lift my hands to hold his face. The prickle of his stubble pressing into my fingers is something I love feeling. It seems like he's okay with the conversation ending when he kisses back and slips his tongue into my mouth.

He groans when I bite his bottom lip. "I know exactly what you're doing."

My lips pull into a smile. "I'm not doing anything." I move to his jaw and then his neck.

"You're avoiding talking about—oh, fuck," he mutters when I tug the back of his hair and nip at his neck.

Tugging at his hair some more, I lift myself onto my knees and straddle his hips. His hands find my ass, and he grips it, moving me back and forth on top of his hard cock. A small moan vibrates through my throat when I feel it rub against me.

"You really want to avoid talking, don't you?" he says. I answer him with another thrust against him. "Motherfu— okay, fine. You win." The grip on my ass turns solid when he lifts us up. "If this is your way of ignoring life problems— making me fuck you until you can't speak—then you're too smart for your own good."

I wrap my arms around his neck and giggle into his neck.

# FORTY-TWO

## ROWAN

"Hey." I walk up to Addie when she's in the middle of folding shirts on the display shelf with other merchandise.

"What's up?"

"Let's have lunch."

She stops what she's doing and peers at me with a puzzled look. I don't take lunch breaks. Never have. So I expected the sudden questioning on her face.

"What happened?" She places the last shirt on the wooden shelf.

"Can a big brother take his little sister out to lunch without a reason?" I tilt my head.

"No," she says flatly. "But, since you're paying, then I can't say no."

When we cross the street to The Pizza Joint across from the brewery, we can already smell fresh bread and cheese the closer we get. They offer a full pan or individual slices. The single slices also come on a full pan because of its size. It's bigger than my head.

It was a popular spot when the guys and I were

younger. We'd get hammered and stagger to get pizza at two in the morning.

She finds a place to sit, then I order two pizzas, plus two drinks, at the counter. I slide into the booth with our drinks.

"Thanks." Addie grabs hers, ripping the paper off the straw and stabbing it into the lid. "What toppings did you get?"

"Half cheese, half Hawaiian," I say before stabbing my lid on my drink. The ice-cold fizz of my soda tingles my throat.

"You know Bella is going to give you shit? And Ellie. I'm surprised she stuck around with you after she realized you like pineapple on your pizza."

"I'm willing to take the risk with Bella, and Ellie adores me too much. Anyway, I want to talk to you about Dad. My visit with him." I can't help but break eye contact out of nerves, and glance around at the photos on the walls. That family, who manage the business, hangs in a frame near our booth. They stand in front of a home in Italy with extended family.

Addie sips her drink and narrows her eyes. "What happened?"

"Neapolitan and...Hawaiian pizza," the server—Bella—says when she places the pans down. "Anything else you need?" She brackets her hips, her brown hair pulled back into a bun.

As I peer at her, her lips press into a hard line, and then I give her a friendly grin. She hates when I order this. She calls it an abomination. "Thank you, Bella."

"Ananas sulla pizza, cosa c'è che non va in queste persone?" She says under her breath in Italian as she saunters away.

Addie chuckles when she picks up a slice of cheese pizza. "You know she hates it when you order this."

"Then why is it on the menu?"

"Because her father loves you. I'm sure she's argued with him about this." She takes a bite and

"I can't help that I'm adorable."

Addie's facial expression stays neutral, bored even. "What do you need to tell me?"

"Obviously, you know that me and Ellie went to see him this past weekend." I take a bite of my pizza; the sweet taste of pineapple mixed with Canadian ham melts on my tongue. A hum of appreciation leaves my throat.

"Mhm." Addie takes another drink before she continues on her pizza.

A heavy sigh blows through my lips. "I'm going to see him again."

Addie stays silent, eating her food as if I'm not telling her anything important. She continues to hold my gaze.

"Do you care how the visit went?" I say with an undertone of annoyance.

"You can tell me whatever you want to share. I'm here to support you."

"Then stop looking at me like you're bored out of your mind and don't care what's coming out of my mouth."

She rolls her eyes and tips her head back. "Okay, sorry. How did it go?"

"Honestly? I don't know. It started out awkward, then it was fine, and then there was some yelling."

Addie sits up straight, and her eyebrows pinch. "Yelling? What happened?"

My body mimics hers in my seat, before whispering, "Ellie doesn't know this, so you can't go to her—or anyone—okay? I trust Ellie; you know this, but I'm not ready to talk about it with her. The only reason I'm talking about it with you is that you're my sister, and I'm just trying to protect Mom."

"What the hell is going on, Ro?" Addie leans in, whispering.

"Dad's married, and we have four step-siblings."

"Okay, that's expected."

It doesn't surprise me that it doesn't shock Addie. However, I need to share that bit of information.

"Have you talked to Mom lately?" I ask.

She shakes her head. "No, I haven't."

"Fuck," I mutter under my breath. "I can't really tell you what happened until you talk to Mom."

"Rowan." She carries heaviness in her eyes. "Tell me what's going on? What don't I know?"

Guilt crawls up my throat. I know it's Mom's job to sit down and tell Addie everything I know. I need to talk to someone about what happened. I'm not going to Mom or Aunt Rosey.

She angles her head at me and pierces me with her gaze. My sister's an angel, but she isn't one to cross. It takes a lot to make her mad.

"Mom's gonna kill me," I mutter, both hands running through my hair. "Dad has been helping Mom out since he left," I spit out.

Addie leans back in her seat. "What do you mean?"

"He's been sending her checks to help with school, clothes, things that Mom wouldn't have been able to keep up with."

She crosses her arms. "Okay."

"And they still keep in touch. She knows where he lives, and I assume she knows he's remarried."

She lets out a choked laugh and shakes her head. "So

you're telling me he left us, gave Mom money to help, and she still talks to him?"

I nod.

"And she's kept this from us this entire time?"

I nod again. "But you cannot be angry with her for that. We never asked about any of it. Why would we?"

"You don't think she owed it to us? I mean, she still talks to him. We didn't know that. We're over here thinking that he wants nothing to do with us." Her tone sounds more like hurt than anger. "I'm not angry." She scratches her forearm, peering down.

"What's wrong? Talk to me."

"Why do I feel like a dick?"

"What do you mean?"

She shrugs. "I don't know. I thought—I thought he didn't give a shit about us. Twenty something years later, we find out he's been helping us this entire time and still connects with Mom."

"Hey, look at me," I say sternly, and she does as I ask. "You had every right to be mad. Honestly, I felt annoyed that Mom had hidden it from us. I think she wouldn't have said anything if I hadn't seen him."

"Okay." She shakes her head like she's clearing her thoughts. "Go back to you seeing Dad. What happened?"

"Dad said they drifted apart. He wasn't ready to be a dad like he thought. He hated himself for what he had done and figured it'd be better if he left." I pause. "Oh, and he said Aunt Rosey scares him."

She chuckles. "Good." We're quiet for a beat before she continues. "I still don't think I'm ready to have him in my life. It's a lot to process. I'm used to his not being around. Springing back into our lives is overwhelming."

"I understand. He invited me back for dinner." The

pizza in front of us has gotten cold, but we have lost our appetite.

"Are you gonna go?"

I nod. "You need to talk to Mom. She's gonna be mad I told you this, but I felt guilty for keeping it from you. I didn't want you to be in the dark much longer. You wouldn't have brought it up, and I don't think Mom will unless you do."

"Sounds about right."

We both fell silent while processing everything we spoke about. She hasn't run to the bathroom to throw up like I did. Maybe that's a good sign.

"Thanks for telling me this," she breathes.

"You're my little sister. Of course, I'm going to tell you this."

"Yeah, but now you'll get Aunt Rosey's wrath if she knows you're not supposed to tell me this."

"I can handle her." I sip my drink.

"Uh-huh, sure. Just know I'm getting front row to that conversation."

# FORTY-THREE

## ELLIE

My gaze stays fixed on the ceiling while I lie on the couch. Numerous thoughts occupy me. I haven't moved my body in two hours while I play out scenarios in my head.

The other day, I made my decision. Reject the promotion, keep the current position, and continue my existence. But that didn't happen.

This morning, my boss—Chef Roberts—called me. The conversation started out nicely. She asked about my summer, how the kitchen misses me, then asked if I considered taking on the new position.

Chef Roberts and I don't have a typical professional relationship in the kitchen. We're more mentor and mentee. I've been by her side since I graduated culinary school. She comes to me to help come up with solutions to problems we may come across.

My heart hammered in my chest. She needs my answer in a few days. Everything changed once I spoke with her. Disappointing her affected me more than her words.

I'm her star chef (her words, not mine).

Before ending our conversation, I told her I'll give her

my answer soon. The thought of taking on this new role sets off my anxiety. The thought of going back to New York makes it worse. I think I have an ulcer.

A groan slips out of me before my phone vibrates on my stomach. When Rowan's name appears on my screen, giddiness replaces the anxious thoughts.

> Rowan: I'm taking you out tonight.

> Ellie: Oh? Why's that?

> Rowan: Because I have a crush on you. Why else?

> Ellie: You have a crush on me? Oof, good luck with that. Three out of ten stars would not recommend it.

> Rowan: I don't know. I'm looking at the reviews right now, and you've got high ratings.

> Ellie: 😳

> Rowan: I'll pick you up at 7pm.

---

"THE BEACH?" I study Rowan, who's carrying a basket of goodies, a blanket, two hoodies, and a lantern.

We continue walking toward the beach as the sun sets in the sky. A slight breeze pushes off the ocean, blowing my hair back behind my shoulders. Rowan told me to wear something comfortable. I wasn't sure what that meant.

Comfortable can mean a lot of things.

I played it safe, wearing leggings and an oversized shirt with my sneakers. Rowan is wearing gray sweatpants and a simple shirt. My eyes betray me as I continue to look down near his crotch. If I don't stop, I'll need to rip my eyes out.

"It's chill, nothing fancy except I have chocolate-covered strawberries to set the mood."

"Who are you?"

"I'm your best friend-turned-lover again."

"Lover? Bold of you to assume that."

"I know you love me as a friend. Considering our history, you never know. We're grown adults now. We have more control over our lives now than we did at nineteen."

With no words, he's clarified that he wants something between us again. It's beyond a casual summer considering we've slept together twice. We know the feelings are there, but it's complicated, and he knows that.

Rowan puts the basket and then the lantern on the sand before handing me his hoodie. I can't help but bring it up to my nose and smell the scent. A manly smell, but also comforting. I can't explain it. It makes my knees weak, and that's all that matters.

"Help me with this." He opens the blanket, which is much larger than I expected. It could fit at least four people.

I grab the other end and help him place it on the sand. Once that's done, we settle ourselves onto the blanket, and he grabs things out of the wicker basket.

"Where did you get the basket from?" I point.

"Aunt Rosey."

"Okay, that makes sense." I nod.

He glances at me. "What? You thought this was mine?" He gestures to it with his head.

"For all I know, it was helping you get back to Kansas, Dorothy."

I make him laugh, his dimples showing off. My mind

pushes me to kiss them before they disappear, and so I do, catching him off guard.

He stops what he's doing and looks at me with a shy smile. "What was that for?"

I shrug. "I really wanted to kiss your dimples."

"My dimples? You've kissed them plenty of times before."

"They're just so darn cute."

He looks down, trying to contain his small smile that wants to grow into a grin, then watches me again. "Thank you."

Rowan empties the basket, and my eyes travel over everything.

A small charcuterie board with assorted breads, cheese, and meats, with another small platter of chocolate-covered strawberries.

I gasp when I see the sandwich-shaped foil that he pulls out last. He passes it to me and then takes out a tiny container filled with ketchup. Only Rowan wouldn't judge me for my weirdness.

"I can't believe you made this for me." I carefully open the tinfoil. "Everyone finds it weird that I like my grilled cheese cold. They just don't get it." I marvel at the perfectly toasted bread. I look back at him with raised brows in question, expecting him to read my mind.

"Yes, I used mayo and not butter along with four slices of white American cheese," he says.

An evil laugh pours out of me as I wiggle my fingers that pick up the sandwich. I rip a piece off and dip a bit in the ketchup. "Mmm."

"Accepting this took a long time. Normally, people will have grilled cheese with tomato soup, both warm. It's like you're doing the complete opposite."

"And then you realized that I'm a genius." I take another bite.

"Good thing you bake," he mumbles.

"Hey." I slap his arm. "I heard that."

He laughs and digs into the sandwich he made. A "regular" sandwich. Whatever that means.

"Now you don't get your gift." I turn up my nose.

"You have a gift for me? In that case, you're the best cook in the world. Whoever said cold grilled cheese is gross has no taste buds."

"That's what I thought."

When Mom and I went to lunch, we stopped at The Surf Shack to see Dad and August. I figured since I was there, I'd get Rowan some new board shorts. I'm a gift giver. It's one of my favorite love languages.

He holds them out in front of him, examining the shorts. "Oh, hell yeah. You bought me new board shorts. I love the color." He turns to me and gives me a kiss on the cheek.

"Yeah? I was hoping the color was okay. August suggested a salmon color, which is not you, like at all."

"No way. These are perfect. Thank you." He gives me another kiss on the cheek, and I feel his scruff brush against my skin in the most pleasurable way. "What's the occasion?"

I shrug. "I just wanted to get you something. Do I need a reason?"

"No way. Buy all the gifts you want for me. I need to get you a gift."

"No, you don't." I take another bite of my sandwich.

"Well, we'll see about that." He winks at me.

# FORTY-FOUR

## ROWAN

When Ellie takes a bite of the strawberry, chocolate smears the corners of her mouth. She looks at me when I let out a chuckle.

"What?" she says with a mouthful.

"You have chocolate all over your face."

"This is a giant strawberry, okay? I'm sorry that I can't fit my mouth around it without getting chocolate on my face." She takes another bite.

"You've proved you can fit giant things in your mouth, what are you talking about?" I joke.

"Rowan," she exclaims. "Why are you always in the gutter?"

"Because I'm a red-blooded man?"

She tilts her head, and her facial features drop, as if it's a silly excuse.

"You're telling me you never have dirty thoughts in your head?"

Her eyes narrow, and she's careful about how she answers. It's too late because I'm grinning like a fool and my eyebrows rise triumphantly.

Before she can rebuttal, I say, "Let me get that chocolate off you." And gently wipe my thumb across her lips. "Hm. It won't come off." I lean in and kiss the corner of her mouth, letting my tongue slip out discreetly when I lick the chocolate off.

The sound of a small gasp makes my lips curve up, and I pull away. Her cheeks flush when she looks at me with hazy blue eyes.

"Now tell me," I say into her ear. A smile still plays on my lips. "Are you thinking about us?"

"Are you trying to turn me on to prove a point?" she whispers.

"Did it work?" My lips trail around her ear, and my hand wanders to her thigh.

She lets out a quiet whimper that no one would hear unless you were as close as I am. "I refuse to let you win this silly game of yours."

"Aw, come on. All I'm asking is you to admit defeat. You think about us, and probably have dirtier thoughts than I do."

I can't get a boner. Especially since I wore sweatpants instead of jeans. Ellie's turned on. She doesn't need to say anything. The breathing patterns and small noise that come from her lips tells me enough.

She bites her lip and shakes her head. "No. You're not winning. I'm not thinking about anything." Ellie inhales. "Especially when you groan in pleasure." She breathes out.

"I can bet anything in the world that your nipples are hard." My voice rasps, and I hear her whimper. "If I could guide my hand to your pussy, I bet you're as wet as I think you are. Completely soaking through your leggings." Another whimper. "Am I right?"

Her breathing unravels, but she quickly controls it. "No. I'm not wet."

"You don't want me to take you back to my house and fuck you until you beg me to stop?" I smirk, my lips still hovering near her ear. There's a sort of thrill in knowing that what we're talking about is driving us both crazy, and everyone else here doesn't even know it.

When I pull my head away to gaze at her, she's biting her lip so hard that it's turning white.

"What do you say?" My lips press into hers, light enough that she wants more. "Wanna go back to my place? Keep the date going?"

Ellie smothers a smile. "Only because it's getting cold."

"Of course, my love."

THIS IS an unexpected turn of events. Not that I'm complaining. But we lasted twenty minutes until my cock throbbed, begging for her pussy.

With each passing day, I know that I'm going to lose her again. I'm consumed with her. I want to remember how she tastes, sounds, and feels when we're wrapped in each other. I'm not sure I can convince her to stay.

Would she stay if I went on my knees and begged? Would she think less of me? Or feel bad for me? Her decision about staying needs to be her idea, not mine. The thought of her packing up her car and leaving rips my heart into shreds.

So right now, I need her.

We get to my house in record time and walk into the living room where Milo greets us. We give him a quick hello and then run upstairs, eager to rip each other's clothes off. Ellie never admitted to losing, and that's okay, because in five seconds, she's going to be in my bed naked.

My foot kicks the door shut behind me while I tug my shirt off. She doesn't waste a second either before throwing hers on the floor. I grab her face in my hands and kiss her hard.

"I need you so fucking bad, Ellie. You have no idea," I pant.

She nips at my bottom lip, pulling a groan out from me, while I guide us to the bed. When she sits back, I crawl on top of her. Our pants are still on along with her bra. I can't have that. Before she lies on her back, I make quick work of taking it off, freeing her incredible breasts.

My mouth drops to one, and I suck on her taut nipple. She moans loud enough to make my cock twitch in my sweats. Her hips move against me, causing my hand to grip the blanket to control myself.

"Bite it. Bite my nipple. Please," she begs.

I do as she says, and it's so fucking hot when she tells me what to do. She yells in desire when I suck and bite it. Then I shift towards the other, repeating the same thing as my grip holds her other breast.

"You're so fucking perfect." My hips grind into her before I let go of her breast and put my hand between her legs. A guttural groan comes out of me. She's soaked. Knowing that this is because of me makes me almost feral.

"I'm not wearing any underwear," she says with a teasing tone.

"Are you pushing me to rip these off you? I already gave you money to buy a new dress." I smirk against her skin as I kiss her neck.

"That would be insanely hot."

"Yeah, baby? You want me to rip these off you? Then I can eat that beautiful pussy of yours."

She gives me a nod and grips her fingers in my hair. Another groan escapes me. I lift myself up onto my knees, grabbing the thin fabric. The strength of my hands lifts her hips up, and we hear fabric ripping apart.

We both work our hands to tug them off her, and I don't waste anymore time. I need to taste her now. Holding my hand out for her, she takes it, and I take her off the bed. A yelp slips from her.

"What are you—"

She doesn't have time to finish her question when I lift her from her thighs and place her on the wall next to my bed. I want to stand while I eat her out. I need to feel her body shiver and shake when she hits that pleasurable orgasm I've been so lucky to hear.

"Oh my God," she cries out. Her hands run through my hair, and I feel her body slump against the wall. Then her thighs wrap around my head tighter than before when I continue to lick her sensitive bud.

Currently, I entertain the possibility of being choked. I've done it to women who ask for it, but nobody has ever done it to me. Her legs are doing just that, and my cock hardens more than I didn't think possible.

The sound of her hand slapping the wall as she holds her body up. My mouth sucks on her clit, and I nip at it, testing to see if she likes the pressure.

"Do that again," she breathes. "Do it again."

Pleased with myself, I obey her commands, and bite down. Not soft or hard, but just enough to give her pleasure.

When I'm satisfied with her being secured on my shoulders, I slowly explore her entrance with a finger. She breathes out a satisfying moan before I slip another finger inside her.

I pump my fingers and suck her clit while she tugs my hair and squeezes me with her thighs.

"Faster," she pants.

My fingers go from pumping to pounding, my tongue flicking, and my lips sucking. She cries out my name and rocks her hips into my face. The taste of her on my lips and in my mouth can make me come in my pants alone, but I'm not done with her tonight.

"I'm gonna come," she says in a shaky breath.

At those words, I crook my fingers inside her, hitting that spot that I know will set her off. She rides my face and cries out in pleasure. My tongue keeps gliding down her slit while my fingers continue to slip in and out.

As she comes back down to reality, her legs are shaking, and her body goes slack.

"Oh, fuck," she mutters through her deep breaths.

Wrapping my hand around her thigh again, I set her down on the bed, her breasts rising and falling with each breath. I grab my sweatpants and pull them down with my briefs, my cock springing free.

Ellie's eyes widen when she realizes what's coming next. My laugh is all gravel as I gaze at her.

"I'm not done with you yet."

# FORTY-FIVE

## ELLIE

I'm still trying to uncurl my toes after having that out-of-body orgasm. The sight of Rowan's cock builds this pressure of need deep in my belly. My body is already asking for more.

I use my palms to lift myself, then sit on the bed's edge. When I look up at him through my lashes, his breathing is labored, and his eyelids are heavy. A devilish smirk pulls at my lips before my hand grips his length.

The sound of sharp air comes from Rowan's mouth when my tongue licks his tip. His firm grip holds my neck, then goes into my hair and wraps it around his fist.

"You look goddamn beautiful holding my dick. Pump it for me, baby," he rasps.

My hand moves in a hypnotic rhythm, and I wrap my lips around the tip and then suck until I hear a deep groan come from him. I peek at him and watch his head tilt back with his eyes closed. I continue the same motion until I feel ready enough to take his entire cock into my mouth.

Of course, I choke once the tip hits the back of my throat and again, I'm only halfway. My eyes become watery.

Unfortunately, since I don't want to throw up on his dick, I'm careful and take in what I can, letting my hand pump the rest. He doesn't seem to mind since he's busy enjoying getting his dick sucked altogether.

I love the taste in my mouth. The feeling of him in my hand, hard and desperate for touch. God. I'm already soaked again. I took my other hand to play with my nipple, rolling and pinching it. My moan vibrates through him.

"I love watching you take care of yourself while you suck my cock." He slips his hand away from my head, sliding it onto my cheek.

The praise he gives makes me want to pleasure him more until he can't stand it. I pump faster and suck harder, pulling groan after groan from him. I moan when I pinch my nipple and clench my thighs together.

"Get up," he breathes.

When I stare up at him, I whine, wanting to keep his dick in my mouth.

"Are you my good girl?" he rasps.

With him still in my mouth, I nod.

"Then take my cock out of your mouth and stand up," he orders, while holding his hand out.

I wonder whether I should see a therapist. The way he spoke to me just now, in that demanding tone. Fuck me.

I take my mouth off him and stand. Then, I place my hand in his as he lifts me up. He spins me around and presses my back against his chest.

"You're going to get on your knees and show me that perfect ass. Can you do that for me?" he asks, and lifts my chin with one finger and kisses me on the lips before I give him a nod.

I'm still floating on clouds from my orgasm, and my knees feel like jello. But I do what I'm told.

The bed dips when Rowan gets on his own knees, then his large, muscular hands grip my ass before he spanks me. I cry out, not in pain, but in pleasure.

"Did you like that, baby?" His tone was gentle.

"Yes," I breathe out.

"Let me know if it's too much for you, okay? I don't want to hurt you."

I shake my head and look over my shoulder. "You won't. I promise."

Then, he lowers his hand between my legs and down my slit. I'm still wet, and I get a pleasant groan from him. His fingers disappear for a moment before I feel the tip of his cock push into me. Crying out in pleasure, he pushes deeper.

He places his hand on my back, nuzzling me down some more. My head dips into the pillow. "There we fucking go," he says before filling me up.

We both moan out as he pumps in and out of me. The sound of skin on skin. My hands let go of the headboard and instead of pushing against it, my ass pushed into Rowan.

"You're pussy is so fucking tight. Fuck." He's gentle, but I need more.

"Harder," I demand.

"You need more of my cock?" His left hand grips my hair, pulling another moan out from me. Then his other hand grips my hip, sliding down to my ass, and slaps it.

"Yes," I cry out.

"Yes, what?"

"Yes, please—" My sentence cuts off with a loud moan when his hips slam against my ass.

My breathing becomes sharp with each thrust that allows my lungs to take in gasps of air. The hard muscles of his chest press into my back as he leans over me. Then I feel his fingers trail along my slit as he plays with my clit.

"I want you to come all over my cock. Can you do that for me, baby?" He whispers in my ear. The graze of his lips sends shivers down my spine.

With his fingers on my cunt and small breaths near my ear sends me over the edge. I bury my face in the pillow as I cry out in pleasure, muffling the noise that is so loud it could crack the windows.

Rowan's thrusts become faster as he pushes himself over the edge with me. He groans, not holding back, cursing under his breath.

We both collapse on the bed as we catch our breaths in a synchronized rhythm. When he turns over to me, he caresses my face, brushing his knuckles along my dewy skin. His lips meet my nose, and then his eyes stare back into mine.

"I love you," he whispers.

I peer into his stormy grey eyes that hold so many emotions and so much love. There are a million reasons I should stay here and start my life over. He's the number one reason. Can I let myself give in, taking what I want?

With summer coming to an end, I need to figure it out. Quick.

"I love you, too."

# FORTY-SIX

## ELLIE

"I think your fry has enough ketchup on it," Hailey says.

There's a beat of silence.

"Ellie," Riley says.

My brain is on autopilot. I'm zoning out on my plate, swirling my fry around in the puddle of ketchup. Around and around. Last night repeats in my thoughts.

We both said I love you and then fell asleep. Just like what happened before. Except this time, I answered back. He disappeared early this morning, giving me a forehead kiss, explaining he needed to go to work. Incoherent words fell from my lips, and then I drifted back to sleep.

A warm hand stops mine from moving, and when I glance up, both Riley and Hailey stare at me with concern etched in their features. Riley is opposite me, with Hailey to my right.

The sounds of chatter and silverware grab me from my hypnotic trance.

"Are you okay?" Riley asks.

Hailey cocks her perfectly shaped eyebrow while Riley strokes my skin with her thumb. I fight with myself, wondering if I should spill my guts. They know me better than I know myself.

Picking up my cup, I bite the straw, thinking before I take a drink. My teeth scrape over my bottom lip, and I choose my words carefully.

"Rowan and I... we had sex... three times." I bite my thumbnail.

The girls are silent. They both stare at me with complete shock. Hailey's eyebrows rise, but a smirk tugs at the corner of her lip. And Riley, well, she's gaping at me like a fish.

"Okay, can you guys stop staring and say something?" I beg.

Riley blinks a couple of times, and Hailey leans back in her chair, folding her arms, and grins.

"Good for you," Hailey teases.

"Oh... my God. When. Did. This. Happen," Riley exclaims in confusion.

I fidget in my seat and straighten my shoulders. "It happened after we went out. Wait, that doesn't count; we only fooled around. I mean, we almost slept together, but I stopped it because I was overthinking." I pause, and they say nothing. "First it was after the art exhibit. And then, a couple of days ago. And last night."

They blink at me while I pick up my drink, the last of the fizzy water going through my straw in a crackling noise.

"And you're just telling us now?" Riley shouts.

"Don't yell." I chide and look around the diner. "I don't need the entire town in my business."

Riley looks at me, stunned, and stutters her words before forming a sentence. "Ellie, this is a big deal." She places her palm on the table and leans in. "You're leaving like, next week, and you're telling us you and Rowan hooked up, not once, not twice, but three times."

Hailey gives her sister a bored look while remaining calm. She tussles her dark hair, the icy white strand of hair getting mixed in.

"So... what? Do you want our advice?" Hailey asks as I bite the inside of my cheek. "We're not telling you what you should or shouldn't do. We can voice our thoughts, but what we think or feel shouldn't sway your decision."

Hailey is always the realistic one with her head on straight. She always keeps her feet grounded, and sometimes people seek her guidance. Hence, that's why I told her and Riley. But now? Now she doesn't do that.

"You're the realistic one in the group. You don't daydream; you say it like it is."

"She's got you there," Riley says before biting into her cheeseburger.

I let my head fall on the table, banging it lightly, causing our glasses to shake on the table. "Hailey," I drew out her name in desperation.

I'm one year away from turning thirty, and I still need life advice.

Life is like a book. Better yet, a series. I'm stuck on book three of five because I've been in a slump—with my life. Maybe this is how book three ends? Rowan will never give up on the idea of our being together. And what if I give us that chance again?

Does that mean he leaves Dove Point so I can continue my career? I'd rather be alone than do that to him. His life here is stable, while mine is crumbling apart like a dry cookie.

"Ellie," Hailey says, placing her hand on my arm. She isn't one for physical touch. If someone tries to hug her, she squirms. This simple touch speaks volumes to me. "You know what you should do? Go talk to the person you're asking for advice about."

---

MY KNUCKLES RAP on the wooden door in front of me, and I hear a small bark.

"Come in," Rowan shouts from inside his office.

When I open the door, I peek my head in. "Hi."

Milo gets up from his giant bed and runs into my arms. Before I sit on the couch with him, I close the door, and he jumps on the cushion. Golden fur already covers my black leggings. But I give him what he wants and scratch his jaw and behind his ear.

Rowan smiles and walks around his desk before bending down to give me a kiss on the lips. My heart melts.

"How's my favorite girl doing?" He sits on the edge of his desk and crosses his arms. His biceps bulge out of his shirt sleeves, making his tattoos pop more.

"I just came from lunch with Riley and Hailey." I continue to pet Milo while he sleeps on my lap.

"So you came over to give me some hot gossip?" He smirks.

"Oh, totally." I nod. "Riley and her mom are best friends now. Oh, and Hailey is dating Beau."

He snorts. "The day Hailey and Beau date, I'll get a tattoo on my ass."

"I guess I need to make it happen then, huh?" I laugh. "Being near you eases my thoughts; there's a lot weighing on me."

"Penny for your thoughts?"

How do I tell him what's wrong when everything feels chaotic? So, I word vomit.

"What is this?"

Rowan looks around us and smiles. I need to force down a squeal when I see his dimples. "Uh, my office?"

I huff out a breath of annoyance. "No. I mean us."

The smile that was on his lips a second ago has disappeared. His mouth opens, then closes, like he's lost for words. It wouldn't be a surprise if he did considering I just dropped a bombshell of a question.

"Look," I say. "What are we doing? Where is this going? I—I'm leaving soon. My career, this fictional bakery, plus where my home lies, still take up space in my head. But you." I gesture to him. "You are at the top of my list. I need to know what we're doing."

He runs a hand through his hair, dragging it down to his neck. "I can't tell you what to do, El."

"Oh my God." My voice comes off harsher than expected. Milo lifts his head up from my lap, then picks himself up to go back on his bed. "Why can't anyone give me a fucking answer? My life is falling apart, and all I need is advice."

"Whoa." Rowan holds his hand up, like he's telling me to pause. "Relax."

My eyebrows shoot up to my hairline. "Relax? Really? I'm so tightly wound, I don't know how to, Rowan." I stand up. "I'm leaving soon. This summer, what we've been doing, it's made my decision much more complicated."

"What do you need from me? How can I help?" His voice is gentle.

"I need to know what we're doing. What do you want out of this? We can't ignore this conversation anymore." My hands splay out and then slap on my thighs.

Rowan's lips raise into a small, sad smile. His sensitive blue-grey eyes roam over my face, like he's taking in every freckle, crease, and birthmark to remember.

Panic runs through my body as we stand in silence. Fear gripped its hand around my heart, trying to steal it from me.

Finally, he pushes himself off the desk and takes two steps toward me, then grabs my hand.

"If going to New York feels important, then do it."

Air becomes trapped in my lungs, and I feel like I can't breathe. A prickling sensation comes over my body. My throat, eyes, fingertips. Dread grips at the idea of leaving him.

"And I'll come with you," he says.

Like a balloon, my chest deflates. I take a step back, speechless at his words. He can't do that. I won't let him do that. If he does, then I'll watch him turn into me and spiral and become depressed and stuck.

"No," I tell him.

"No?"

"You can't do that for me. I won't let you leave all this." I gesture around us. "Behind. This is your life."

"You're my life, El. Only you. And you're mine. I'm not giving up this time." His callous hands cup my face, and he kisses me.

"I'm not gonna let you drop everything for me. You still have things to work out between you and your dad. That's bigger than me."

"I go where you go," he says. "This may be the universe's way of pushing us back together."

I pick up his hands and kiss his knuckles, which are still wrapped in mine. "Yeah. Maybe."

"El, I can't lose you again." He lets go of my hands and rubs his face, like he's frustrated. "When you stayed in New

York for good..." He brackets his hips as his head falls. "The day we ended things, I had a ring with me."

Tears form in my eyes; the wall that was keeping the tears at bay cracks. He was going to propose. And then I left him. Only for things to fall apart. What did I do?

Does anyone else know? Does Addie know? Is that why she gave me such a hard time about his seeing their dad? I'd just end up leaving again, and she'd have to pick him up.

"You were going to propose," I say in disbelief.

# FORTY-SEVEN
## ROWAN

.

The swirls of blue become glassy when she realizes what I've just confessed. What I don't need her to do is blame herself.

"I wanted you to follow your dreams, El. I wasn't going to keep you from doing that. I'm not selfish. You're a star in my eyes." A piece of her hair falls in front of her face, and I gently brush it back before kissing her forehead.

"I'm so sorry," she croaks.

"Don't be sorry. We were young and had our entire lives ahead of us. Challenges presented themselves, and now here we are." I kiss her soft, plump lips and then press my forehead into hers. "And you didn't leave me. I'm the one who let you go."

"But what if I hadn't gone? We would have a home and kids. Maybe you wouldn't have The Salty Dog."

"There's no point in wondering. What's done is done. Now you're here with me. I'm done thinking about the past and what could have happened. I'm too busy planning my future with the girl who stands in front of me."

Ellie places her hand on my cheek, stroking the stubble, and I close my eyes while soaking in the touch.

"You don't need to come with me," she whispers.

"El, I go where you go."

"No," she continues. "I mean—I can stay here for good. I can leave my job. Come back home. Give us a fresh start."

My brows pinch together, and I shake my head. "You won't leave that life for me. You've worked too damn hard just to abandon all of that. We could work through it and figure it out together. Okay?"

"Rowan." A warm smile pulls at her lips. Sweet and caring. "I've been considering things. The thrill I had for New York and that fast-paced environment doesn't exist anymore. All my thoughts and dreams are consumed by you and the possibilities we have. You're the reason I've found inspiration again."

I'm forcing myself not to run out of the building, climb to the rooftop, and scream in victory.

"I think it's time that I came back home, Ro. Start over. Maybe..." She scrunches her nose. "Open a bakery? Who knows? I'm getting ahead of myself, but when I think about all those possibilities, I get excited."

"Do you really want this?" I ask in a shaky breath, and I hope this isn't a dream. I'd really hate to wake up right now.

"The stars brought me back home to you. And I am so deeply and madly in love with you, Rowan Williams."

ELLIE'S PACING back and forth in my living room, talking to herself, while I sit on the couch and watch. After yesterday's conversation, we've both decided it was best for her to call her boss and lay it all out there.

"I feel sick to my stomach," she says. "This is the worst feeling ever. I'm letting her down."

"You won't let her down. You'd disappoint yourself if you forced yourself into something you dislike."

She stops pacing and starts biting her nails instead.

"I can pretend to be you." I clear my throat. "Hi, Mrs. Chef, it's Ellie." My voice squeaks.

"Stop that. I don't sound like the mice from Cinderella."

"Maybe Milo can do it for you?" I joke.

We look at Milo, who's lying on his back, and snoring. Ellie mutters something under her breath and taps on her phone before putting it up to her ear. Then she covers her eyes with her free hand.

"What are you doing? She's not here," I say.

She swats her hand at me, mouthing 'shut up', and her posture straightens. "Hi, Chef Roberts. It's Ellie."

Although I'm screaming inside out of fear, I'm keeping my composure. This conversation could go anywhere. The plan is to pass up the opportunity and leave her job to pursue her passion here. If they pursued her enough, she could change her mind at the drop of a hat.

"Yes, I needed to talk to you about that." She places her hand on her forehead and continues to pace around. The plaid cotton pajama pants hang low on her hips; the material drags on the floor. "Of course, I know this is an incredible opportunity."

With my arms still crossed, my knees bounce in anticipation. She isn't frowning, her eyebrows aren't shooting up, but she isn't smiling either. She's calm and collected. Maybe there's a professional switch in her when she speaks to her head chef.

Since I own and manage the brewery, I wouldn't know. I've also been lucky not to have any awkward conversations with my employees because they're all outstanding. I've fired no one either.

Ellie looks at me, and I give her a thumbs up and smile wide.

"Chef Roberts, I can't take the promotion," she spits out. Her movements stop, and her shoulders slump. "I'm so lucky to have this opportunity, and I'm happy that you considered me, but I'm not the right person for you."

She walks toward the end of the couch and sits on the armrest. Then, she gets up and goes to the kitchen to walk around the island. "Uh-huh." She nods to herself. I watch her open the fridge and glance inside before closing it. "Of course."

Milo's still snoring, oblivious to the world around him. I can only imagine what his dreams are like. Running through fields and having a pile of dog bones in front of him.

"I've been grateful to have worked for you these past nine years. The thought of letting you down—" She stops mid-sentence and nods. "I just feel burnt out, and it's pulling away the passion I have for this industry." Ellie smiles and lets out a small laugh. "Yep, everyone else is saying that too."

I quirk an eyebrow at the last sentence. My elbows rest on my knees, which have stopped bouncing, keeping my focus all on her. Then I see her wipe a tear, and I shoot up to my feet. Her hand stops me from overreacting and smiles at me.

"Of course. Anything." She sniffles, then walks toward me, wrapping her arm around my waist, and tucks herself into me. My own arms grab onto her. "How soon do you need it? Two weeks?" I can feel her nod against my chest. "Yes, I can do that. Thank you so much. Bye."

We pull away, and her eyes glow. The light inside her

ignites again. After she hangs up, she gazes up at me with a look of disbelief.

"Is everything okay? It sounds like the conversation went well," I say.

"It did." She looks behind her at the kitchen. "Um, mind if I take over your kitchen?"

# FORTY-EIGHT

## ROWAN

Ellie hasn't stepped out of the kitchen for four days. But when she did, it was by force. I'm in love with the woman, but she desperately needed to shower.

It's astonishing how little sleep she gets.

When she sat me down and told me everything, a wave of relief washed over me. According to Ellie, Chef Roberts understood where she was coming from. She noticed Ellie was losing her self-esteem in her work. Apparently, it happens a lot. Chef Roberts didn't give her a hard time and instead pushed her to do what's right for Ellie.

She also mentioned opening her own bakery, and I think that's what sealed the deal for Ellie. I guess she needed Chef Roberts—the person she looked up to the most—approval to move forward with her life and not waste the amazing talent she has.

The only request she asked for from Ellie was to create a limited dessert menu to honor her work and creativity. I think it's pretty badass that a special menu will be presented at The Red Table. Celebrities go there. It's a huge deal.

One night, I forced her to go to bed with me. Then I woke up a couple of hours later, hearing her repeating a recipe in her sleep.

Call me crazy, but when she started talking to the ceiling about the measurements she needed, I grabbed my phone and took notes. Ellie swears up and down she doesn't remember doing that, but she kissed me for an entire five minutes, thanking me over and over.

That dish involved blueberries and a crust. Having played hero, my hope was to get some time with her in bed. Unfortunately, that didn't happen.

I look at Ellie in the kitchen, gaining insight into her experience at The Red Table. I've watched Ellie bake, but this is on another level. It's not just brownies and cookies. This is straight-up fancy shit.

She's made a key lime tart with berries and white choco-late. It took her an hour to perfect just one. Then she made a raspberry foam (and I told her it sounded like a cleaning product). I was wrong about the foam. It was delicious.

"Okay!" Ellie claps her hands, and a puff of flour wafts in the air. "There are four out of five desserts. The key lime tart, the mini blueberry mousse cakes, the caramel apple mascarpone vanilla mousse cake, and the three chocolate Plaisir sucre." She lets out a breath and brackets her hips. "Now, I need one more. My brain feels like mush."

The four desserts sit in a neat row on the island in front of us. They're too pretty to eat, and I can't believe I'm thinking that.

"Plenty of time exists to mull it over. These four took one week to make. Take the extra time to give yourself a break."

She stomps her foot and whines. "I can't. I have a rhythm now, and I don't want to stop."

Ellie moves things around the kitchen: bowls, plates, whisks, spoons.

"Utilize this time and give your brain a break. Let your mind and body recharge. If you force it, you won't be happy with your choice."

"I know that. I just don't want to stop."

Walking around the kitchen island, I splay my arms out and hug her. "I get that. But it's healthy to give yourself a break. And shower."

Ellie steps back from me and then tilts her chin up. "Are you saying I smell?"

I pinch two fingers together. "Only the tiniest bit."

She deadpans and walks around me toward the stairs. "Fine. I'll go scrub my ass nice and clean just for you."

"I'd be happy to help." I turn to look at her and give her a cheeky smile.

When she peeks over her shoulder, she glares at me with deadly eyes. I hold up my hands in surrender.

"I'm joking."

"No, you're not."

"I'm not. But I'll clean the kitchen for you."

She leans against the railing. "Thank you. I love you."

Our gazes turn soft toward each other, and my heart reaches out to hers. "I'll never get sick of hearing you say that."

AN HOUR LATER, Ellie is sparkling clean and wearing a smile. "That feels much better." She sits next to me on the couch while I scroll through my phone.

The sun is setting, and the crickets are singing outside. The house smells of dough and butter. It's perfect.

"Good," I kiss her damp hair, continuing to browse on my phone.

She lays her head on my shoulder before asking, "What are you looking at?"

"The lineup of vendors for the Taste of Dove Point."

"Shit, it's already coming up?"

I nod and say, "Mm-hm."

She peeks at the list. It has about fifty businesses taking part, which is more than I thought we'd have this year. Addie rented a table to offer free tastings to the tourists who would soon pour into town. No pun intended.

"I think you should do it," I say. "It doesn't hurt to try it out. Maybe plan out your next steps?"

"Crap," she whispers. "I hadn't considered what's next. I just knew I wanted to be back home and fuck everything else." She waves a hand.

"Well, it's a good thing you're staying with me. Decide what to do, and I'll figure out the finances."

She pulls back her head to look at me. "I'm not doing that."

I angle my head and give her a 'don't be stubborn' look. She pokes her finger in my ribs.

"I will not mooch off you." She folds her arms. "I'd live with my parents until I figure things out."

"You're not going anywhere. You're staying here, and you're gonna figure out what your next move is. I don't want you to worry about anything else. Don't feel any pressure."

"Do you know who you're talking to?" She squints at me.

"Fine. Let's start with the festival. We can sign up right now." I wiggle my phone in my hands.

"Right now?"

I nod. "Right now."

"Do they have any spots left? When is it happening?" Her body leans against mine, almost slumping into me.

My finger scrolls on the screen, finding the vendor signup sheet. Sure enough, it's still open, but the deadline shows today.

"It's next weekend," I say as I type away on my phone.

"A week?" Ellie exclaims. "I can't do everything in a week."

"El," I side-eye her. "I just witnessed you create crazy desserts that I assume would take someone else forever. Fortunately, you can do what you want. It can be simple: cookies, brownies, cupcakes."

"Okay," she drawls. "What about everything else?" She gestures at nothing with her hand. "Booth, branding, bakery name. Where will this money come from, hmm?"

"We'll ask our friends for help."

"What will this cost me?" She looks at the screen. "Two hundred dollars?" She shouts. "I barely have two dollars to my name."

My eyes roll. "I'll pay the fee. It's not a big deal."

"No, you're not." She reaches for my phone, but I snatch it away to the opposite side of her.

"Ellie," I say sternly. "You're letting me do this for you. You can try to stop me now, but I'll just do it later."

She sits back down on the couch and crosses her arms. "Fine. But I'm paying you back."

I bring my phone back down and continue to type. "You can pay me back in extra cookies."

I finish filling out the application, pay the fee, and hit send. When I look at her, I smile widely and show her the phone screen that confirms acceptance.

"I still need one more dessert for Chef Roberts." She covers her face and groans.

"Continue to brainstorm, but not today. Start again tomorrow. The guys and I will look at the list of everything you'll need. I can buy all the baking items and help with the baking."

She leans back and stares at me. "You want to help me bake?"

"It'll be fun."

A snort leaves her nose. "If you say so."

When I stand up from the couch, I stretch my body, raising my arms over my head.

I get up from the couch while she keeps her eyes on me. I hold out my hand to her, and she looks at it.

"What?" she asks.

"I want to take you somewhere. Come on." I gesture with my head.

She hesitantly takes my hand, trying to hide her smile. "Okay."

We walk outside into the backyard, where a ladder leans against the side of the house. I look at it and then back to Rowan.

"What are we doing?" I ask skeptically.

He points upward and says, "We're going to go on the roof and star gaze."

I let out a laugh. "What? Ro, we haven't done that in years. I don't know if it's actually safe to do that."

He starts to walk while holding my hand. "We did it all the time."

"Yeah, when we were dumb kids who didn't know any better. We're adults now, and we definitely know better."

We stop at the ladder, and he turns to me. "I promise we will be fine. I will not let you fall, and if you do, I will soften the fall for you. I will throw myself under you."

"Have I ever told you how dramatic you are?"

"I'm only ever dramatic when it comes to you, my love." He kisses the top of my head and then gestures to it. "After you."

I stare at him and then back to the ladder.

"Go on." I gesture with my hand.

I walk past him and carefully start to climb it step by step, taking my sweet ass time because I am *not* going to die today. I know I called Rowan dramatic, but I have every right to be. As I've gotten older, I've gotten afraid of heights. If I look down now, it's over.

I can feel myself gripping onto the sides of the cool metal, still moving carefully, one step at a time.

"You're almost there. I'm holding it, so don't worry," I hear Rowan call up to me.

He's holding it. Okay, that's fine. My head gets to the top, and I can see the roof and the dark gray shingles. How did I do this as a teenager? I lean on the roof; thankfully, it's a flat area, and I baby crawl on it.

I slowly turn around, and when I do, I see Rowan already at the top.

"I was afraid we'd end up seeing the sunrise by the time you got up here," he tells me jokingly with a chuckle.

"Hey, I'm not as risky as I was when we were younger. I developed my frontal lobe long ago," I say, turning slowly and sitting down.

He sits next to me, and the sun fully sets, bringing out the deep blue sky above us with specks of sparkles. It's incredible up here. If you close your eyes, you can hear grasshoppers chirping and the waves crashing.

The town has plenty of lights to guide us, but we still have the pleasure of getting a night sky full of stars. I feel my body relax, and I take the opportunity to lie down on my back so I can get the full view.

Rowan follows my lead and grabs my hand. We lay there in complete silence. Comfortable silence makes me feel grateful. I feel his thumb brush the top of my hand, and I count out all the stars I can see.

"I never told you this," I say, "but I used to go on the roof at my apartment and try to spot any stars I could. There would be moments when I thought I saw some, but they were just planes passing by. When I didn't see any stars, I'd just look at the moon, wondering if you were looking at it too. And if we were looking at it together."

I see his head turning toward me, but I keep my eyes on the sky.

"Every year on your birthday, I would come up on my roof," he says, and his voice is deep and quiet.

I turn my head to look at him, and it's like the stars never left because I see them in his beautiful dark blue eyes and the way they sparkle.

"Why?" I ask.

"After we would get off the phone, when I would call you to tell you a happy birthday, I'd wish I had more of you. The only way I could think of having that is by coming up here at night and looking at the stars."

"Are you trying to make me cry, Rowan Williams?" I laugh through what sounds like a cry. I can feel my eyes prickle with tears.

"I would never try to make you cry. Not if it's a tear of anger or hurt or worry."

I can feel a single tear fall down my temple, but Rowan gets closer to me and kisses it onto his lips. He sets his head back down and cradles my face with his other hand.

"I'd like very much to kiss you right now," he tells me.

"I'm all yours."

He leans in while still holding my cheek and presses a soft, warm kiss to my lips. I lean in toward him while my hand finds the nape of his neck. I feel his tongue slide into my mouth, and I suck on it, letting myself taste him in every way.

His strong hand run down my neck, shoulder, and stop at my waist. I can feel his fingers dig into my skin in the most sensual way. I let out a small whimper when I feel him nip at my bottom lip.

A second later, I find my body turning itself toward him, wanting to feel him on me. He lets go of my hand and slides it on the other side of my waist, gently bringing me on top of him while our lips are still locked together.

My body shivers when I start to feel him pressed against me in the most delicious way. I can feel my knees start to get bothered with the material of the roof, but I don't care. Let them get scratched up.

"I want to fuck you. Right here," I tell him desperately against his lips.

I move my lips to his neck, his jaw, and the back of his ear.

"We will need to be very, very quiet." His large hands caress my ass, moving my hips. "Do you think you can stay quiet?"

I moan quietly into his ear before telling him, "I can try. But I can't make any promises." I lift my gaze to him, and he licks my lips with the tip of his tongue before pulling me in for more.

I pull myself up and quickly unbutton his pants and see the pre-cum on his briefs. I look at him with a devilish smirk.

"That's what you do to me, honey," he says with a similar smirk.

I tug down his briefs just enough, and his hard, solid length springs upward. I need to wrap my hand around him. I need to feel the warmth. I only grab it long enough to lick his tip, making him inhale a sharp breath. I look up at him with an arrogant smile.

"Don't tease me, Ellie," he pleads.

I raise myself and go back to him, kissing him while I pull my lace underwear and cotton shorts to the side. I lift my hips up while still holding him in my hand and slide the tip of him back and forth along my clit.

His hand finds my hair and tugs on it so nicely while he lets out a groan. I feel his hips moving up, but I continue to tease him by stroking his tip up and down on me.

"You're so goddamn wet." He pulls me down to kiss him again. The kiss is rough and needy. His tongue plays with mine, begging me to give him more.

I smile against his lips and then drag his tip to my entrance, continuing to tease him while I take full control of him.

"Shit," he groans. "Honey, Ellie, I will beg until my voice is hoarse. Please."

I look at him and kiss him one more time before saying, "Well, since you asked nicely." I kiss him while I lower myself onto him, and we both moan into each other's mouths.

Every inch of him stretches me so perfectly, and I can't get enough of it. I let go of him and lower myself on the rest of him until I feel him completely fill me. We continue to kiss while I rock my hips and move up and down.

His hands hold my hips, and I let him guide me at the rhythm he wants me at. A slow, lazy, loving pace. He wants to enjoy this. Enjoy me and how I feel. Nothing rough or fast, but just the comfortable, slow movement.

"I love you so fucking much, Ellie. You have no idea," he breathes out while he stares into my eyes.

I push myself up and start to control my movements

now. I look down at him, my hair falling into my face. "I love you, Rowan," I say through each breath I take.

"You're a fucking goddess, the way you look under these stars while you fuck me. You ride me so goddamn good, baby." His fingers dig into my hips.

I let my hands roam over my body, going under my shirt and to my hard nipples. I play with them while I look at Rowan and the hunger he carries in his eyes for me.

He takes his hand, slips it under the fabric of my underwear, and starts to play with me, sending a shockwave through my body. I gasp and pull one of my hands from my shirt to cover my mouth, holding in a moan I so desperately want to let out.

Rowan gives me a pleasurable smile. "You like that?"

I nod my head, still covering my mouth. He makes circular motions with his thumb, keeping up with the pace of me riding him. I can feel myself start to lose control and quicken my pace. I bend down, place my hands on his cheeks and kiss him, tugging on his lip, sucking his tongue.

The position I'm in lets me go deeper and quicker. I feel myself reaching the edge of pleasure when he continues to rub me over and over.

"I'm close," he says in a rasp.

We kiss harder, and I move my hips more and more. As fast as I can go. The pain in my knees dulls as the pleasure in my body rises.

"Rowan, I'm close."

"Keep riding me, baby. Let me fill you up."

He tugs my hair, bites on my lip, and tips me over into the best orgasm. I moan into his mouth, and he continues to rub my clit, letting me ride it out. I hear him groan, and his hand tightens on my waist.

"Shit," he whispers into my mouth.

I keep my lips on him, trying to cover all the noise we're making. His breath quickens, and his hips thrust into me when I'm too tired to keep going. I lift my hips while he pumps into me. I bury my face in his neck, taking in the fresh scent of him, and kiss his neck until I feel him start to slow down.

I set myself back down on him and keep him in me while we kiss and pant. His hands cradle my face, and he looks at me. His dark eyes searched mine.

"We just fucked on the roof," he says, out of breath.

I smile and nod. "Yeah, we did."

He looks at me and raises his brows. "That was awesome."

IT TOOK two days to create the final dessert. My focus in my career was to create sleek and sexy desserts that were also considered a delicacy.

I try not to cringe that I've used the words 'sexy dessert' in my career.

The initial four were just that. I've designed them to be a showstopper for influencers who take photos of food and then only have one bite before they're stuffed. However, this last dessert is for me. It's rooted in nostalgia. At least for me.

Cinnamon apple crisp.

A tender, buttery crumble topping on top of Granny Smith apples, with two scoops of creamy vanilla bean ice cream, drizzled with homemade caramel sauce.

I knew not to anticipate an immediate review when passing on the seasonal menu. So I waited. And waited. I blasted the ringer on my phone for this occasion. Adding that last piece of dessert was daring. The Red Table rarely offers something so comforting. They're known for their edginess.

The cozy dessert is a piece that I'd add to my bakery.

"Honey, you need to get ready for the festival," Rowan says.

A deep sigh leaves my mouth, and I stop writing in my notebook.

"I know you're waiting for the phone call from Chef Roberts, but you have a few days left to set up everything." He grabs his hat and sets it backwards. My man is so fine.

"Are you doubting my ability to get things done in a timely manner, Mr. Williams?" I tease, pushing myself off the couch.

Rowan stops what he's doing and turns to me with a sultry gaze. "You've just unlocked a new kink for me."

I cock an eyebrow.

"Mr. Williams sounds sexy coming from your mouth." He wiggles his eyebrows.

A throaty laugh comes out of me, and I cover it with my hand. "You can see I'm prepping in my notebook. Don't worry, I'm on top of it."

"Get on top of me, instead." He walks past me with a chuckle.

"Hey," I shout and smack his butt with the notepad.

Milo follows Rowan around the kitchen; the small tapping of his nails on the wooden floor creates its own little melody. "Please tell me you're making those caramel stuffed brownies. Or the Oreo balls. Ooh, the mini caramel cheesecake bites!"

"The caramel brownies are on the list. But I also need to stick to simple things, like chocolate chunk cookies with sea salt, cinnamon rolls, lemon truffles, and rice crispy treats. Ya know?"

He pours a box of cereal into a blue bowl, then grabs the milk. "That doesn't sound simple." Milo tracks the carton in Rowan's hand before he pours it into the bowl and sets it back in the fridge.

"Do you know who you're talking to?" I say.

He stuffs a spoonful of the colorful cereal in his mouth before saying, "Sorry."

"You can help me with the cookies. I know you've been dying to bake with me," I tease. "Plus, everyone else is helping with the setup. Riley and Addie are handling the decoration and logo."

"Just tell me what to do and I'll do it."

I stop writing and peer at him. "If I'd known you'd do anything for me, I would've stayed here," I joke.

"I guess you have some catching up to do." He winks, and my panties fly off my body.

"So," I say awkwardly, and continue writing. "When are you seeing your dad again?"

Milo paws at his leg, begging for whatever is in that bowl. He doesn't care what it is. He needs it. Rowan finishes the cereal, drinks some milk, and gives the rest to Milo, who makes a complete mess on the floor.

"I'm not cleaning that," I mutter.

"I'm reaching out to him today, to see when he wants to meet up for dinner. You wanna come along?"

"I would love it, but you yourself said I need to focus. Plus, I think it'd be better with just the two of you."

"Yeah. You're right." He sighs.

"What about Addie?" My face winces. I should know better. But maybe she accepted him now.

"I could ask, but I don't feel like getting laughed at for the idea."

"That's fair."

"I guess I should go call him now then."

I lift my gaze to him and tilt my head. My features turn soft, illuminating with so much love for him and what he's doing with his life. "I'm so proud of you, you know that?"

His own smile beams toward me. "Yeah, I do."

## FIFTY

### ROWAN

"Rowan," Dad says on the other line.

"Hey Dad. How's it going?" I rub my sweaty palms on my sweatpants. I've met the man, spoken to him—and shouted—and I still become a nervous wreck around him.

"Better now that you've called," he says excitedly.

The pounding in my heart slows to a steady beat before I force myself to relax. "I was calling to see if you'd wanna grab some dinner? Just the two of us. If that's okay. We don't have to."

The sound of his deep laughter makes me huff out a small laugh of my own.

"That sounds awesome. What were you thinking? I could come to you. Or we could meet halfway?"

"Whatever you wanna do. I'm not picky," I say instead of what I should say.

There's some silence from his end, and I wonder if I've said the wrong thing. I'm overthinking this entire conversation. We're deciding where to eat.

"Sorry," he says. "I was looking at some places online.

This Mexican place sounds pretty good. And it's a halfway point for the both of us."

"Okay, that sounds good. Text me the address. What time are you thinking?" I run a hand through my hair as I wander around the house.

"Is five okay? I want to spend whatever time I can with you."

"That works." My answer leaves my mouth at the speed of light. "Five works."

"Cool. I'll text you the address and see you later."

I'm standing outside the restaurant I'm meeting Dad at. I showed up an hour early because not only do I hate being late, but I hate being late and anxious. So, I tortured myself by leaving way too early, just to stand around.

The restaurant building is lively, like it stepped out of Mexico. It's white on the top half of the building, with tan Spanish tiles that cover outdoor seating. The green-painted square wooden tables sit four people, two chairs in dark blue, and the other two in orange.

There are no windows or doors that lead inside. Instead, it's an open concept, and you can see straight into the space. The mango-colored walls are vibrant, while plants scatter around the room. The long wooden bar is the same color green as the tables outside.

It creates a fun atmosphere where you can have a good time. A place I definitely need to bring Ellie to. She loves herself, a margarita.

As my eyes wander around, I spot Dad coming around the corner. I look at my watch to see the time, and he's forty-five minutes early.

"You beat me here." He splays his arms out and smiles. I feel underdressed. He's wearing a deep blue blazer with a white button-up tucked into his dark, straight-legged jeans. And light brown ankle boots.

"Wow." I look at my outfit; a flannel, dark jeans, and my Vans. "I didn't know we were dressing up."

His forehead crinkles when he raises his eyebrows and then looks down at his outfit. "Oh, this? Is it fancy?"

My eyes peer down at my clothes.

"Hey, you need me to drive back to my place and grab a flannel? Say the word."

I chuckle. "Nah, no need."

When he passes me, he pats me on my arm, and gestures with his head toward the inside of the restaurant. "I reserved a table just in case."

Good thing he did. It's a packed house tonight. Crowds of people gather near the host stand, waiting for tables to open up.

"Hi there, table for two under Williams."

It's an odd sensation when I hear that. Mom didn't change her last name back to her maiden name. I've heard the name my entire life. But hearing it from Dad is different. I think it still hasn't hit me. We're here, in person, having dinner.

The host gestured, grasping two menus plus traveling toward a crowd, parting them akin to the Red Sea. She seats us at a two-person booth. "Your server will be right with you."

Dad sits at the end that faces the entrance. Strings of colorful small banners hang throughout the inside across the ceilings. The floor tiles also showcase more colors in intricate floral designs.

"This place is cool. I've heard their burritos are huge. The size of our heads."

Someone comes by the table to fill out glasses with

water and sets down a basket of tortilla chips and a deep red salsa. Then smiles up at the young boy and thanks him.

"Yeah, I need to take Eli here."

Not a second later, our server comes by. She wears a bright smile; her tan skin complements her light brown eyes. "Hi, my name is Gloria, and I'll be your server for the evening. Have you two dined with us before?" She places her hands in front of her, one on top of the other.

"Hey, Gloria. We haven't," Dad says with the same bright smile.

It's a relief knowing that he doesn't treat waitstaff like an asshole. Maybe that small-town boy is still inside him. My upbringing taught me to always be polite, express gratitude, and respect elders.

"Well, welcome to Casa de Tapas. We have many popular dishes and drinks. My favorite is the Chilaquiles. It's fried corn tortillas soaked in a red or green hot sauce of your choosing, and you can choose shredded chicken, chorizo, or shredded beef. It includes either scrambled eggs or sunny side-up. Of course, our burritos and enchiladas are also very popular."

"Wow. It sounds like we have a lot to consider." He jokes.

"Of course, take your time. Here are your menus, and I'll be back shortly to take your drink orders." She smiles and walks away.

"So, how have things been?" Dad asks.

My greedy hands grab the basket of chips, and I scoop a hearty helping of the salsa, stuffing it in my mouth. The spice is a slow burn. My favorite.

"Things have been going well."

"That's good. And how's Addie doing?"

"She's keeping herself busy with work. She handles the

marketing at the brewery." Another chip flies into my mouth. "She's really amped up the notability for us. The idea of building an outdoor stage drew in more visitors after smaller bands would come and perform."

"Impressive. What about you? How's running the business?" He steals a chip for himself, putting just as much red salsa on it as I am.

"It was stressful at first. Launching a company is kind of crazy. But it's my pride and joy. I'd never trade it for the world. I get to do what I love."

Gloria comes back, asking what we'd like to drink, and Dad orders us two Palomas—a mix of citrus and tequila—along with an appetizer that sounds cheesy and spicy.

"What about you? Where do you work?" I ask.

"I'm the chair and chief executive officer of an engineering firm."

I stop chewing and gawk at him. "That's..." I can't find the words. Incredible? Impressive? That also explains the house. I can't imagine the money he makes. I've also been told never to speak about money. That one came from Aunt Rosey.

"It's not that impressive," he says, as if he's reading my mind.

"You're joking?" I widen my eyes as my eyebrows shoot up. "That is impressive."

"Did you know engineering plays a significant role in the brewing process: fermentation, quality control, malting?"

Huh, I never really thought of that. I understand that brewing involves science. I guess I get the joy of science from Dad.

"Rowan," Dad says, leaning his forearms on the table. "I want to apologize."

"For what?"

"Everything. How I handled this when I was younger. Putting you and your sister through that." His head falls as he stares at the table. His self-inflicted stress in dealing with that is obvious. If I had X-ray vision, I'm sure I'd see his heart broken in two.

"It's fine. You've explained your side of the story." My teeth clench as I feel the stress radiate off him. "I'm sorry for lashing out."

"Don't apologize." He's quick to reply. "Feel free to vent your frustration. Please direct whatever anger or sadness you have toward me. I'm your punching bag if you need one. But most importantly, I'm your father."

He pulls a laugh from me. "It's just a lot to process and digest. It'll take time, and I hope you're patient with me."

"Take all the time you need. All I want is to rebuild our relationship. That's all I'm asking for."

I tap my finger on the table when a certain question hovers in my mind.

"What is it?" he asks.

"Hm?" I glance at him. "Nothing."

"I understand I wasn't in your life, but I still pick up on what you may or may not be thinking. Spit it out."

"You and Amy. How did that happen?"

The corner of his lip tilts up, and he nods. "I was wondering when you would ask about that. We've been together for ten years."

I hesitate. Ten years is a long time. I clear my throat and awkwardly shift in my seat.

"How'd you two meet?"

"Running." He smiles again and glances down at the table, as if he's reminiscing about their past. "We ran the same path every morning near the water. I'm pretty sure I noticed her first because I started saying hello to her when we'd cross paths. We swapped greetings during every run."

"Here are your drinks," Gloria says, placing them in front of us. "And your Queso Flamedo." Steam rises from the skillet, and I need to control myself from burning my mouth. "Are you ready to put your entrée in?"

Dad and I order food and get back to our conversation.

"So, we'd say hello every day. Then one day we finished our run at the same time, I bumped into her in the parking lot, and I asked her out." He shrugs with a smile.

I'm waiting for him to mention anything about my step-siblings. Sure, I could bring it up myself, but that might be awkward. I knew before he could say anything. I don't want to catch him off guard.

"Do you two have any kids?"

Oops.

He gives me a tight smile. "No."

I nod. "Oh."

"She has four of her own, though." He grabs his glass that's filled with a light pink drink—the same as mine—and sets it back down before continuing. "They all live up the coast. That's where Amy's from."

"With their dad?"

"Her husband passed away when they were young."

"What are their names?" I take a drink from my glass.

"Greyson is the oldest; he's thirty-four and has a daughter who's twelve."

"I'm an uncle?" I tease.

"You sure are. It doesn't matter that they're your step-siblings. Your family, so she's your niece."

The role of uncle seemed fun to me. The cool uncle who spoils them and calls me their favorite. The thought of having a niece pulls at my heartstrings.

"Then Amelia; she's thirty-two, and Elizabeth, we call her Birdie, and Theo, they're twenty-seven."

"Twins?"

He nods. "Then there's the baby of the group, Olivia. She's twenty-six."

Damn. He has his very own Brady Bunch.

"I can't wait for you to meet them. They know all about you and Addie."

"They do?"

"Oh yeah. They've known about you two since the moment I stepped into their lives. They'd love to meet you when you're ready."

A lump forms in my throat. It feels like everything is falling into place. The missing puzzle pieces are starting to click together. First Ellie, now this. There's no way I'm crying in public, so I shove down the lump of emotions I have, and smile.

"Yeah. I'd love that too."

# FIFTY-ONE

## ELLIE

My finger taps away on the steering wheel of my car as I drive to Ellie's guesthouse. A container of cookies sits on the passenger seat with me.

Even though I see her every day, I miss her like crazy. She insisted she stay at her parents' place to put all her focus on creating the list of desserts she's come up with. Apparently, I'm a distraction.

I took it upon myself to bake some cookies to give her a taste test. She's letting me help, and I need to instill in her to trust in me. I've got this. If I can brew beer, then I'm pretty sure I can make decent cookies. Baking is also a science.

When I step out of the car, birds fly by, chirping and following each other like they're playing tag. The sound of a bee buzzing by me as it lands on a bed of purple mums.

My knuckles wrap on the glass door, and I see Ellie sprinting—almost falling—to get to me. Flips are happening in my stomach when I spot her beautiful face. There are tan lines on her shoulders from the summer as she sports a ribbed tank top that leaves nothing to the imagination. The white fabric makes her skin glow.

She swings the door open, and I'm hit in the face with a blast of cold air. "Hi," she shouts, and jumps into my arms. Her long, braided hair swings over her shoulder while she snuggles into me.

"What's that?" She points to the full container in my hand.

"What's what?"

"The container in your hand, dummy."

"Oh, shit, yeah. I made these for you."

"Oh?" She grabs it, then shakes it. "What's in it?"

"I guess you need to open it to find out."

She bites the corner of her lip when she glances down, pulling the lid off. She gasps and smiles. Her eyes are soft, pure, and beautiful, like the ocean.

"You made me cookies?"

"Chocolate chip. I figured since you're letting me help you bake the cookies for the festival, that I can show you just how great I am. That way you can put all your faith in me and not worry about me damaging your reputation."

Her head tilts. "You wouldn't ruin my reputation. Now, I'm going to try one of these bad boys." Her fingers wiggle as she decides which one to grab. "I'm sure these will be awesome."

"Fair warning, I haven't tried one yet. I wanted to wait and try it with you." I grab one for myself, not being picky.

I watch her eye the cookie, observing it with a sniff. Why am I nervous? She takes a bite, a generous one, and I wait.

Moving her lips is slow, and her eyes narrow while she looks out in the distance. Is she going through the five stages of grief?

The nod I get is questionable. "Mmm." She covers her mouth. "These are great, Ro."

I'm still holding mine and haven't taken a bite. When I do, I regret every decision I've made in my life. Holy shit, these are atrocious. My feet are already moving to the trash-can, and I spit the cookie out, throwing away the rest.

It doesn't deserve to be swallowed.

"Ellie, spit it out."

She furrows her eyebrows while attempting to finish the cookie because she has a heart of gold. Her head shakes as she waves me off.

"Ellie, please spit it out."

"It's fine." Her mouth is still full. She didn't swallow it.

I fold my arms and stare at her. A smile plays on her lips the entire time through those slow, agonizing chews.

"The best cookie ever." She points to the other half while squinting her eyes, like she's in pain. The other half of the cookie gets shoved into her mouth, and she chews as quickly as she can.

I chuckle and rub a hand down my face. "Ellie, just throw it out."

"No, they were so good! I mean, they could use some work. I think you missed a step, but they were good."

"Maybe I shouldn't help you then?" I wince.

"I'll be right next to you every step of the way. I promise you won't screw up, especially with me in the kitchen. That would be impossible."

"I love confidence." I kiss her forehead.

"Alright, let's get started."

---

"OKAY, now put the mixer on, and I'll grab the chocolate chips."

Before we started baking, I gave him a rundown on how

I bake cookies. It's my recipe, with my own twists. Three different chocolate flavors, small and in big chunks. Gooey on the inside and crispy on the outside.

After taking the expensive chocolate chips out of the freezer, I open the golden bag, stuffing my nose into it and inhaling the rich chocolate.

"You keep them in the freezer?" Rowan asks.

"That's how I prefer them. I think it helps during the baking process. Don't ask me how. I don't know. It just works."

"This is too fancy for me. How much did this thing cost? I made everything by hand."

"See those black levers on each side?"

He nods.

"This one." I push the black lever. "Locks the top in place. And the second lever starts it up. The numbers represent the speed."

"Oh, that's easy." Rowan's hand turns it on before I can finish.

"Wait!"

It's pushed to the highest speed, causing flour to fly out of the silver bowl. I'm hit with flour and turn to Rowan.

"*Shit, shit, shit,*" he shouts.

A laugh abrupt the chaos as I watch him turn off the mixer. Flour flies onto the counter, onto our clothes, into his hair. He stops it and looks at me, flour poofs in the air when he whips his head my way. I keel over in laughter.

His chest rises and plunges. "What the hell just happened?"

"You put it on the highest setting." I point a finger at the lever while still laughing.

"I put it on five. Isn't five slow, and then one is fast?"

My laughter stops, and my face twists in confusion. "Five is the highest speed."

He looks back at it and pushes the lever to number one. The mixer starts up at a calming speed, the ingredients mixing at a slow speed. Rowan drops his head and lets out a sigh. The flecks of flour float in the air. We brush the flour off our clothes as much as we can, but Rowan's hair is pure white.

"I can brew beer, but fail at this. How is that possible?"

"Baking isn't for everyone, and that's okay. You think I could brew beer? I can barely pour a beer without it being half foam." I raise my eyebrows. "Everyone has their own talent that they should stick to."

I hear a defeated sigh coming from his end. "Well, do you wanna continue while we're covered in flour?"

"Actually," I whisper. "I have a better idea."

"Oh?"

"Mhm." I take his hand in my own and guide him to the bathroom.

"Ooh really? The bathroom, huh? Are you gonna wash me up?"

When we step into the bathroom, I take his shirt off, not wasting a second. "We can't finish when we're dirty like this." I wink.

Rowan mutters curse words under his breath when I unbutton his jeans, then take my clothes off.

"Now, let's get that body clean." I trail my finger down the middle of his abs.

The sun beats on my body as I stand in front of the tent, observing everything about it. I'm in a popular area where people stop by the most. I feel both lucky and nervous.

I don't want anyone to question my profession now. It's hard not to. I grew up here, and everyone knows me. They expect—maybe—incredible desserts, and I can't handle criticism right now.

The desserts sit in rows, which makes it easy for customers to look them over.

Riley and Hailey helped put the sweet treats in their own white boxes. Then, Hailey created the logo for me. They both convinced me to use a company name versus just my own. It makes it look more professional.

A round sticker on top of the boxes displays the name Honey Cakes. Underneath, rest a small whisk and spatula, each flanked by curved wreaths.

Hailey designed the banner to hang over the table. Rowan and James set up a canopy for shade, which led to Riley having a freakout. She said it was 'sad and boring' looking and took it upon herself to buy decorations.

Dusty blue and white balloons bunch on either side, giving it a pop of color.

It looks official. My emotions are on a rollercoaster. Happy because I get to share my pastries with the people I love. Sad, because I've left the place that didn't bring me that happiness anymore. And nervous because I'm a people pleaser.

"It looks perfect, El! I'm so excited. I can't wait," Riley shouts in excitement. "Didn't Hailey do such a cool job on the logo? It looks like the real deal."

"I'm happy that I could provide my artistic skills to you." Hailey walks toward us in a cute black dress that hits just above her knees, paired with black platform Dr. Marten sandals.

"Have you seen Rowan today?" Riley glances at me.

"Just this morning. He helped set up, but went back home. His dad is coming to stay for the weekend." A rocket of nerves runs through my body—for Addie.

"Does Addie know?" Riley winces.

"She said it was okay, but she's going to steer clear of him."

"That should be interesting." Hailey laughs.

Closing my eyes, I inhale a long, full breath before letting it out. "Are you guys ready to do this?"

Riley and Hailey nod as we go behind the display table.

"Alright, here we go!" Riley exclaims.

---

TWO HOURS LATER, it feels like we're moving non-stop. A throng of people asked for business cards, seeing if I thought about opening a bakery in Dove Point.

My cheeks hurt from smiling so much. I had to stop and

drink an entire bottle of water from how much I'm talking. Each time someone asked about opening a dessert shop; I didn't have an answer.

"Honey! Ellie!" Mom yells out, her hand popping out from the crowd in a wave.

She strides toward my table with Dad. Mom beams from ear to ear, unable to hold in her excitement for me.

"Hey, guys. Thanks so much for stopping by," I say to my parents.

Mom wraps her arms around me, embracing me while saying how proud she is. "How much have you sold so far?"

"No idea. A lot? I lost count. Sorry you didn't see me for like a week."

"What do you have left?" Dad peers at the table behind me, his tall frame hovering over both me and Mom.

I peer back at the table where Hailey and Riley are still helping customers who keep showing up.

"We've sold out of the cinnamon rolls, considering I only made fifty of those."

"Fifty? How on earth did you do that?" Dad asks in shock.

"Dad, I do this for a living. Did I ever tell you about the event I worked at where I had to make six hundred crème brûlées? You could offer me a million dollars, and I'll say no. I made five hundred mini tarts and mini cheesecake bites. Along with two hundred cookies and Oreo balls."

My parents gape at the numbers I just threw out at them. Considering I chose pastries that were very easy to make in large batches, it didn't feel like I was making six hundred crème brûlées. I'd create tons of cookies instead.

"Come on." I gesture with a tilt of my head toward the table. "Let me see what we have left."

"Not for free," Riley says with a smile.

"Riley," I say.

"What? I know they're your parents, and I love them like they're my own, but this is no exception. We're here to make money, Ellie." Riley peers at my parents. "Mr. And Mrs. Thompson, I love you, but no. Cough up the money." She holds out her hand.

"Of course. You expect me not to support my daughter?" Dad jokes.

"Great, here you go." Riley gives them two cookies, two mini tarts, and two mini cheesecake bites. "That will be twenty-six dollars."

Dad's eyebrows lift in shock. Riley stares back at him. He takes out his wallet and gives her his card. She smiles and packs the goodies she picked for them.

"Enjoy!" she says, handing them the little bag that has a Honey Cakes logo.

Mom grabs the bag and looks at the logo. "Was this your idea?"

"I did." I beam.

"If you open a bakery, hire Riley. She knows what she's doing," Dad says.

"Oh, she has no choice." Riley smiles at me.

My lips tug into a smile before I feel my phone vibrating in my pocket. When I see that it's my ex-boss calling, my heart picks up speed.

"I need to take this." I gesture to my phone and walk away from the festival and noise.

"Hello?"

"Ellie! I've received the menu and have gone over it with the team," Chef Robert says in a pleased tone.

My body stiffens, and I wait for her to continue talking.

"This is a fantastic menu, Ellie. Everyone is so excited

about it. Even Chef Wilson finds your creation impressive. You know how hardheaded he is."

I let out a breath, laughing. "Thank you. I'm glad you approve."

"Ellie, we will miss you in this kitchen. I want you to know that. I look forward to seeing what you do next. Please let me know if you will open a bakery. I'd love to visit to see what you've come up with. Can you promise me that?"

I bite down on a cry and smile. "I promise."

## FIFTY-THREE

### ROWAN

"And this is the beer garden." I walk through the back of the brewery, Dad and Amy following me.

When I reached out to them, asking if they'd like to visit for the weekend, they took up the offer before I finished the sentence. My inner child leaped for joy.

At times, this feels excessively fortunate. All of it. Dad, Ellie, my confidence. The void within the heart, once gaping, is filled, now complete, by two people previously absent.

There's still a small part of me that's hesitant and wary. That might continue for quite a while until I understand his commitment. We've talked a lot since our dinner.

Dad and Amy said they were going to stay at the town's hotel, but I insisted they stay in the guest room. I was relentless, and when they arrived, I took their bags and brought them into the house without question.

Milo is obsessed with them. Of course.

"James and I put in a lot assembling this. This wasn't here when we opened the brewery."

I look at Dad, directing all my attention to him, and

watch every expression he shows. His dark blue-gray eyes round, and I think I see a spark of amazement in them. He places his hands on his hips and meanders in a circle to take everything in.

"You did this all yourself?" Dad asks.

"Yeah." I place my hands on my hips, mimicking him like a child would. "James and I built everything—with the help of Beau and August, of course. Actually, if you look right over there." I point at the sliding doors that lead back inside the brewery. "You'll see our initials from when we poured the concrete."

James and I put our initials on one side of the large sliding doors, and Beau and August put theirs on the opposite side. When we walk through the entrance, it always reminds us we did this together. We celebrated after the final completion with tacos and beer around the campfire.

Hailey, Riley, and Addie were with us. But it still felt empty without Ellie, despite calling and video chatting with everyone in the background. I remember her reaction when she first saw the setup. She was in her chef's coat; her cheeks red, and her hair wrapped in a sleek bun.

*Holy crap, you guys did all that? That's amazing, Rowan. Ugh, I wish I could just fly out there now and be with you guys. I miss you all so much. Especially you.*

I remember my heart tugging, and gave her a lopsided smile.

*I wish you were here too. It doesn't feel the same without you.*

"Do you guys host bands?" Amy asks, pulling me out of my memories.

"We do. We post on our social media pages and usually have a lineup of bands willing to come out to play. Just small bands, nothing huge like Aerosmith." I joke.

"Aerosmith would be lucky to play here." Dad beams.

"You know, my son, Theodore, he's in a band. Maybe he could play here sometime?" Amy suggests.

"That would be cool. What's his band's name?"

"Maybe you've heard of them, Yellow Sundays? He's touring right now."

"Wait." I hold up a hand. "Are you telling me that your son is Theo Grant? Holy shit, yeah, I've heard of them. I've listened to them since they were just a small band. Their music is great. Dad mentioned Theo, but why would I think he's Theo Grant?"

"I'm sure he would be happy to do it. Despite his fame, Theodore still attends family gatherings. Especially when his sisters and brother nag him long enough."

"My stepbrother is Theo Grant. This is wild. Addie is going to flip her shit when I tell her."

Dad puts on a smile, but it carries a lot of sadness behind it. He knows Addie doesn't want to see him, and even though he's upset about it, he understands.

We haven't run into Addie. I've been careful to stay away from the area where our table is set up.

But if Dad runs into her and sees her at the table, I will not stop whatever he does. Yes, I want to protect Addie. But I'm hoping she changes her mind. I would love it if she changed her mind.

"Would you guys mind if we checked in on Ellie? I saw her only this morning before the festival started. Maybe she still has some desserts left."

"Oh, yes, please. I would love to." Amy looks at Dad.

"Yeah, let's go see how she's doing. I'm excited to see what she's made." Dad smiles at me and places a hand on my shoulder, guiding us back inside the brewery.

# FIFTY-FOUR

## ELLIE

By the end of the night, I couldn't feel my feet. They've disappeared and no longer exist. Sometimes I forget about comfort in being cute. My white Converse didn't provide the comfort I needed, and I should have known better.

Within the tent's shade, I stand from the chair I was in, observing the festival's attendees. It's crowded, yet somehow I've spotted one person who's been on my mind all day. The smile he sends me is brighter than the sun, and we lock eyes.

His dad and Amy walk behind him, and right now, my heart is so full and happy it could burst. He looks like he's floating on air, and nothing can bring him down.

It feels like all the pieces are coming together, and I don't regret one moment of leaving it all behind in the city. I should be here. With my friends, my family, and *him*.

"There's my girl," Rowan shouts as he walks closer toward us.

He's in a simple dark blue shirt, a hat that's turned backward (please calm down, ovaries), and black jeans with black Vans.

I can feel my cheeks heat, and I tuck my bottom lip in my mouth and bite down on it, trying not to giggle like a teenage girl. *His girl.* I'm his. My sole view centers on him, along with his sapphire eyes glittering in the sunshine. The dark gray swims along the edge.

Raising my chin, I touch his firm chest, then reach him for a kiss. His full lips melt away the aches in my body.

"Hey, handsome." I grin.

"How did everything go today? Did you sell out of everything like I said you would?"

"I did. But I saved some goodies for your dad and Amy, of course. We just sold the last of everything we had about twenty minutes ago." I let out a breath of relief. "I just want to go home and lie on the couch while you rub my feet. They are painfully sore."

He looks down at my shoes and shakes his head before saying, "I told you not to wear those. You should know better, chef."

I pull my head back, and a smile grows on my face. "Did you just call me chef?" I bite my lip and glance away, blushing again.

He bends down, his lips near my ear. "Yes, chef."

"Well, I guess I found a new praise kink," I utter, trying to suppress my laugh.

His lips leave my ear and trail below on my neck while he says it over and over. I can feel my knees weaken and my body screaming for him. I raise my shoulder to cover my neck and let out a laugh.

"Rowan, not here."

"Mmm, fine." He groans in my ear. He stands up straight and nods to Riley and Hailey in greeting.

"Here, take this," Riley tells him, handing him a white bag filled with desserts. "This is for your dad and Amy. Do not steal any of this. It's only for them." She points. "Ellie, go have fun. Hailey and I can handle it from here."

"Are you sure? I don't mind staying."

"Rowan, take your woman and go," Riley commands.

"Aye, aye, captain." He takes the bag before we walk over toward his dad and Amy.

They're standing in front of a table that's covered in homemade jewelry. Necklaces, bracelets, earrings, rings. I scan over everything; all the sparkles and pretty colors draw me in like a moth to a flame.

"Look at these; aren't they beautiful?" Amy asks, showing me a pair of amethyst stone earrings.

"Oh, wow, those are gorgeous," I say.

"Do you really like them?" She hands them to me so I can look closer. The little purple crystals glimmer in the sunshine. If you turn them toward the light, you can see the different shades of purple that run through the stone.

"This is my birthstone color." I hand them back to her with a smile.

"Oh? When is your birthday?"

"It's in February." I smile.

She walks toward the other portion of the table, where a girl is crafting jewelry. "Hello, I'd like to buy this, please."

She raises her gaze, smiles toward her, sets aside what she held, and readies a tiny box. When I realize what's happening, I walk to Amy.

"Are you getting those for yourself?" I ask.

"I'm getting them for you, darling," she tells me in her sweet voice.

"You don't have to."

"I want to. As a thank you. I see the way you've helped Rowan. He told your dad so much about you at their dinner. He is absolutely in love with you, and it makes me so happy that he has someone like you in his life."

I swallow down the lump in my throat, fighting the tears that are creeping up on me. I've only spoken to Amy a few times since we first met, and she's the sweetest person I know. She welcomed both me and Rowan with open arms. No judgment, no questions.

"Thank you," I say.

"Of course." She turns to me and hands me the small box. I see her arms open, and she gestures for a hug. I take her in embrace.

When we pull back, she looks at me and asks, "Are you coming to dinner with us tonight?"

"Oh, uh, maybe. What time?"

Amy looks at her watch and then goes back to me. "In about three hours. I would love for you to join us."

"Okay, that sounds great."

An hour later, Rowan is taking me home. I couldn't be happier to have them help me with all of this. It was such a whirlwind. All the excitement that surrounded me. I must admit, it's pushed me even more toward the idea of making Honey Cakes a real thing.

I told Rowan I wanted to walk home and change for dinner. He insisted on giving me a piggyback ride because of how much I've complained that my feet hurt. I didn't pass up the opportunity.

"From this height, the view is insane. No wonder you can see the next town over, you giant," I mock.

He jokes back, saying, "I can see the craters on the moon from where I stand."

"I've never seen the top of a shelf at a grocery store. It makes me jealous considering I need to climb on the bottom shelves to get something from the top."

"Trust me, you don't need to see the top."

Everything feels perfect. I'm finding myself again, and having Rowan by my side makes this adventure fun. After ending things ten years ago, we let the flame that once burned bright between us fade. I guess the universe wasn't having any of that and threw a curveball into our lives.

Thank you, universe.

"I have something for you," Rowan says.

"A present?" I slide off his back when we reach the door to his house.

His hand digs into his back pocket, and I see a shiny, silver key pinched between his fingers.

"What's that?"

He cocks his head, giving me an exasperated look. "Ellie. It's a key to my house. Our house."

My eyes widen, and before I grab the key from him, I go back down the stairs where a fake rock sits. When I lift it up and check the bottom for the spare key, it's still there.

"This is yours, silly. It's not the spare key." He laughs.

"Wait, are you asking me to move in?" I run back up the stairs and snatch the key from him.

"Well, I'd ask you to marry me, but we just started dating and I'd like to see where things go." He stuffs his hands in his pockets.

"Shut up," I say, slapping his arm with the back of my hand.

He gives me the honor of opening the door to my new home. The grip from Rowan's large hands wraps around my stomach, and his chin dips into the crook of my neck.

"Welcome home," he whispers.

He pulls away, twirling me toward him, gazing into my eyes, then toward my lips before kissing me. With his lips against mine, all I feel is happiness. Me in Rowan's arms.

Him in mine. He dips his forehead to mine while I stand on the tips of my toes.

He smells of saltwater and citrus.

"I'm the luckiest person to have you in my life, Ellie Thompson. One of my wildest summers—I'd keep every minute. I can't wait to spend the rest of my life with you," he whispers. "Only if you'll have me forever."

"You *are* my forever. Maybe someday I'll be Mrs. Williams." I smile.

He looks at me for a beat and then throws me over his shoulders. I let out a scream and a laugh as he walks to the bedroom. "What are you doing?" I slap his butt while I yell.

"I'm going to make love to my woman. We might be late for dinner, but my folks will understand. Get ready for a long night, honey." Rowan lays me down on his bed, the soft sheets pressing against my body.

A wicked grin tugs at my lips before I say, "Bring it on."

# EPILOGUE
## NEW YEARS EVE

"Thank you, everyone, for coming to celebrate with us," Rowan announces to the crowd in the cavernous room.

I peer up at him and admire his good looks. He's wearing a sleek black suit. His jacket is unbuttoned, and so are the first two buttons of his crisp white shirt. A small strand of his hair falls onto his brow as he pushes the rest back.

My lips want to feel his clean-shaven jaw that the Greek gods blessed him with. Even though I woke up with him between my legs this morning, I want to take him back home and tangle up together in bed.

"We had our New Year's party here because this is the space that will soon be Honey Cakes," he says.

"Hold on, this bakery belongs to you?" August asks, looking around with his hands in his pockets.

"Yes, Clark Kent," Riley says, glancing at him with a smart-ass smile.

"You think that's an insult? Superman is very handsome." August pushes his glasses up his nose with a finger.

"Riley will help when she isn't working at the yoga

studio. Just with accounting. I'll hire someone to help with other tasks, although I'll deal with that when the time comes."

Riley takes a large gulp of her wine. "And I'm going to rock the shit out of it."

"How exciting!" Rowan's mom exclaims.

I glance over at Mom, who's brushing a tear off her cheek. "Mom, please don't cry."

She fans herself with her hand. "I'm sorry. I'm just so happy. You've been so happy since you moved back home. Now this."

Dad wraps an arm around her shoulders and pulls her in.

"Alright, we have two minutes until the clock strikes twelve," Rowan shouts to everyone.

There's music playing in the background, and everyone gets their drinks refilled, making sure they find their loved ones to share a kiss with. At least, the people with company. Which isn't many.

August and Riley exchange playful remarks, revealing hints of flirting between them. Riley thinks she's slick, but she isn't. The corner of her lip twitches, but she puts her emotions back in control after August makes a joke.

"Okay, here we go!" Addie shouts.

We all count down from ten. I'm wrapped in Rowan's arms, and we gaze at each other. He places his thumb on my cheek and strokes it.

"Happy New Year!" everyone shouts.

Rowan kisses me just the way I like it. Rough, but also soft. Then, I turn to give everyone else a hug, wishing them a happy new year. The rest of the year was amazing.

Riley and I went to apply for a business loan after we decided Honey Cakes would be my next big step. It was an agonizing wait, but we were fortunate enough to get approved.

We've already started mapping out what the shop will look like. Right now our head is swimming with powder blue walls, Victorian-style paintings with golden frames.

Rowan's gotten better at letting other people handle things at The Salty Dog. He's adapted to handing over some control. Only a little. Addie still nags him about it, and James rolls his eyes at every disagreement Rowan and Addie have because he's stuck in the middle.

Riley grabs my hands, and her mouth curves into a smile. "You know I'm the greatest best friend you've ever had, right?"

I give Riley a smile that says, 'Of course I know that'.

"And because we've known each other since we were in diapers, I can only assume that I'd be your maid of honor, right?" She brushes her buttery-blonde hair over her shoulder.

"Of course."

"Cool." She beams. "So I'm going to be your maid of honor? That's a promise?"

I furrow my eyebrows, still smiling. "Ry, what's going on with you?"

"Nothing. Can't a girl be excited for her best friend? I'm excited for you to start the next chapter of your life."

"Aw, thanks, Ry. It's a new chapter of *our* lives. The new chapter of Honey Cakes Bakery."

"Yeah, and you'll be able to call yourself Mrs. Williams too." She wears a smirk.

I let out a dreamy sigh. "Someday, yes."

She laughs and peers over my shoulder. My heart picks up.

If I'm about to catch Rowan kneeling down on one

knee, *I'm going to lose my mind*. My eyes find him, and he is, in fact, down on one knee.

His piercing smile makes me giddy, and I hold myself back from kissing his dimples again. He holds up the forest-green velvet box and opens it.

"Oh my God," Addie exclaims.

"Oh, shit," Beau follows in excitement.

"Ellie, you're the love of my life. You whisked me away the day you came over with a Funfetti cake. My favorite, by the way." He looks around the room, grabbing a laugh from everyone around us. "I've let you get away once. That mistake won't happen again. Ellie, will you—"

"Yes," I shout, forcing myself not to jump up and down.

His shoulders shake with laughter. "You didn't even let me ask you—"

"Yes. Yes, yes, yes." I throw myself at him, wrapping my arms around his neck. When I pull back, I hold his face in my hands. "Yes, yes, yes." I kiss him between each yes, over and over.

"You didn't even see the ring." He kisses me back.

"I'll take a ring pop and be happy. I don't care."

Everyone around us claps and hollers in excitement. His dad's booming voice carries from the background, while Mom cries more. But all I see is my future husband in front of me. My best friend. He places the small box in my vision, and I look at the ring.

"Holy shit," I exclaim, taking the box. Inside sits a pear-shaped diamond that's placed on a rose gold band with smaller diamonds spaced out around the band.

"You like it?" He glances up at me.

I gape when my eyes set on the sparkle of the diamond. My eyebrow quirks. "Is this...*the* ring?"

"It is. With a few upgrades." He takes it out of the box and slides it onto my finger, and it fits just right.

Now I'm the one who starts crying. I wipe away the tears so I don't mess up my makeup—that I spent a long time doing—and I hate doing my makeup.

"I was thinking," Rowan says. "What about Milo being the ring-bearer? He looks pretty snazzy in a bowtie."

"I'd have to think about that. It's my day after all. He'll steal all the attention." I joke.

"Trust me, no one can steal your spotlight. You're my shooting star, El. All eyes will be on you." Rowan nuzzles his face into my neck. "What if we leave early to celebrate?"

"What do you have in mind?" I whisper.

"You. Me. The bed... no clothes."

A heavy sigh leaves my chest, trying to play off as if I'm not thinking the same thing. "I guess it's the right thing to do... since I'm not wearing any underwear."

"Excuse me, everyone," Rowan shouts, and everyone turns toward us while we both stand up. "My fiancé and I want to thank all of you for coming."

*'My fiancé.'* I like the sound of that.

"However, we're going to continue the celebration alone," he says with a smirk.

Heat shoots up from my belly and to my chest. Did he actually share that with everybody? I cover my face.

"Ew, Rowan, you don't need to announce that," Addie says, downing the rest of her champagne.

"Really, Rowan? In front of your entire family?" Aunt Rosey shakes her head.

"Get out of here, you lovebirds," Beau yells before saluting his drink to us.

Rowan whispers in my ear, "I'd throw you over my

shoulder, but I don't think that'd go over well with everyone here."

I chuckle. "Uh, yeah, that wouldn't be good."

"But I can do this." Rowan bends and swoops one arm under my legs, then picks me up. A squeal comes out of me, and my arms wrap around his neck. "Goodnight everyone," Rowan shouts as he walks toward the door.

Everyone I love looks back at us. All my friends and family who have been there for me since day one.

I never imagined this chapter's end. I would have laughed if someone had told me I'd be engaged to Rowan and opening a bakery in Dove Point this new year.

I'll never question the universe again.

# SWEPT AWAY: PROLOGUE
## RILEY

"Ellie," I whisper toward my best friend, who's sleeping next to me.

The moon's light illuminated the opposite side of the big room, while the wind stirred the curtains. I hear Ellie let out small snores every five seconds. She looks so peaceful while I'm next to her, wide awake.

I drum my fingers on my stomach while I stare up at the glow in the dark stars. All different sizes, scattered along the ceiling.

This week marks the end of summer break, and the start of a new school semester makes me giddy. I'm not sure if it's the extra school supplies, or getting the cute, colorful gel pens and organizers. Or that I'll be in precalculus during tenth grade.

Math makes me happy. Math doesn't lie. It's like what Cady in Mean Girls said, *'Because it's the same in every country'* and Damon was right, it's beautiful. I also really like yoga and decorating.

I wonder if I can combine math and decorating into one. That'd be awesome.

Mom doesn't understand my interests. I remember telling her about being in pre-calc, and all she did was give me a confused look. She wants me to be on the cheerleading team just like she was when she was my age. Or focus on winning Homecoming Queen in sophomore year. Things that aren't interesting to me.

Before school started, I wanted to cut my hair. But Mom wasn't having it. She says I'm too pretty to have short hair. This year I turn sixteen, and I need this year to be about my interests.

But how do I tell Mom that without hurting her feelings?

A dramatic sigh escapes from me, and I grab the soft blanket that's covering me, and uncover myself. My feet touch the cold, wooden floor as I get up from the bed, trying not to wake up Ellie.

Since I'm awake, I'll grab a drink, maybe watch television, hoping for some sleep.

Everything is quiet until I walk toward August's room, which sits across from the top of the stairs. I stop myself, my feet making no sound on the plush carpet, and hear him talking.

Since his door wasn't shut, it's easy to overhear him.

"What the hell is wrong with you?" August hisses.

*Who is he talking to?*

"It's simple math, moron," he grumbles.

I've never heard August talk like this to anyone. He's always been nice to me.

"Why can't I get this? Oh, I'm a dumbass, that's why."

My face shifts from confusion to annoyance. I can feel my lips part in questioning while I hear him talk to himself like this.

Mom is constantly condescending toward Dad. It gets to a point where you start to believe the words that are being spewed at you.

I know this feeling all too well.

Before intervening in his self-directed torment, I pause, then consider my own words. This isn't a situation that I can throw myself into. We don't have that type of friendship.

We don't have a friendship. We're acquaintances.

Knocking on his door, I poked my head in. August turns to me, his hair in disarray like he was tugging on it.

He's gotten taller this past summer. I'm tall myself, for a girl, but he's maybe an inch taller than I am. My eyes scan behind him and onto his desk. The small lamp shines down on a textbook and papers spread throughout.

"I—I heard you talking. Didn't know if someone else was in here," I whisper.

August gestures around the room. "Nope, just me, and..." He turns to look at the messy desk behind me.

"Homework?" I raise an eyebrow. "School doesn't start for another week? Are you taking an honors class? Did they give you homework already?"

"Honors?" His dark blue eyes stare at me like I've just asked him what color his underwear is. He lets out a laugh. "Thank you for thinking I'm smart enough to be in any honors class."

The awkward silence pushes me to glance around his room.

A giant poster of a surfer hangs on the wall behind his full-size bed. An extra pair of glasses sits on the wooden nightstand, along with what looks like an empty can of Mountain Dew.

"I need to pass a math test so I can take algebra," he mumbles.

I tilt my head. "Why?"

Is this really a thing? Is this testing required to enter this class? Especially math. It's an easy subject.

"Because I don't want to be in pre-algebra while I'm in ninth grade. Eighth graders take pre-algebra." August scratches the back of his neck. "I've been studying for weeks, and I keep getting stuck." He lets out a heavy breath. "Maybe giving up is easier than this. Accept that I'm just a dumb idiot," he mutters the last part.

I feel something inside me ignite when he says those last words. I see myself in him. His emotions, I experience them constantly. Maybe I can help him.

"I can help," I blurt out, then bite my tongue.

Crap. I hope I didn't offend him.

"Help?" He scrunches his eyebrows.

"With your math?"

My palms feel clammy, and the way he looks at me makes my stomach flutter. A small smile tilts up on his lips. Right now, I'm seeing August in a different light.

His struggles mirror mine. Self-doubt.

"Are you sure you want to spend the last week of freedom staring at a math book?" he asks.

"I love math." I lift a shoulder and smile.

August raises his brows. "Oh, well." He looks back at his desk again. "I don't want Ellie thinking I'm stealing you away from her for a week."

Before I can stop, I roll my eyes. "She knows how much math makes me happy, and I don't think she would take that away from me. I can also help you organize your desk."

"Uh." He scratches his head again. "I—are you sure?"

"August, it's not a big deal. I'll tutor you for the week, and that's it."

A smile spreads across his face. "Alright." He extends his hand out to me. "Deal."

When I take two steps toward him and reach for his hand, it's soft and warm. Something I wasn't expecting. Although I'm not sure what I was expecting. But the way he holds mine, it's delicate, as if he isn't trying to hurt my hand.

August looks at our hands clasped together and then at me. I watch his lips part. Something in me clicked when I felt this simple touch.

We make awkward sounds, clearing our throats, and letting out small laughs before pulling away.

"We—uh," I say.

"Do you?" he says.

What is happening right now? Why do I feel shy and awkward with August? I've never experienced this emotion toward him.

*Teenage hormones. Yep. That's it.*

"Do you want to start now? We can wait until tomorrow too." His tone carries so much eagerness that it's too cute not to smile at.

"I couldn't sleep, so I was going downstairs to get a drink, maybe watch some TV." My cheeks heat and I push a strand of hair behind my ear.

"Oh, okay. I can get you something?"

"No, it's okay. I'll grab something real quick and then we can go over what you're studying."

"Okay, cool." His smile is bright and electrifying. Hopeful.

Suddenly I feel thirstier than I did when I got out of bed.

"Hey, Riley," August calls out.

I paused, gripping the doorknob, and spun to view him over my shoulder. The small lamp casts a glow around him.

"Thanks," he says with a sheepish smile.

The corner of my lip twitches, but I let it grow to a grin before saying, "Of course."

# ACKNOWLEDGMENTS

To everyone who has supported me from the beginning of
this crazy ride.

# ABOUT THE AUTHOR

Monica is a born and raised midwest girl, when really she believes she should have been born in California by the beach. Deep down, she loves being a Chicagoan.

When she isn't writing, she's reading her own TBR list, hanging out with her best friend/spouse, and their two cats Bobby and Romi, or watching her favorite TV shows.

This is her debut novel and has already started to plan her next series, amongst other books that she can't wait to write.